JAYNE ANN KRENTZ

DANGEROUS AFFAIRS

MIRA™

CONTENTS

THE WAITING GAME 7

LEGACY 225

First Published 1985
Second Australian Paperback Edition 2004
ISBN 1 741 16154 1

Published by
Mira Books
3 Gibbes Street
CHATSWOOD NSW 2067
AUSTRALIA

Printed and bound in Australia by
McPherson's Printing Group

JAYNE ANN KRENTZ

THE WAITING GAME

One

Sara Frazer paused in the act of searching Adrian Saville's desk and told herself for the hundredth time that what she was doing was illegal and potentially dangerous. And while she had her faults, as her family had only recently pointed out to her in some detail, she had never, until that moment, sunk to the level of doing something of this nature.

But Sara was concerned, worried, anxious and more than a little suspicious of the stranger whose study she was going through with such haste. Besides, she told herself with her customary impulsive enthusiasm, the opportunity had been too good to let pass. The door to Saville's isolated home had not been locked when she had arrived twenty minutes earlier. And she had, after all, no intention of stealing anything. She just needed some answers.

Impatiently Sara scanned the room as she closed the drawer of the desk. The study was a clean-lined, orderly room. It was a quiet, solid, masculine room, and she couldn't help wondering how accurately it reflected its owner. Hardwood floors, simple, substantial furniture and a great deal of shelving were the main features. If the den did mirror its owner with any degree of accuracy, she would be in trouble should Saville happen to walk in the door. Something about the place seemed to resist and resent her intrusion.

A greenhouse window that overlooked the cold, dark water of Puget Sound provided the main source of light. Dusk was settling in on Bainbridge Island, where Adrian Saville made his home, and across the expanse of water the lights of Seattle began sinking into life. Sara didn't dare turn on a lamp for fear of alerting a neighbor to her presence. The house was tucked away by itself amid a stand of fir and pine, but one never knew who might pass by on the road outside. It was late summer and she ought to have enough fading twilight to get her through the rest of the search.

She was turning away from the desk, intent on exploring the bookshelves, when she noticed the apple. Startled, Sara reached out to pick it up. In that moment she was forced to acknowledge that she might have been mistaken in her suspicions of Adrian Saville. After all, she had an apple just like this one and there was only one person who could have given it to Saville.

Sara held the object up to the fading light and studied it intently. It was not just any apple, of course. It was fashioned of heavy crystal, and the stem with its leaf was of intricately worked gold. The person who had made a gift of the apple believed in substantial things such as gold, Sara knew. Small bubbles had been captured inside the apple by the artist. They reflected the light in an intriguing manner, making anyone who held the object want to examine it more intently.

All in all, it was a very attractive paperweight, and the fact that it sat on Adrian Saville's desk put a whole new light on the situation. Sara stood still, turning the apple so that the crystal caught the light, and wondered what she was going to do next.

''Offer me a bite.''

The deep, graveled voice came from the doorway. Sara chilled for an instant as fear and embarrassment washed through her. She nearly dropped the crystal apple as she spun around to face the man who was lounging calmly against the doorjamb. Frantically she struggled for self-control and a reasonable explanation of her presence in his study. Unfortunately the situation did not do wonders for her presence of mind. Sara found herself wishing very badly that she had never succumbed to the temptation his empty house had provided.

''I'm sorry,'' she managed, stumbling over the words. Vaguely she realized that her hands were trembling. ''I didn't hear anyone. I mean, there was no one at home when I arrived, and the door was unlocked. I had no business wandering in to wait for you, but it seemed pointless to sit outside in the car and I—'' She broke off abruptly as something occurred to her. ''You are Adrian Saville, aren't you?''

Eyes that were either unusually colorless or else were washed of color by a trick of the dim light swept curiously over her. Sara had the feeling that the stranger had taken in every detail in that brief glance.

''If I'm not Adrian Saville, this situation is going to get even more complicated, isn't it?'' he noted softly.

Sara's fingers tightened on the paperweight as she forced herself to sound reasonably cool and collected. ''It would mean that there are two intruders in Mr. Saville's home instead of just one. Yes, I would say that would complicate things. But I don't think that's the case. You are Adrian Saville.''

Arms folded across his chest, the man regarded her with mild interest. ''What makes you so sure?''

''You're leaning much too casually in that doorway, for one thing,'' Sara retorted. Whatever he was thinking, he didn't seem intent on doing her any immediate harm. Actually, he really didn't look like the sort of man who would harm someone unless greatly provoked. The fear died away, leaving only the embarrassment. ''Look, I can explain this, Mr. Saville.''

''I can't wait to hear the explanation.''

Sara felt the warm flush paint the line of her cheekbones. Carefully she set the crystal apple back down on his desk. It was a relief to have an excuse to look away from that strangely colorless gaze. ''Then you're going to acknowledge your name, at least?''

''Why not? This is my home. I might as well use my name,'' he murmured easily.

''I'm Sara Frazer,'' she said quietly, turning her head to meet his eyes once more. ''Lowell Kincaid's niece. I have a paperweight just like this one at home.''

''I see.''

She hadn't expected the silence that followed. It made her feel uneasy and awkward. Hurriedly she tried to fill it with further explanations. ''I came looking for you because I couldn't locate Uncle Lowell. I just arrived from his place in the mountains late this afternoon. I caught the ferry here to the island and by the time I found your house it was getting quite late. There was no answer when I knocked on your door, and when I tried it, it was unlocked. I'm afraid I just came on in to wait for you,'' she concluded with a tentative smile.

''And wound up searching my study as a means of passing the time?'' He didn't return her smile but he didn't seem unduly upset.

Sara took a deep breath. ''I happened to notice the paperweight,'' she lied politely. ''It really is just like the one I have. Uncle Lowell gave it to me a few months ago. I assume he gave you this one?''

''Umm.''

Sara decided the noncommittal sound was an affirmative. ''They're quite beautiful, aren't they? I have mine on my desk at home.''

He ignored her determined chattiness. ''What were you looking for, Sara?''

Something about the calm manner in which he asked the question convinced her that Adrian Saville wasn't going to accept her explanation of why she happened to be in his study. Sara exhaled slowly, considering her options. This might be a clear-cut case of honesty being the best policy, she decided ruefully. Folding her arms across her small breasts in a subtle mockery of his own stance, she leaned back and propped herself against the edge of the desk. She met his gaze with a level one of her own.

''I was looking for something.''

He nodded as if it were the most natural thing in the world. ''For what?''

She shrugged. ''That's the problem. I don't know. Anything that might give me a clue about where my uncle is.''

Adrian continued to regard her with solemn interest for another long moment. This time Sara resisted the impulse to fill the silent void with attempts at explanations. She could be just as remote and laconic as Adrian Saville could, she promised herself.

''What makes you think I might have some answers for you?''

''I'm not sure you do. But Uncle Lowell once told me that if anything ever happened to him, I was to notify you. He gave me your address several months ago, shortly before he sent the apple, in fact.''

''And you think something has happened to Lowell?''

''I don't know,'' Sara admitted. ''I only know that he's not at his home up in the mountains.''

''Perhaps he's taken a short trip. Was he expecting you?''

Sara swallowed uneasily. ''Well, no. I just showed up on his doorstep unannounced, I'm afraid. I did try to call but all I got was his answering machine.''

''Then why the concern?'' Adrian pressed quietly.

Sara looked at him searchingly. ''How well do you know my uncle?''

''Well enough.''

Not much to go on, but she might as well see what happened when she told him the reason for her concern. ''His neighbor said he went hunting.''

Adrian Saville greeted that bit of information with more silence. Then he straightened away from the door. ''Have you had dinner, Sara?''

Sara frowned as he turned away and started down the hall. ''Wait a minute! Don't you understand?'' she demanded, hurrying after him. She caught up with him just as he rounded the corner and walked into the small, rather old-fashioned kitchen. ''They said he went *hunting*.''

''And Lowell Kincaid doesn't go in for blood sports. Yes, I understand.'' Adrian opened the refrigerator door, examining the contents with a wary eye.

"It's because of his old job," Sara said quickly. "Before he retired he worked in a rather violent world, you see."

"He worked for the government, you mean." Adrian finally decided on a plastic-wrapped chunk of cheese. He removed it from the refrigerator and set it on the counter. Then he opened a cupboard and reached for a box of crackers. "I know what your uncle used to do for a living, Sara."

She blinked, watching him carefully. "Oh."

"You didn't answer my question. Did you have any dinner?" Adrian began slicing cheese with smooth, methodical strokes of a knife.

"Uh, no, I haven't had time," Sara said vaguely. Her mind was on other things and had been all afternoon.

"Neither have I. Cheese and crackers and some vegetables okay?"

"Look, Adrian...Mr. Saville...I'm really not very hungry. I just came here to see if you knew anything about Uncle Lowell."

"And stayed to rifle my study." He nodded. "Sorry I can't offer anything more interesting. But it's kind of late in the evening to start something more elaborate. And I'm really not that good a cook in the first place."

"I didn't rifle your study!" Sara exploded, beginning to lose her patience. She didn't have a great deal of that commodity in the first place. Life was short enough as it was, she felt. What good was an excess of patience? "Now, about Uncle Lowell..."

"There's some wine in that cupboard next to the sink. Why don't you open a bottle while I slice up a few carrots and some broccoli?"

"But I don't want any wine!"

"I do." He glanced back at her over his shoulder, a faint smile playing at the corner of his mouth. "I'm celebrating, you see."

That stopped her. "Celebrating what?"

"The sale of my first novel."

Sara stared at him, astonished. "Are you really?"

"Umm."

Again she assumed the noncommittal sound was a yes answer. Her enthusiasm sprang up, as usual, out of nowhere and rushed into her voice. "Adrian, that's fantastic! Absolutely fantastic! A once-in-a-lifetime event. I can't believe it. I've never even met an author before."

"Neither have I," Adrian said dryly. He finished slicing the cheese and opened the refrigerator to pull out a handful of carrots. "Choose whichever bottle of wine you want."

A little bemused, Sara found herself obediently reaching into the cupboard and selecting a bottle of Oregon Pinot Noir. She'd heard the Northwest wine industry was starting to flourish but she hadn't yet had much experience with the products. They hadn't yet become chic in California. "You must be very excited."

He thought about that. "Well, it was a relief to make the sale," he began consideringly.

"A relief! Why, it's marvellous! Terrific! Thrilling! What's the matter with you? I should think you'd be doing handsprings or something."

"I imagine it's easier to get excited when there's someone else around to get excited with you," he murmured, arranging raw vegetables on a platter and putting a dollop of mayonnaise in the center. "I did go out and have a beer down at a local tavern. That's where I was when you arrived, in fact."

Sara poured the wine and handed him a glass. With a smile she raised her own glass in a grand salute. "Congratulations! And here's to nice, fat royalty checks." She sipped her Pinot Noir with attention. It was good. She made a mental note of the fact. There appeared to be a future in Northwest wines. Then she remembered belatedly that she didn't have to worry so much anymore about being on top of the latest culinary trends. "Too bad you can't tell Uncle Lowell. I'm sure he'd be very happy for you."

Adrian regarded her over the rim of his glass as he took a deep swallow. ''Yes, I think he would be quite satisfied.''

Sara smiled at him quizzically. ''Did he know you were writing a book?''

''He knew.''

''Then you really are a close friend of his?'' she went on doggedly.

''Umm.''

Sara shot him a narrow glance. ''Can't you just say yes or no?''

''Sorry. Yes.''

''Then you do realize that it was odd he would tell his neighbor he was going hunting?'' she continued more seriously.

''Is that exactly what his neighbor said? That Lowell said he was going hunting?'' Adrian picked up the platter of vegetables and led the way into the rustic living-room. He set the plate down on a low wood-and-brass table in front of the couch and went over to the old stone fireplace. Going down on one knee, he reached for a handful of kindling. Although it was still technically summer and the day had been sunny and warm, the first hint of the coming fall was in the air tonight.

Sara sat down in the corner of the worn black leather couch, studying the man in front of her. ''That's what the woman who had the cabin near his said. Her exact words.''

Adrian didn't respond, his attention on constructing the fire. Sara sipped her wine and continued to watch him. There was a certain fluidity to his movements that intrigued her. There was also a definite logical precision to the way he built the fire. A coordinated, controlled man. He was dressed in a pair of faded jeans and a black denim workshirt. The clothing molded a lean, tautly built body that seemed totally balanced. On his feet he wore a pair of dusty, soft-soled canvas sport shoes. Now that she had a moment to think about it, she decided the strange eyes were really a shade between blue and gray. In the right light they might appear as silver.

He was a friend of her uncle's and that took the nervousness out of contacting him, even if he had caught her going through the contents of his desk. Although he gave the impression of being easygoing and very friendly, Lowell Kincaid was actually quite cautious in his friendships. He had worked too long in a world where few people could be trusted. If he liked Adrian Saville, then Sara knew she, in turn, could trust the stranger in front of her. Her uncle had always been an excellent judge of people. Sometimes his life had depended on those judgments. The fact that he had survived and been able to retire at the normal age was evidence of just how accurate his analyses of other people had been over the years.

Adrian set a match to the kindling and the yellow flames leaped to life. He crouched for a moment in front of the fire, making certain it had caught properly, and the flickering light illuminated the hard line of his profile.

He was far from being a handsome man, Sara reflected. The planes and angles of his face had been carved with a dull knife, not finely chiseled. But there was a primitive strength in the aggressive nose and the austere cheekbones. He wasn't the kind of man who would smile easily; the grim set of his mouth wasn't shaped for such expressions. Sara guessed his age at somewhere between thirty-five and forty; probably closer to forty. She thought she saw something of the fundamental sureness and strength in him that her uncle must have seen before he decided to make Adrian a friend. Lowell Kincaid was sure of this man and therefore Sara knew she could be sure of him, too. She relaxed even more and took another sip of her wine. She sensed she had done the right thing by seeking out Adrian Saville.

She just wished he'd show a little more interest in her concern for her uncle. But then, a man who had just sold his first book probably had a right to be thinking of other things at the moment.

''What's it called?'' she asked as he got to his feet and paced back to the couch.

''My novel?'' He seemed to have no trouble following her

abrupt shift in the conversation. Adrian picked up a cracker with cheese on it and downed the whole thing in one gulp. ''*Phantom.*''

''Is it a horror tale?''

He shook his head slowly, his eyes on the fire. ''Not in the sense you mean. It's what's called a thriller.''

''Ah, secret things, espionage, plots and counterplots. That sort of thing. I read a lot of thrillers.'' She smiled. ''Are you writing under your own name?''

''I'm writing under the name Adrian Saville.''

''Good, then I won't have to jot down your pseudonym. You'll have to autograph a copy of your book for me when it's published. I'm sure Uncle Lowell will want one, too.''

''Lowell's already seen the manuscript,'' Adrian said quietly. ''Because of his, uh, background, I thought he might be able to give me a few ideas that would make *Phantom* sound more authentic.''

''Did he?''

''Umm.'' Adrian stared into the fire. ''He was very helpful. You're really worried about him, aren't you?''

Sara resisted the temptation to say ''umm.'' ''Yes. My uncle doesn't hunt. He doesn't even like to fish. Why would he tell his neighbor he was going hunting and then drop out of sight?''

''Beats me.'' Adrian swirled the wine in his glass. ''But don't you think you may be overreacting? You should know your uncle can take care of himself.''

''He's in his late sixties now, Adrian. And he's been out of the industry a long time.''

Something close to amusement gleamed briefly in Adrian's eyes. ''The industry? You sound like an insider. Lowell uses words like that.''

Mildly embarrassed, Sara's mouth turned down wryly. ''That's how he always referred to his government work. I guess I picked up the term.''

''And some of the skills?'' he asked too blandly.

She looked away, reaching for a carrot. Sara knew he was

referring to the fact that he had found her prowling around his study. ''Obviously I didn't pick up the skills. If I had, you would never have caught me the way you did this evening. How did you sneak up on me so quietly, anyway? Must be those sneakers you're wearing. But I was certain I'd hear any car pulling into the drive.''

''I walked back from the tavern. The car is still in the garage behind the house.''

''Oh.'' Chagrined, Sara chewed industriously on her carrot.

''You'd better practice checking out those sorts of details if you plan to follow in your uncle's footsteps.''

''Don't worry, as much as I like my uncle, and in spite of the fact that I happen to be in the market for a new career, I do not intend to go into intelligence work. I can't think of anything more depressing and grim. Imagine living a life in which you couldn't trust anyone or anything. Besides, I like to limit my close association with violence to reading thrillers,'' she added with a small smile. ''It's okay on a fantasy level but I certainly wouldn't want to make a career out of it.''

''If you feel that strongly about it, you'd better give up the habit of going through other people's desks. You could have just as easily turned around and found yourself facing an irate homeowner holding a gun as a friendly, trusting soul such as myself.''

She eyed him thoughtfully for a moment. ''Actually, you did take the whole thing quite calmly.''

''You didn't look that dangerous,'' he informed her gently. ''In fact, you appeared rather inviting standing there in the twilight, gazing into the apple. Besides, as soon as you said you had one just like it, I knew who you were.''

''You were certain I was Uncle Lowell's niece?''

''When he gave me the crystal apple he told me he'd given a second one to you. He had them made up specially for us, you know.''

''No, I didn't know. That is, I didn't realize he'd had a second one made until I saw it sitting on your desk. When I spotted it, I decided I probably didn't have any reason to go on being suspicious of you,'' she added apologetically. ''Unfortunately, I came to that brilliant conclusion a bit late. You'd already snuck up and found me in what I guess qualifies as a compromising situation. You really don't know where Uncle Lowell might have gone or why he would say he was off hunting?''

''No. But I do think Lowell can take care of himself. My guess is he'd want you to stay out of the way until he's handled whatever needs handling.''

''Then you do believe something's happened to him!'' she pounced.

''I didn't say that,'' Adrian protested mildly. ''I only meant that he probably had his reasons for disappearing. Maybe he just wanted to take off by himself for a while. Maybe he's got a woman friend and didn't feel like explaining all that to his neighbor. There could be a hundred different reasons why he's not at home, none of them particularly sinister.''

''I don't like it,'' Sara muttered, feeling pressured by the logic.

''Obviously, or you wouldn't have taken the trouble to find me. So Lowell told you to look me up if you were ever worried about something having happened to him?''

''He said you'd want to know, or something like that. I wasn't exactly certain what he meant. He doesn't have a lot of close friends. I assumed you might be one of them.''

''But you weren't sure where I fit in so you decided to take a quick look around my desk drawers while you waited for me to return. Are you always that impulsive?''

''It seemed prudent, not impulsive, to take the opportunity to find out what I could about you before I confronted you,'' she said cautiously. ''Some of my uncle's old acquaintances aren't the sort with whom you want to get involved on a first-name basis.''

''You've met a lot of them?'' Adrian inquired politely.

''Well, no. But Uncle Lowell has told me about a few of them.'' Sara shuddered delicately, remembering one particular tale. "He's got a great collection of stories and personal recollections, although he always changes names and locations to protect the guilty. I suppose he's mentioned a few of the more colorful characters to you if you used him as resource material for *Phantom.*"

"We've shared a few beers and talked on occasion," Adrian admitted.

"You see a lot of my uncle?"

Adrian moved his hand in a vague gesture. "He doesn't live that far away. I get out to his place once in a while and sometimes he makes it over here. What about you? See a lot of him?"

Sara grinned. "Not as much as I would have liked over the years. I'm afraid Uncle Lowell has always been considered the black sheep of the family. As you can imagine, though, I found him quite fascinating. He was the unconventional relative, the one who had the mysterious career, the one who showed up when you least expected him. He was unpredictable, and kids like that, I suppose. The rest of the family thought he was a bad influence on me and, of course, that made him all the more interesting."

Adrian leaned back against the sofa, slanting her a glance. "Why did they think he was a bad influence?"

"Because he always encouraged me to do what I wanted to do, not what my family wanted. And he had a way of understanding me, of knowing what I was thinking. He told me two years ago, for instance, that I wasn't going to be happy for long as a mid-level manager in a large corporation. Said I didn't have the proper corporate personality. He was right. I think I knew it at the time but everything seemed to be on track and running smoothly in my life. I was living the perfect yuppie life-style, and to be honest, it had its moments."

"Yuppie? Oh, yes—" Adrian nodded. "—Young Urban Professional."

Sara gave him another laughing smile. "I was into the whole scene down in California. I had a lifetime membership in the right athletic club, dressed for success, had my apartment done in the high-tech look and kept up with the trends in food. I ground my own coffee beans for my very own imported Italian espresso machine, and I can tell you the precise moment when pasta went out and Creole cooking came in, if you're interested.''

''No, thanks. I eat a lot of macaroni and cheese. I don't want to hear that it's 'out.' So Lowell advised you to dump the yuppie life?''

''Macaroni and cheese does not count as real pasta,'' she told him forcefully. ''Yuppie pasta is stuff such as linguini and calamari or fettuccini Alfredo. And, yes, Uncle Lowell did advise me to dump the yuppie life. Along with the yuppie males I was dating at the time,'' Sara confided cheerfully. ''I think he thought they were all wimps. He said none of the ones I introduced him to would be of any use in a crunch. I explained I didn't plan to get into any crunches but he just shook his head and told me to come visit him when I came to my senses.''

Adrian regarded her assessingly. ''And that's why you went to his place today? To tell Lowell you'd come to your senses?''

Sara stirred a little restlessly on the couch, tucking one jeaned leg under her as she shifted her focus back to the fire. ''Something like that. I quit my job last week. I think I'm going through a mid-life crisis.''

''You're a little young for that, aren't you?''

Sara ignored the underlying trace of humor in his question. ''Don't patronize me. I just turned thirty. As it happens, I've been through several mid-life crises and I know them when I see them. I'm ready to make some changes in my life again.''

''You're sure that change is what you want?'' Adrian got to his feet to throw a bigger log on the fire.

''Oh, yes,'' she whispered with great certainty, ''I'm sure.''

She sounded quite resolute, Adrian decided as he fed the flames. He'd heard that quiet certainty in Lowell's voice from time to time. Must be a family characteristic.

For some reason, Sara Frazer wasn't quite what he'd expected, though, even if she did have some of Lowell's iron-hard determination. Adrian toyed with the flames a moment longer, considering the female who was curled on the couch behind him. When a man had waited nearly a year to meet a woman, it was perfectly natural that he would have developed a few preconceptions.

The few expectations he had, however, had never been fully formed. Lowell had given him some vague, odd bits of information about his niece but little that was concrete enough to build a picture in his mind. Just like Lowell to deliberately leave a great deal to the imagination. He was, after all, a man, and he knew what a man's mind could do when it went to work on a mysterious woman.

Adrian realized that he hadn't expected Sara Frazer to be a flaming beauty and in that regard he'd been correct. Taken individually, her features didn't add up to those of a beautiful woman. What surprised him was that the hazel eyes, long light-brown hair and slender figure somehow went together to create a subtly appealing combination.

On second thought, it wasn't the collection of physical characteristics that made for that appeal. There simply wasn't anything that unique about eyes that hovered between green and brown or about hair that was worn parted in the middle and clipped casually behind her ears. The red knit top she was wearing emphasized small, pert breasts rather than lush voluptuousness.

Adrian turned the matter over in his mind for an instant longer before he decided that Sara was somehow more than the sum of her parts. There was intelligence, ready laughter and more than a dash of impulsiveness in those hazel eyes. And when she had learned of the sale of his first book, her spontaneous enthusiasm had been very real even though he was a stranger to her. It was her inner animation that somehow pulled the ordinary together and made the total package strangely intriguing.

He'd been consciously and unconsciously anticipating her

arrival for several months but the end result had still taken him by surprise. He simply hadn't expected to feel such an immediate and compelling attraction. He hadn't thought he'd react to the reality of Sara with such intensity. It was unsettling but he'd lay odds that Lowell would probably say "I told you so" the next time he saw him.

Satisfied with his analysis, Adrian turned and moved back toward the couch. He'd long ago accepted the fact that for some things there were no answers, but he still preferred situations that could be taken apart, analyzed and understood. He liked to have a handle on things, Adrian told himself. No, it was more than that. He liked to know he was in control of his environment. Having everything accurately assessed and properly analyzed gave him the only real sense of security one could have in this world. Sara Frazer was a new and disturbing element in his environment and it was good to know he was already beginning to comprehend her. More importantly, he was comprehending and accepting his reaction to her. He rather thought Lowell Kincaid would be pleased at the progress of the situation.

"It's getting late," Sara mused as she munched the last cracker. "I suppose I'd better be on my way. If you really don't have any idea of where Uncle Lowell is, there's no point imposing on you any longer."

"Where were you planning on going tonight?" Adrian sank back down on the couch, aware of an unexpected and totally irrational sense of disappointment. She had just arrived. It didn't seem right that she should already be planning to leave. That wasn't the way it was supposed to be. A part of him was disturbed that she seemed oblivious to the fact that things were different now. Clearly Kincaid had not given her any idea of what he'd had in mind when he'd set about engineering a meeting between Adrian and his niece.

He wondered how much to tell her about her Uncle Lowell's plans for her. He wondered how she would take the news. She might be furious or she might treat the whole thing as a joke.

Women were tricky. It occurred to Adrian that in spite of being nearly forty years old he didn't know nearly as much about them as he should. It would probably be better not to bring up the subject of Lowell's plans this evening. On the other hand, Adrian found himself fiercely reluctant to let Sara go without putting the first delicate tendrils of a claim on her. Something elemental had come alive deep within him, something hard to deny.

"There's an inn on the outskirts of Winslow. It's only about a mile from here. I'll stay there tonight and be on my way tomorrow."

Adrian frowned. "You're planning on returning to California?"

Sara shook her head vigorously. "Not until I satisfy myself about Uncle Lowell. I'm worried, Adrian, even if nobody else is."

Adrian rolled his empty wineglass between his palms. "I don't think you have anything to be concerned about."

"Maybe I've got an overactive imagination. People are always accusing me of it." She lifted one shoulder in careless disregard for the fact. "But Uncle Lowell's former career must have contained some loose ends. And I know that at times he was involved with some dangerous people. There was one in particular he once told me about—" She broke off abruptly, eyes narrowing.

"What do you think you can do about the fact that he's not available at the moment?" Adrian asked reasonably.

Sara gave the matter some thought. "I think I'll go back to his cottage in the morning and break in. Maybe he left some notes or something on his desk." Her eyes grew pensive with the plans running through her head.

Adrian looked down at the glass in his hands. "The last time you tried that trick you got caught."

She laughed. "Well, no harm done if Uncle Lowell comes home unexpectedly and catches me in his house. In fact, it will be a great relief. The mystery will be solved, won't it?"

Adrian experienced a flash of amused amazement. "You're going to do it, aren't you?"

"Why not? Maybe I'll get some answers."

"I think you'll be wasting your time."

Sara grimaced. "At the moment I have time to waste. As I explained earlier, I'm unemployed."

"There are probably more productive things you could do with your newfound time," Adrian suggested dryly.

"I know. Such as look for another job. But I think I'll see what I can find out about Uncle Lowell first."

"Are you always this impulsive and stubborn?"

"Just since I turned thirty," she told him with benign menace, her eyes mirroring an amused challenge.

Adrian found himself smiling back at her. Her gaze went to his mouth, and he realized she was very interested in his expression. Did the smile look that odd on his face? "Well, if you're intent on another act of breaking and entering, I suppose I'd better go along with you."

She was startled. "Why? There's absolutely no need for you to come with me."

"You're wrong," Adrian said gently. "There are several good reasons why I'd better tag along, not the least of which is that Lowell Kincaid would probably nail my hide to the wall if I didn't."

"Why on earth should Uncle Lowell care?"

"You're worried about him to the point where you're willing to break into not one but two private homes. Lowell would expect me to take your concerns seriously, I think. He'd also want me to make sure you didn't get into trouble. What if a neighbor saw you going through a back window and called the law? You'd have some difficult explanations to make. Messy. Lowell likes things neat and tidy." Adrian paused a moment. "So do I."

"Well, I still don't see why Uncle Lowell would expect you to take the responsibility of keeping me out of trouble," Sara declared firmly.

Adrian deliberately kept his voice casual even though he was oddly aware of the strong, steady beat of his own pulse. ''Don't you? The explanation's simple enough. Lowell Kincaid has plans for you, Sara. You've arrived a little ahead of schedule. I think he was planning on you coming to visit him in a couple of months, but the timing doesn't change things.''

For the first time since he had caught her in his study, a degree of genuine wariness flared in Sara's gaze. Adrian immediately wished he'd kept his mouth shut. But the strangely primitive desire to let her know she wasn't quite as free as she assumed was pushing him.

''What plans?'' she demanded suspiciously.

He'd already said too much, Adrian decided. In a way it was alarming. He'd allowed his unaccustomed emotional response to push him in a direction he'd guessed would be awkward. Odd. He usually had a much better sense of discretion. Having gone this far, however, he was committed to finishing the business. He couldn't take back the words he'd already spoken. The next best thing he could do was concentrate on keeping his tone light and whimsical.

''Didn't your uncle tell you that he has decided to give you to me? You're my reward, Sara. My gift for finishing *Phantom* and a couple of other things that were hanging fire in my life.''

Two

"Uncle Lowell has always had an odd sense of humor. If you're really a close friend of his, I imagine you know that by now. I've always thought he would have made a good cartoonist. Between his constant doodling and his offbeat notion of what's funny, he'd have been very successful."

An hour later Sara lay in the unfamiliar inn-room bed rerunning her response to Adrian Saville's casually outrageous remarks. She decided she'd handled the scene reasonably well. She would have suspected Saville of having a warped sense of humor except for the fact that she knew her uncle. It was entirely possible that Lowell Kincaid had "given" her to his friend. He'd told her more than once that she didn't know how to pick her men. It was Lowell who had the fractured sense of humor, Sara decided grimly. What worried her was that under that trace of whimsy, she sensed Adrian might have taken him seriously.

She turned onto her side, bunching the flat pillow into a more supportive shape, and thought about what her uncle had done. It was annoying, irritating and totally in keeping with Lowell Kincaid's somewhat bizarre way of arranging things. His affinity for the unexpected was probably some sort of survival trait. A good secret agent couldn't afford to be too predictable, Sara thought with a sigh. Normally, however, Lowell didn't allow his penchant for the unique approach to infringe too much on the lives of friends and family. He knew intuitively where to stop.

But he'd let himself go overboard this time, and Sara found herself wondering why. Couldn't he see that Saville was a man who took life seriously? You didn't play jokes on people like that. They either got mad or hurt. There was always the possibility that Lowell was deadly serious about handing her over to a man of whom he approved, of course. He'd made it clear often enough he didn't think much of her own choices in male companions. Yes, Lowell might have been very serious in his intent. In which case she would be sure to give him a piece of her mind when he showed up again.

Sara watched the shadows behind the gently blowing curtains. The window was open a few inches, allowing the fresh, crisp night air into the room. She knew a lot about her uncle's sense of humor. Over the years she'd seen enough examples of it. Strange that he was such good friends with Saville. No one would ever accuse him of having much sense of humor, warped or otherwise. The faint flashes of amusement she had seen in him that evening disappeared so quickly she might have imagined them. She had the impression that when they did appear they surprised him as much as her. Saville was a controlled, quiet man who not only seemed quite different from her uncle but who was also a perfect opposite to the kind of men who circulated in her world.

Her ex-world, Sara reminded herself. Yuppiedom was another ex-world to add to the pile of such interesting experiments. It had been fun, but she had known when she'd gone into it that it wouldn't be permanent. Sara knew she would recognize the life she wanted to live on a permanent basis when she found it. Until then she played games with the world. She wondered if she was getting a little too old for games.

Restlessly she switched to her other side and plumped the pillow again. Still, she had learned some useful skills during the past few years. For example, she knew how to slide out of a socially awkward situation such as the one that had occurred tonight. A light laugh, a wry expression and an easy comment.

Adrian had accepted her withdrawal from the topic, although he had insisted on accompanying her to the inn in her car. He'd offered her a bed at his house but had not seemed surprised when she politely declined. There was no sense complicating an already complex situation, Sara had told herself. As much as she had been intrigued by Adrian, she had been a little wary of him toward the end of the evening.

She was accustomed to men who didn't take anything except their careers, their running and their new Porsches seriously, men who knew the socially acceptable vocabulary of the new male sensitivity by heart but who didn't really know how to make commitments. Sara knew how to handle men such as that. She wasn't so sure about Adrian Saville. She sensed he took a great deal in life very seriously.

There was more age in his eyes than on his face, she thought. And there was quiet, implacable strength in that pale gray gaze. She thought she understood why her uncle liked him. But she could also picture her unpredictable uncle trying to lighten the somberness that surrounded the younger man like an aura. She could just see Lowell Kincaid laughing and telling Adrian that his niece would be good for him and that he could have her when he'd finished his novel.

Sara made a rueful face. Perhaps her easygoing uncle hadn't realized just how seriously a man like Adrian Saville would take such an outrageous comment. Ah, well. She would do her best to keep things light and easy between herself and the budding author on the drive back into the mountains tomorrow. And when this was all over she would give Lowell a lecture on interfering in the private lives and fantasies of his friends. Assuring herself of that, Sara finally drifted off to sleep.

It was sunny and warm the next morning as Sara showered and dressed for breakfast. Accustomed to that kind of weather in San Diego, she didn't think much about it. She buttoned the wide cuffs of the oversized men's-style shirt she had chosen to wear and fastened the yellow belt that clasped the tapered olive-green trousers. Hastily she clipped her bluntly cut hair with two clips and wondered if Adrian Saville would be on time for breakfast as he'd promised. She decided he would be. Authors were entitled to be erratic in their habits, Sara felt, but Adrian was the kind of man who would be exactly where he said he would be at the specified time. Dependable.

She hurried downstairs and across the street. The coffee shop Adrian had pointed out last night when he'd escorted her back to the inn was full of people who weren't nearly so inclined as she was to take the local weather for granted. There seemed to be a kind of desperation in the air, as if everyone was determined to grab the last of summer before the Northwest winter took hold. Everyone from the hostess to the busboy commented in a dazed fashion on the fact that the Seattle area was getting another day of sunshine.

"Yes, it certainly is marvelous weather," Sara agreed politely as she was seated. Privately she thought that no one in San Diego would have even bothered to comment on it. "By the way, I'm waiting for someone." Something made her glance back toward the doorway. "Oh, there he is now. Would you show him to my table?"

The gray-haired, middle-aged hostess chuckled. "Sure." She waved energetically at the man who stood in the doorway surveying the room. "Hey, Adrian. Over here."

Not just Adrian but everyone else in the room looked around. Sara experienced an acute twinge of embarrassment. She should have guessed that in a small community like this everyone knew one another. Determinedly she smiled as Saville walked toward her.

Striving for a casual pose of polite welcome, Sara was astonished to realize that she was actually mildly fascinated with Adrian's approach. His stride was a deceptively easy, flowing movement that covered the distance between the doorway and her table very quickly. He had a coordinated, masculine grace that went beyond the kind of athletic motion her male friends developed by running or working out. Sara had a feeling Adrian's physical control and smoothness had probably been born in him, the way a cat's coordination was.

The pelt of dark hair that he obviously kept disciplined with a scissor was still damp from his shower and combed severely into place. He wore jeans and a cream-colored button-down shirt. On his feet were the usual sneakers, Sara noted in amusement. The shoes made his progress across the coffee shop quite soundless. If Sara hadn't been watching him, she would never have heard him approach the table. Just as she had never heard him come down the hall to the study last night, she reflected as he greeted the hostess.

''Good morning, Angie. How's it going today? Looks like a full house this morning.''

The hostess nodded, pleased. ''Give these Northwest folks a little sunny weather and they crawl out of the woodwork in droves. We've been doing real good this past week. Real good. Have a seat with your lady friend here and I'll send Liz on over for your order.'' Beaming impartially down at Sara and Adrian, the hostess bustled off to find the waitress.

''Lady friend!'' Sara winced. ''I've always heard that in small towns people pay a lot of attention to what their neighbors are doing but I hadn't realized they were so quick to jump to conclusions! Better be careful, Adrian. When everyone finds out you've gone off to the mountains with me for the day, you'll be a compromised man.''

''I can live with it.'' He appeared unconcerned, turning his head to greet the teenage waitress as she hurried over to the table.

''Morning, Adrian. Coffee for both of you?'' Liz began filling Adrian's cup without waiting for confirmation and then glanced inquiringly at Sara.

''Please.'' Sara smiled.

''Ready to order?'' Briskly Liz whipped out her pad.

''Try the scones,'' Adrian suggested before Sara could speak.

''Scones?''

''Ummm. Homemade. They're great,'' he assured her.

''Well, I usually just have a croissant and coffee,'' Sara began uncertainly.

''You're leaving that yuppie life-style behind, remember?'' Adrian pointed out seriously.

Sara felt a wave of humor. ''All right. An order of scones and a poached egg,'' she said to the waitress.

''Got it,'' Liz responded. She glanced at Adrian. ''The usual for you? The number-three breakfast without the bacon?''

''Fine, Liz.''

Liz giggled and hurried off toward the kitchen.

Sara stirred cream into her coffee and slanted a glance at Adrian. ''Okay, I give up. Why the giggle over your order of a number-three breakfast?''

Adrian's mouth twisted wryly. ''Because a number three without bacon is really a number one. The first time I ate here I didn't notice the difference on the menu and just told Liz I wanted the number three minus the bacon. For some reason she's made it into a standing joke between us.''

''I see. You don't like bacon?''

''I don't eat meat,'' he explained gently.

Sara was instantly intrigued. ''Somehow you don't look like a vegetarian.''

He leaned back against the cushion of the booth and picked up his coffee cup. ''What do vegetarians look like?''

''Oh, I don't know. Maybe like leftovers from a sixties' commune or like a member of some exotic religious cult. Do you avoid meat for health or moral reasons?''

''I avoid it because I don't like it,'' Adrian said too quietly.

Feeling very much put in her place, Sara managed a faintly polite smile. She knew when she was being told to shut up. ''I guess that's as good a reason as any other. So much for that topic. Let's try another one. When will you be able to leave for the mountains? I'd like to start as soon as possible, if you don't mind.''

Adrian's dark lashes lowered in a thoughtful manner and then his steady gaze met Sara's. ''Was I rude?''

''Of course not,'' she assured him lightly. ''I should never have pried. What you eat is entirely your own business.''

''I didn't meant to be rude,'' Adrian insisted.

''You weren't. Forget it. Here come the scones and they do

look good.'' Sara flashed her best and most charming smile. The one she reserved for cocktail parties and management types.

''Don't.''

She blinked and arched a brow in cool question. ''I beg your pardon?''

''I said don't,'' Adrian muttered as his plate was set in front of him.

''Don't what?''

''Smile at me like that.''

''Sorry,'' Sara said rather grimly. Perhaps she would go to the mountains without him.

''It looks like something left over from your yuppie days,'' Adrian explained carefully. ''Kind of upwardly mobile. A little too flashy and not quite real. I'd rather have the real thing.''

Sara couldn't resist. ''Choosy, aren't you?''

''About some things. I can leave right after breakfast if you like.''

''Actually,'' she began forbiddingly, ''I'm on the verge of changing my mind.''

''About breaking into your uncle's cottage?'' Adrian slid a piece of egg onto a piece of toast.

''About taking you with me,'' Sara said sweetly.

He glanced up, surprised. ''Just because I was a little short with you a few minutes ago?''

Put like that, it did sound rather trite. Sara was at a loss to explain exactly why she was vaguely reluctant to have him accompany her, but the feeling had been growing since she'd awakened that morning. She didn't really have a valid excuse for refusing his companionship, however. After all, she was the one who had sought him out and she had done so precisely because Lowell Kincaid had advised it several months ago. The sense of ambivalence she was feeling for Adrian was a new emotion for her. Sara drummed her berry-tinted nails on the table and decided to lay down a few ground rules. Normally she didn't think too highly of rules, but there were times when they represented a certain safety.

"I suppose I can't stop you from coming with me, although I'm not at all sure it's necessary. But I would appreciate it if you would keep in mind that this whole plan to get into the cottage is my idea."

"Meaning you're in charge?" Adrian munched his toast, watching her with intent eyes.

"Something like that. Forgive me if I'm jumping to conclusions, Adrian, but I have this odd feeling that you might be the type to take over and run the show." Even as she said the words, Sara realized the truth of them. Perhaps this was the source of her vague wariness regarding this man.

"Think of how nice it will be to have someone else along to share the blame in the event you get caught breaking and entering."

Sara's eyes widened. "Not a bad point," she conceded. Then her sense of humor caught up with her. "What did you do before you became a writer, Adrian? You seem to have a knack for getting what you want. Were you a businessman?"

He considered the question. "I guess you could say I was sort of a consultant."

"A consultant?"

"Umm. Someone you call in when things go wrong and have to be fixed in a hurry. You know the type."

"Sure. We used a lot of consultants in the corporation where I recently worked. What's your area of expertise? Engineering? Design? Management?"

"Management."

Sara nodded, familiar with the field. "Get tired of it?"

"More than that. I got what is casually known as burned out."

"I can understand that. I think that in a way that's what happened to me. Uncle Lowell is right. It takes a certain type of personality to be really happy in corporate management. I guess neither you nor I is the type."

A slight smile edged Adrian's hard mouth. "Maybe we have more in common than you thought. We're both in the process of changing careers and we both like Lowell Kincaid."

Sara laughed. "Do you think we can keep each other company on a long drive given those two limited things in common?"

"I think we'll make it without boring or strangling each other."

An hour and a half later Sara was inclined to agree with Adrian. The drive east of Seattle into the Cascades had passed with amazing swiftness. There had been stretches of silence, but the quiet times had not been uncomfortable. Adrian was the kind of man a woman didn't feel she had to keep entertained with bright conversation. In fact, Sara was privately convinced that Adrian would be disgusted if he thought someone was deliberately trying to entertain him with meaningless chatter. It was rather a relief to feel so at ease with him in this area, she realized. Her early-morning tinglings of ambivalence faded as Adrian guided the car deeper into the forest-darkened mountains.

When they did talk, the topics varied from the spectacular scenery to speculation on Lowell Kincaid's whereabouts. In between they discussed Adrian's fledgling career as a writer and the turning point Sara had reached in her own life.

"Are you in a hurry to find a new job?" Adrian asked at one point.

He had calmly assumed the role of driver and Sara had acquiesced primarily because she suspected he would be excellent behind the wheel. She was right. His natural coordination and skill made her feel comfortable at once. He had insisted on using his car and Sara couldn't complain about that, either. The BMW hugged the curving highway with a mechanical grace and power. Normally Sara wasn't particularly enthusiastic about being a passenger in a car being driven by someone whose driving techniques she didn't know well.

"I've got enough of a financial cushion that I can afford to take my time,'' she told him, her eyes on the majestic mountains that rose straight up from the edge of the highway. Small waterfalls spilled over outcroppings of granite. A crystal-clear stream followed the path of the highway on one side. Heavily timbered terrain stretched endlessly in front of the car. It was hard to believe such mountain grandeur lay so close to the heart of a cosmopolitan city. ''But I'll get restless if I sit around too long trying to make up my mind about what I really want to do with my life.''

''Any ideas?''

''Well...'' She hesitated realizing that she hadn't discussed her tentative plans with anyone else, not even her family. ''I've been thinking of going into your old line of work.''

Adrian's head came around in a sudden, unexpected movement. ''My old line?''

She nodded, smiling. ''That probably seems odd to you, but to tell you the truth, I think I'd be a fairly good management consultant. I'd like the opportunity to be my own boss, though. I wouldn't want to work for a firm of consultants. And I'd pick and choose my contracts. I know it sounds like a contradiction in terms, Adrian, but even though I don't like working within an organization, I do have a flair for management techniques that work in an organization. It's one of the reasons I hesitated so long about quitting my last job. I was good at it in a lot of ways.''

Adrian's attention was back on the road ahead. ''I don't think it sounds like a contradiction. A lot of people can give objective advice about things they wouldn't want to make a living doing.''

''It would take a long time to build a clientele,'' Sara said slowly.

''I know the feeling. It will take a long time to build a writing career.''

''But I do have some good contacts who would be glad to recommend me to companies looking for a consultant,'' Sara went on more enthusiastically.

''And I've sold my first book. Sounds like we both have a toehold on the future,'' Adrian said with the first hint of a smile that day.

Sara grinned. ''Assuming we both don't wind up in jail because one of Uncle Lowell's neighbors sees us breaking into his cottage!''

It was shortly after noon by the time Adrian pulled into the drive of Lowell Kincaid's mountain cabin. They had stopped for lunch at a small roadside café en route.

The weatherworn house was one of a number of such cottages scattered about the forested landscape. Many were filled with summer visitors but a few, such as the one just over the next rise, were owned by permanent residents. Lowell Kincaid liked his privacy, however, and had purchased a cottage that was not within sight of the next house. Unless his nearest neighbor happened by on a casual walk, no one would notice two people jimmying the back window, Sara told herself.

''Have you ever done this before?'' Adrian asked blandly as he climbed out of the BMW and stood surveying the cottage.

''I got into your place, didn't I?'' Sara reminded him.

''The front door was unlocked, remember?''

''You should probably start locking it,'' she told him seriously. ''You can't be too careful these days.''

''I'll try to remember to do it,'' he said dryly. ''Now, about this little business...''

''Well, I'll admit I have no direct experience of prying open a window, but how hard can it be? People break into houses all the time.''

''And occasionally get shot doing so.''

Sara gave him a bright smile. ''Maybe we should knock on the front door first, just to make certain no one's home.''

''Good idea.''

Adrian strode to the front door of the cottage and pounded loudly. There was no response. There was also no sign of Lowell's car.

''Looks like we'll have to do this the hard way,'' Adrian

observed morosely. ''We'll probably wreck the window and Lowell will send me the bill.''

Sara started around the corner of the house looking for a window at the right height and of the right size. ''Don't be so pessimistic. I brought you along to help and to lend moral support, not to paint a picture of doom and gloom.''

''It's just that I have this image of Lowell coming home and finding his window broken. He won't be pleased.''

''I'll leave a note,'' Sara offered as she stopped in front of an appropriate window. ''What do you think about this one?''

Adrian frowned and stepped forward to examine it more closely. ''I guess it's as good as any of the others. We'll need something to jimmy it with. Maybe the jack handle in the car. I'll go see what I can find.'' He swung around and then halted abruptly, staring at the next window on the side of the cottage. ''Well, hell.''

''What's wrong?'' Sara turned to follow his gaze. ''I don't...''

''Looks like someone else has been here ahead of us,'' Adrian said softly.

Sara peered more intently. ''Do you really think...oh.'' For the first time she felt a distinct chill of unease. It was obvious the window had been crudely but effectively forced open. The frame was badly marked from whatever instrument had been used, and the window itself was still half raised. ''Vandals?''

Adrian was examining the damage. He didn't look around. ''Surely you're not going to be satisfied with the notion that a couple of young punks broke into your uncle's house. Not after all the exotic mischief and mayhem you've been imagining.''

''Don't be sarcastic. What are you doing?''

''I'm going inside to have a look.'' Adrian shoved the window completely open and casually swung a leg over the sill.

''Wait!'' Sara grabbed for his arm. ''What if someone's still in there?'' she hissed.

He glanced inside the house and shook his head. ''The place is empty.''

"You can't be sure. It's very dangerous to corner burglars in a house. You're supposed to go call the cops before going inside."

"Is that right?" Adrian said vaguely. Then he swung his other leg over the sill and dropped lightly to the floor inside.

Annoyed, Sara leaned through the window to lecture him further. But the words caught in her throat as she took in the chaos of the room. "Oh, my God."

"Umm." Adrian walked past a bookcase that had been ransacked and came to a halt in front of the old roll-top desk.

Feeling stunned, Sara followed him through the window. Inside the house she stood staring in speechless dismay as Adrian examined the desk. She remembered the desk well. She had helped Lowell select it at a junk shop in Seattle. Her uncle had spent hours refinishing it.

Now the surface was a jumble of strewn papers, books and magazines. The drawers had been unceremoniously hauled open and emptied. Folders of personal business papers had been tossed on the floor along with a notebook of Lowell Kincaid's sketches.

Infuriated more than anything else by the way the sketchbook had been dumped on the well-worn Oriental rug, Sara bent down to retrieve it. "Stupid bastards," she muttered as she tried to smooth the pages and close the cover. "Whoever it was just wanted to make a mess. I thought we had all the mental flakes down in California."

"We have a few up here in the Northwest." Adrian walked slowly through the living room into the adjoining kitchen. "Looks like someone really enjoyed himself."

"It's sick." Sara wrinkled her nose at the smell of decaying food. The contents of the refrigerator had been thrown against the walls. "Absolutely sick."

"Or else someone wanted it to look that way," Adrian murmured slowly.

Sara swung around to stare at him wide-eyed. "Good heavens, I hadn't thought of that. That's a possibility, isn't it? Whoever broke in might have deliberately tried to make it look like the work of vandals. That way no one would be able to figure out what he or she had been looking for.''

''On the other hand, it might have really been a couple of genuine vandals.'' Adrian shrugged, moving on into the single bedroom.

''Make up your mind!'' Sara hurried after him.

''How can I? I don't know what's going on here any more than you do.''

''Good point.'' Sara couldn't keep the sarcasm out of her voice. ''Given that basic fact, I guess we'd better go find the local police or sheriff or whatever passes for the law here.''

Adrian paid no attention to her. He was looking at the phone-answering machine that still sat on the table beside the bed. Whoever had gone through the room yanking open drawers and closet doors had ignored the telephone. The red light was gleaming, indicating a message had been recorded.

''The message on there is probably from me,'' Sara said quietly. ''The one I left when I called him a couple of days ago to let him know I would be arriving. There was no answer, so I just kept driving.''

Adrian pressed the button that rewound the tape. The first voice on the machine was Sara's, as she had predicted.

''Uncle Lowell? I'm driving up from California to see you. Just wanted you to know I took your advice. Mom and Dad are in a deep depression over the whole thing but I think they'll survive. Maybe they're getting used to my life-style changes. Personally, I feel great. You were right. See you tomorrow.''

Sara caught her breath when she heard the next voice on the tape. Her uncle's easy growl was as unconcerned and laconic as ever.

''Adrian, if you and Sara are the ones listening to this, then you'll have realized I have a small problem on my hands. I can't explain everything just now but don't worry. We'll talk later. Pay attention to me. This isn't anything I can't handle but I need a little time and privacy. Some unfinished business regarding your wedding present, I'm afraid. It's tough enough to find just the right gift for a special couple like you and Sara. I didn't realize it would be even harder to protect it. Do me a favor and don't bother the local cops. This is a personal matter. Oh, and Adrian, Sara tends to have a rather vivid imagination and she doesn't handle waiting very well. A distinct lack of patience in that woman at times. I heard her message on the tape when I phoned to leave my own. I know she's on her way here and when she doesn't find me she'll probably look you up. Which, of course, explains why you're standing there listening to this tape. Aren't you impressed with my wondrous logic?'' There was a rough chuckle. ''Take care of her for me and keep her out of trouble until I get back. I'll see you as soon as I can.''

The tape wound on into silence while Sara stood utterly still, staring at the machine in astonishment and dread. ''Wedding gift?'' she finally got out very weakly.

Adrian punched the stop button. ''I told you Lowell had plans for us,'' he reminded her dryly.

''Adrian, none of this makes any sense!''

''Yes, it does.'' Adrian turned to look at her. His light eyes were unreadable, but the set of his harsh features was intently serious. ''Lowell says that whatever's going on is private business. He'll take care of it. He doesn't want any help or he'd ask for it. And he wants me to keep you from getting involved. I'm supposed to take care of you. It all seems clear enough to me.''

''Don't be ridiculous. There is nothing clear about this mess.'' Sara spun around and stalked back into the living room. ''Damn Uncle Lowell anyway. Why couldn't he have left a simple straightforward message or called you and told you exactly what was going on?'' She headed toward the rifled desk. ''Just like him to leave a lot of questions lying around for us to try to answer.''

''He says it's a private matter. He doesn't want us involved. He probably didn't call because he didn't want to alarm us unnecessarily. On the other hand, he figured if we got this far he'd better leave some sort of message.'' Adrian followed her on silent feet, stopping to examine the stack of books that had been stripped from the bookcase.

''If it's such a personal matter, what was that business about protecting our wedding present?'' Sara shot him a scathing glance as she began picking up the scattered magazines that had been spilled from an end table. Lowell Kincaid was an inveterate magazine reader. Sara had frequently teased him about the number of subscriptions he maintained.

''You know your uncle. There are times when he simply can't resist throwing out a teaser.'' Adrian seemed unconcerned.

''It's his unfortunate sense of humor, I suppose.'' Sara sighed and shuffled a stack of insurance papers. ''Adrian, this whole thing is going to drive me crazy. How are we going to know he's all right?''

''We won't until he gets back. But I've told you before, Sara. Your uncle can take care of himself.''

''I don't like that comment about 'unfinished business,''' she went on unhappily. ''It sounds dangerous. Like something from his past coming back to haunt him.''

''Lowell was right. You do have an active imagination.''

''Well?'' she challenged. ''How would you interpret that message?''

''Like something from his past that has come back to haunt him,'' Adrian admitted in resigned tones. He picked up a stack of books and put them back on the shelf. ''The real problem is that food on the walls in the kitchen. That's going to be a mess to clean. It's going to take quite a while, too.''

''Stop changing the subject! This is important. We have to figure out what's going on.'' Sara frowned intently down at the papers in her hand. Predictably enough, many of them, even the most important-looking ones, contained small sketches and doodles. Lowell Kincaid was forever covering books, papers and notepads with his drawings. He did them almost unconsciously, Sara knew. He could be talking about one thing and sketching a totally unrelated subject. She remembered once having coffee with him in a restaurant and discussing her growing dissatisfaction with her latest job. Lowell had carried on a detailed and logical conversation while making comical character sketches on a napkin of the people in the next booth. ''What do you suppose whoever did this was looking for?''

''That's something we can't even guess until Lowell shows up.''

''Except that we know it has something to do with our so-called wedding gift,'' Sara muttered in growing annoyance. ''What in the world could Uncle Lowell have been talking about?''

''If he'd wanted us to know, he would have told us.''

''You're awfully casual about this, Adrian.'' Sara glared at him over her shoulder.

''I know your uncle very well, Sara,'' Adrian said. ''He doesn't want us getting involved.''

She ignored that, her sandaled foot tapping impatiently under the desk. Thoughtfully Sara stared out the window toward a stand of fir. ''He said he'd already gotten the gift. Now he has to protect it.''

''Something like that.'' Adrian reshelved another batch of books.

''So whoever did this must have been looking for whatever Uncle Lowell calls our wedding present.''

''Are you going to give me a hand cleaning up the kitchen?''

''You know, Uncle Lowell once told me he believed in the old theory that the best hiding place was the one that was in full view. People really do tend to overlook the obvious. He says answers are always quite clear when you know where to look.'' She glanced around the room with narrowed eyes. ''He'd had some experience along those lines. He ought to know what he's talking about.''

Adrian went into the kitchen. ''If whoever made this mess didn't find what he was looking for, the odds are you won't find it, either. It may not even be here. Or Lowell might have removed it and hidden it somewhere else. Or this chaos might really be the work of casual vandals who happened on an empty cabin. A coincidence. Sara, we don't have a clue. There's no point beating our heads against a stone wall. Let your uncle take care of his own business.''

Sara heard water running in the kitchen sink. Reluctantly she put down the stack of insurance papers and got to her feet. Adrian was right. They should clean up the kitchen first.

''Uncle Lowell said he was thinking of putting in a fancy alarm system. Too bad he didn't get around to it in time to prevent this,'' she commented.

''I know. I was going to help him install it,'' Adrian said from the kitchen.

Sara took a step forward and her toe brushed a thick sheaf of papers that had been lying on the floor beside the chair. The pile of neatly typed pages was still bound with a rubber band. Automatically she leaned down to pick it up. Halfway down the first page a single word, underlined, leaped out at her. *Phantom.*

''Adrian! Here's a copy of your manuscript,'' she called, aware of a surging sense of interest in what she held. Curiously she flipped through a handful of pages.

''I think I mentioned that I had given a copy to Lowell,'' Adrian said softly from the doorway of the kitchen.

''Would you mind if I...?'' Sara's request to read the manuscript died on her lips as she looked at the penciled sketch in the right-hand corner of the first page. There were other doodles at the bottom of the page, but it was the one at the top that made her grow cold.

The drawing had been done hurriedly, but Lowell Kincaid's talent lay in the quick character sketch. Strong, simple lines defined the figure in only a few brief strokes. It was the head of a wolf.

''No,'' Sara whispered as she stared at the drawing. ''Oh, no.''

"Sara? What's wrong?" Adrian tossed aside the sponge he had been holding and came toward her, his expression one of grave concern.

Feeling decidedly unnerved, Sara sank back down into the desk chair and looked up at him. "See that drawing on your manuscript?"

Adrian glanced at the page and then back at her strained face. "What about it? Your uncle is always doodling and sketching. You know that." He leaned down to flip through the rubber-band-bound stack. "Look. There are little drawings on nearly all the pages."

"I know. But this is more than just an idle sketch." She swallowed, struggling to remember details. "There was a real wolf in his past, you see. A renegade killer. Never mind, it's a long story. Uncle Lowell told me about him one night over a few drinks." Dazedly she stared down at the drawing. "Adrian, if this is the 'unfinished business' my uncle is taking care of, he's in real trouble. We've got to do something."

Adrian's mouth tightened. He reached down and picked up the manuscript. "We are going to do something. We're going to stay out of Lowell's way and let him handle his unfinished business."

"Adrian, we have a responsibility!"

"My responsibility is to take care of you. Very clear—very simple. That's what your uncle wants and that's what I'm going to do. Now, if you really want to do something useful for Lowell, come on into the kitchen and help me clean up the mess. If we don't take care of it, some helpful, foraging skunks or worse will take care of it for us."

Three

She was genuinely scared, Adrian reflected a few hours later. Tense, nervous, restless and scared. He had spent the past three hours alternately trying to reassure her that Lowell Kincaid could handle his own problems and trying to convince her that she was letting her imagination play havoc with her common sense. Neither attempt had been particularly successful. But then, he hadn't had a lot of experience attempting to soothe the fears of others.

It had been late by the time they'd finished cleaning up Lowell's cabin, and when Adrian had suggested they spend the night at a motel instead of driving all the way back to Seattle, Sara hadn't argued. He'd scrupulously booked two rooms at a charmingly rustic little lodge located just off the main highway.

Now, as he studied her across the restaurant table, it occurred to Adrian that he was going to have his hands full trying to carry out the task Kincaid had assigned him in that damned recorded phone message.

Nothing was going the way he had thought it would, and the knowledge irritated him. For the better part of the past year the unknown Sara had been hovering in the back of his mind, her nebulous image planted there by Lowell Kincaid.

''The two of you are going to be great together,'' Lowell had told him with vast assurance. ''But you both need a little time. You've got to get *Phantom* out of your system and she has to reach a few conclusions on her own. I figure in another few months—''

''Lowell, you may be my best friend but I don't want you playing matchmaker. Understand?'' Adrian had been very firm even though he'd already downed a great deal of beer before the conversation had gotten around to the subject of Kincaid's niece.

"You're going to love her, pal. Trust me. The two of you have a lot in common."

"That's rather doubtful, isn't it?"

"I know people, Adrian. You should realize that by now. She's perfect for you. She's intelligent and full of life. She's also fundamentally genuine and honest. She'll help you keep your life in balance. You need a dose of enthusiasm and optimism. You're too cautious. Furthermore, she's capable of making a commitment to the right man. Luckily for you, she hasn't found him yet. And she won't as long as she hangs around those wimps she's been dating for the past few years. She's smart enough to play with the dross but wait for the real gold." Lowell had grinned. "She's really very good at playing with life. In college she played at being pseudo-intellectual. She used to spend hours arguing about philosophical treatises. A lot of people thought she was serious, including her teachers. Got good grades. When she graduated she decided to play at being an artist for a while. Rented a genuine garret, wore her hair long and went around in paint-stained jeans. She actually sold a couple of paintings through a gallery that made the mistake of taking her seriously. Then she went through an activist phase during which she went around protesting against environmental polluters. Eventually she wound up as the epitome of the young, upwardly mobile urban professional. She always did have a good sense of timing. She also has a real flair for management. She enjoys life the way some people enjoy a game."

"And just what am I going to be offering her in return?" Adrian had asked roughly as he popped the top on another can of beer. The discussion was outrageous, but such conversations were allowable when you were sharing several beers with your only real friend. Besides, there was something about the unknown Sara that intrigued him more than he wanted to admit.

He found himself wondering what she would think of him if Lowell ever got around to introductions.

''She needs someone strong, someone who can appreciate what she has to offer. She also needs a counterfoil for her natural enthusiasm and impulsiveness. Someone stable and steady. When she does give her heart for real, it will be completely. She'll need someone who will make the same commitment to her that she'll be making to him. A lot of men aren't capable of that. They might know several fancy names for spaghetti or how to select the right brand of running shorts but that's about the extent of their sensitivity.''

''Been reading those articles on the 'new male,' I see. I warned you about that. You should cancel some of those magazine subscriptions. Bunch of garbage and you know it.''

''Is that so? Well, how many men would you trust with your life or your wallet or your woman these days?'' Lowell had countered.

That had struck a chord, Adrian remembered. ''Not many. Maybe you. That's about it.''

''And you're the only one I would trust with anything I value. I value my niece, Adrian. Perhaps because there's something in her that reminds me of myself.''

''So you're going to give her to me? I'm not sure that you're taking your responsibilities as her uncle seriously enough.''

''I know what I'm doing. You should be thanking me. You need a woman who can give herself completely. You also need someone who has a real understanding of loyalty. You could also use someone who occasionally shakes you up a bit. You're so damned controlled, son, that it worries me at times. It's as though you've built a carefully organized, well-defined little world for yourself and nothing gets in unless you've fully analyzed and comprehended it first.''

''I like to be sure of things, Lowell. You know that.''

The older man had grinned complacently. ''Once you get to know Sara you'll realize you can be sure of her in all the ways that count. There's a lot of love and loyalty in that woman, and the man who taps it is going to be very rich. You'll see."

The conversation, as Adrian recalled, had gone downhill from there. The beer had flowed freely, and mercifully it had inspired Lowell Kincaid to bring up other topics for discussion. Adrian couldn't remember too many of them the next morning, but he definitely recalled the little matter of Kincaid's niece.

Phantom had absorbed most of his time and energy in the ensuing months. He hadn't seen a great deal of anyone, not even Lowell Kincaid, but the older man had known what he was doing. As usual.

The seed had been planted, and as he'd worked steadily, often painfully, on the novel, Adrian had found the presence of the mysterious Sara hovering in the corners of his mind. Sometimes late at night after he'd put in hours on the manuscript he'd dosed himself with brandy and gone to bed thinking about what he would do if he had Sara there. He'd let himself fantasize about having a woman who loved him, a woman who knew what loyalty meant. And then he'd gone to sleep with a body that still ached from the stirrings of an irrational passion.

On the rare occasions when he did talk to Kincaid, Adrian had heard himself ask after the woman with what he hoped was deceptive casualness. Lowell had supplied information readily enough, telling him about her success in her job or the latest "wimp" she was seeing.

When he'd begun to realize he didn't like hearing about the newest males in Sara's life, Adrian had finally acknowledged to himself that he might have a problem. It was ridiculous and quite asinine to start wanting a woman you'd never met, but the sense of anticipation had taken firm root. That anticipation had been followed by a curious sensation of possessiveness that was even more perplexing than the fantasy-induced desire.

Her undefined image had remained on the borders of his mind, always waiting for him. She was there when he took a break during the day from *Phantom.* She emerged to haunt him before he went to sleep at night. And she casually made herself felt when he sat by himself in front of the fire in the evenings sipping a lonely glass of wine.

Lowell had said he'd see about introducing Sara to Adrian when the book was finished. Over a period of months she had begun to seem like the prize at the end of a quest.

Last night when he'd returned from his small celebration of the sale of *Phantom* and walked home to find the lady in his study, Adrian had experienced the disorienting sensation of having met his destiny. The quest had been completed and now his gift was within reach. The fantasy hadn't diminished since the previous evening.

It should have, Adrian thought objectively as he watched Sara prod a sun-dried tomato in her pasta salad. Fantasies were supposed to die quick deaths when reality took over. But reality was proving very interesting in this case, far more gripping than fantasy.

''So what are we going to do?'' Across the table Sara finally gave up on her salad and set down her fork. Challengingly she waited for Adrian to say something brilliant.

Adrian realized he couldn't rise to the challenge. ''Nothing.''

''As an answer, that lacks a certain something,'' she muttered. ''In management training I learned that you're always supposed to sound confident and in charge.''

''Maybe I should take the course.''

''This is not a joke, Adrian. We can't just sit around and wait.''

''Why not? It's what your uncle wants us to do. We'll drive back to Seattle in the morning. You can stay with me on the island until Lowell returns.''

She eyed him with abrupt wariness. ''I don't think that's such a good idea.''

''It sounds perfectly reasonable to me. You're certainly not going to spend the time waiting in Lowell's cottage. If you think I'd leave you there knowing that whoever went through that place once might return, you're out of your little ex-corporate skull.''

He hadn't raised his voice, but Sara felt the diamond-hard determination in him more clearly than if he'd shouted the words.

"Don't worry," she said bluntly, "I'm not particularly eager to stay alone at Uncle Lowell's cottage. Not after seeing that sketch of the wolf."

Adrian glared at her and picked up his wineglass. "What the devil is all this nonsense about the wolf, anyway? You've been acting as if you'd seen a ghost ever since you saw Lowell's dumb doodle on my manuscript."

"I did. In a way." Moodily Sara stared at the tablecloth in front of her, remembering. "It's a long story, Adrian."

"We've got a long evening ahead of us," he noted grimly. "You might as well tell me the tale."

"I only know bits and pieces of it." Sara sighed and pushed aside her half-eaten meal. "Uncle Lowell never told me all the details. He probably couldn't because of security reasons, although lately my uncle has begun to demonstrate an amazing disgust for all the bureaucratic paranoia that generally controls matters of security." A brief flicker of amusement lit her eyes for a few seconds as she thought about that. She heartily approved of the trend.

"So what did he tell you about this wolf business that has you so upset tonight?"

"There was a man," she began slowly, recalling the conversation with her uncle that had taken place nearly a year ago. "A man who carried the code name of Wolf. Uncle Lowell said it suited him." Sara gave Adrian a level glance, willing him to understand the importance of what she was trying to say. "Lowell said he was so good at what he did, so dangerous, that when he walked into a room the temperature seemed to drop by twenty degrees."

Adrian considered that in silence for a moment and then murmured very distinctly, "Bull."

Sara scowled at him. "It's true."

''Your uncle's right. You do have an overactive imagination.''

''It was Uncle Lowell who told me about the guy. That business of the room going cold was his description, not mine. He meant that the man could literally chill your blood. Even Uncle Lowell's blood, apparently. Now do you want to hear the rest of the story or not?''

Adrian shrugged and buttered a roll. ''Go ahead.''

''All right. But only if you're going to listen seriously to what I'm saying. This is not a wild tale, Adrian. Uncle Lowell meant every word the night he told me the story. He was... upset.''

''Lowell was upset?''

''Yes. You see, he knew the man they called Wolf. The guy was supposed to be his replacement. Uncle Lowell had the job of grooming him to step into his shoes when he retired.''

''Lowell officially retired five years ago.''

Sara nodded. ''But my uncle kept tabs on his replacement, I guess. He must have been very uneasy about him right from the beginning. He said this Wolf was almost frighteningly ruthless. He seemed to have no emotions, no human sensitivity. Sending him on a mission was like aiming a gun and pulling the trigger. From what Uncle Lowell said, the man would probably qualify as a sociopath. You know, someone who doesn't really function in society. No emotional equipment. Sick. Working for the intelligence group Uncle Lowell was in gave him an outlet for his antisocial tendencies and his ruthlessness. If he hadn't gotten that kind of job, he probably would have ended up as a first-class criminal.''

''Lowell said all this?'' Adrian seemed both skeptical and reluctantly fascinated.

''Some of it I've inferred from his description that night. My uncle was very restless about something that evening. He wanted to talk to someone, I think. I've never seen him in quite that mood. And he'd certainly never made a habit before of talking about his, uh, former business associates. Sometimes he'd tell me stories and tales but they were always deliberately vague on details. I could tell that the story wasn't being embroidered or altered for security reasons this time. Anyhow, he'd come down to spend a weekend with my family in San Diego. We had all gone out to dinner, and when we were finished he drove me over to my apartment. I knew something was bothering him, and when he started talking, I just let him go on until he'd gotten it all out of his system."

"Did he give you any specific details on this character he calls Wolf?" Adrian asked softly.

"You mean like a description or his real name? Of course not." Sara smiled wryly. "Even when Uncle Lowell's in a chatty mood, he knows how to watch his tongue. I guess he spent too many years being cautious. All I know about Wolf is that Lowell was worried. I think he believed his protégé might be slipping over the edge. Wolf was dangerous enough when he could still be aimed by his superiors and fired like a weapon, but if he could no longer be at least minimally controlled... If he decided to go into business for himself, for example..."

"You're saying Lowell thought the guy might have gone renegade?" Adrian demanded.

Sara took a breath. "That's the impression I got that night. I only know that Uncle Lowell was tense and worried about what he had helped create."

Adrian chewed meditatively on another chunk of his roll. "Dr. Frankenstein and his monster."

"I know it sounds melodramatic," Sara admitted, "and if I hadn't seen that little drawing of a wolf's head on your manuscript, I wouldn't have thought twice about that conversation with my uncle. But after hearing the message on the telephone-answering machine and seeing the mess that cottage was in and then finding the drawing—" She broke off, her anxiety clear in her eyes.

"Why do you suppose your uncle happened to make that little doodle on the front page of my manuscript?" Adrian asked reflectively.

Sara lifted one shoulder negligently. "You know him. He's constantly sketching and doodling. He uses whatever's handy. I've seen him make the most intricate little drawings on cocktail napkins or paper towels or the back of his income-tax forms. Your manuscript probably happened to be nearby when he was thinking of this Wolf person. Or..." Sara's eyes widened as a thought caught her attention. "Maybe something in your manuscript reminded him of the wolf."

"Not likely. Not from the way you've described the guy," Adrian said flatly.

Sara thought about that. "Then he must have been thinking of the wolf at a time when your manuscript was lying nearby. Which means that something was making him uneasy. He tells us in that recorded message that he's going to take care of unfinished business. I think...I think Uncle Lowell always considered Wolf unfinished business."

"Because he'd trained him and then turned him loose?"

"Something like that. How would you feel if you'd been assigned to train someone and had him turn into a...a criminal or worse. Perhaps a renegade killer. Wouldn't you feel you had to do something about it?"

"Not a pleasant thought," Adrian said slowly.

"But wouldn't you feel responsible?"

"I might."

"Then maybe—"

Adrian interrupted abruptly. "But, Sara, that doesn't explain Lowell's message completely. Remember, he said he was out to protect our, er, wedding present."

"I know. I can't figure out that part," she admitted morosely.

"Face it. We don't stand a chance in hell of figuring any of this out until your uncle gets back and tells us just what was going on. The only thing we can do is wait." Adrian's rare smile flickered briefly at the corners of his mouth. "At least I got assigned a task to keep my mind off Lowell's problems."

"What task?" She frowned at him across the table.

"Taking care of you. I'm supposed to keep you out of mischief, remember?"

"Oh, that." She waved the entire matter aside. "That was just a casual comment on my uncle's part."

"Nevertheless, I feel obliged to take it seriously. After all, you're worried, and if someone doesn't keep an eye on you, I can envision you getting into all sorts of trouble."

"Don't be ridiculous."

"You might," Adrian concluded without any trace of amusement at all, "even manage to make some trouble for your uncle."

That caught her attention. "What on earth do you mean?"

"I think that, left to your own devices, you'll convince yourself that Lowell really is in trouble. You'll start poking around, perhaps asking questions. There's no telling what small waves you might set in motion that could ripple back to Lowell."

Sara studied him, stricken. "You're serious, aren't you? I wouldn't do anything to jeopardize my uncle."

"I know you wouldn't do anything deliberately, but how could you even begin to guess what might or might not have an effect?"

"Oh, come off it, Adrian, I'm hardly in a position to do anything dramatic one way or the other," she protested.

"No?" He pushed aside his plate and leaned forward, his arms folded on the table in front of him. "What if you go back to talk to that neighbor of his? What if you decide to do a little investigating on your own? Find out if anyone noticed someone hanging around your uncle's cottage recently, for example. And what if someone notices you and takes exception to your involvement? I can see you doing all sorts of little things that could blow up in Lowell's face. Or worse yet, your own face."

"That's ridiculous and you know it. Now you're the one whose imagination is running wild," she scoffed. But deep down she felt a prickle of guilt. It had occurred to her only a few minutes earlier that it might be interesting to talk to her uncle's neighbors. A vague plan to talk to some of them had been formulating in the back of her mind. She knew her flushed cheeks betrayed her.

Adrian gave her a very deliberate look. "Going to deny you were making a few plans?"

"Well, no, but I certainly don't think..." She trailed off, flustered.

"Umm. I think my little assignment is going to be the tough one," Adrian groaned. "I have a hunch Lowell knew exactly what he was doing when he asked me to keep an eye on you. If you're finished playing with your food, let's head back to the rooms. It's getting late." He stood up without bothering to wait for her agreement. The waiter hurried over with the check.

Disgruntled at the abrupt termination of the meal and the conversation, Sara got to her feet more slowly and allowed Adrian to walk her out of the small restaurant. Her head was spinning with worry, speculation and half-formed plans. In fact, her attention was focused so completely on her thoughts that she didn't notice where Adrian was guiding her until she suddenly became aware of flagstone under her strappy little sandals. He was leading her along a path that wound around the motel.

"A little late for a walk, isn't it?" she asked, glancing into the shadows of darkened stands of trees. Behind them the lights of the motel flared in the night.

"I thought a walk before turning in might calm you down a bit." Adrian took a firmer grip on her arm as she stumbled lightly on a cluster of pebbles. "Watch your step."

"That's tough to do since I don't see well in the dark," she complained.

"I'll guide you."

"You can see in the dark?" she asked very politely.

"Umm. I've always had good night vision."

"That must come in handy for this sort of thing," she allowed still more politely.

"What sort of thing?"

''Enforced midnight marches with unsuspecting females,'' she drawled.

''It's only nine-thirty and believe it or not I can't even remember the last time I went for an evening walk with a female, unsuspecting or otherwise.'' He hesitated, mulling that over. ''It's very pleasant.''

''Even though I'm having trouble walking in a straight line?''

''That's the best part.''

''Oh.'' Her brief amusement vanished as suddenly as it had appeared, and Sara went back to thinking about her missing uncle.

''It won't do you any good, you know,'' Adrian said after a moment.

''What won't do any good?''

''Worrying.''

''But I'm so good at it.'' She sighed.

''What you need is something to take your mind off your problems.'' Adrian came to an unexpected halt, catching hold of her with both hands as she stumbled into him. ''And I think I need the same thing,'' he added almost under his breath as he stood very close in the darkness and ran his palms down her arms.

Sara felt the strength in his hands as he pulled her close. She looked up, aware of a fierce surge of sudden awareness as she realized he was going to kiss her. For an instant she tried to read his shadowed gaze, seeking answers to questions she couldn't formulate. But in the almost nonexistent light his eyes were colorless and infinitely unintelligible. She was enthralled by her own reaction to that gaze. It lured her, promising something she wasn't sure she wanted. Before she could fathom the strange sensation, Sara felt herself pressed against him, and in the next moment Adrian's mouth was on hers.

What startled her most about his kiss was the urgency in it. It seemed to wash over her, a combination of male curiosity, hunger and carefully restrained desire. The first kiss from a man was usually tentative, polite and as practiced as he could make it. This was something else again. There was nothing tentative or polite about it. Nor was there any element of practiced seduction in the damp heat of his kiss.

Sara was tinglingly aware that it was the most honest kiss she had ever received. She wasn't sure how she knew that with such certainty but there was absolutely no doubt in her mind. It was like finding gold after years of sorting through scrap metal. The vivid realization brought forth a response from her that she'd had no intention of indulging until it flared into life. Then it could hardly be denied.

Slowly, savoring the moment of unexpected awareness, she slid her arms around his neck and found the dark pelt of his hair with questing fingertips. She was thirty years old, she thought, and not given to such episodes of instant attraction. This was something unique and she was wise enough to know it.

''Sara?''

Slowly, reluctantly, Adrian lifted his mouth from hers. He raised one hand to tangle in her hair while with the other he stroked the length of her back. She could feel the intensity in him as he urged her soft thighs against the hard planes of his lower body.

''I believe you said this was supposed to give me something else to think about?'' she murmured gently.

''I don't know about you, but I may have given myself a little too much to think about tonight. Forgive me, honey, but I've been wondering what you would taste like for a long time.'' Once again he lowered his mouth to hers.

Sara felt her lips being parted and then he was deep in her unresisting mouth exploring her with such intimacy that she trembled. For countless moments time stood still for her there on the narrow path. She gave herself up to the intriguing, captivating touch of a man who qualified as a near-stranger and wondered why he seemed so right to all her senses.

She offered no resistance as Adrian drew her deeper and

deeper into the embrace. When his palms slipped down to cup the contours of her derriere, she stood on tiptoe, nestling closer. His leaping desire made itself felt through the fabric of his jeans and her own body struggled to answer the ancient call. Sara had never known such driving urgency. When Adrian freed her mouth to seek out the sensitive place behind her ear, she heard herself murmur a throaty response. His breath was exciting and warm in her hair.

Then, slowly at first but with gathering strength the night breeze began to make itself felt. Sara became vaguely aware of the gathering chill as it swirled and eddied around her. The warmth of Adrian's body warded off some of it but not all. He seemed to realize what was happening at about the same moment and slowly lifted his head.

''I think it's time to go back,'' he said huskily.

''Yes.'' She didn't argue. He was right. It was time to go safely back to her own bed. But she felt unexpectedly weak and she found herself holding on to his arm.

For a moment longer Adrian's palms framed her upturned face. She sensed the hesitation in him and was warmed by it. He was reluctant to break the spell and that pleased her. She didn't want to be the only one caught up in the magic, Sara realized.

''If it weren't so cold out here and if you'd had a little more time to get used to the idea...'' Adrian let the rest of the sentence trail off as he took her hand and started back toward the lights of the motel.

''Get used to what idea?''

''Never mind,'' he told her laconically. ''My imagination is proving to be as vivid as yours, although it seems to be running along different lines.''

Sara smiled serenely to herself in the shadows, knowing exactly what was going through his head. He wanted her, and the knowledge sent a primitive thrill through her veins. Adrian wouldn't do anything about it tonight, of course. It was much too soon. They barely knew each other and there were a great many factors that might get in the way of a relationship between them. Still, tonight she would go to sleep with a sense of anticipation that was entirely new to her.

But an hour later as she lay in bed in the room next to Adrian's Sara realized that, anticipation or not, sleep was not going to come easily that night. Adrian had succeeded in distracting her for a while, she decided ruefully, but now that she was alone again, too many jumbled thoughts were swirling in her head. Her mind skipped around from worries about her uncle and his ''unfinished business'' to memories of Adrian's urgent kiss. She needed something to relax her.

''Like a good book,'' she decided aloud, pushing back the covers. And she knew just where to get one.

Padding barefoot across the carpet, her long cotton nightgown trailing behind her, Sara went to the suitcase in the corner. Opening it, she reached inside and removed the manuscript of *Phantom* that she had picked up off her uncle's desk. For a moment her gaze rested thoughtfully on the sketch of the wolf in the upper corner, and then she told herself to ignore it. She was after relaxation, not added worry.

A deep curiosity filled her as she climbed back into bed and started *Phantom.* Silently she admitted to herself that it was the desire to learn something more about the man she had spent the day with rather than a wish to see how the story ended that prompted the feeling. How much could you tell about a man by his writing, she wondered.

On the surface, *Phantom* was high adventure. It involved the perilous race to retrieve a cache of gold that had been smuggled out of South Vietnam during the last, chaotic days of the war. The treasure had been hidden near the Cambodian border and had been inaccessible for years because it was simply too dangerous to go after it. Only a handful of men knew the location.

As the story opened, it was learned that more than a treasure had been hidden. Secret documents that could destroy the career of a powerful government official had been buried along with the gold. Suddenly any risk was worth taking to retrieve the cache.

The action was well plotted and moved with the swiftness of an avalanche, but what held Sara's attention until nearly two in the morning was the inner conflict of the protagonist, the man called Phantom.

He was portrayed as a man who had clearly reached the limits of his emotional and physical endurance. Too many years of tension and violence had taken a savage toll. Now he had been assigned one last job by the government agency for which he worked. He was told to retrieve the gold and the documents hidden with it. At any price.

In the end the man called Phantom did the job he had been assigned to do, but it had nearly destroyed him. Then he had accidentally discovered that the incriminating documents buried with the gold constituted a shattering indictment of the man who ran the very agency for which he himself worked. The secret papers pointed at treason at the highest levels. Phantom had learned far too much. He had not been expected to survive his mission, but now that he had, his life was in jeopardy.

By the time Sara finished the harrowing and emotionally gripping tale, she felt exhausted but not at all relaxed. The writing had been lean and stark, which didn't surprise her. Adrian Saville struck her as the kind of man who wouldn't use one more word than necessary to tell his story. But she was left with the same question she'd had when she'd begun reading. How much insight could you gain into a man by reading his fiction?

Restlessly she restacked the manuscript pages and climbed back out of bed. She put *Phantom* back in the suitcase and turned to eye the rumpled sheets. She really didn't feel like climbing back into bed just yet. The book had left her far too keyed up and strangely tense.

On impulse she walked over to the sliding-glass door that opened onto the balcony and unlocked it. Taking a deep breath of the chilled mountain air, she stepped outside.

"You should have been asleep hours ago."

Sara jumped at the sound of Adrian's voice. Whirling, she saw him lounging against the railing of the balcony next to hers. He had one foot propped on the lowest rung and his elbows planted on the top one. The shadows hid the expression on his face, but she was aware of a strange tension in the atmosphere between them.

"I couldn't sleep," Sara whispered. "I've been reading."

"*Phantom?*"

"Yes."

"Learn anything?" he inquired sardonically.

Sara half smiled. "Only that I think you're going to have a very successful career as a writer of suspense novels. I couldn't put it down, Adrian."

"But did you learn anything?" he pressed softly.

She wished she could see his face. "You know I started it out of curiosity, don't you?"

"Umm."

"Well, I finished it because it was a very gripping tale. But I don't think I learned much about you in the process." She paused, thinking. "No, that's not true. I guess I did pick up a few things along the way."

"Such as?"

"You have a set of rather fundamental values, don't you? You believe in integrity and justice. Things like honor and loyalty are important to you. If they weren't you wouldn't have been able to portray the hero's emotional turmoil so well. You tore that poor man apart, Adrian. Halfway through the book I almost hated the writer for doing that to his protagonist. And then in the end, even though you pull together all the strands of the story and see that justice is done, you leave us wondering a little whether or not Phantom will survive emotionally."

Even as she spoke Sara realized the truth of her own words. She had learned something about Adrian Saville by reading his manuscript, and what she had learned was disturbing on some levels. This was not a man who would ever understand games, let alone a lighthearted approach to life. On other levels Sara was aware of a strong feeling of respect. There were so few men who knew what it meant to have a personal code of honor and integrity. Adrian must know or he would never have been able to create Phantom. On still another level of awareness Sara experienced a sensation of compassion. Adrian must have known what it felt like to hold yourself together by sheer willpower. She wondered what he'd gone through in order to comprehend the depths of that kind of struggle.

"You wanted a miracle cure?" Adrian turned his head to look out toward the night-shrouded forest.

"I like happy endings," Sara admitted with a soft smile.

"I'm not sure there are any."

Sara leaned sideways against the rail, the chilly breeze whipping the hem of her nightgown around her ankles. "Adrian, I swear, if you turn into one of those cynical New York-style writers I won't read your next book."

He looked at her then and she saw the flash of a genuine grin. "Maybe the trick is not to write endings. Just cut the story off after the main issues have been resolved and let everyone go their own way. Readers like you can assume it all ends happily."

"You won't be able to fool me," she warned. "I know a real happy ending when I see one."

"I'll work on it," he promised so quietly she could barely hear him.

"Adrian?"

"What is it, Sara?"

"About the basic story line of *Phantom*..."

"What about it?"

"Where did you get the idea of the gold being hidden during the last days of the Vietnam war? It was very ingenious. And you made all the action so realistic."

"I got the idea from your uncle. He told me the tale of the gold."

"Really? It's a true story?"

''It's just a legend, of course. There are always a lot of tales and legends that come out of a situation like the last days of South Vietnam. Lowell told me the story one night about a year ago. Supposedly the gold was used by U.S. intelligence to buy information and finance certain clandestine operations. Your uncle told me privately that it's far more likely the gold was a payoff from some big drug deals that were going on in the south. Vietnam was a hotbed for that kind of thing toward the end of the war. At any rate the last man to actually see the gold was a U.S. agent. He arrived at his rendezvous point minus the treasure. No one really knows what happened.'' Adrian shrugged. ''And thus are legends born.''

''You added the bit about the secret incriminating documents?'' Sara hazarded.

''It's called literary license. I needed an extra fillip to make the tale more than just a treasure hunt.''

''You certainly accomplished that.'' Sara shuddered. ''I really empathized with your hero. I think I fell a little in love with him.''

There was a moment of silence from the other balcony and then Adrian said very calmly, ''I'd much rather you fell in love with me.''

Four

Perhaps it was the knowledge that she was concealed in the shadows of her balcony and that Adrian was isolated, in turn, on his own little island that made Sara feel safe enough to indulge the dangerous curiosity. Or perhaps she was still wondering just how much she had learned about him from reading his book. Then again, it might have been simply a woman's endless need to probe a man's words, searching for the real meaning. Whatever the cause, she couldn't resist asking the question.

"Why?"

"Because I think it might be very pleasant to have you fall in love with me."

The answer was straight enough, Sara had to admit to herself. Straightforward and honest. Just like the man. The bluntness of it served to wilt the small blossom of excitement within her before she'd even had a chance to fully analyze it. She stifled a small sigh of regret.

"Pleasant," she mused. "That sounds a little insipid."

He seemed surprised at her interpretation. "No. Not at all. I've learned to value the pleasant things in life," he continued slowly. "Pleasant things are civilized. They bring an element of grace and gentleness and peace into our lives. A glass of wine before dinner or a can of beer on a hot afternoon, a late-night walk on a beach, a friend you can trust with your life, a woman whose love is unshakable even if she knows you've been to hell and back. A wise man values such things."

"It must be the writer in you that can put the love of a woman in the same category of pleasantness as a glass of wine.

Don't expect a woman to be impressed, however. We like to think we're special,'' Sara said with a degree of lightness she wasn't feeling.

''You're not going to take me seriously, are you?''

''Not tonight. It's two o'clock in the morning and we've had a disturbing day. I feel a little strange after reading *Phantom;* restless in some way. And as for you, you're a man whose understanding of life's pleasures seems to be different from the way other men view them. I'm not sure I understand you. All in all, I think there are too many jumbled emotions and unknown factors hanging around tonight for me to risk taking you seriously.'' She said it all very easily but Sara believed every word she was uttering.

''You may be right,'' Adrian agreed. He paused before asking, ''Are you always this cautious with a man?''

She laughed in spite of herself. ''It's the only area of my life in which I am careful. Or at least that's what my family would tell you. A woman can get burned falling in love with a man who's only interested in the superficial pleasures and pleasantries life has to offer. And there are so many men out there who are only interested in the superficial things. Uncle Lowell is right. But then, he usually is when it comes to judging people.''

''I'm different, Sara,'' Adrian told her as he faced the sea. ''I'm not one of your superficial wimps.''

''No, I don't think you are. But I'm a long way from figuring out just exactly what category of male to put you in, Adrian Saville. And until I do...''

''You'll be cautious?''

''I think so. Good night, Adrian.'' Deliberately breaking the spell, Sara turned and stepped back into her room. Resolutely she closed the sliding-glass door and pulled the curtain. She stopped for a moment, listening to the silence, trying to examine the strange emotions swirling within her. Perhaps she was only feeling the remnants of the passion Adrian had ignited with his kiss.

But that kiss had ended hours ago. Perhaps she was simply

disquieted by the tale of Phantom, she thought. No, there was far more to it than the restlessness left by the powerfully told story of a man on the brink. She had to face the fact that her suspicions concerning Adrian's serious approach to life were true. In all probability he really did look upon her as the prize he'd been promised by Lowell Kincaid.

What made her deeply uneasy was that she wasn't resisting the idea of being handed over to Adrian nearly as much as she ought to. Was it because she couldn't bring herself to take the notion seriously? Or was it because she was finding herself attracted to this stranger in a way that she'd never experienced with any other man?

Pleasant! Adrian thought it would be *pleasant* to be loved completely by a woman he could trust. Sara gritted her teeth. The man had a lot to learn emotionally. Either that or he needed a new vocabulary! After having read *Phantom,* though, she couldn't believe he lacked emotions.

But after having read his novel she could believe he was the kind of man who was determined to stay in control of the emotional side of his nature. The story of Phantom told her that on some level Adrian viewed the emotional side of life as full of risk. He would want to be very certain of a woman's love before he could allow himself to trust it, Sara realized.

It was all too complicated to figure out tonight and there were so many other things to worry about. Sara took a deep breath and went back to bed.

It was the kind of conversation that neither of them would want to mention the next morning. She felt certain of that. The late hour and the inherent safety of being on separate balconies with the soft rustle of the wind in the trees as background had combined to create a strange mood that had infected both of them. The mood would be gone by morning, and she had a hunch Adrian was wise enough to let it go.

Besides, she didn't really care to be lumped into the same category as a glass of wine or a can of beer.

Out on his balcony Adrian watched the shadowy sway of a

tall pine and decided that, as a writer, he really ought to pay more attention to his choice of words.

Obviously words such as ''pleasant'' and ''pleasure'' were not the right ones to use around Sara Frazer. To her they were part of the games one enjoyed in life. Not matters of seriousness. She just didn't realize how much he valued the softer things in this world, or how seriously he took everything. Well, he'd try to watch it in the future.

After all, he sure as hell didn't want to fall into the same category as all those lightweight males Kincaid claimed she dated.

Straightening away from the railing, Adrian paced back into his room and closed the door. He had been unable to sleep earlier, his body far too aware of the fact that Sara was awake next door. The glow from her room while she read had lit her balcony and had been plainly visible from his own room. Now that she'd finally turned out her light perhaps he'd be able to get some rest.

THE NEXT MORNING Sara decided to take the initiative. She would put the mood and the conversation back onto a safe track. Setting an assured, easygoing tone was second nature for her. It was a skill she'd picked up early on in the world of corporate management and perfected even more in the world of casual dating.

''I've been thinking,'' she said as Adrian held the car door for her the next morning, ''that you never really got a chance to properly celebrate the sale of *Phantom.* You had a beer by yourself and a glass of wine with me later, and that was it. Since then, I've had you running around helping me break into a private house, clean up a nasty mess and calm my fears. This evening I think we should celebrate properly.''

''How?'' Adrian turned the key in the ignition.

''I'll cook dinner for you. How does that sound?'' She smiled.

''It sounds very pleasant.'' His mouth twisted. ''I mean it

sounds very nice.'' He cleared his throat and tried again. ''It sounds great.'' He appeared pleased with his final choice of words. ''Can you cook?''

''A good yuppie can fix the current gourmet fad food at the drop of a hat,'' she assured him.

''How about an ex-fad food like pasta?''

''No problem, as long as it's not macaroni and cheese. Imbedded in my brain cells is a recipe for a wonderful pasta and vegetable dish that will knock your socks off.''

''No meat?''

''Absolutely not. Meat would ruin the delicate flavor of the dish, anyway. We'll need a nice Chardonnay to go with it.''

He nodded. ''Sounds like we'd better make a stop at the Pike Place Market before we board the ferry home.''

''Terrific. I'd love to see the market. I've heard about it for years. I keep meaning to go whenever I visit Uncle Lowell, but somehow we've never had the time.'' Her sudden enthusiasm bubbled over.

''It's one of Seattle's main attractions. The only problem is finding a place to park. The place is usually crawling with tourists on a day like this.''

They followed the highway down out of the mountains, crossed the bridge that connected Bellevue and Mercer Island to Seattle and then descended the steep streets downtown to First Avenue. Seattle's aggressive new skyline faced Elliott Bay, hugging the western coast of the continent and waiting eagerly for the daily traffic of cargo ships from around the world. The Pike Place Market, an old and honored institution, occupied prime territory a block from the waterfront. But if anyone had dared to suggest that it be razed and replaced by a high rise, he would have been lynched by the local citizens, Adrian told Sara. Seattle loved its market, with its blocks of vegetable stands, craft shops, bakeries and restaurants.

Adrian pulled off the neat coup of finding a parking space not more than a block from the busy outdoor market. He seemed quite proud of himself for being able to avoid one of the expensive parking garages. Men always seemed to see it as a challenge to find street parking, Sara realized with an inner grin. She congratulated him as he reached for her hand and led her up a flight of steps into the bustling atmosphere.

"I got lucky," he acknowledged modestly. "Stay close. I don't want to lose you."

Street musicians, a mime, a puppeteer, craftspeople and various and assorted panhandlers added noise and interest to the basic color of a working public market. Sara was fascinated by the array of intricately arranged vegetables in the produce stalls. The fish vendors hawked their wares in loud voices, waving live lobsters around to attract attention. Meat vendors offered every cut imaginable. Tourists and locals thronged the crowded aisles and spilled out onto the cobbled street that ran down the center of the market. Sara noticed that Adrian did not glance at either the fish or meat stalls.

"There's a shop where we can get the pasta at the far end of the market," Adrian advised as Sara halted to study an artistically arranged pyramid of red peppers. "And there's a wine store across the street."

"Why don't you go select the wine and pick up the pasta while I choose the vegetables?" Sara suggested. "I'll meet you back at the flower stall on the corner. That way we can save a little time. It's getting late."

Adrian hesitated. "Sure you won't get lost?"

"I'll be fine. The flower stall in fifteen minutes." She smiled up at him.

"Well, all right. You said you wanted a Chardonnay?"

"Right." Sara turned to plow through a gaggle of tourists who were trying to photograph the red peppers forming a pyramid. She was intent on finding the perfect broccoli. And she mustn't forget some Parmesan cheese, she reminded herself. There was a cheese vendor up ahead.

Somewhere between selecting the broccoli and choosing the fresh peas Sara began to lose track of time. Fifteen minutes went by very quickly and she was in the process of ordering the grated Parmesan when she happened to glance at her watch and realized she was going to be late meeting Adrian back at the flower stall. But surely he wouldn't hold her to the exact minute, she decided. He'd realize she was bound to be a little late what with all the hustle and bustle and the endless distractions around her. On the other hand, she had a hunch Adrian Saville was a man who valued punctuality. No sense kidding herself, she thought wryly. He would insist that she be where she said she would be when she said she would be there. Demanding punctuality was an element of control one could exert, and Adrian liked exerting control.

She thought about that as she ordered the cheese, realizing she had just had a strong insight into Adrian's personality. He needed to be in control of his environment. He needed to be sure of things. Maybe she'd better hurry.

She handed her money to the cheese vendor and accepted the package of Parmesan. It was as she turned away to plunge back into the stream of foot traffic that a large, male tourist careered into her.

"Excuse me," Sara said hastily, hanging on to her armful of packages. "It's so crowded here, I—" She broke off as the man gripped her arm.

"Your uncle wants to see you," the stranger grated. His fingers tightened, digging into her skin through the fabric of her shirt. He began pushing her deeply into the passing crowd.

Sara nearly dropped her parcels. Her mouth fell open in shock. "My uncle!"

"Come on, lady, we don't have time to waste."

She looked up at him, taking in the narrowed dark eyes, the gray-streaked black hair and the aquiline cast of his features. She was suddenly very scared.

"Who are you?" she managed, aware that she was being pushed toward the far end of the cobbled street. Around her the crowd ebbed and flowed. A string of cars vainly searching for the few parking spaces right next to the market stalls inched through the crowds. The flower stall was in the opposite direction. ''What do you know about my uncle? And let go of my arm!''

The man didn't answer, intent on making progress through a cluster of tourists wearing name tags that declared they were all from New York. They seemed to resent his insistence.

''Hey, watch it, buddy,'' one of the group snapped.

''I thought folks out here were supposed to be laid back, not pushy. I coulda stayed home if I wanted this kinda treatment,'' muttered a heavyset woman with a huge camera strung around her neck.

The man with the face of an eagle didn't bother to respond. He simply forced his way through the grumbling tourists, pushing Sara ahead of him.

''Wait a minute,'' Sara gasped, beginning to panic. ''I'm not going with you until you tell me who you are and what you know about my uncle! Now, unless you want me to start screaming—''

''Sara!''

She turned her head at the sound of Adrian's voice. ''Adrian! Over here.''

With a savage oath the man holding her arm released her. Sara spun around to watch him as he melted into the crowd. He disappeared in an instant.

''Sara, what the hell is going on?'' Adrian came up beside her, pushing aside a few more New Yorkers in the process. He paid no attention to their enraged lectures on manners. ''When you didn't show up at the flower stall on time, I figured you'd gotten lost. You're just lucky I spotted you when you stepped out into the street a minute ago. Who was that guy?''

''He said my uncle wanted me,'' she gasped. ''He grabbed my arm and started pushing me along as though I were a sack of potatoes or something. Adrian, he knew who I was! How could he possibly know me? I've never seen him before in my life. And how could he know about Uncle Lowell?'' She felt a wave of relief as she huddled against Adrian's side. His arm wrapped around her waist, fastening her securely as he began propelling her back toward the car.

"What did he look like? Tell me his exact words, Sara," Adrian ordered.

Sara clutched her packages and tried to think. "He looked very vicious. Sort of like a hawk, and his eyes were mean."

"Sara, that's not exactly a description, that's an emotional reaction, for heaven's sake."

"Well, I can't help it. I didn't have a lot of time," she defended herself. "He—he had dark eyes and dark hair that was turning gray. I'd say he was probably in his mid-forties. He was wearing very nondescript clothes. I can't even remember what color his jacket was. He said my uncle wanted to see me and that we didn't have a lot of time to waste."

"Those were his only words?"

"I think so. He was quite rude. Just ask those New Yorkers."

"He simply walked up to you and said that?" Adrian demanded. "Nothing else?"

She shook her head, trying to think. "No, I don't think so. I asked him who he was and what he knew about Uncle Lowell, but he didn't answer me. I was getting ready to start screaming when you showed up, Adrian, I have to tell you, I was very glad to see you! In fact I was never so happy to see anyone in my life as I was to see you a few minutes ago!" It was the truth, she realized. The sight of Adrian had meant safety.

They reached Adrian's car and he unlocked the door. His eyes narrowed as he took her arm to settle her in the front seat. "You're trembling."

"That man scared me," she said evenly. "There was something very frightening about him."

"Given the fact that it looks like he was trying to abduct you, I imagine he was somewhat scary," Adrian growled as he slipped into the seat beside her and started the car. "The bastard. I should never have left you alone."

"You know, I said he had hawklike features but you could describe them another way," she noted thoughtfully.

He slanted her a sharp glance. ''How?''

''You could say that with those dark eyes and those strict features he looked a little like a wolf. Ruthless and potentially violent.''

Adrian froze, his hand resting on the steering wheel. ''You're letting your imagination get carried away again, Sara.''

''I don't think so,'' she whispered, staring out the window. Behind them an impatient driver who wanted the parking space honked loudly.

With an oath Adrian put the car in gear and pulled away from the curb. He headed down toward the wharf and the ferry docks. ''Sara, listen to me. I'm the writer in the crowd, remember? Leave the melodramatic touches to me.''

''But I didn't get a really *cold* feeling,'' Sara went on, remembering her reaction. ''I was scared and my palms got damp, but it wasn't like the temperature dropped twenty degrees or anything.''

''For pete's sake, it's eighty-three degrees today! The meanest-looking guy in the world is hardly likely to make you feel as though the temperature dropped into the low sixties.''

''True,'' she admitted dryly. ''And I suppose Uncle Lowell only used that bit about the temperature drop for effect.''

''Your uncle likes to tell a good tale and he's quite happy to embellish it for a willing audience.''

Sara's mouth curved upward. ''I know. I've been a willing audience since I was five years old.'' But there had been something different about the way her uncle had described the man called Wolf. Sara hadn't had the impression that her uncle was embroidering a story for her benefit. He had been in an oddly reflective mood the night he'd told her about the man he'd trained. Lowell Kincaid had been uncharacteristically quiet that evening. Almost morose.

''Forget your uncle's descriptive turn of phrase,'' Adrian said grimly as he guided the car into the line of traffic waiting for the white ferryboat. ''We've got more important problems on our hands, thanks to him.''

Sara shivered. ''You mean the fact that someone knows who I am and managed to find me in the crowd at the market?''

''Exactly. We have to assume someone followed us. Probably from your uncle's cabin. Must have been watching it. The freeway was busy coming into Seattle today. It would have been hard to spot a tail if I'd had the sense to be looking for one.''

Adrian's self-disgust was plain in his voice and it bothered Sara. ''It's certainly not your fault that man found me in the market. For heaven's sake, don't blame yourself, Adrian.''

''Well, he's not going to find you alone again.''

''What are you talking about?''

''I'm going to start doing my job,'' he stated resolutely.

She smiled. ''You mean keep an eye on me?''

''Umm. You'll stay at my place, not the inn, while we wait for Lowell to get in touch. I don't want you out of my sight again.''

Sara absorbed the deep determination in his voice and knew he meant every word. Adrian had decided he had a job to do, so he was going to do it properly. That meant in his mind that he had to be in complete control of the situation. She would be spending the next few days with him. On the whole, she wasn't inclined to object at the moment. The man in the market had scared her. The relief of having Adrian appear at the critical moment was still with her. She wouldn't forget that sensation soon. The instinctive knowledge that he offered safety and protection was one more element to add to her growing list of things that seemed to fascinate her about Adrian Saville.

''What do we do about him?'' she asked after a moment.

''The man you think is Wolf?'' Adrian shrugged negligently. ''Nothing right now. There isn't anything we can do except take care to keep him away from you.''

''But we have no idea when Uncle Lowell will get back from wherever it is he's gone. We can't just wait indefinitely,'' she protested.

''Sara, honey, a long time ago I learned the value of patience. We'll wait.''

''I think we ought to do something, Adrian.''

''We'll wait,'' he repeated stonily.

''But that man seemed to know where Uncle Lowell was,'' she pointed out.

''If that character knew where your uncle was, why would he need you?'' Adrian asked simply.

''Good point. Why *would* he need me?''

''Possibly because he intended to use you to lure your uncle out into the open.''

Sara swallowed uneasily. ''You have a devious turn of mind, Adrian.''

''Umm. Probably an occupational hazard of being a writer of thrillers.''

''So we wait?''

''It's either that or try the police—and your uncle specifically asked us not to do that.''

''I doubt there's much they could do anyway,'' Sara said unhappily.

''No, I don't think there is.''

''I guess we'll have to start locking your front door, won't we?'' she offered, trying to keep her tone light.

''Lock the front door?'' He glanced at her quizzically. ''Oh, you mean the door you walked through so easily the other night.''

''No offense, Adrian, but I got the distinct impression you haven't had to be too security conscious on your island,'' she said gently.

''Don't worry about it. You'll be safe. There's an alarm system installed. Lowell helped me install it a year ago.''

''It wasn't on the night I walked in the front door?''

''It was on.''

''But I never heard an alarm and no police came,'' she protested.

"My system works on a slightly different principle from most alarm setups."

"What principle?" She was deeply curious now.

Adrian parked the car inside the ferry and reached for the door handle. "The idea that it's sometimes simpler and more effective to trap an intruder inside the house than attempt to keep him out. I can set it in reverse mode, however, and keep intruders out just as easily as I can let them in. When I'm inside the house I set it that way. But when I'm gone, I use the first setting."

She blinked, not finding the idea either simple or effective sounding. But what did she know about alarm detection systems, Sara asked herself. "I see," she responded vaguely. "If I had tried to get back out of the house the other night, would I have found myself trapped?"

His mouth picked up at the corners in one of his brief flashes of humor as he helped her out of the car. "Weren't you?"

"Hardly. I mean, you just walked in and happened to find me in your study," she grumbled. He was leading her up to the passenger deck and it was hard to hear him distinctly in the noisy stairwell.

"I knew where you were in the house before I came through my own front door, Sara. I carry an electronic device that warns me when the system's been activated. The device starts working within a mile of the house."

"Really?" She was impressed.

"You never had a chance," he drawled.

She laughed. "Is that supposed to reassure me?"

"If you don't like my alarm system, blame your uncle. He's the one who helped design it."

"It sounds like something he'd come up with," Sara admitted. "It's that sense of humor of his. It would be just like him to design a system that can reverse the general principles of burglar detection. It fits in with some of his other theories, such as hiding something right out in the open where the whole world will see and overlook it. Well, if you're convinced it's safe, I'll trust your judgment.''

''I'll take care of you, Sara,'' he said very seriously.

He meant it, Sara realized. The knowledge touched her on a very deep, perhaps primitive level. She hadn't met a lot of men who would say that sort of thing these days. And if they did say it, a woman couldn't risk believing it completely. Adrian Saville, Sara decided, meant it. And she could trust him.

She thought of something as they took a seat in the passenger section where they could watch the Seattle skyline recede into the distance. ''Did you remember the pasta?''

''How could I forget the featured item in my celebration dinner?'' he asked whimsically.

In spite of the unnerving scene at the public market, Sara found herself enthusiastically preparing her specialty pasta and vegetable dish later that evening. Adrian poured each of them a glass of wine and lounged in the kitchen, watching as she put the finishing touches on his dinner. He seemed to be fascinated with her every move. The kitchen took on a cozy feeling that made Sara almost forget her fear that afternoon.

''I can see you're going to expand my culinary horizons,'' Adrian noted as he sat down at the kitchen table he had set while Sara had fixed the Parmesan-flavored sauce for the pasta. ''This sure beats macaroni and cheese.''

''When did you stop eating meat?'' she asked casually. Too late she remembered the last time she had asked him a question on the subject he had cut her off rather quickly.

''A little over a year ago,'' he answered calmly.

Relieved that he didn't seem to be taking offense over the issue, she decided to risk another question. She couldn't seem to stop wondering about every aspect of this man, Sara realized. ''You don't miss it?''

''No.'' He plucked up a spinach leaf from the salad bowl. ''Great dressing on the salad.''

''Thank you.'' She hesitated and then tried again, delicately. ''Did you just suddenly lose your taste for meat?''

''In a way.'' He eyed her silently as she sat down. ''I was going through my mid-life crisis at the time. When I emerged, a lot of things in my life had changed. I quit my job, moved to a new state, started a book and decided I really preferred being a vegetarian.''

''All those changes sound wonderful.'' She smiled. ''I'm in the mood for some massive changes myself. Have you ever married?''

He arched his eyebrows as he forked up a mouthful of pasta.

''Sorry. I didn't mean to pry,'' Sara mumbled, lowering her eyes to her plate. It was difficult to know just how far she could push with this man.

''It's all right,'' he surprised her by saying after a moment. ''I'm just not used to personal questions. No, I've never married. There's never been time. What about you?''

''No. I always seem to be changing careers and that tends to keep the available pool of men changing, too. The right one never seemed to come along.''

''You'll know him when you find him?''

''Definitely.'' Sara laughed softly. ''Uncle Lowell has been telling me for two years that the right man never was going to come along in the world in which I was living. He's always been a bad influence on me. Just ask my parents. They think I get my occasional bursts of unpredictability and unconventional behavior from his side of the family.''

Adrian nodded. ''He can be unpredictable and unconventional but he has a way of getting things done. He really did give you to me, Sara. I'm not making that up.''

The camaraderie she had been feeling faded into a new kind of uneasiness. ''It was a joke, Adrian. I'm sure of it. Even Uncle Lowell wouldn't go that far.''

''Then why the matching gifts?''

''The crystal apples? They probably just took his fancy in some shop and he decided to buy a couple.''

''He told me he had them specially made by a craftsman on the coast who works in glass,'' Adrian said.

"Adrian, I really don't know why he would give us a matching set of crystal apples, but I don't see that it matters one way or the other!"

"And what about that message on the tape at his cottage? The bit about protecting our wedding gift?"

"Now that," she admitted dryly, "was fairly bizarre. Your guess is as good as mine. But knowing Uncle Lowell, he was probably referring to something obvious."

"It would be just like him," Adrian agreed thoughtfully.

"When he shows up," Sara went on forcefully, "I'm going to have a few pointed remarks to make to him."

It was after dinner that Sara began to experience a strange nervousness. She knew the focus of it was the inevitable approach of bedtime and the necessity of making a dignified exit that was neither provocative nor rude. You learned to distinguish such subtle variations of behavior when you'd been through as many different careers as she had, she decided ruefully.

It wasn't that she was expecting a heavy-handed pass from Adrian. He didn't seem to do things heavy-handedly as far as she could tell. Just very deliberately. He certainly wouldn't pressure her into bed. But there was no denying the sexual tension that now existed between them, and if he alluded to it, she would find it difficult to deny.

The graceful approach was to keep things light and casual, she decided. That's the tone she would strive to maintain. After this first night it would be easier. Tonight would set the tone for the rest of her stay under his roof. She sensed it instinctively.

"Ah, a checkerboard," she exclaimed as she followed him into the living room after dinner. It struck her as the perfect answer to the question of how to spend the rest of the evening. "Are you any good?"

"At checkers? Fair, I guess. I'll give you a couple of games." Adrian poured two brandies and carried them across the room to the table where Sara was busily setting up the game. ''I've played your uncle a few times.''

''He prefers chess.''

''So do I, usually.''

''I only played it during my college years,'' she confided cheerfully. ''It seemed to fit the academic image. Haven't played it since. I didn't really like it.'' She lined up the checkers in their little squares. ''All that business about strategy and having to think several moves ahead was far too much like work to me. When I play games, I like to *play.*''

''I see.'' He gave her a half-questioning, half-amused glance. ''Checkers may be simpler but it's a game of strategy, too.''

''You play it your way and I'll play it mine,'' she ordered, reaching out to make the first move.

Four games later they faced each other across the width of the table. Adrian's expression was one of wry wariness. Sara was feeling quite cheerful.

''That's two wins apiece,'' she pointed out. ''One more game to settle the matter.''

''Who the hell taught you to play?'' he grumbled as he set out his pieces.

''I'm strictly self-taught,'' she acknowledged brightly. In truth, she was secretly pleased with her two victories. They had been achieved with wild, haphazard moves that clearly offended her opponent, who had won his two games with careful, precise strategy.

''It shows. You didn't win those two games with hard work. You got lucky on some wild moves. You have an extremely off-the-wall manner of playing, if you don't mind my saying so.''

''You're just envious of my inborn talent. The way you play, a person would think the fate of the nation hinged on your next move. You're much too serious about the game, Adrian. You'd have more fun if you'd just loosen up a bit.''

He looked at her, light eyes intent. ''I'm afraid I tend to be a serious sort of man.''

"Not given to fun and games?"

"No."

Sara caught her breath as she realized that they were suddenly inexplicably discussing more than a game of checkers. For reasons she didn't want to analyze she was afraid of the new direction. Desperately she tried to find a casual way of turning the conversation around before it strayed into the realm of the personal again. "Well, we'll see whose approach works best with this next game. I warn you, I'm going to be at my most off-the-wall!"

"In the long run, strategy and planning always succeed more often than wild luck, Sara."

"Prove it," she challenged rashly.

He shrugged and proceeded to do so. Fifteen minutes later Sara was left staring in vast annoyance at the board. She didn't have one single playing piece left on it. Adrian had beaten her with cool, deliberate ease, never relenting for a moment. Every move from first to last had been plotted and carried out with ruthless intent. Her cheerfully haphazard approach had netted her only a few of his playing pieces. Even those, she was convinced, he had deliberately sacrificed at various points to lure her into traps he had set.

"I demand a replay! You don't play fair. You play exactly like my uncle."

"What's unfair about it?" he asked, tossing the checkers back into the box.

"I don't know, but there must be something sneaky and underhanded about all that strategy," she complained. "It must be quite terrifying when you and Uncle Lowell play together."

"The games tend to last a long time," Adrian said with a faint smile.

"Who wins?"

"We're fairly evenly matched."

"You mean you win frequently?" she asked curiously.

"Umm."

"That's interesting. I don't know of anyone who can consistently beat Uncle Lowell at checkers or any other game. But sometimes I can take him,'' she added proudly.

''With one of your wild moves?''

''Yes.'' She grinned. ''The thing about people who always use intense strategy is that you can occasionally upset them with my technique.''

''Only occasionally. Not consistently,'' Adrian informed her politely. ''You got lucky twice tonight, but that was about the best you could do, playing with your style.''

''Something tells me that people who play with your style will never appreciate people who play my way.''

And on that note, Sara decided suddenly, she had probably better make her gracious, unprovocative exit to the bedroom he had given her earlier.

Five

Adrian watched moodily as Sara went off to bed and wondered how he was going to get to sleep himself. When she had disappeared into the bedroom, he sprawled in an armchair and considered having another brandy. He needed something to squelch the restlessness that seemed to be thrumming through his veins.

This sensation was far worse than the disoriented feeling he'd had when he'd finally finished the book and put it in the mail. Then he'd felt suddenly at loose ends, as if everything had ended too quickly. But tonight's uneasiness was multiplied a hundred times by the dull ache of desire.

He could not remember the last time he'd desired a woman as intensely as he wanted Sara.

Adrian stared across the room at the waiting brandy bottle and decided against pouring himself another glass. He needed it, but this was not the night to indulge. Not when he was standing guard over a lady who had no real conception of the kind of trouble that might be waiting outside the door.

"Kincaid, you old devil, you really pulled out all the stops this time, didn't you?" he muttered, leaning his head back against the chair. "Who or what are you hunting?"

Whoever Kincaid's quarry was, Adrian didn't have any doubts about the outcome. Lowell had been out of the business for a long time, but he'd once been the best there was at what he did. He'd get his man. In the meantime, Adrian knew exactly what was required of himself. Kincaid had assigned him the task in that phone message. His responsibility was to take care of Sara.

"We also serve who only sit and wait," he paraphrased, mockingly solemn.

The fact that someone had actually approached Sara that afternoon was eating at him, fueling his unease and gnawing at his mind. His instincts were to run with her, take her as far away as he could, and hide her well. But when he left emotion out of the process and concentrated on logic, he knew she was safest here in the house. The alarm system Kincaid had helped him install was good. The best. The place was a walled fortress. Actually, when he thought about it, most of his life had become a walled fortress. Strong, secure, protected, with everything under control.

Until he'd walked into his den the other evening and found the lady with the crystal apple standing in the filtered gold of a setting sun.

He really should be trying to get some sleep, Adrian thought. He wasn't doing himself any good sitting here fantasizing about a woman with an apple. And there was no need to stay on guard all night in this chair. There would be ample warning if anyone tried to get to Sara while she was here. But somehow the thought of going off to a lonely bed was depressing. It didn't make any sense, because he was used to a lonely bed. But tonight the prospect bothered him.

Forcing his mind away from the tantalizing image of Sara undressing for bed down the hall, Adrian wondered just where Lowell Kincaid was at the moment. The older man had dropped out of sight and would probably stay out of sight until it was all over. Good, logical strategy. In the meantime all Adrian could do was wait and keep watch over the woman in his care.

Patience, he had told her that afternoon, was of great value. He wasn't sure she had believed him. The thought edged his mouth with a wry flicker of amusement. The lady did things with a certain impulsive flair. He could see why she probably wasn't cut out for the corporate world in the long run. She didn't have the patience for elaborate strategy and she didn't show any interest in restraining her impetuousness. In the short time he'd known her she'd enthusiastically broken into two private houses, comprehended and been a little shaken by the gut-level action of *Phantom,* nearly gotten herself abducted, and fixed him a celebration dinner with all the excitement of a woman who genuinely cared about his success. She'd topped that off by serenely taking herself off to bed as though she were simply a visiting relative rather than a woman who'd been subtly tantalizing him all evening.

Yes, he could see why she probably couldn't have gotten too much further in the corporate world. They liked flair in that world, it was true, but they liked it coupled with a certain amount of predictability and internalized respect for the corporate image. Adrian had a strong hunch Sara didn't have any such thing as an internalized respect for that type of image. Just as she probably hadn't had any for the academic image or the artistic image. She would play at maintaining the corporate facade the same way she played at being a yuppie. After a while, upper management would probably have figured out that she wasn't one hundred percent committed to their world. Apparently she had figured it out first and decided to make a graceful exit.

The same kind of exit she'd made tonight, Adrian concluded grimly. Did she know he was sitting here, his body in a state of semiarousal while his mind tried to anticipate the next move the guy outside in the shadows might make? He wished to hell Kincaid would call and provide some clue as to what was happening. In the meantime all he could do was sit tight and practice the virtue of patience. It was a virtue he'd learned well.

Two hours later Sara came drowsily awake and lay still in the wide bed wondering what had brought her up out of a light sleep. It had been hard enough to get to sleep in the first place. She was momentarily annoyed at the intrusion.

Then the reality of where she was and why came back and she sat up, absently rubbing her eyes. She listened for a moment but heard nothing. A wary glance at the curtained window showed no menacing shadows. Why on earth was she awake?

Perhaps it was simply nerves. She certainly had a right to a severe bout of nervous tension, she assured herself. Patting a yawn, she thought about getting up for a drink of water or a glass of milk. Then she noticed that light was seeping under her bedroom door from the hall. Adrian must still be up, she realized in concern.

If he wasn't able to sleep, it was because of her. He was sitting out there in the living room, worrying. Sara was certain of it. The man took his responsibilities too much to heart. She didn't want him staying up all night to stand guard over her.

Pushing aside the covers, she climbed out of bed, found her robe and went to the door. The hall outside her room was empty and the light left on in it seemed to be the only light in the house. Perhaps she was wrong. Maybe Adrian had gone to bed after all. She would feel much better if he had.

As long as she was up she might as well see if there was any milk in the refrigerator. Stepping out into the hall, Sara walked toward the living room, intent on reaching the kitchen. It was as she left the lighted hall and moved into the shadows en route to her goal that she saw him.

"Adrian?"

He was standing near a window, his lean frame a dark silhouette amid the various dark shapes of the living room. She knew he was watching her, although the silvered eyes were lost in pools of shadow.

"Do you make a habit of running around a lot at night?" he asked gently. "This is the second evening in a row that I've found you out and about instead of tucked into bed."

She smiled. "The fact that you've been awake to observe my nocturnal habits means yours are a little odd, too. Why aren't you in bed, Adrian?"

"I wasn't sleepy," he said simply.

"I don't believe you." She took a few steps forward, her bare feet silent on the wooden floor. "You're worried, aren't you? I thought you said the house was safe."

"It is."

"Then you should be in bed, not prowling around out here."

"Is that what I was doing?" He seemed vaguely amused. "Prowling?"

Sara moved still closer. She came to a halt a foot away from him and lightly touched his arm. "I don't think I'm going to be able to sleep unless you do. I'm not used to someone fretting over me like this. It makes me feel strange, Adrian. You don't need to assume this kind of responsibility toward me."

"I don't have any choice." His tone was suddenly grim.

"You mean because of that message my uncle left on the tape?" She groaned. Her fingers tightened urgently on his arm. "Adrian, you mustn't take that too seriously. I'm not really your responsibility. There's absolutely no need to feel that you have to play bodyguard."

"After what happened this afternoon?" he asked dryly.

She shook her head resolutely. "When it comes right down to it, Adrian, that was my problem, not yours. I mean, I certainly appreciate your interest in my welfare, but I don't want you to feel you have to get so involved."

"I've already told you; I don't have any choice." He lifted his hand to touch her cheek. "And I think you know it."

Belatedly she remembered that he could see much better in the dark than she could. Sara was very much afraid he might be able to read the uncertainty in her eyes as she looked up at him. "Adrian, please…"

"What are you afraid of, Sara? That you might come to rely on me? Your uncle says you move in a world where you can't count on a man when the chips are down."

"Sometimes my uncle exaggerates," she said huskily, acutely conscious of the roughness of his fingertips. She wanted to move away from his touch and couldn't.

"Your uncle knows a lot about human nature. He learned it the hard way."

"But he's prone to sweeping generalizations," she protested. "He met a couple of the men I've dated and decided everyone in my world was like them. I don't think he approves of the 'new male,''' she added, trying for a spark of humor.

Adrian didn't respond. His hand slid down the side of her throat, resting just above the collar of her robe. ''I don't think you approve of the 'new male' either, Sara, or you would have been married by now.''

''It sounds as though you're prone to sweeping generalizations, too! Actually, there's a lot to be said for the new breed of male. He acts as if he's sensitive, communicates his thoughts and feelings with all the right words; he's into things like art and gourmet cooking and he's able to handle the idea of a woman in the professional world, or says he is...''

''And he thinks in terms of relationships instead of commitments. But a woman like you needs commitment, according to your uncle. That says it all, Sara. Your uncle is right. You would never have found what you were looking for in your old world.''

''How can you know so much about me?'' she whispered, feeling confused and unsure.

''Your uncle has told me a lot about you. For nearly a year he's been feeding me bits and pieces of information about you. Enough to torment me and bait me and tease me. I've remembered everything he said. And now that I've had you with me for a couple of days I've had a chance to learn a few things on my own.''

''You're an expert on human nature, too?''

''Umm.'' The hand on her throat was warm and compelling. He traced the curve of her shoulder as if deeply intrigued by it.

''And did you gain your knowledge the hard way, also?'' she demanded, striving to maintain her sense of balance, both emotional and physical.

''There is no easy way.''

''Adrian...''

''There's nothing else to say, Sara. We're together in this.

I'm going to look after you, whether you think I have the right to do so or not.''

She moved her head in a slow negative. ''Because my uncle 'gave' me to you?''

''Perhaps. I haven't had a lot of gifts in my life. I've learned to take care of the ones I do get.''

''Just as you've learned to value life's little pleasures?''

He muttered something under his breath, something that sounded disgusted. ''You misinterpreted what I meant last night.''

''Did I?''

''And now you're using that misinterpretation as an excuse to withdraw from me tonight, aren't you?''

''Yes,'' she acknowledged, aware of an ache of pain and regret because of her own defensive behavior. She wanted to toss it aside and give into the promise of the moment. Feeling torn in a way she had never known before, she couldn't bring herself to release her grip on his arm and walk back to the bedroom. It should have been a simple enough action. She knew it would certainly be the wisest thing to do under the circumstances.

''Sara, you don't have to be afraid of me,'' he said so softly she almost didn't hear him. It was the urgent need in his voice that got through to her.

''I know that.'' The bluntly honest words were out before she could halt them, a response to the urgency in him. Hastily she tried to retreat. ''It's not that I'm afraid of you, I simply don't want you assuming so much responsibility toward me.''

''I know. Because you're afraid that if you give me that right, you'll come to rely on me and at some point in the future that could be dangerous, couldn't it?''

''Dangerous?''

''You're afraid that one day you'll turn around and I won't be there or I won't be the man you think I am at the moment you need me most.''

Sara took a deep breath and tried to control the trembling in her fingers where they rested on his sleeve. "That's quite an analysis."

"I told you; I've been studying you. Between your uncle's observations and my own, I've got a fair amount of data," he murmured.

"So you think you know a great deal about me now, is that it? What about you, Adrian? What do you need?"

"You."

The single word was a monolith between them. Sara knew there was no way around or over the starkness of his answer. She could only retreat or accept it. It was not possible to ignore it.

Intellectually she knew she should retreat. But her intense emotional reaction anchored her to the spot. She could not move. In that moment she knew she wanted him, too. The one element of caution that she had always practiced in an otherwise playful approach to life seemed to be disintegrating. The strange swirl of emotions she experienced around this man was blowing into a full-scale storm. Sara was no longer certain she could resist the impact.

"Adrian," she heard herself whisper, "are you sure?"

"Do you have to ask?"

"No." She looked up at him wonderingly. "No, I don't think I do. I've never met anyone like you."

"I know. I've never met anyone like you, either." The hand on her throat held her very still as he brought his mouth down to hers.

Sara trembled a little beneath the warm onslaught of his kiss, and there was a soft sound far back in her throat that was lost against his lips. She felt the need in him and the leashed hunger and knew that the honesty of his desire was going to be overwhelming.

Slowly her palms lifted to rest against his strong shoulders as her mouth flowered open.

"Sara..."

Her name was a husky groan uttered deep in his chest and

then he was tasting the damp warmth behind her lips. The aggressive intimacy of the kiss seemed to swamp her, making her sway against him. Adrian steadied her, holding her with a kind of fierce gentleness that provided all the strength she needed.

Slowly he lifted his head until he could look questioningly down into her face. His eyes gleamed with a silvery brilliance that captivated her, and she knew in that moment that she was lost. Or found. She couldn't be sure which. Nothing seemed normal or totally rational. But one fact seemed to emerge from the shimmering world of her emotions. If Adrian wanted her tonight, she was his.

He must have read the vulnerable response behind her lowered lashes because he let out a long sigh and lifted her into his arms.

''It's all right, Sara.'' His voice was a dark and passionate stroke along her nerves. ''It's all right, honey. I'll take care of you. I'll take care of everything. I've waited and wondered so long. I didn't even realize how much I needed you until you finally walked into my life.''

Sara felt the easy power in him and rested her head against his shoulder. Unconsciously she surrendered the last remnants of her caution. She didn't care where he was taking her or what would happen when they arrived. Never had she been so certain that it was safe to abandon the future for the moment. There was no longer a distinction between the two in her mind. In fact, it seemed to her that there could be no real future without this timeless interlude. Adrian needed her and she needed him.

She was vaguely aware that he carried her into his own bedroom, not hers. Carefully he stood her on her feet while he turned back the covers. His eyes never left her face. When he'd finished the small task, he stood in front of her and put his hands at the base of her throat. There was more than passion in his touch, Sara realized. There was that sense of need and urgency she had responded to last night on the balcony of her motel room. Once more it enthralled her and this time there was no barrier to keep her from tumbling into the glittering net.

''Don't think about anything else except us,'' he whispered as he slowly slid his hands inside the robe and pushed it off her shoulders. ''Please, Sara. Just us.''

''I don't think I could concentrate on anything else even if I wanted to,'' she said truthfully. Again she shivered. The light robe fell to the floor at her feet.

''Are you afraid of me?''

Sara shook her head. ''No.''

''You're trembling.'' He seemed incredibly concerned over the fact. His fingertips stroked her bare arms and then he touched the rising swell of her breast just above the edge of the nightgown.

''I know, but not because I'm afraid.'' She smiled a little as she covered one of his hands with her own. ''You're trembling a bit, too.''

''I'm shaking like a leaf. I want you, Sara. I've been wanting you all evening. No, longer than that. I've been wanting you for months.'' The words were raw with honesty.

''Adrian, it's probably much too soon—''

''No,'' he interrupted roughly. ''It couldn't possibly be too soon. Not for us.''

His hands moved down over her breasts and she felt the tantalizing heat of his palms through the thin material of the nightgown. She knew he must realize that her body was already responding. Sara could feel the tautness of her nipples as they came tinglingly alive. She caught her breath and began to fumble with the buttons of his shirt.

''Please, Sara,'' he breathed into her hair. ''Yes, please.''

His need filled her with a longing to satisfy and comfort him. Slowly she made her way down the front of his shirt until it parted, exposing the dark hair on his chest. So entranced with the vivid sensuality of the moment was she that Sara was hardly even aware of her nightgown floating to the floor.

But when Adrian's hands slid down her back to the full curve of her hips, she moaned softly and stumbled a little against him. She glanced up into his face and read the masculine anticipation there.

"You're so soft," he murmured in tones of wonder. His fingers sank luxuriously into the flesh of her derriere and he pulled her tightly against him.

"You're not soft at all," Sara said unthinkingly and then buried her flushed face against his chest as he growled his amused response.

"No, I don't suppose I am. I feel as though I'm made up of angles and rough edges. You, on the other hand, are composed of curves and gentle valleys. Places where a man can lose himself."

He let his fingers trail into the cleft between her buttocks and Sara's nails dug lightly into his skin as he followed the path to the dampening juncture of her thighs.

"Adrian…"

"Say my name like that again," he demanded hoarsely as he picked her up and settled her on the bed. "It sounds different when you say it."

"Does it?" She lay watching as he yanked off his shirt, stepped out of his shoes and unclasped his jeans. A moment later he stood nude beside the bed, the light from the hall emphasizing his lean, hard body. He was wonderful, she thought dazedly. Everything she could ever want in a man. It was strange to be so certain of that, because until now she hadn't been quite sure just what she had wanted in a man. She had only known that she hadn't found it.

"Oh, Adrian," she whispered as he came down beside her. "Adrian, I didn't know…"

"Didn't know what?" He flattened his palm on her stomach and smoothed her skin down to the curling hair that veiled the heart of her femininity.

"Never mind. I don't think I can explain it just now." She curled into him, shifting languidly under his touch. "I can't even think right now."

"There's nothing to think about." He leaned down to kiss

the peak of her breast. His tongue teased the firm bud of her nipple until she cried out and pulled him closer. ''That's all you have to do right now,'' he told her approvingly, the words heavy with desire. ''Just give yourself to me. Let me open my present. I've been waiting so long for you, sweetheart.''

She obeyed, wrapping her arms around his neck as he touched her with growing intimacy. When his prowling fingers found the hot damp center of her need she said his name again, this time with an urgency that matched his own.

''Sara, my sweet, Sara.'' He pinned one of her legs with his strong thigh and probed her deeply with a deliciously questing touch. When she shuddered, he muttered hot, dark words of encouragement into her ear.

She lifted herself against his hand, unable to resist the caress. Never had she responded so completely and so readily. Her senses seemed inflamed, thoroughly alive and aware in a way that was new to her. Fascinated by the world of sensation that was beginning to spin around her, she stroked his smoothly muscled frame. Her palms slipped over the sleek contours of his back, down to the hard planes of his thigh. Then, with gentle boldness she moved her fingertips around to find the flat terrain of his stomach. For an instant longer she hesitated. Then her hand went lower.

''Yes,'' he grated with harsh need when she dared to tease his male hardness. ''Take me inside, sweetheart. Let me have all of you. I need you so.''

She couldn't find words but he seemed to know she was ready. With passionate aggression Adrian pushed her into the pillows and lowered himself down along the length of her.

''Put your arms around me, Sara, and never let go,'' he commanded. ''Never let go....''

She did as he instructed, pulling him to her until she felt the blunt hardness of him waiting at the gate. The knowledge that he was on the verge of entering her fully and completely brought a brief, startling flicker of alarm. For an instant Sara had a vision of the reality that lay beyond tonight. *This man was unique. After tonight nothing would ever be the same.*

The fleeting glimpse of the future was gone an instant later as Adrian moved heavily against her. All of Sara's senses returned to the moment, lost once more in the pulsating excitement.

"Oh, *Adrian*..." The words were torn from her as she felt the full impact of his body taking possession of hers.

"Hold me, Sara."

Instinctively she obeyed as she adjusted to his sensual invasion. Then he began to move within her, slow, tantalizing strokes that pushed her senses into tighter and tighter bundles of energy that strove for release.

The end was a revelation to Sara, a new understanding of her body and its responses. She found herself clinging to the man above her with an abandon that she would never have believed if she hadn't experienced it firsthand.

"That's it, honey," he rasped as she cried out his name once more. "Let go. Just let go. I'll take you with me all the way."

Willingly, unable to do anything else, Sara gave herself to him completely and gloried in the knowledge that he was returning the gift in full measure. She heard the sound of her name as it was wrenched from him and then he was pushing deeply into her one last time. His hard body shuddered for a long moment and then collapsed. Outside the window the night breeze briefly stirred a stand of fir and then all was silent.

It was a long while before Sara became aware of the sprawled weight that still trapped her in the depths of the bedding. She opened her eyes to find Adrian lying on top of her, his head on the pillow beside hers. He was watching her from behind half-closed lashes.

"Am I too heavy for you?" he asked lazily.

"Umm."

His mouth flickered in brief amusement as he recognized her deliberate imitation of his characteristic response. "What does 'umm' mean?"

"I don't know. You're the expert. You tell me."

"It means 'uh-huh.'" He sighed regretfully and slowly rolled onto his side. Then he gathered her close. "Too bad. You're very comfortable."

"Am I?"

His head inclined downward once in a short nod. "Incredibly comfortable. I can't recall when I've been this comfortable. Or this relaxed. Or this content."

"Neither can I," she said honestly. It was the truth. Tonight there were no pretenses or games or caution. Her fingertips worked small, idle patterns on his chest. "Adrian, I've never felt quite like this before in my life."

"You don't sound as if you're sure you like feeling this way." He touched her cheek.

Nothing will ever be the same. "It feels strange."

"We'll get used to it," he assured her.

"Will we?"

"You're nervous all of a sudden, aren't you?"

"No," she denied quickly.

"Sara, honey, don't try to fool me now. You can't do it," he told her gently.

"Well, maybe I am a little nervous. It was too soon, Adrian."

"It was inevitable, so the timing doesn't really matter."

"We hardly know each other."

"You were a gift to me, remember? I was bound to open you as soon as I could."

She flushed. "I thought you were a great believer in patience."

"Only when it's the best option."

"You don't think we should have waited awhile longer? Made certain of our feelings?" she asked anxiously.

"I am certain of my feelings," he told her roughly.

"I don't want you confusing your feelings of responsibility for me with...with your, uh, more personal feelings."

He looked down at her in mocking pity. "Believe me, I'm

not mistaking a sense of responsibility for raw passion. From my point of view the two are quite distinct. You're the one who sounds confused."

"You're not?"

"Not at all, Sara. If anything, tonight just makes everything even simpler and more straightforward."

She eyed him curiously. "What does that mean?"

"It means we don't have to have any more arguments about my right to take care of you, for one thing." He brushed her parted lips and then drew back to study her expression. "You belong to me now. That gives me all the rights I need."

"I've never met a man so anxious to assume responsibility," she tried to say lightly. But she was very much afraid her voice cracked a little on the last word.

"I've never been particularly anxious to assume responsibility for anyone else," he told her seriously. "With you, it's different."

"And what do you want from me in return?" she asked carefully.

"I've already told you, remember?" He pushed a strand of hair back behind his ear. "I want you to love me. I like the idea of having you love me. I like it very much."

"You think it would be 'pleasant,'" she couldn't resist saying somewhat tartly.

"You said you fell a little in love with the hero in *Phantom.*"

"So?" she challenged softly.

"How do you think he would treat a woman whose love he wanted?"

The question startled her. She frowned. "I think he would take care of her. She could trust him."

"I want you to trust me the same way."

She half smiled. "You're not Phantom."

"I created him. There must be something of me in him and vice versa."

Sara studied his intent features. She had asked herself so many questions about the similarities between Adrian and his hero the previous night when she'd read the manuscript. "Yes, I think there might be."

"Trust me, sweet Sara," he grated, rolling onto his back and pulling her down on top of him. "Trust me with your love. Like your uncle, I know what has value in life. I'll take good care of you."

"Aren't you worried about how well I'll take care of you?" she parried, aware of the renewing tautness in body.

"You won't play games with me."

"What makes you so sure?" she demanded, rather irritated with the certainty in his voice.

"Because it would tear me apart if you did," he said simply. "You wouldn't do that to me, would you, Sara?"

Horrified at the thought, Sara cradled his face between her palms. "No, Adrian. Never that," she vowed.

Unaware of how deeply she had just committed herself, Sara kissed him, translating the verbal promise into a physical one. His hands came up to wrap around her waist and he arched his lower body demandingly into hers.

"Adrian?"

"Umm."

She didn't bother to ask him what he meant. It was becoming very obvious. Sara parted her legs for him and her mouth locked with his as he began the spiraling climb to passion.

THE FIRST HINT OF DAWN was in the sky the next time Sara came awake. There was a moment of lazy curiosity as she opened her eyes and absorbed her surroundings. Adrian's room was a thoroughly masculine affair, with its warm cedar walls and heavy, clean-lined furniture. It was as orderly and controlled-looking as the rest of his house. She was finding it interesting until she became aware of the weight of his arm across her stomach. Then she awoke completely.

Memories of the night filtered back in a haze of lingering passion and midnight promises. She turned to look at Adrian and was grateful to discover he was still sound asleep. What exactly had she agreed to last night, she wondered with a sudden feeling of panic.

There had been talk of love and responsibility and a promise not to play games. But it seemed to her that most of the dangerous, reckless promises had come from her. The only thing he had vowed in return was to take care of her.

It was crazy, Sara chided herself as she cautiously slipped out from under his arm. She hadn't intended to let things go so far. She had never meant to wind up in bed with him, at least not so soon. She had barely met the man. This was exactly the sort of behavior she had instinctively avoided in the world she had just left. What on earth was the matter with her?

Adrian stirred restlessly when she slid off the bed but he didn't awaken. On silent feet Sara fled down the hall to her own room and scrambled about for her jeans and a shirt. She badly needed to get out of the house for a while. She needed time to think and reevaluate the whole situation. Her family had often warned her that her periodic bouts of impulsiveness would land her in real trouble someday. Even Uncle Lowell had felt obliged to point out that there were some risks involved in playing games with life.

But last night had been no game. Last night had been for real. Twenty-four-karat real.

Shoving her feet into a pair of sandals, Sara yanked a lightweight Windbreaker out of her suitcase and hurried down the hall to the living room. She let herself out the front door and stood on the porch, inhaling deeply of the sea-sharpened morning air.

For a moment she hesitated, unable to think clearly enough to decide on a destination. Then she remembered the car she had left parked in the inn parking lot. With a small sigh of relief at having provided herself with a focus for the morning walk, she hurried down the steps and out to the road. She would walk back toward town and pick up her car. Wonderful. It would give her something useful to do while she tried to sort out her future, she thought. Sara patted her jeans pocket to make certain she had the keys.

Behind her she was unaware of the house purring to life with news of the unauthorized exit. Adrian came instantly awake as the nearly silent vibration in the headboard jolted him. The alarm-clock radio beside the bed was blinking in a fashion that had nothing to do with its normal function. The message was quiet but clear.

The house was doing its duty. Faithfully it undertook to warn its owner that Sara was gone.

With an oath that was half rage and half pain, Adrian threw off the covers and reached for his clothes.

Six

The flash of rage and pain gave way to another emotion even as Adrian slipped out the front door. Fear began to claw at his insides, and in that moment he could not have said whether it was fear for Sara's safety or fear that she was leaving him. The two seemed to combine in the bottom of his stomach, forming a knot of tension that increased as he realized she was already out of sight. He was at a loss to explain how he could have been so sound asleep that he hadn't even felt her leave the bed. Normally he never slept that deeply. Last night had altered something as fundamental as his sleeping patterns and that was unnerving in some ways.

The truth was he hadn't handled last night all that well. He'd practically pushed her into bed, Adrian berated himself. He should have waited. He'd known it was much too soon. She hadn't spent nearly a year with a fantasy nibbling at the edge of her mind the way he had. She couldn't know what it was like to have a fantasy become reality. As far as Sara was concerned she'd only known him a couple of days. She must have awakened this morning with a head full of doubts and anger aimed at him.

So she'd taken off without bothering to say good-bye.

Damn it, he thought furiously, where the hell could she have gone? There had been no sound of a car. She must be on foot and that meant she couldn't have gone far.

The car. Hers was still at the inn and it probably represented escape to her. The road would seem the fastest way into town to her, Adrian decided. Without hesitating a second longer, he loped down the steps and started up the drive toward the winding road that led into the Winslow.

He saw her just as he reached the pavement. She was walking briskly along, her light-brown hair catching a sheen of gold from the dawn light. It complemented the faint gleam of gold from the little chain on her wrist. He remembered the way the tiny little bracelet had glittered last night against her skin. She had told him that her uncle had given it to her a long time ago. Her slender, soft body moved with an ease that seemed to emphasize the intriguing roundness of her hips and the subtle, feminine strength he recalled so vividly that morning. Adrian watched her in silence, remembering the sweet passion he had tapped during the night.

The year's wait had been worth it, he acknowledged to himself as he began to pace silently a few yards behind her. He had not set himself up for disappointment by allowing Lowell to build an image in his head. In his wildest imaginings, though, he could not have envisioned that she would wrap her arms around him with such abandoned demand. Nor could he have dreamed up the clean, womanly scent of the real Sara Frazer. It was unique to her and he would never forget it. There was no way his fantasies could have created the exact feel of her soft thighs as she opened herself to him and there was nothing in fantasy that approached the real-life sensation of sinking himself deep into her soft, clinging warmth.

But it was the words he remembered with such stark clarity that morning. Her soft words of need and the promises he had coaxed from her lips. He had thought the words would hold her even if the lovemaking could not. She had told him she would not play games with him and she had said she wanted him.

But this morning she was running from him.

It would be easy enough to catch her. She wasn't even aware of him prowling along behind her on the empty road. Her mind seemed focused on her destination, whatever that was. Was she planning to take the car and head back to San Diego? Or would she go to Kincaid's house and wait there for her uncle?

Not that it mattered, Adrian thought grimly. His hand curled and uncurled briefly in a subtle act of tension. He couldn't let her leave.

He ought to just catch up with her and explain very succinctly why he couldn't let her off the island. Perhaps she would be rational about the matter. Or he could simply overtake her, scoop her up and carry her back to the house. She'd probably start screaming. Then again maybe it would be simplest if he caught her and swore never to touch her again as long as she did as she was told. And just how would he manage to keep a promise like that?

None of the alternatives seemed viable. With a savagely stifled oath, Adrian continued to trail her along the narrow road. It was ridiculous following her like this, unable to make up his mind about how to handle her. Kincaid would collapse in laughter if he could see him now. The Adrian Saville he knew had never been prone to indecision or uncertainty.

Several yards ahead Sara walked toward town with an energy that was fueled by a sense of impending fate. She couldn't explain the feeling of being caught in a trap, but the sensation was strong in her mind. A part of her could not regret last night no matter how hard she tried. But another side of her warned that everything had happened much too quickly. It was so completely alien for her to catapult herself into a situation like that. She shook her head morosely, unable to comprehend her own emotions. Throwing herself into bed with a virtual stranger was one game she had never played.

There was no denying that the unfamiliar blend of emotions she had experienced around Adrian had taken her by surprise. In a way, it seemed almost logical, almost inevitable that they had culminated in last night's sensual conclusion. That sense of inevitability, however, was new and disturbing. What irony that Adrian had been worried about her playing games with him! Nothing had ever seemed less like a game than her own fierce response in his arms. Perhaps if it had seemed more like a game, she would be feeling far more comfortable this morning.

Of course, Sara decided caustically, she could always reassure herself that Adrian wasn't exactly a stranger. Hadn't Uncle Lowell apparently chosen him for her? Dear outrageous, unpredictable and not infrequently brilliant Uncle Lowell. The man should be dangled over hot coals for creating this mess.

Uncle Lowell.

Her uncle's name brought a dose of common sense. This whole mess had been precipitated by Lowell Kincaid. Where was he and when would he return?

Sara's brows were shaping a thoughtful line above her hazel eyes when she finally reached the inn on the outskirts of the small town. Her car was still waiting patiently for her in the parking lot. She hoped the inn management wasn't upset about her tardiness in picking up the vehicle. Digging into her pockets for the keys, Sara started forward.

She had her hand on the door handle, absently trying to identify the slip of paper she noticed resting on the front seat when the shock of Adrian's voice behind her spun her around.

''You can't just disappear into the mists, you know. Only fantasies can evaporate like that and you're not a fantasy any longer.'' The remark was made in a cool, conversational tone that completely belied the shimmering intensity of his gaze. He stood a few steps behind her, his hands thrust into the back pockets of his jeans. The familiar canvas shoes were on his feet and Sara dimly realized that he must have followed her for nearly a mile without making a sound in those shoes.

For an instant the unlikely combination of the easy tone and the fierce demand of the silver eyes caused Sara to feel as though she had somehow lost her balance. Her hand closed tightly around the door handle behind her as she steadied herself.

''I didn't realize you were behind me,'' she finally managed, pulling herself together quickly. It was ridiculous to let him throw her like this. "You should have said something."

"If you'd wanted company, you probably would have mentioned it before you decided to sneak out of the house."

She was taken aback by the tightly reined emotion she sensed in his voice. Was it anger or pain? In that moment she couldn't be certain. But she knew she'd prefer that it was anger. Even in her uncertain state of mind this morning she realized that the last thing she wanted to do was hurt Adrian Saville. On the other hand there was such a thing as self-preservation. Sara acknowledged that she felt more than a little on the defensive.

"I didn't sneak out of the house. I simply went for a walk and decided to pick up my car while I was out. You're the one who was sneaking around! You and those sneaky shoes you wear!"

"The last time I let you go off by yourself you nearly disappeared, remember? It's my job to keep you out of trouble until your uncle gets back."

"Is that what you were doing last night?" she challenged, goaded by the accusing tone of his voice. "Keeping me out of trouble?"

"If we're going to talk about last night, let's do it somewhere else besides this damn parking lot," he growled. He stepped forward and closed his fingers around her upper arm. "We can get a cup of coffee down at the wharf."

"Adrian," she began firmly, and then decided against an argument. Uneasily Sara acknowledged that she couldn't tell what he was thinking this morning. Nor could she be sure of the state of his emotions. Given the uncertainty in his mood and her own odd feelings, it seemed wisest to avoid an outright confrontation.

He led her down the hill from the inn to a pier that thrust out into the beautiful, sheltered cove that was called Eagle Harbor. A marina full of peacefully tethered boats of all shapes and sizes extended out from the pier. On the other side of the cove Sara could see private homes tucked away above the water's edge. At this early hour there were several people lounging on the rail, or working on their boats. Fishing rods and tackle were in evidence as folks came and went from the marina to the small wharf buildings. Near the entrance to the short pier a small shop featured coffee and fresh pastries. Adrian bought two containers of coffee to go and wordlessly handed one to Sara.

"Thank you," she murmured with exaggerated politeness.

He didn't bother to respond to her comment. Instead he seemed to be deep in thought as though he were struggling to find the right words. The idea that he was having trouble made Sara relax a bit. She had the impression Adrian was not accustomed to dealing with this morning's sort of situation. She was glad.

"I wasn't exactly going to disappear into the mists," she tried tentatively.

"No?" He sounded skeptical.

She shook her head, sipping at her coffee as they walked out onto the pier. "No. I only intended to pick up my car and drive it back to the house. If I'd been planning to duck out, I would have taken my suitcase. Or at the very least, my purse."

"Umm."

She slanted him a glance. "What is that supposed to mean?"

"That you've got a point," he said grudgingly. "I should have thought of it. I just figured you were so upset about last night that you raced out of the house without bothering to pack or say good-bye."

Sara focused on the far end of the pier. "I was upset about last night." She felt him examine her profile but she didn't turn her head to look at him.

"I rushed you into bed," he said finally.

"*We* rushed into bed," she corrected firmly.

"You're not going to let me take all the blame?"

"Do you want all the blame?"

Adrian took another sip of coffee. "No. I'd like to think you had a hand in the final decision. I don't have much interest in playing the role of seducer of unwilling females.''

The response that came to Sara's lips was cut off abruptly as a fisherman who had been unloading his morning's catch walked past with a bucket of water in which two fish swam lethargically. The man turned to wave to a comrade who hailed him from a nearby yacht. Quite suddenly he stumbled over a fishing-tackle box that someone had left on the pier. In the next instant the bucket of fish tilted precariously and one of the silvery, wriggling creatures fell out. It landed right in front of Adrian's foot and lay shuddering as it began to die.

''Whoooeee, look at that sucker!'' a young boy exclaimed excitedly.

''Must be six pounds if it's an ounce,'' another man said approvingly. ''Nice catch, Fred.''

The man named Fred grinned proudly as he caught his balance. ''Thanks, Sam. Thought I'd do 'er over a mesquite fire tonight. The wife's having the neighbors in for cards.''

Sara was aware of a familiar pang of regret at the sight of life going out of the fish. She understood about the food chain and that humans were inclined to be carnivores but she preferred her fish neatly filleted and packaged in plastic in a supermarket.

She glanced away from the fish before realizing that Adrian had come to a halt and was staring down at the creature that lay dying at his feet. There was no expression on his face. He simply stood silently watching the wriggling, flopping fish. The man who had caught it leaned forward to retrieve it.

Without stopping to think, Sara reached out and grabbed Adrian's wrist. He glanced up as she pulled him firmly around and led him toward the pier entrance. He followed her lead, not saying anything as they walked away from the sight of the now-dead fish.

''That sort of thing is hard enough on us supermarket carnivores,'' Sara heard herself say casually. ''I imagine it's rather sickening for a vegetarian.''

''Don't worry, I'm not going to be sick out here in public,'' he said dryly.

She cast him a quick, assessing glance. ''No, you're not, are you?''

''I'm a realist, Sara. I don't eat meat but I understand how the world works,'' he said quietly.

''Yes, I suppose you do.'' She dropped his hand, feeling foolish at having made the vain effort to protect him.

''That doesn't mean I don't appreciate the thought,'' he told her softly.

''What thought?''

His mouth was edged with quiet amusement and a hint of satisfaction. ''You were trying to shield me from a bit of reality back there. It was very—'' he hesitated, hunting the word ''—very compassionate of you.''

''Forget it,'' she said sturdily. ''Now about our plans for the immediate future...''

''Does this mean we've finished our discussion of the immediate past?'' he inquired politely.

''There's nothing to talk about. We've both agreed that we were equally to blame for rushing into the situation.'' She straightened her shoulders. ''We're adults and we should be able to analyze our actions and learn from our mistakes. We are stuck here together until my crazy uncle sees fit to get in touch, so we will have to conduct ourselves in an intelligent manner. Now, I suggest we both put last night behind us instead of trying to rehash it.''

Adrian shrugged. ''Suits me.''

''I'm so glad,'' she muttered too sweetly.

''You weren't running away this morning?'' he confirmed quietly.

''No, I was not running away. I just wanted a little time by myself. I felt as if I needed some fresh air.''

He nodded and then said calmly, ''I think I can understand that.''

''Kind of you,'' she drawled.

"Just make damn sure you don't do it again."

A faint trickle of unease went through her at the cool way he spoke. "I beg your pardon?"

"I said, don't do it again."

They were back in the inn parking lot, approaching Sara's car. She had the keys in her hand but her mind was on his quiet command. "Adrian, one of the reasons I decided to get out of the corporate world is that I don't take orders well. We'll get along much better if you don't get carried away with your sense of responsibility."

"I hear you," he said agreeably.

"Good." She reached down to open the car door and slid into the front seat.

"Just don't go running off again without me," he concluded as he settled smoothly on the seat beside her. He held out his hand for the keys.

Sara felt goaded. "The next time I try it I'll be sure to look back over my shoulder to see if I'm being followed."

He lounged into the corner of the seat, never taking his eyes from her stormy gaze. "I thought we were going to act like adults about this."

She drew a deep breath, aware of feeling extremely childish. "Sorry," she mumbled. "You're right, of course. I should never have left the house alone this morning. I wasn't thinking. I was feeling rather, er, emotional. I assume you don't have that problem frequently yourself?"

He didn't smile at her sarcasm. "Wasn't I emotional enough for you last night?"

Sara felt a flush suffuse her face. "What you appeared to be feeling last night is often referred to by an entirely different name."

"Passion?"

"Try lust," she bit out.

"I thought we just got through agreeing that we're adults. If that's the case, then I think it's safe to say both of us know the difference between lust and...'' He hesitated. ''And other feelings.''

She stared at him in silence for a long, troubled moment. She knew the difference, she thought. She just wasn't quite ready to admit that what she had felt last night went by a very dangerous name of its own. It was called love.

Instinctively Sara moved a bit farther over in her seat, seeking to put some distance between herself and Adrian. The car seemed filled with him, she thought. As she slid across the upholstery something crackled beneath her thigh. Belatedly she remembered the slip of paper she had noticed earlier on the car seat. Grateful for the minor distraction, she reached for it.

''You'll give me your word you won't take off alone again?'' Adrian asked in a neutral tone as he switched on the ignition. He glanced at the paper in her hand as she unfolded it.

''Oh, I'm nothing if not cooperative.''

''I appreciate it. What's that?'' He put the car in gear, ignoring her sharp tone.

''I don't know. Just a piece of paper that was lying on the seat. I don't remember...'' Sara's voice trailed off in stunned amazement as she read the short message she held.

Adrian frowned at her, his foot on the brake. ''I said, what is it, Sara?''

''A problem. A very big problem.'' Mutely she held the typed message out to him.

Adrian stared at her wide eyes for a second longer before switching off the ignition again and reaching out to take the note from her hand.

It wasn't a long note. Sara had it memorized after reading it through twice.

The one-fifteen ferry to Seattle. Come alone.
You'll be safe.

''Well, hell,'' Adrian said thoughtfully.

TWO HOURS LATER he was still acting and sounding very thoughtful. It infuriated Sara because she had argued herself hoarse in the meantime. She no longer felt in the least thoughtful. She felt quite desperate in fact. For the hundredth time she paced to the far end of the living room and whipped around to glare at Adrian, who was lounging quietly on the sofa. He had one foot on the coffee table in front of him and was flipping through a magazine with absent attention.

''Listen to me, damn it!'' Sara was sure her voice would give out at any moment. It seemed to her she had been yelling at him for hours. ''I haven't got any choice! I have to be on board that ferry at one.''

''You don't have to be anywhere at one.'' Adrian's responses had been quiet and reasonable for two solid hours. They were driving Sara up a wall. How could anyone remain quiet and reasonable and totally inflexible for two solid hours?

''How else are we going to discover what this is all about?''

''People who leave notes in cars are no doubt creative enough to think of alternatives when Plan A doesn't work.'' Adrian turned the page of his magazine. ''Under the circumstances I think it would be better to make them resort to whatever it is they didn't want to do first. No sense letting them have the easiest option. Gives them an advantage.''

''Adrian, I don't want to wait around for Plan B!''

''That's what the guy is probably counting on. Be patient, Sara.''

Sara swung away, striding restlessly back to the other end of the room. Anger and nervous dread alternated relentlessly in her head. She was furious at Adrian's refusal to even consider letting her go alone on board the one-fifteen ferry. The nervousness was a growing fear that whatever her uncle was involved in was proving to be more than he would be able to handle. She braced a hand against the window frame and stared out at the stand of trees that guarded the drive.

''Uncle Lowell must be in very big trouble,'' she forced herself to say carefully.

''Or someone wants you to think he is.''

"Since when are you the expert on how people such as that man Wolf think and operate?" she snapped. "You've only written one thriller, for heaven's sake. That hardly qualifies you as an authority on the real thing."

Adrian put down the magazine. "Sara, I'm only doing what your uncle asked me to do."

"I understand," she said, trying to be patient. "But you're taking his instructions much too literally. The situation calls for a little improvising. Something's gone wrong, don't you see?"

"No."

Her fingers closed into a futile fist and she leaned her forehead against the window. She was rigid with exasperation. "Adrian, please listen to me."

He came up behind her, moving soundlessly across the floor to rest his hands on her shoulders. "Honey, if I let you go on board that ferry by yourself, we wouldn't be exactly improvising. We'd be following someone else's plan. Surely you spent enough time playing corporate manager to know that following the opposition's game plan is usually not to your advantage."

"We've got to find out what he wants!"

"What he wants," Adrian said distinctly, "is to use you."

"We don't know that. Maybe he has news. Maybe he wants to give us some information. For heaven's sake, Adrian, whoever left that note might not even be what you call the 'opposition.' He might be a friend of my uncle's trying to get a message to me."

"Sara, your uncle has a strange sense of humor but I don't see him pulling a stunt like this."

"Whoever is going to be on that ferry is someone who knows something about Uncle Lowell. I'm going to find out who it is and what he knows." Sara lifted her head away from the window, aware of Adrian's fingers sinking heavily into her shoulders.

"Sara..."

She shook her head, tired of arguing, her mind made up. "No, Adrian. I'm through discussing the matter. I'm going to be on the ferry. Be reasonable. What can happen to me on the boat? It will be full of people commuting to Seattle. Whoever is going to meet me will be trapped on there, just as I will be until the ferry docks. He can hardly pull a gun and shoot me, can he? After all, he'd be stuck with the body until he gets to Seattle.''

He turned her around beneath his hands, his face drawn and grim. ''Sara, this isn't a game like corporate management or checkers. You can't handle it with your casual off-the-wall style. You don't know what you're getting into.''

''I'm already into it,'' she pointed out stiffly. ''And I can't stand the waiting, Adrian.''

He searched her face. ''I can force you to stay here.''

''Not unless you tie me up and throw me in a closet,'' she retorted.

''That's a possibility.''

''Don't be ridiculous!''

He dropped his hands to his sides and turned to walk back toward the sofa. ''You can't go alone,'' he finally said flatly.

She frowned, trying to decide if she'd just won part of the battle. ''But the note said—''

''Damn the note!'' He glanced at her over his shoulder. ''You can't go alone.''

''Are you saying you're going to come with me?''

''If you're refusing to listen to my advice, then I don't have much choice, do I?'' he asked, sounding bleakly resigned.

''Not unless you really do tie me up and throw me in a closet.'' Sara tried for a tremulous smile, hoping to lighten his mood now that she appeared to have won the confrontation.

Adrian just looked at her. ''The temptation is almost overwhelming.''

Sara let the smile fade abruptly. ''You're not a good loser, Adrian.''

''No. I never was.''

She'd won half of the concessions she needed, Sara realized.

It shouldn't be tough to get him to agree to the rest. The note had specified that she be on the ferry alone.

"I'm glad you've decided to be logical about this, Adrian," she began cautiously.

"I generally am logical and reasonable."

"Then you can understand why I have to go alone today."

"Forget it, Sara. I'm not that logical and reasonable. Try to get out of this house alone and you'll find me standing in the way. Think you can walk over me?"

At ten minutes to one, Sara was sitting beside Adrian as he drove down the ramp onto the ferry. The crowd was a small one for the afternoon crossing and they easily found seats in the main lounge. Scanning every face that went past her, Sara suddenly realized that her palms had grown damp around the strap of her shoulder bag. She wasn't accustomed to this kind of tension, she decided unhappily. Her body felt unnaturally alert, poised for the unknown. There had been no sign of the wolf-faced man in the ferry terminal.

"It's very stressful, isn't it?" she muttered to Adrian, who was sitting across from her in the booth they had chosen by a wide window.

"Very," he agreed wryly.

"You can jot down your feelings and put them in your next book," she suggested with false lightness. "It'll add a note of realism."

"I'll do that."

Sara twisted the shoulder strap. "What if he doesn't show because you're with me?"

"Frankly, I'll be relieved."

She glowered at him. "Are you going to drag this little incident out every time we quarrel in the future? Throw it at me and use it to illustrate how headstrong and foolish I am?"

"I doubt I'll need any additional evidence. You seem to provide enough on a day-to-day basis." He paused, thinking, and then asked interestedly, "Will we be doing it a lot?"

''Doing what?'' she grumbled, watching people as they filed past to the snack counter.

''Quarreling.''

''I hope not,'' she said feelingly. ''It's wearing. I feel as though I've been through the wringer today and the main event hasn't even taken place.''

''Umm.''

The ferry moved out of its slip, beginning its crossing to Seattle. In the distance a giant freighter loaded with containers of cargo headed toward the bustling port of Seattle. Sea gulls hoping for tidbits kept pace with the ferry, wheeling and gliding alongside.

''You know, Adrian, there's something to be said for living in this area,'' Sara remarked wistfully. ''It's beautiful country.''

''Umm.''

Sara was about to demand an explanation of his monosyllable response when she caught sight of the man who was walking into the lounge from the outside deck. She went very still as she recognized the grimly handsome aquiline features. He looked at her down the length of the passenger lounge.

''Adrian,'' Sara whispered tightly, ''it's him. The man who tried to grab me in the market.''

With a casual movement that Sara couldn't help but admire, Adrian turned calmly to stare at the hawk-faced man. He examined him in silence for a moment and then swung his gaze back to Sara. ''Looks like he's going to go ahead with Plan A, even though some of the details have been changed.''

''You mean the fact that you're with me?'' She watched the stranger make his decision and walk firmly down the aisle of window seats. ''If you want to know the truth, Adrian, I've changed my mind. I'm glad you're here. Very glad.''

''It's always nice to be appreciated,'' he muttered just as the other man came to a halt beside Sara.

''Miss Frazer?'' His voice was quiet and unruffled.

Sara swallowed, trying to keep her face unemotional. ''Yes.''

''I'm Brady Vaughn. I'd like to talk to you.''

''We assumed that from the rather melodramatic note you left in her car,'' Adrian said before Sara could respond. ''Why don't you sit down and tell us what this is all about.''

Brady Vaughn coolly examined Adrian and then appeared to dismiss him. He returned his attention to Sara. ''This concerns your uncle, Miss Frazer. It's a very private matter.''

Sara stared up into the darkest eyes she had ever seen. The man was towering over her, and if Adrian hadn't been sitting quietly across from her, she would have felt terribly vulnerable. As it was she instinctively took her cue from Adrian and gestured at the seat beside her. ''Whatever you have to say can be said in front of my friend. He is as concerned about my uncle as I am. Please sit down, Mr. Vaughn.''

''For your own sake, Miss Frazer, I think the fewer people involved in this, the better.''

''I'm already involved,'' Adrian growled softly. ''Sit down, Vaughn, or leave us alone.''

Sara held her breath as the tall man flicked another assessing glance at Adrian, who returned the look expressionlessly. Then the aquiline-faced Vaughn shrugged and sat down beside Sara. When he spoke he ignored Adrian.

''This is rather a long story, Miss Frazer.''

''Perhaps you could summarize?'' Adrian suggested easily. ''We've got short attention spans.''

Sara saw the flare of impatience in Vaughn's eyes. ''Please, Mr. Vaughn. Tell us what's going on.''

Vaughn rubbed the side of his jaw with an air of contemplation. Then he nodded slowly. ''To put it simply, Lowell Kincaid is in trouble.''

Sara caught her breath. ''Do you know where my uncle is at the moment?''

''We think he's in Southeast Asia.''

''Southeast Asia!'' Sara glanced in astonishment at Adrian, who kept his gaze on Brady Vaughn. ''What on earth would he be doing there?''

Vaughn sighed. "I told you this was a long story. The truth is it goes all the way back to the last days of the Vietnam war."

Sara went still. "Go on."

"Your uncle was working for the government in those days, Miss Frazer. He was assigned to the embassy in Saigon but he spent a lot of time in the countryside. He knew his way around South Vietnam as very few Americans did. He had friends in the oddest places." Vaughn looked a little pained. "If you remember the news reports, you'll recall that things were very chaotic toward the end. Panicked crowds from the city tried to overrun the embassy walls in Saigon. Everyone wanted a seat on one of the evacuation helicopters. Things were in turmoil. A lot of men such as your uncle had to play it by ear when some of the normal chains of command broke down."

With a disturbing sense of déjà vu, Sara listened to the tale. She never once looked at Adrian to see how he was reacting. Something told her she should respond to Brady Vaughn as though she were hearing the story for the first time. Not as if she had read the nucleus of it in a manuscript called *Phantom*.

"There was a lot of valuable material that had to be salvaged during the U.S. evacuation of the country," Vaughn was saying quietly. "Some of it was taken out by helicopter but some of it was sent out through less obvious routes. Your uncle was in charge of handling a particularly valuable shipment. He was to take it across a border. To be blunt, Kincaid reached his rendezvous point in Cambodia but the shipment he was assigned to safeguard never made it."

"I see." Sara's throat felt constricted.

Vaughn looked at her with a cold, even glance. "We think he's decided to go back and bring out the shipment he left behind, Miss Frazer."

"Who's 'we'?" Adrian inquired politely.

Vaughn frowned. "The people for whom Kincaid used to work."

"The government?" Sara pressed.

Vaughn inhaled slowly. "Yes and no."

''That's a little vague, isn't it?'' Sara asked tartly.

Vaughn's handsome features twisted ruefully. ''I should make it clear, Miss Frazer, that while I have ties to the same agency for which your uncle worked, this is something of a personal matter for me. I am not representing the government in this.''

''You want that shipment for yourself?'' Adrian drawled.

Vaughn shook his head tiredly. ''There's no chance of getting that shipment out of Southeast Asia. Kincaid will only get himself killed trying. I'd like to prevent that. Your uncle and I go back a long way together, Miss Frazer. I owe him. He was my friend.''

''Who would kill him if he went back?'' Sara whispered.

''The story of that lost shipment of, uh, material, is not exactly a secret, Miss Frazer. There have been rumors and speculation for years. A couple of very dangerous people are aware of its existence and of the fact that only your uncle knows where it is. They've dropped out of sight since Lowell Kincaid did. I have reason to believe they've gone after him. I want to get to Kincaid before those others do.''

''And just where do I fit into all this?'' Sara demanded urgently.

''Your uncle is a very independent man. Especially now when he no longer has any ties to his former employers. He probably won't listen to me but I think he might listen to you. I want you to come with me, Miss Frazer.''

''Come with you where?'' she asked dazedly.

Vaughn slid a speculative glance at Adrian and then refocused intently on Sara. ''I'd rather not say our destination. But it will be in Southeast Asia. There are ways of getting a message to your uncle once we're in contact with certain local people.''

''I don't have a passport,'' she heard herself say.

''That detail can be handled. Leave it to me.''

Adrian stepped in, his voice remote and restrained. ''She needs time to think it over, Vaughn.''

''How much time?'' Vaughn kept his gaze on Sara. ''We haven't got a lot to spare.''

''Forty-eight hours,'' Adrian answered for her.

Sara glanced at him and once again instinct made her follow his lead. ''Forty-eight hours, Mr. Vaughn. Please. I have to think about this.''

Brady Vaughn got to his feet. The Seattle waterfront was rapidly filling the horizon. He touched Sara lightly on the shoulder. ''Forty-eight hours, Miss Frazer. For Kincaid's sake, please don't take any longer.'' He turned and walked away.

Sara sat staring at Adrian as the ferry bumped gently into the dock. She ran her damp palm over her shoulder where Brady Vaughn had touched her. ''Does it feel as if it's gotten colder in here?'' she asked vaguely.

Seven

Sara concentrated on another bite of the chocolate-chip ice cream she was eating as she strolled along the Seattle waterfront. Beside her Adrian neatly devoured the pecan-flavored cone he had chosen. The ferry wouldn't be leaving for another half hour. It had been Adrian who had suggested they take a walk on the picturesque wharf before they caught the boat. Neither had said much until after they bought the ice cream at one of the many fast-food stalls that dotted the wharf.

Sara knew the reason for her silence was probably the same as Adrian's. They were both lost in contemplation of the scene on the ferry with the man who called himself Brady Vaughn. Finally Sara polished off the last of her cone and flipped the napkin into a trash container outside the entrance to the aquarium.

"You know what I think?" she announced, thrusting her hands into her pockets.

"What?" Adrian seemed fascinated with his disappearing ice cream.

"I think that legend Uncle Lowell told you about the gold is not pure fiction."

"Brilliant deduction."

She slanted him a disgusted glance. "Either it's for real or else—"

"Or else other people such as Brady Vaughn believe it's for real, which amounts to the same thing," he concluded grimly.

"Know what else I think?" Sara went on determinedly.

"Let me guess. Your uncle's idea of the perfect wedding gift is a cache of gold buried somewhere in Southeast Asia.'' Adrian swore softly.

Sara sighed. ''He always did like gold. Said it was the only real hedge against an uncertain world. I can imagine him thinking gold would be the perfect present for me. Whenever he's given me a gift, it's usually been made out of gold.'' She extended her wrist briefly, displaying the thin gold chain. ''And he did say something about going off to protect our, uh, wedding gift.''

''Does chronic idiocy run in your family?''

''My uncle is not an idiot!''

''I know,'' Adrian agreed derisively. ''He just has a bizarre sense of humor. You'd think I'd realize that by now.''

Aware of Adrian's irritation, Sara felt obliged to turn the conversation away from a defense of Lowell Kincaid's odd actions. There would be time enough to defend her uncle later. With any luck he would return to take up his own defense. Heaven knew it had always been a little tricky making excuses for him. Sara decided to go on the offensive.

''Are you quite certain that Uncle Lowell didn't say anything about the legend being for real when he told you the story?'' she demanded.

''He told me it was only a tale. There are others like it that came out of the war, you know. I turned up a lot of them while doing research for *Phantom.* It certainly isn't unique.''

''Really?'' Momentarily distracted, Sara stared up at him, her eyes widening. ''Tell me some of them.''

Adrian lifted one shoulder in a heedless shrug and tossed away the end of his cone. A trolley car designed to carry tourists from one end of the waterfront to the other clanged past along tracks that paralleled the street. Adrian didn't speak until the sound of the whistle had faded. ''Well, there's a story about the CIA agent assigned to destroy vital documents in the hours before the embassy was overrun.''

''And?'' Sara prompted.

''According to the legend he kept some of the more interesting ones, such as a list of agents and their covers operating in Asia. Then he tried to hold an auction.''

''He was going to sell the list to the highest bidder?''

''That was the plan, I gather.''

''Did he?'' she demanded interestedly. ''Hold the auction, I mean?''

''Sara, it's just a legend. How should I know what happened?''

''Oh.'' Disappointed, Sara pushed for more information. ''What other tales did you hear?''

''Leftover legends from that particular war?'' Adrian's heavy brows came together in thought. ''I think there was a story or two about businessmen who were supposedly hired by the U.S. government to supervise construction projects in Saigon and the surrounding area. Apparently they used their visits to South Vietnam to establish heroin connections that continued long after the war ended, making them very rich men. Then there are the tales of gold deals made in the north. The list of such stories is endless, Sara. Wars breed them. Just think of all the stories and legends that came out of World War II. People still write novels based on them.''

''I see what you mean. So when Uncle Lowell told you the story of the gold, you assumed it was just that: a story.''

''Umm.'' Adrian appeared lost in thought. ''It still might be just that.''

''I don't know,'' Sara mused. ''I can see Uncle Lowell doing something like this—hiding a cache of gold in a bizarre location and then telling me it's supposed to be my wedding gift.''

''*Our* wedding gift,'' Adrian corrected. ''Don't forget he gave me the story first.''

Sara ignored that. ''What I can't see is him stealing the gold in the first place.''

''We don't know that he did. At this point all we've got is Vaughn's version of things.''

Sara shivered. ''Creepy guy, isn't he?''

Adrian looked at her with a wry expression. "That's one way of putting it."

Sara came to a halt and leaned over the railing to stare out across Elliott Bay. Several long piers on either side of her, many full of import shops and souvenir stands, poked fingerlike out into the water. Around her, children ate popcorn and other assorted goodies while their parents browsed around the shops and enjoyed the sun. Another large ship was making its way into port flanked by tugs. Its deck was stacked high with containerized cargo. The ship carried a strange name and a foreign flag. A sailing yacht skirted the tip of a pier, seeking a place to tie up so that its passengers could come ashore for a meal at one of the many restaurants featuring fish. The sight of all the seagoing traffic made Sara think of places she had never been to and which, under normal circumstances, she would probably never go to, places that had bloody histories stretching back a thousand years.

"Have you ever been to Southeast Asia, Adrian?"

There was silence for a moment and then Adrian moved to lounge against the rail beside her, his eyes following her gaze. "Why do you ask?"

"Just curious. I was wondering what it's like."

"You're not going to find out in the company of Brady Vaughn," he told her roughly.

Her head came around, her face mirroring her serious mood. "I may not have a choice, Adrian."

His fingers tightened on the railing. "You think I'm going to let you get on a plane with him forty-eight hours from now?"

Sara moved restlessly, not quite certain how to handle the harshness in him. "That reminds me," she said, not answering his question. "What made you think of asking for a couple of days' leeway?"

"I didn't ask."

"That's right." She nodded, remembering. "You just told him that we were going to take that much time, didn't you? That was very quick thinking, Adrian."

"I try," he murmured sardonically.

She frowned. "Maybe writing thrillers helps you think fast on your feet in situations such as this."

"I was sitting down at the time."

She peered suspiciously at his profile, wondering if he'd actually attempted a small joke. "Well, I'm just glad you were there. I'm not sure that he wouldn't have been able to pressure me into going with him if I'd been alone."

"You're not accustomed to dealing with people like him. They can be very convincing, especially when they're using the fate of someone you love as bait."

"You really think Vaughn is lying?"

"There's a hell of a lot we don't know about this mess, Sara."

She was silent for another moment or two as she turned things over in her mind. "He must be who he says he is, Adrian."

"Who? Vaughn? What makes you think he's telling the truth?"

"Well, there was that business about being able to get me a passport on two days' notice, for one thing. I mean, no one but a real government agent could accomplish that."

"Money and the right connections can buy just about anything in this world."

"Oh, yeah?" She was beginning to resent his calm, cynical superiority. "And just where would someone like Vaughn go to buy a fake passport?"

There was a slight pause and then Adrian said quietly, "He might try Mexico City."

"Mexico City!"

"Umm. It's huge, Sara. One of the largest metropolitan areas in the world. Here in the western hemisphere it's one of the places frequented by a certain kind of 'in crowd.' A man can shop for anything, including a fake passport. He can also get lost there and reappear on the other side of the globe without bothering to answer a lot of inconvenient questions."

She stared at him. ''More lore you've picked up from writing thrillers?''

Adrian watched the sailing yacht make another pass along the piers. ''Legends and tales, honey. A writer of thrillers collects them.''

''Which is probably why Uncle Lowell couldn't resist feeding you that story of the gold.''

''Probably. Lowell knows a sucker when he sees one.''

''Well, we'll deal with him later,'' Sara vowed. ''In the meantime, we have to deal with Vaughn.''

''Sara, we can't trust that guy one quarter of an inch,'' Adrian said evenly. ''You said yourself he's a, uh, creep.''

''But he knows where Uncle Lowell is,'' she protested.

''He *says* he knows where he is. But if we go on the assumption that we can't trust Vaughn, we have to assume we can't trust anything he tells us, right?''

''It's very confusing, isn't it?'' she groaned. ''And in the meantime Uncle Lowell could be in real trouble.''

''I think we're the ones in real trouble, thanks to good old Uncle Lowell,'' Adrian said, pushing himself away from the rail. ''Come on, honey. The ferry will be leaving soon. We'd better get going.''

''Forty-eight hours isn't a very long time, Adrian.''

''I know.''

''What if my uncle doesn't get in touch before the deadline?''

''I didn't set the deadline because I hoped Lowell would have sense enough to contact us. I set it to give myself some time.''

Sara glanced at him in astonishment. ''Time to do what?''

Adrian wasn't looking at her. He appeared to be concentrating on the brightly dressed crowds of casual strollers who were ambling along the waterfront. ''Sara, I'm going to leave you alone for a while tomorrow.'' He spoke slowly, as though measuring each word.

''Why?'' she demanded, utterly startled.

He hesitated. "There's something I want to check out. A man I want to see."

"Are you going to try contacting that government agency my uncle used to work for?" she demanded.

"No. I'm not sure we could trust any answers we got from that source," he told her honestly. "Look who we're dealing with from that department now."

She wrinkled her nose. "Vaughn. I see what you mean. So who are you going to contact?"

"Somebody who may know for certain whether or not Lowell really is in Southeast Asia."

"But if we don't know it for certain, who would?"

"Sara..." Adrian reached out and threaded his fingers through hers. His tone was low and urgent. "Sara, would you please not ask any more questions? Your uncle and I have talked a great deal during the past year. He's told me things I don't think he's told anyone else."

"But, Adrian..."

"Please, Sara. Just trust me, okay?"

She wanted to scream that no, it was not okay. She wanted to tell him it had nothing to do with trust, that she simply deserved some explanations. Sara was infuriated and frightened and she felt like lashing out but she realized with an instinct that went to the bone that it wouldn't do any good. Her uncle had apparently shared some confidence with Adrian that neither of them had seen fit to share with her. Adrian would not tell her anything else at this point. She was certain of it.

"If you've known someone we could contact all along, why haven't you already done it?" she asked in a carefully controlled voice.

"Because your uncle wouldn't want me doing it unless I thought we had a full-fledged crisis on our hands. Up until now I've been going by what he said in that taped message."

"You've been assuming he could handle his 'old business.'"

"Yes."

Sara pulled her hand free from his, putting a small distance between them. ''All right. There's not much I can say if you won't tell me what's going on. Go ahead and contact whoever it is you think can give us some information.''

''You're angry, aren't you?''

''I'm feeling a little annoyed at the moment, yes,'' she bit out. ''I don't like being kept in the dark.''

''I'm sorry, Sara,'' he began but she cut him off.

''Forget it. Just don't ever again accuse me of playing games. You're turning out to be a real pro at the art.''

That stilled him for a moment. He said nothing until they were back at the ferry terminal and walking on board the boat. Then Adrian told her the rest of his decision. ''It will take me most of tomorrow to do what I have to do. You'll be alone at the house.''

Sara threw herself down on a seat, her arms folded across her breasts in cool disgust. ''Why? Or is that part of the game?''

He sat down beside her, his hands clasped loosely in front of him. He studied his linked fingers. ''I'm not playing games, Sara. I have to leave you alone because I wouldn't dare risk using the phone to contact your uncle's friend, even if I thought I could get through to him.''

She watched his profile through suddenly narrowed eyes. ''You think the phone's tapped?''

''After meeting Vaughn, I'd say we have to assume the worst, wouldn't you?''

''Probably. What do you mean, you aren't sure you could reach this man on the phone even if you did dare use it?''

''From what your uncle says, this guy isn't the sort who trusts people over the phone. I'll have to see him in person.''

''Where is he?''

''Not far,'' Adrian answered evasively. ''I can catch a plane and reach him in a few hours. I'll leave as soon as I can book a flight in the morning. I should be home by late tomorrow afternoon.''

"And in the meantime I just sit patiently waiting, is that it?" Sara muttered.

"Sara, you'll be safe in the house," he told her quietly.

"I'd rather go with you."

He shook his head, staring down at his clasped hands.

"Can't you at least tell me why I can't accompany you?"

"Sara, please—"

She interrupted whatever it was he intended to say with an exclamation of impatience. "Forget I asked."

They were politely remote with each other for the rest of the day. They walked up the street from the ferry docks and into Winslow so that Adrian could make his plane reservations at a pay phone. Sara was too proud even to attempt to overhear his conversation with the airline clerk. Later she berated herself for not having tried to eavesdrop. At least she could have found out where he was going. When he rejoined her to walk back to the cottage, she asked only if everything was settled.

"I can't get a flight out until nearly seven tomorrow morning."

"I see."

"That means I'll have to take the first morning ferry to Seattle."

"Yes."

His mouth thinned as he listened to her aloof responses. "Sara, there's one thing I want to make very clear."

"That would be a change."

He ignored that. "You're not to leave the house for any reason after I've gone."

"I understand." She didn't look at him, her gaze fixed stonily ahead.

"Good. You're safe in the house after I've set the alarms. No one can get in unless he decides to use explosives."

"What a pleasant thought."

"Don't worry about it," Adrian said dryly. "Just give me your word of honor you won't leave the house until I get back."

''Or until Uncle Lowell gets back,'' she amended smoothly.

He nodded. ''Promise?''

She wondered briefly what would happen if she didn't promise and decided not to push the matter. ''All right. Word of honor.''

''I swear I'll return within a few hours, Sara. I'll be back on the five-fifty-five ferry.''

''I believe you.''

''Then can't you stop giving me the ice treatment for a while?'' he asked gently.

''Speaking of cold,'' she drawled slowly.

He gave her a sharp glance as they walked down the drive and opened the door of the house. ''Is that your imagination I hear cranking up again?''

''I think Vaughn might really be the one they called Wolf,'' Sara told him in a low voice. ''It would make sense, wouldn't it? He was once very close to my uncle, so he might know about the gold.''

''There's no sense speculating about it, Sara.''

''Why not? Maybe if we speculate long enough and hard enough, we'll come up with some answers.''

''Not on that subject.'' He stood in the hall for a moment, listening. Then he ushered her inside.

''Just think, Adrian. That creep is probably the renegade. Uncle Lowell might have gone to Southeast Asia thinking he could hunt him down and remove him before he got the gold.''

''Sara, all we've got at the moment are a lot of questions. Not answers.''

''But why would Vaughn be hanging around here if he was after Uncle Lowell's gold?''

''How the hell should I know?'' Adrian stalked into the kitchen and put a kettle of water on the stove.

Sara trailed after him. ''Adrian, I think we're missing something. Something crucial.''

''Like your uncle?'' he suggested bluntly.

''I mean a clue!'' she gritted. ''Listen to me, Adrian. Let's assume Uncle Lowell really does have some connection with that gold and that he had some fantastic notion of giving it to us as a…a wedding gift.''

Adrian leaned against the stove waiting for the water to boil. He crossed his arms on his chest and eyed Sara deliberately. ''All right, for the sake of argument, let's assume it. Now what?''

Sara tried to construct her thoughts into a logical sequence. Frowning intently, she began to pace the kitchen. ''Okay, he knows where that gold is but he hasn't made any attempt to date to retrieve it. At least no attempt that we know of. In that taped message he didn't say he was going to *fetch* our wedding gift. He only said he was going to *protect* it.''

''True.'' Adrian watched her closely.

''Now if he suddenly decided he had to protect it for us, it must be because he got word that someone was out to steal it. We have to assume that very few people would even know for certain that the tale was anything more than a legend. The most logical person my uncle might have confided in besides you or me is his ex-protégé.''

''We're back to Wolfie?''

''This is not a joke!'' she hissed.

Adrian exhaled heavily and turned around to pour the boiling water into two cups. ''I know. Go on.''

She glared at his broad shoulders. ''Not only is Wolf or Vaughn or whoever he is the one man who might know about the gold and might even know its approximate location but we have the evidence that Uncle Lowell was definitely thinking about him before he left for parts unknown.''

''You mean that sketch on my manuscript. Sara, that's pretty damn slim evidence.''

She shook her head. ''I don't think so. I think it means that the man called Wolf was on Uncle Lowell's mind recently and that could easily be because he had reason to fear the guy was going to make a move on the gold. Something or someone we don't even know might have tipped him off. Who knows how many mysterious contacts my uncle has left around the world? You yourself are going to try to find one of them tomorrow!'' She flung her hands outward in a sweeping gesture. ''Don't you see? Uncle Lowell is trying to protect our so-called wedding gift from the one man who might be able to steal it.''

''Then what's Vaughn doing hanging around the Northwest?'' Adrian asked logically. ''Why isn't he in Southeast Asia?''

''Because he doesn't know where exactly in Southeast Asia the gold is hidden. No one knows except Uncle Lowell. Vaughn is probably looking for my uncle. Maybe he thinks he can use me somehow.'' Sara nibbled on her lower lip while she considered that. ''My uncle has dropped out of sight. He told the neighbor he'd gone hunting. Guess who the quarry is?''

''Wolfman?'' Adrian asked mockingly.

''Go ahead and laugh if you want, but I think I'm getting a handle on this.''

''I'm not laughing at you, Sara.'' Adrian handed her a cup of tea. ''You may be right for all I know. But I think the first thing to establish is whether or not your uncle is where Vaughn says he is. And I only know one way to do that.''

''Find that man whom Uncle Lowell mentioned. I know. I'm not going to argue with you any more on that score, Adrian. I can see your mind is made up,'' she said wearily.

It was over a rather strained dinner a couple of hours later that Adrian brought up the subject again. Sara was poking idly at the roasted red pepper salad she had made when, after a long silence, Adrian spoke.

''There's one other thing,'' he began thoughtfully.

She glanced up. ''What's that?''

''Lowell told me the story of the gold for a reason. He knows it forms the kernel of the plot in *Phantom.*''

''That's right.'' Sara set down her fork.

''If you're right about the wedding gift being that cache of gold, then what he was really doing was—''

''Giving you the first clues about what your wedding gift

actually was and where it was located,'' Sara finished on a note of excitement. ''I can see him doing something like that.''

''So can I. Damn it, I may pound the man into the ground if and when he finally does show up,'' Adrian growled. ''He knows I don't like games.''

THE SPARSE CONVERSATION at dinner faded into a very long silence by mid-evening. The strain in the atmosphere grew stronger as bedtime approached. Adrian watched the clock move slowly toward ten and knew from the remote expression in Sara's eyes that he would be sleeping alone tonight.

He'd been expecting to find himself in a cold bed, of course, ever since he'd awakened that morning and realized that for Sara everything was happening much too quickly. She had a right to some time to adjust to the idea of having him as a lover. After all, she didn't have all those months of fleshing out a fantasy that he'd had. He was too much of a stranger yet, too much of an unknown quantity.

Adrian inclined his head politely when she excused herself and disappeared down the hall to her own room shortly after ten. He sat in his chair, legs stretched out in front of him, and repeated the admonitions he'd been giving himself all evening.

Not enough time.

Too much of a stranger.

Too many other problems at the moment. Big problems.

And she was mad as hell because he wouldn't take her with him tomorrow.

All in all, a formidable list, he thought wryly. But the logic and the rationalizations didn't seem to be making much of an impact on the pulsing desire that was going to keep him awake tonight.

He thought about what he had to do in the morning and told himself that he needed sleep, not a night spent brooding in an armchair. He'd already had enough of those during the past year.

No doubt about it. He needed sleep; he could do without the

brooding and he had no right at all to go to Sara's room. All three things were perfectly clear and logical in his head. But, as he'd learned the hard way, clear logic didn't always chase away the shadows of emotions. Adrian wondered briefly at that. Emotions were odd things. There had been a time when others had sworn he didn't have any. Adrian knew better.

Slowly he got to his feet and began a silent tour of the house. Sara would be safe here. The house could keep out intruders. And he would be back for her as soon as possible. Quietly he checked and double-checked the hidden alarms and the exotic barriers Kincaid had helped him install. Lowell, with his skillful hands and his crafty, convoluted mind. *Where are you tonight, my friend?*

His soft-soled shoes making no sound on the hardwood floor, Adrian walked from one checkpoint to another, reassuring himself that the gift from Lowell Kincaid would be safe. Keeping Sara secure was the most important priority in his world, Adrian realized. It was a strange feeling to accept such total responsibility for another human being. Almost primitive in a way. He considered just how completely she had infiltrated his thoughts and then he headed down the hall toward his bedroom.

He would not pause in front of Sara's door. He would not listen for a moment to see if she was restless in her bed. He would not stand in the hall and let himself think about what she would do if he opened her door. He was a disciplined man and he could deal with his body's hungers.

It was the hunger in his mind he wasn't sure about, Adrian admitted as he approached Sara's closed door. How did you discipline the need for another person? Especially when you'd spent a lifetime not really needing anyone?

His steps slowed in spite of all the logic and discipline, and Adrian was vaguely aware of his hand curling tightly against his thigh. She would be asleep by now.

Sara lay very still in the wide bed, her hair fanned out on the pillow, and watched the shifting light under her door. She couldn't hear him but she knew he was standing there. She sensed the tension in her body and realized she was waiting for the door to open. She'd been lying there waiting for it since the moment she'd turned out the light and climbed into bed.

Because, Sara thought grimly, there was no way she could allow him to leave in the morning without letting him know that he had a right to be in her bed tonight.

The knowledge was sure and complete in her mind. She couldn't account for the certainty, but it was there.

Sara threw back the covers and sat up on the edge of the bed. She was reaching for her robe when the door of her room opened soundlessly. Adrian stood framed in the doorway, his face in deep shadow. Sara's fingers froze around the fabric of the robe as she looked up at him.

"You're not asleep." His voice was low and gritty; the words a statement, not a question.

"Neither are you." Sara let the robe drop from her hand. The wave of longing that swept through her was startling in its intensity. She was afraid that if she tried to stand up she wouldn't have the strength.

"You should have been asleep," he told her very seriously.

"Should I?"

"It would have made things...easier." He didn't move in the doorway.

"Easier for whom?"

"For me."

Sara drew a deep breath. "But not for me," she whispered, and held out her hand in an ancient gesture of feminine invitation.

"Sara?" Adrian's voice was raw with the question.

"Come to bed, Adrian. Please."

He hesitated for a timeless moment. Then he moved forward in a dark, silent glide that swept her up and bore her back onto the bed.

"Adrian..."

"Hush, Sara. There's no way on earth I could let you change your mind now." He was sprawling heavily on top of her, his hands pinning her passionately against the pillows as he sought her mouth with his own.

She wanted to tell him that she had no intention of changing her mind, that she wanted him, needed him, that she had never felt like this about a man before in her life. But the words seemed to be locked in her throat as he began to make love to her.

Adrian pushed the canvas shoes off his feet without even bothering to sit up on the bed. Sara heard them thud softly to the floor. She felt him fumble with the fastening of his jeans and then the buttons of his shirt. And all the while he kept her achingly close to him, deliciously trapped under his strength.

''I told myself I shouldn't stop at your door,'' he grated as he kicked his clothing to the floor.

Sara's head moved from one side to the other on the pillow. ''No, this is where you belong.'' She circled his neck with her arms, pulling him close.

''Sara, my sweet Sara.'' He tugged at the nightgown, pushing it off her shoulders and down to her waist. Flattening the palms of his hands across her breasts, he grazed her nipples with a rasping, tantalizing touch that brought them to taut peaks.

Sara uttered a soft sigh into his mouth and dared him with the tip of her tongue. He responded instantly, thrusting deeply behind her teeth. She traced the contours of his sleek back with her fingertips until he groaned heavily.

Lifting himself for an instant, Adrian pulled the nightgown down over her hips and let the garment fall to the floor beside his jeans. Then he came back down beside her and Sara felt the demanding hardness of him against her thigh. She could feel the almost violently taut need in him and her own body reacted to it with fierce awareness.

Slowly, with deliberate provocative strokes, Adrian caressed her. His fingers played an enticing game on the inside of her leg until Sara thought she would go out of her mind with excitement. When he moved his hand upward, she cried out against his mouth.

Then she was struggling passionately to return the heady thrill and the throbbing anticipation. She slid her hand down his back to the slope of his thigh, feeling the crisp curling hair. Then she explored him more and more intimately until she cupped the heavy evidence of his desire.

"Sara, you're driving me wild," he groaned out.

"Yes, please," she whispered breathlessly.

"Sara, are you sure?"

"I've never been more certain of anything in my life." She used her nails with excruciating delicacy, and he muttered something soft and savage against her throat.

"Adrian?"

"I couldn't stop now if all the forces in hell got in the way," he said, and then he was parting her legs with his own, sliding toward her warmth until he was only a pulse beat away from possessing her completely.

Sara whispered his name again and again, lifting herself with undisguised longing.

"That's it, sweetheart. Give yourself to me. Just give yourself to me. I need you so."

She gasped as he entered her, the shock of his passionate invasion ricocheting through her whole system. Then she tightened her arms and legs around him, wrapping him as close as possible.

Lost in the embrace, Adrian knew only that he wanted Sara to cling to him forever. There was nothing else besides this shattering moment and Adrian seized it with all of his strength. There would be time enough tomorrow to wonder at the intensity of her need, time enough to worry that she was only reacting to the drama of the situation, time enough to reconsider the wisdom of letting himself be swept up in her hot, damp warmth. There was always time enough to regret the past. But he was living for the moment tonight, he told himself, and for this hour he would revel in it. He would allow himself to believe it was all for real.

When he felt the telltale tightening of her body, it precipitated an echo in his own. For an instant he forced himself to raise his head so that he could watch her face during the fiery release. He had a few seconds to wonder at the compelling possessiveness he felt for the woman in his arms and then he was trapped in the vortex of their combined desire. It swept them both to a violent, throbbing climax, left them hanging for a sweet moment and then slowly, slowly ebbed.

The moment in which he had been living was already becoming the past, Adrian thought distantly as he lay beside Sara. Soon the morning would arrive and with it another slice of the past. Perhaps there was some sense of balance in nature. Perhaps one piece of the past could offset another. He would have the memory of Sara's warmth tonight to carry with him as a talisman against the chill of tomorrow.

She stirred in his arms. "Adrian?"

"I'm here, Sara."

"Good," she murmured drowsily. "See that you're here tomorrow night, too."

When tomorrow night comes will you really want me here, my darling Sara, he wondered silently.

HE LEFT AT DAWN and Sara was at the door to watch him go. She had awakened the instant he did, her senses aware of his every movement. He'd lain quietly for a long moment looking down into her face and then he'd brushed his lips lightly against hers. Words flooded his head but he couldn't find a way to say them aloud. There wasn't time now to say the things that should be said. Perhaps it was better this way.

Pushing aside the covers, he'd climbed out of bed and headed for the bath. Without a word she'd fixed coffee for him while he dressed and then she'd stood on tiptoe to kiss him goodbye.

"Be careful, Adrian. Please be careful."

"Hey, I'm only going to talk to a friend of your uncle's," he protested gently. He was afraid of the intensity he saw in her gaze. He liked it better when she was laughing up at him with her eyes or watching him with passion. Adrian realized just how much he had come to value the impulsive warmth that was so much a part of Sara. Life would be very cold without it. ''I'll be home by sundown.''

''Yes.'' She didn't argue.

''You won't leave the house,'' he said again, making it an order.

She shook her head. ''Not unless you or Uncle Lowell tell me to leave the house,'' she answered obediently.

''Sara...'' He hesitated on the porch, turning back to her one last time.

''Just hurry, Adrian. I'll be here when you return.''

He looked at her, nodded once and left without glancing back again.

Eight

The house seemed incredibly lonely after Adrian left. Sara wandered around from room to room, wondering if doing a little housekeeping might help her deal with the strange mood in which she found herself. The thought brought to mind the question of who actually did Adrian's housecleaning. Something told her he probably took care of the chores himself. Certainly no one had been in during the few days she had known him to sweep the hardwood floors or dust. But everything seemed orderly and reasonably clean. Keeping his environment neat and precise was undoubtedly a part of his nature. It fit with what she knew of his preference for being in control of his world.

Sara wondered if Adrian had ever felt out of control. When had the need to be in command of everything around him come into existence? Perhaps he had been born that way. Or perhaps something in his past had made him so cautious and controlled. Surely the average person didn't install the kind of sophisticated electronic gadgetry that protected this house unless some event had instilled a raging desire for security. Adrian was definitely not the type of man to let his imagination make him paranoid. He must have his reasons for his self-control and the controls he had imposed on his surroundings. The only time she sensed that he slipped his own leash was when he made love to her.

The images engraved on her mind from the previous night rose to warm her now. She remembered the passion and intensity of the man who had held her. And she recalled her own ungoverned responses.

She drifted into the library and drew a finger along the top shelf of the bookcase. There was a smudge on her hand afterward but nothing really terrible. Just a normal amount of dust. The kind she herself collected on the top shelf of her bookcase. The kind people living alone tended to collect. She wondered how long Adrian had lived alone. Most of his life, apparently.

Finding the thought depressing, she turned away from the bookcase and walked over to his desk. Having been through it once, she felt there was no point amusing herself by browsing through it again. She sat down in the swivel chair and remembered the way Adrian had caught her here a few nights ago. She hadn't heard his approach, she recalled. You hardly ever heard the man. He moved very quietly in those well-worn sneakers.

A shaft of morning light caught the crystal-and-gold apple, making the trapped bubbles come alive for a moment. Sara leaned forward and studied the shimmering effect. She liked the notion of Adrian having sat here at his desk for months, the apple in front of him, while he worked. How many times had he glanced up idly and found himself studying the apple? Perhaps as many times as she had.

But she hadn't known there was a duplicate crystal apple in existence, Sara reminded herself. While Adrian had known all along that there was another apple and that someday he would encounter its owner. She wondered what he had expected her to be like. What picture had her uncle sketched for him? It was suddenly very important to Sara that Adrian had found his gift satisfactory. She wanted to be sure he would return to collect it this evening.

"Adrian," she whispered aloud, "remember what I said about taking care of yourself. I don't think I should have let you go alone." As if she'd had a choice.

Uneasily Sara stood up and walked slowly back out of the study. She'd make herself another cup of coffee and see if she couldn't find something to read. It was going to be a very long day.

She was pouring the coffee when she realized that what she wanted to read was *Phantom.* Perhaps if she went through it a second time, this time knowing her uncle had deliberately been planting information, she might pick up something useful. Digging the manuscript out of her suitcase, she carried it back to Adrian's study and sat down to read it with the cup of coffee at her elbow.

She wrinkled her nose at the sketch of the wolf on the first page and then deliberately set herself to go through the manuscript with an alert eye. There must be something in it. Didn't Lowell believe in hiding things in plain view? He certainly had doodled a great deal on the pages. But then, that was standard operating procedure for Lowell Kincaid whenever he found himself with a pencil in hand and a sheet of paper nearby. The man should have been an artist instead of a secret agent.

Just as had happened the first time through *Phantom,* Sara once again found herself caught up not in the intricacies of the plot but in the hero's pain and savage determination to survive. The feelings of protectiveness she had experienced the first time she read it returned anew. She longed to comfort the hero even as she told herself that only he could endure his own survival both emotionally and physically. In the end she knew she would again be left wanting to know for certain that there really was going to be a happy ending. And once more the question of how much of Adrian existed in the guise of *Phantom* returned to haunt her. This was a first novel. Somewhere she had read that they tended to be the most autobiographical.

Sara was into chapter three when the phone on the desk rang shrilly. The unexpected sound startled her. In the time she had been staying at Adrian's home, the thing had never rung. She hesitated a few seconds before reaching out to pick up the receiver. Then the thought that it might be Adrian calling for some reason made her fumble with the instrument.

''Hello?''

''Sara.''

''Uncle Lowell!'' Sara sat stunned as she heard her uncle's

distinctive growl of a voice. ''Uncle Lowell, where are you? I've been absolutely frantic. This whole thing is—''

''Sara, don't talk, just listen to me,'' Lowell Kincaid said quickly. ''Come back to my place as soon as you can.''

''But Uncle Lowell—''

''As soon as you can, Sara. I can't explain. I'll be waiting.''

He hung the phone up in her ear before she could get in another question.

Her first instinct, Sara realized, was to panic. She had no way to reach Adrian to tell him what was happening, no way to find out if her uncle needed immediate help such as an ambulance, no way even to begin to figure out what might be wrong. All she could do was obey Lowell Kincaid's summons as swiftly as possible. Desperately she tried to reassure herself with Adrian's words about her uncle's competence. *He can take care of himself.*

Whatever else was happening, at least she knew he wasn't in Southeast Asia! If only she could get in touch with Adrian to call him off that wild-goose chase. Frantically Sara tried to think. It took her a moment to break through the paralysis engendered by her uncle's phone call. Then she was on her feet and running toward the bedroom. Her purse was where she had left it, slung on the bed. She grabbed it and scrabbled around inside for her car keys.

Sara was almost to the front door when she remembered the elaborate warning devices built into Adrian's house. Forcing herself to slow down and concentrate, she went into Adrian's bedroom and programmed the alarms as he had taught her so that she could leave without causing a disturbance. Almost as an afterthought she pushed the reset button so that the house would be able to detect intruders. Adrian wouldn't thank her for leaving the exotic alarm system completely turned off. She was afraid to set it to keep out intruders because Adrian hadn't told her now to bypass the alarms if she were to leave and then try to reenter. There was always the chance that she might be coming back here this evening with her uncle. This way the house would recognize that it had been entered, but she would be able to get back inside if she wished. When she was finished, the alarms were set just as they had been the night she'd walked so easily into Adrian's study to search it. She'd better leave a note, too, just in case Adrian returned before she got back.

She dashed back down the hall to the study and found a pen and a piece of paper. Hastily she jotted down the facts about the phone call and Lowell's summons. Then she glanced around for a means of anchoring the slip of paper. The crystal apple caught her eye. She picked it up and a shaft of morning light broke into a rainbow as it passed through the apple and touched the frozen bubbles inside. Sara found herself staring into the depths of the crystal for a split second. The apple had been the start of this whole mess, she realized. And it had provided the first link between herself and Adrian.

Shaking off the momentary sense of distraction, she plunked the crystal apple down on top of her note. Time enough later to figure out whether the apple was more significant than it seemed.

Finished with the task, she flung herself out the door and down the steps to where her car was parked in the drive. She was furious with her own nervous tension and her anger just served to make her more nervous. It seemed an incredible chore to get the key into the ignition. The wait at the ferry dock was interminable. The Interstate was jammed through the heart of Seattle and over the bridge to Mercer Island. Everything seemed to be conspiring to keep her from making good time out of town.

When at last she was free of the city's congestion, she found it difficult to keep within shouting distance of the speed limit. Every instinct was to hurry. Uncle Lowell's words had sounded extremely urgent. But there had been an oddly flat quality to his voice, she thought as she drove. She'd never heard him sound quite that way.

On the other hand, she had never been around him when he was "working." For her he had always been the laughing, witty man who had seemed to understand her even when the rest of the family hadn't. There had been an affinity between her and her uncle since she was a small girl. Her parents tolerated it good-naturedly most of the time. But there had been occasions when she had been warned that it wasn't right to play games with life. The black sheep of the family might be a lot of fun but he didn't set a responsible example for a young person.

With every passing mile Sara wondered what had gone wrong with Lowell Kincaid's latest game.

It wasn't until nearly two hours later when she was turning off onto the narrow road that led toward the cottage that Sara remembered to wonder why her uncle hadn't mentioned Adrian. If there was anything really wrong, would Lowell have asked her to come alone?

Impatiently she slowed to take the twists and turns of the old road. Quite suddenly she was furious with both her uncle and Adrian. Men and their little macho schemes. And they had the nerve to say she played games! When this was all over, Sara decided as she braked for a sharp curve, she would give them both a piece of her mind. More than that. She'd tear a wide strip off each of them.

The car that blocked the road on the far side of the curve came as a distinct shock. It was sitting across both lanes, making it utterly impossible to get past. Sara, who had her foot on the accelerator again as she came out of the curve, hurriedly slammed on the brakes.

"Damn it to hell!" It was the last straw, Sara told herself as she came to a halt. Well, at least she could walk to the cottage from here. Angrily, her mood fueled by a firestorm of mounting concern, she pulled over to the side of the road, pushed open the door and climbed out. There was no one in the other car as far as she could tell. Who on earth would be stupid enough to leave a vehicle in the middle of the road? Probably some drunk driver who hadn't made it home from a local tavern.

Leaning down, Sara reached inside her own car to yank her purse off the front seat and remove the keys from the ignition.

It couldn't be more than a mile now to her uncle's house. Luckily she'd worn comfortable sandals. She straightened up, stepped back to slam the car door, spun around and found herself staring straight into Brady Vaughn's hawklike face.

''Congratulations, Miss Frazer. You made excellent time.'' He motioned almost negligently with the compact, snub-nosed gun he held in his right hand. ''I just put the car across the road fifteen minutes ago. Thought you'd take a little longer to get here.''

''I shouldn't have hurried, apparently,'' Sara managed in a tight little voice. She couldn't take her eyes off the gun. The casually efficient way Vaughn held it seemed as frightening as anything else that was happening. A man who held a gun that coolly must have had plenty of practice. ''Who are you, Mr. Vaughn?''

''Let's just say I'm an old acquaintance of your uncle's.'' He nodded toward his vehicle as he spoke. ''Now I think we'd better get these cars off the road. This isn't a well-traveled area but I wouldn't want some stranger coming along and starting to ask silly questions.''

''Such as why you're holding a gun on a woman?'' Sara didn't move. She wasn't certain she could.

Vaughn's smile was an odd travesty of humor. ''Take it as a compliment, Miss Frazer. I learned long ago that the female of the species can be just as dangerous as the male. I don't take chances. Get in the car. You'll drive.''

When he stepped toward her, Sara discovered that she could, indeed, move. She edged back toward the nondescript compact that was lodged across the road. ''Drive where?''

''To your uncle's cabin, of course. That's as good a place to wait for him as any.''

''I thought you said he was in Southeast Asia!''

''I lied. I do that quite well. You should start getting used to it. A lot of men in your life lie to you. Now move, Miss Frazer. And please, for both our sakes, don't try anything too tricky, okay?''

There was no opportunity to try anything clever even if she had been able to think of something truly brilliant, Sara discovered. At the point of the gun she slid into the driver's seat. Her fingers trembled as she took the wheel. Her red shirt was turning dark under her arms from nervous perspiration. Vaughn got in beside her, his eyes never leaving her for an instant.

The drive to Lowell Kincaid's cabin was a short one. Sara fantasized briefly about stomping down on the accelerator and trying some wild maneuver that might dislodge the weapon from Vaughn's hand but common sense warned her it wouldn't work. There was no way she could get the car up to a fast rate of speed before he could put a bullet in her. There would be plenty of time for him to kill her and grab the wheel.

The cottage appeared exactly as she and Adrian had left it. When Sara obediently switched off the ignition, Vaughn ordered her out of the car.

"Now we'll walk back and get the other one." He stood aside and waited for her to start back down the road ahead of him.

"Why the stunt with the car across the road? Why didn't you simply wait for me in the cabin?"

"I was afraid you might be suspicious about entering the house when you noticed the strange car in the drive. And there wasn't any convenient place to hide it and still have it readily available." He indicated the clear area that extended from the drive to the front of the house. "I also didn't know if you and your uncle might have some particular signal."

"You're giving me a lot more credit for caution and observation than I deserve," Sara told him dryly. "I doubt that I would have thought twice about the car. I would have assumed it was my uncle's. And we don't have any special greeting signal! Good grief, I'm his niece, not a secret agent."

"Oh, I'm aware of who you are, Sara Frazer. Very much aware. I'm counting on your identity to lure your uncle out into the open, you see."

She turned to glance back at him over her shoulder. The gun

was still pointed unwaveringly at her back. "But that was my uncle's voice on the phone. I don't understand. Where is he?"

Vaughn arched an eyebrow. "It was your uncle's voice, all right. Right off the tape on his answering machine."

"His answering machine! But he didn't say those things on the machine," Sara gasped, startled.

"Sure he did," Vaughn told her with a soft chuckle. "He just didn't say them in quite that order."

"You mixed his words from the tape into different sentences?"

"And recorded them onto another tape. It takes a little work and the right equipment, but it can be done. I had both his recorded message to callers and the message to your friend Adrian with which to work. Plenty of material from which to get a few simple sentences."

Sara stared unseeingly at her car as she rounded the bend. "You appear to be very professional at this sort of thing, Mr. Vaughn," she whispered dully.

"Very," he assured her. "It would be best if you didn't forget it."

She drove the second car back to the cottage under the same circumstances as she had driven the first. When she finally parked it beside Vaughn's compact, he motioned her into the house.

"What now?" she asked quietly as she stepped inside.

"Now we wait. Make some coffee if you like. It's probably going to take a while." Vaughn appeared unconcerned.

"But what exactly are we going to wait for?"

"Your uncle should be contacting us in the near future."

"But why would he do that? How would he even know where I am or that I'm with you?" The shock of the situation was affecting her mind, Sara thought vaguely. She couldn't seem to think properly. Perhaps she ought to take Vaughn's advice and make some coffee. At least it would give her something to do. She was very much afraid that if she sat down or stood still she would begin to tremble uncontrollably.

''Your uncle is looking for me. It's only a matter of time before he figures out I'm waiting patiently right here on his home stomping grounds. And when he does, he'll discover I have you with me.''

Sara turned on the tap in the kitchen sink, aware of Vaughn watching her from the doorway. ''You're going to use me?''

''I'm going to trade you to your uncle for the information I want,'' Vaughn confirmed. ''I see it all as a business deal.''

''And what information is it that you want, Mr. Vaughn?'' she demanded softly.

''Don't you think you should start calling me Brady?''

''I don't see us ever getting together on a social basis,'' she gritted out as she set the pot into place in the drip machine.

''But we are together, Sara,'' he drawled smoothly. ''Perhaps for some time. You made it very easy, really. I was a little worried about how to get rid of the boyfriend. I wasn't sure until yesterday where he fit into the scene. I had a couple of plans I thought would work but he simplified matters considerably when he obligingly left on the morning plane to Mexico City. His leaving for Mexico also confirmed his part in all this.''

''Mexico City!''

''I got the clerk at the airline counter to verify that he bought a one-way ticked to Mexico. What's the matter, Sara? Didn't he tell you where he was going?''

''Yes, but I…I just don't see how you could find out that sort of information.'' Sara was surprised that she could get the lie fairly glibly past her lips. Mexico City! It didn't make any sense. You didn't pop down to Mexico City for the day and return by early evening. And just yesterday Adrian had been telling her tales of how a man could disappear into Mexico City and reappear on the other side of the world.

''You can get all sorts of information out of people if you flash the right badges at them,'' Vaughn informed her. ''Poor little Sara. You still don't realize what he's done, do you? You've been had, lady. In more ways than one.''

''He's a writer,'' she explained, struggling for something logical to say. ''He does a lot of research and he's had this trip planned for some time. My showing up got in the way of his schedule, I'm afraid. He's setting the next book in Mexico.'' Did that sound reasonable? ''I didn't have the time to go with him.''

''Is that a fact?'' Vaughn said musingly. ''So he just left you up here all by yourself to worry about your uncle? After asking for forty-eight hours to think over your problem?''

''I...yes.'' It was probably better not to weave any more strands into the story. She wouldn't be able to keep it straight in her own head.

''Not terribly gallant of him, was it?''

Sara said nothing. She focused on the pot filling with coffee.

''You're a fool, Sara,'' Vaughn finally said calmly. ''You've been dumped. As long as Saville figured you were the easiest way to get at the gold, he was willing to play lover. But yesterday when I let him know that others were getting close to the prize, he panicked and decided you were no longer the quickest or safest means to an end. I know better. I know that you still are the best means to this particular end. I'm a patient man, Sara.''

She cast him a quick, frightened glance. He smiled again. ''Want me to tell you the real reason he's gone south?''

''What's your explanation, Mr. Vaughn?''

''Oh, it's simple enough. Mexico City is a wide-open town. It has a certain reputation in the industry. Among other things it's a jumping-off point for people who want to head for such places as Cambodia without letting the U.S. government know where they're going. You can buy anything in Mexico City, including alterations on your passport. Your boyfriend has skipped out on you. He's probably heading for Southeast Asia.''

''I thought,'' she said weakly, ''that the stories about Mexico City were just the product of espionage fiction. Legends and tales.''

''Fact, I'm afraid. Your lover has skipped.'' Vaughn seemed amused.

Sara lowered her lashes. ''Why would he do that?''

''Because he's decided to risk going after the gold on his own instead of waiting for your uncle to return. As I said, he got nervous yesterday when he realized others were closing in on it. He's obviously a friend of your uncle's and Kincaid made the mistake of trusting him, both with his niece and with the information about the gold. Kincaid never used to make mistakes like that, but he's getting old. He's trusted the wrong man with the details of what was probably intended to be your dowry. The race is on, Sara, but I'm the one with the inside track. I've got you. I'm not worried that Saville tried to buy himself forty-eight hours for a head start. It won't do him any good because he's obviously an amateur. A greedy amateur, but an amateur nonetheless.''

''Why do you say he's an amateur?''

''Because a professional would have realized that you're the most useful key around. And that I'm the biggest threat. A professional would have made a try for me before leaving town, if for no other reason than to find out just how much I know. Southeast Asia is a big and dangerous place to go hunting without specific directions and a few contacts. Saville will probably just succeed in getting himself killed trying for your uncle's gold. And it does nothing to change my plans. One way or another I wound up with you, and ever since you appeared on the scene so conveniently, that's been my goal. I'm a highly adaptable man. Before you came along I was using a different approach. I'd been through this cabin with a fine-tooth comb. I was just realizing how useless that method was going to be when you showed up out of the blue. Couldn't figure out who you were at first, but after you'd left the first time I remembered seeing the phone-answering machine. I played it back to see if I could pick up any information about Kincaid's unexpected female guest, and sure enough, all the news I needed was on that tape. That's how I found out you're Kincaid's niece.''

"You want that gold, don't you?" Sara reached for a cup and poured coffee with exaggerated care. She was afraid that if she wasn't extremely cautious she would spill the hot liquid all over her feet. "The gold you said my uncle left behind in Southeast Asia."

"Yes, Sara. I want the gold. Pour me a cup, too. Just set it on the counter. I'll get it. Wouldn't want you trying to throw it in my face with a grand, heroic gesture."

"So you're going to use me to force my uncle to tell you exactly where he hid the stuff?" Sara persisted, standing back so that Vaughn could pick up his coffee.

"Precisely."

"You said Uncle Lowell thinks you're in Hawaii," she began with a frown as she tried frantically to put the pieces of the puzzle together.

"I made certain he got information to that effect. Rumors are very effective in our crowd, even among the, uh, goldenagers. I wanted him sidetracked for a while so that I could try getting the data I needed the easy way."

"You searched this place," she whispered, remembering the chaos she and Adrian had discovered.

"Unfortunately, as I said, my search didn't turn up anything so convenient as a map or a set of coordinates that would have made my task a straightforward one. I really thought I'd have a chance of finding what I wanted because I knew your uncle rather well at one time, Sara. I know his theories on hiding important data, for example. He always got a kick out of concealing things right in front of someone's nose. Kincaid had a sense of humor, you can say that for the man. When I didn't turn up anything, I realized matters were going to get complicated. I made the search look like the work of punks and decided to keep watch on the cabin for a while. It paid off. You happened along and greatly simplified my life."

Sara leaned back against the counter, her hands braced against the cool ties. "Why would my uncle go tearing off to Hawaii just because he thought you were there, Mr. Vaughn?"

"He thinks that after all these years I've decided to go after the gold. He's got a couple of other reasons for following my trail, too. He and a few others, I believe, have some private suspicions about me." Vaughn sipped tentatively at his coffee. "Not bad," he declared. "I enjoy good coffee."

Sara took a deep breath before plunging in with the next question. "My uncle has other reasons for hunting you down?"

"'Hunting' sounds a bit melodramatic, don't you think? Let's just say he couldn't resist the hint that I might have surfaced and that he might be able to find me."

Sara met his gaze unflinchingly. "Do you by any chance go under the code name of...of Wolf?"

Vaughn went still, the coffee halfway to his mouth. Slowly he lowered the cup, his dark eyes narrowing speculatively. "Now what would you know about the man called Wolf?"

Her fingers tightened around the counter's edge. Sara was beginning to wish she hadn't brought up the subject. "Not much. My uncle mentioned him once. That's all."

"And you've been assuming I might be...Wolf?"

She didn't like the cold amusement that was suddenly in his eyes. "The thought occurred to me."

"Fascinating."

"Well?" she challenged bravely.

Vaughn's mouth drew back in a humorless smile. "Your uncle always could tell a good story."

"Is that all Wolf is? A Lowell Kincaid tale?" she breathed. It was getting difficult to tell legends from reality, she realized.

Vaughn chuckled, shaking his head. "No. As usual with your uncle, there's a germ of truth in the story. There really was a man called Wolf. I never met him. Few people did and survived to tell about it. His cover was very deep and he protected it. They said he had a thing about maintaining his cover."

A man who liked to be in total control of his surroundings. Sara shivered. "What do you mean his cover *was* deep?"

"He's a legend, Sara. Just like the gold that never made it out of Vietnam. But he was real like the gold, too. Lethally real, from what I understand. In my business legends can be real.'' His mouth twisted ironically.

''But you're not him?''

''Hell, no.'' Vaughn grimaced. ''Give me some credit. The guy cracked up completely, according to the old gossip. Went bonkers on his last mission. He never returned.''

Sara was very still. ''What do you mean, he cracked up?''

''Just what I said. The story goes that he broke like a fine-tuned violin string. Came apart. Went crazy. Cracked. Couldn't handle what he was paid to handle. Got himself killed on his last assignment. Why the interest? Because you've been assuming I'm him?''

''The thought had crossed my mind,'' she admitted softly.

''I'm not especially flattered. The guy may once have been good, the best there was, in fact, but I sure as hell don't intend to lose my nerve the way he did.''

''What are you going to do with the gold if you get it?'' she pressed, desperate to keep the conversation moving. She had no particular wish to chat the afternoon away with Brady Vaughn, but she somehow felt safer when he was talking.

''I'm going to retire, Sara. Somewhere far, far away. Some nice island, perhaps where a lot of gold will buy a lot of silence and a lot of what I want out of life. I've been living under a great deal of tension for the past couple of years. And you know what they say about the dangers of too much tension. I've done well financially, but as the magazines say, stress takes its toll.''

''Like it did on the man called Wolf?'' she flung back.

Vaughn shook his head. ''That was an entirely different sort of situation. According to the story, he simply broke. With me, dropping out is more of a reasonable, strictly pragmatic business decision. You see, I've been working very hard lately. And I'm a little tired. Holding down two jobs will do that to a man.''

''Two jobs?'' she questioned, confused.

''Never mind.'' Vaughn shifted his position in the doorway. ''I really don't feel like discussing it any further at the moment. Let's go into the living room and sit down. We might have a long wait ahead of us. But have no fear. Sooner or later your uncle will figure out that he's been sent on a wild-goose chase. When he does he'll rush back here. We'll be waiting for him. I bought some food. Enough to last us a couple of days, if necessary. But I doubt we'll have to put up with each other's company for that long. Your uncle is a smart man.''

What did you talk about when you found yourself whiling away the hours with a man who kept a gun in his hand while he conversed with you?

Sara was still asking herself that sometime later as she sat almost immobile on the sofa in front of the cold fireplace. She hadn't moved in so long that she was afraid her foot might have grown numb. When she did move it cautiously, Vaughn glanced at her sharply.

''Going somewhere, Sara?''

''The bathroom, unless you have any objections,'' she muttered, rising slowly to her feet. There was a tingling sensation in her left foot but it wasn't completely numb.

Vaughn eyed her thoughtfully. ''None. There's no way out of that room. I've checked. Try to resist the temptation to forage for a pair of scissors or a razor blade. You'd only wind up cutting yourself.''

Sara didn't respond. She turned away and went down the hall to the bathroom. When the door closed behind her, she sagged against the sink and stared at her drawn face in the mirror.

She had to do something. She couldn't bear this endless waiting. What was it Adrian had said about the value of patience? In her case it bought nothing but anxiety. It didn't seem to bother Vaughn particularly, she reflected. He was very professional about the whole thing. Or at least he seemed professional. Hard to judge, given her limited experience in this kind of business. Sara winced.

Vaughn had the ability to wait but would he bother with that route if he thought there might be a shortcut to his goal, she asked herself as she splashed her face with cold water. He'd tried a shortcut once before when he created the diversion that had sent her uncle off to Hawaii. If she could make him think there was an alternative to this interminable waiting, perhaps he would go for it. She dried her flushed face and thought of Adrian's promise to return by early evening.

There was no way he could make it back tonight if he'd actually gone to Mexico and Vaughn seemed convinced he'd gone.

But Adrian had promised her he'd be back. And the house was set on its alarm status. If she were inside the house with Vaughn, Adrian would know as soon as he returned that there was trouble. His small signaling device would warn him there had been an unauthorized intrusion when he came within a couple of blocks of his home.

That scenario would only work if Adrian really was planning to return tonight. If he was even now en route to Mexico City, she was in very bad trouble. Heaven only knew where her uncle was.

Sara wrenched herself away from the mirror. It was an incredible disaster, and if she didn't act, it was going to get worse. She didn't have any illusions about the man in the next room. He was quite capable of casually raping her tonight and killing her later after he had what he wanted from her uncle.

Her only real chance was to bank on the fact that Adrian had told her the truth about returning this evening.

Legends and reality. How could a woman be sure of the difference, she asked herself.

A few minutes later Sara opened the bathroom door and went down the hall to the living room. She saw the fleeting spark of interest in Vaughn's eyes as she resumed her seat on the couch. No, the last thing she wanted to risk was spending the night here with him.

"In another couple of hours we'll have to discuss the sleeping arrangements, Sara," Vaughn mused, tossing a magazine into the bin beside the chair. "I think that could be interesting."

"Really? Do you sleep with your gun in your hand, Mr. Vaughn?"

He chuckled. "I think I can dispense with the gun once I've tied you up for the night. You'd look interesting spread-eagled on a bed."

Sara shuddered and nerved herself for the next bit. "I'm not interested in sharing a bed with you."

"Perhaps I will find it a challenge to see if I can create a little interest," he suggested coolly.

"I doubt it. I'm going to be married soon."

"Are you?" he murmured blandly. "To the boyfriend who just skipped town? You'll have to catch him first, won't you?"

Sara chose her next words carefully. "That gold you're after is supposed to be my wedding gift from my uncle."

Vaughn's eyes narrowed thoughtfully. "Just how much do you know about your uncle's little social-security cache?"

She tried for a mild shrug, her arms wrapped around her drawn-up knees as she sat on the couch. "About as much as you do. You know my uncle. He's fond of dropping little, uh, hints."

"Kincaid never does anything without a reason. And in spite of that easygoing facade, I worked with him long enough to know he's a shrewd and careful man. If he was dropping hints to you about the gold, then he must have truly believed it was safe for you to know about it. No reason he shouldn't think it was safe after all these years, I suppose."

"In addition to being shrewd and careful, my uncle also likes to plan for the future," she added deliberately. "He wanted Adrian and me to know enough about the gold to be able to find it someday in the event something happened to him."

Vaughn leaned forward on his chair, the gun cradled loosely in his fist. "That's very interesting, Sara. Very interesting. It puts a whole new light on the situation. Up until now I've assumed that no one except Kincaid knew the truth about the gold. It's a fact that your uncle tries not to leave much to chance, though. Tell me more, little Sara. Tell me what made

Saville think he's got a shot at the gold. I've been wondering who he plans to contact after Mexico City."

She caught her lower lip between her teeth, watching him the way a small mouse probably watched a hovering eagle. *Adrian, where are you?* "Mr. Vaughn, I'll make a deal with you."

He smiled and she could almost hear the way he must be laughing inwardly at her naiveté. The knowledge made her grit her teeth.

"I'm listening, little Sara."

"If I…if I show you where I think the information is hidden, will you take it and go away?"

"I'd have no reason to hang around any longer if I had a map showing the location of the gold," he murmured.

Sara wanted to cringe, but she managed to project a hopeful expression. "It's at Adrian's."

"Your boyfriend's house?"

"He's the man I'm going to marry. Uncle Lowell gave us each a copy of the map. If what you say is true about Adrian being in Mexico, then he must have taken his copy with him. But I have my own. Or at least I have information that will lead me to the gold. I'm not sure that it's exactly a map."

"I can't quite decide whether or not to believe you, little Sara," Vaughn finally said.

She clenched her fingers tightly together. "I can show you."

"But first we have to drive all the way back to that damn island? I don't like islands, Sara. A man can get trapped on islands. So few ways off, you see."

"I thought you were going to retire to an island," she shot back.

"Ah, but that will be different. Much different. There I will have my own means of transportation."

She let out her breath. "Then you're not interested in getting your hands on the information my uncle gave to me?"

Vaughn was quiet for a long while and then he suddenly seemed to come to a decision. "It would make things much simpler if it turned out that you're telling the truth, although I have a few doubts. Still, your boyfriend is several thousand miles away by now following some lead. I'd give a lot to know exactly what kind of lead he thinks he has. Who knows when your uncle will show up." He drummed his fingers on the arm of the chair, his eyes hooded and speculative. "I suppose there's no harm in checking out your story. We could be into the city and over to that damn island within a couple of hours."

"Yes." She could hardly breathe as she waited for the final decision. Was greed finally going to swamp this man's patience?

He nodded once. "All right, Sara. We'll go. But I warn you that if you've lied to me, I will make things most unpleasant for both you and your uncle. And probably your boyfriend, too."

"I'm not lying," she said with great conviction. "I know where my copy of the information is hidden. I had finally realized it just before you made that fake phone call this morning."

"I do believe you're telling the truth," Vaughn mused as he studied the certainty in her expression. "Fascinating. Remind me to thank you later."

Sure, thought Sara as she got to her feet. *I'll remind you. Just before you pull that trigger.*

Nine

The drive back into Seattle was the longest and most exhausting traveling Sara had ever done in her life. She decided that the normal stresses and strains of rush-hour traffic are not enhanced by the fact that your passenger is casually holding a gun in his lap.

Brady Vaughn didn't say much during the drive. He was undoubtedly contemplating his imminent retirement, Sara thought as she navigated the off ramp from the interstate and found the street that led down to the ferry docks. He kept the gun discreetly shielded under a jacket but he kept it aimed in her direction. She had a hunch that once she had parked her car on the ferry Vaughn wouldn't allow her to go up onto the passenger decks. The thought of sitting on the car deck for the entire length of the ferry ride was depressing.

She was right, of course. Vaughn simply lounged in his corner of the car and watched her speculatively. Unobtrusively Sara glanced at her watch. Her timing, at least, was good. If Adrian had told the truth this morning, he would be catching the ferry that would be leaving Seattle forty minutes from now. She would have forty minutes to entertain Brady Vaughn. Her fingers flexed uneasily on the wheel.

The whole exercise would be extremely pointless if Adrian didn't show up on the right ferry. Halfway across the bay Sara had a wild thought or two about flinging herself from the car and making a dash to the passenger decks. It would be a futile move and she knew it. Even if he chose not to use the gun, Vaughn could probably run her down easily in the close confines of the parked cars. Besides, she reminded herself, that wasn't the plan. She had a much better one in mind.

If it worked. *Legends and reality.* Where did the truth stop and the legend begin? Perhaps in some cases there was no difference. Perhaps a woman just had to make the leap to faith.

"You look nervous, Sara," Vaughn observed politely. "I trust you're not wasting my time with this little chase? It won't do any good, if you are. I know what I'm doing."

She shook her head. "All I want is for you to take the information about the gold and leave."

"Sounds simple enough. I do like simple plans; don't you?"

"Yes." How simple was hers?

"Will you dream about the gold you could have had, Sara? Will you think about it occasionally in the future? Wonder what it might have been like to have your hands on your uncle's cache?"

Again she shook her head. "Even if the gold is still there, I don't see how I could get it out. How are you going to accomplish that little feat, Vaughn? Just walk into that part of the world and tell the current government officials you'd like to do a little digging on their borders?"

He chuckled. She was learning to hate that poor excuse of a laugh. "Nothing that obvious. I prefer quieter techniques. I have contacts and I'll have cash with which to grease the way. I'll be going in through Cambodia. That gold must be somewhere near the Cambodia-Vietnam border."

"Gold is heavy. You won't be able to simply hoist it over your shoulder and hike out of the country with it. Not if there's as much there as you seem to think."

"I'll have help," he explained absently.

Sara slanted him a curious glance. "Help?"

"There are men who will undertake a great many risks for a promise of a split of the profits." He shrugged.

"You'll find some mercenaries to help you get the gold out?"

"They undoubtedly think of themselves as entrepreneurs," Vaughn murmured.

Sara closed her eyes and willed the ferry to a faster speed. She couldn't take much more of this unremitting tension. Whether her scheme worked or not, all she wanted to do at the moment was get it over and done with. She didn't see how anyone could live constantly under the stress of genuine danger. It was easy to see how a man or a woman might crack.

The ferry docked eventually and Sara turned the key in the ignition with a sense of fatalism. Forty minutes from now, if she was very, very lucky, Adrian would be driving off a similar ferry. If she was not so fortunate... Sara pushed the thought aside. There wasn't much point dwelling on that possibility. She would deal with it when the time came.

She drove slowly along the narrow road that wound around the island's perimeter, more slowly than was really necessary. Any time she could eat up this way was that much less that had to be used up at the house waiting for Adrian.

For the first time since she had arrived in the Seattle area the weather was finally beginning to live up to its reputation. The day was rapidly turning gray and overcast. A light mist began to fall.

"Come on, let's get going." With one of his first hints of impatience Vaughn moved the gun in an ugly gesture.

Sara tried to think of something calming to say. "You don't have to use the ferry to get back off the island, you know. You can drive across a bridge on the far side. It's the long way around if you're trying to get back to the airport or Seattle, but—"

"Just shut up. I know my way around."

Of course he did. He was, after all, a *professional.* He wouldn't trap himself on an island. Sara pulled into the driveway in front of Adrian's house. The windows were still dark, so that removed the possibility that by some miracle Adrian had actually arrived home ahead of her. *Forty minutes.*

"Is it true?" she began tentatively as she slowly opened her car door.

"Is what true?" Vaughn reached out and snapped the keys from her hand. He pocketed them.

"That you really have a chance of getting that gold out of Southeast Asia?"

"Believe me, I wouldn't be going to all this trouble if I didn't think it was possible." Vaughn made a careful outside inspection of the house, reassuring himself that no one was around. Then he cast an amused glance at Sara. "What's the matter, honey? Having second thoughts about giving me that map?"

She stopped at the top of the steps and looked back at him. "I admit that until now I assumed the gold was completely inaccessible."

He chuckled. "For years I believed it probably didn't exist at all! Kincaid hid the truth well behind the legend. He made everyone think it really was just one more wild tale set in the last days of the war. There were a hundred other similar stories and there was no real reason to think this one was for real. But a year ago I came across an old file that had been sealed since shortly after Saigon fell. The one thing that damned war generated was paperwork. Files and memos and reports will probably still be turning up twenty years from now. At any rate this one contained some notes by a journalist who claimed he'd interviewed some villagers in the south. He said they told him a story about an American agent who had worked with them toward the end of the war. They described him as a man who knew how to laugh and how to hold his whiskey. A man who was always telling stories. A man who could sketch your face before you even realized he was holding a pencil."

Sara caught her breath.

"Exactly." Vaughn nodded grimly. "A perfect description of Lowell Kincaid. The reporter's notes went on to tell a fascinating story. It culminated in Kincaid's departure for the Cambodian border with a jeep full of gold. The villagers didn't actually see the gold in Kincaid's jeep but they did see the share of it he left for them. He apparently stashed it in the village well and told the elders to wait until the North Vietnamese had passed through before digging it back out. Just like Kincaid to make a grand gesture like that. He was a brilliant agent, but he had some definite weaknesses. When I put that report together with the legend I'd first heard back in 1972, I began to believe I might be dealing with more than just another war tale. It's taken me months to piece together some idea of what might have happened and where. The file with the journalist's notes led to other files. Eventually I knew I was onto the real thing.''

''What happened to the journalist?'' Sara heard herself ask.

''He died,'' Vaughn said carelessly. ''An accident down in South America earlier this year, I believe.''

''I see.'' She wondered how much Vaughn had had to do with the ''accident.''

His mouth twisted wryly. ''I do believe I recognize that look in your eyes, little Sara.''

''What look?''

''Greed, love. Pure unadulterated greed. I saw it in your boyfriend's eyes yesterday and it's in yours today.''

She feigned a nonchalant movement of her shoulders and turned to open the front door. There was no sound from within. The house was as quiet and innocent-looking as it had been that first night when she'd arrived and searched Adrian's study.

''Doesn't your boyfriend believe in locking his front door?'' Vaughn drawled as he followed Sara into the house. He held the gun at the ready while he verified that the place was empty.

''He says there's virtually no crime around here.''

''A trusting soul.'' Vaughn smirked. He took in his surroundings with a quick, professional eye. ''I take it back. It goes beyond trusting. I think we can safely say your friend Saville is probably a fool.''

''And what about me?'' She slung her purse down on the sofa and turned to face him.

''Oh, you're very smart, Sara. Very smart indeed, if you're telling the truth.'' Vaughn's eyes hardened. ''Where's the map?''

She grabbed for her courage, using all of her willpower to keep her expression cool. ''I've tried to tell you, it's not exactly a map,'' she began carefully.

''What the hell are you talking about?'' The violence in Vaughn was very close to the surface.

''My uncle has his own unique way of doing things. You know that. He made sure I'd have the information I needed but he hid it in an unique manner. I don't know how he gave Adrian his information, but I think I know where my copy is.'' Her fingernails dug into her palms. She wondered if Vaughn realized just how scared she was.

''Sara, let's not play any games. You'll lose, believe me. Where's the map?''

''It's not a map. I'm trying to explain. It's a sort of...of code.''

Vaughn stared at her. ''A code? You told me you and your uncle didn't go in for codes.''

''I said we didn't have any prearranged greeting signals.''

''Then what are you saying?''

''I'll show you.'' Moving cautiously so as not to alarm him, Sara turned and started down the hall toward the study. This business of trying to think two steps ahead of a man with a gun was tricky. The ferry that might or might not be bringing Adrian to the rescue had left Seattle by now. Her fate was in the hands of the Washington state ferry system. They claimed to have an excellent safety record.

Vaughn was close behind her as she stepped into the study. The crystal apple gleamed on Adrian's desk, still pinning her note. Beyond it the manuscript of *Phantom* waited.

''There,'' she whispered, indicating the pile of typed pages. ''Everything you want to know about that gold is in that manuscript. My uncle has jotted down little doodles and notes all over the margins, you see.''

Vaughn stared first at the stack of papers and then gestured viciously at her with the nose of the gun. ''You little bitch. What kind of game do you think you're playing?''

She hugged herself, trying to master the faint trembling that threatened to weaken her limbs. Her head bent forward and a sweep of her hair hid her expression. ''It's there. I promise you. And I know how to get at the information you want. It's in code and my uncle once taught me the code. It will take a while, but I can do it.''

''Why you little fool!'' he snarled. ''Stalling isn't going to get you anywhere. There's no one around to come to your rescue. If there was any likelihood of that, I'd never have agreed to let you drag me here.''

''No.'' She shook her head and lifted her chin defiantly. ''I'm not trying to stall. I'm...I'm trying to make a deal. You said you were going to be hiring professional help to assist you in getting the gold out of Southeast Asia. Well, I want you to consider me as hired help, too. I can decode Uncle Lowell's doodles on that manuscript. I can do it here and now, in fact, and prove that what I'm saying is true. In return, I want you to cut me in for a piece of the action.''

He studied her derisively. ''You've got your uncle's nerve, little Sara, I'll say that for you. Decode the manuscript. What a crock of—''

''It's true,'' she insisted. ''You know Uncle Lowell. It would be just like him to hide the information so I would be sitting right on top of it all the time. That manuscript was waiting for me at his cabin the other day. It was right out in the open. You'd overlooked it, naturally. He says people always overlook the obvious. But I recognized the doodles on the margins. It's the code he taught me when I was a little girl. It was a game we used to play together. Give me half an hour and I'll have the information you need to find that gold.''

Vaughn was clearly and dangerously undecided. His eyes slid from the manuscript to her face and back again. ''Half an hour?''

She nodded quickly. "Is it a deal?"

"I can afford half an hour's wait. I was prepared to wait for much longer than that for Kincaid to return. And your boyfriend is no doubt getting ready to land in Mexico City so there's plenty of time on that end. All right, my greedy little Sara. You've got yourself a deal."

"You'll cut me in for a slice of the profit?" She had to make it sound real, Sara told herself. She tried to inject just the right note of hopeful greed.

"Sure. Why not?" He threw himself down into a chair in the corner. "Half an hour. And if it turns out that you're lying, little Sara—"

"I'm not lying." She sat down slowly behind the desk. From there she was looking through the study door and into the hall beyond. Brady Vaughn would be able to see anyone who came through the door but from his seat in the corner he could not see into the hall as she could. Sara figured she would have a couple of seconds' advance notice if and when Adrian arrived. Nervously she reached out and pulled the manuscript toward her.

She found herself staring down at the sketch of the wolf. For an instant it almost paralyzed her. Then, with excessive care, she turned over the first page of *Phantom* and picked up a pencil.

Time ticked past with a slowness that made Sara think she was waiting for eternity to end. She would have no way of knowing until the last moment whether or not Adrian would arrive. He would have the warning about the invasion of his house shortly after he drove off the ferry. He would probably leave the car down the road and walk the final few yards, she decided. Neither she nor Vaughn would have the sound of a vehicle to alert them.

Carefully she went through the manuscript, occasionally stopping to jot down a meaningless number or word on the notepad beside her. It would be particularly ironic if there really was a code imbedded in her uncle's margin doodles, Sara decided at one point. A real joke on her. As far as she knew she was looking at nothing more than meaningless notes and drawings.

Time crept past. Outside the window the mist turned to rain. Sara turned on the desk lamp. Vaughn's eyes never left her as she went page by page through the manuscript. His patience was as amazing to her as Adrian's had been. Where did they learn that kind of skill? Perhaps some people were just born with it. It was a cinch she wasn't one of those lucky souls. She shuddered and turned over another page. She would force herself not to sneak another glance at the clock or her watch for at least ten minutes, Sara decided resolutely at one point. The last thing she wanted to do was give Vaughn the idea that she was waiting for someone. She kept her head bent over the manuscript for what she estimated must surely be at least ten minutes if not more and then, unable to resist, she slid her gaze upward to the clock on the wall near the door.

She almost didn't see Adrian standing in the shadows of the hall. When she did, she thought her breath had stopped permanently. He was simply waiting there, watching her in absolute silence. It was as if a ghost had materialized out of thin air and in her odd, light-headed state of mind she might have believed just that if it hadn't been for the rain-dampened Windbreaker he wore. It took her another instant to see the gun in his hand.

''Something wrong, Sara?'' Vaughn asked conversationally from the corner. He lifted his gun in an easy threat. ''You seem a little tense.''

Sara swallowed and dropped her eyes from Adrian's still, shadowed figure to the crystal apple in front of her. ''I've just realized that I made a mistake.''

''Did you?'' Vaughn seemed only politely interested. ''Just what kind of mistake would that be, little Sara?''

She picked up the apple and held it so that it caught the light from the desk lamp. ''The information you want isn't in the manuscript.''

''Then you have a problem, don't you, Sara,'' he said with brutal emphasis.

She shook her head. ''No. I don't think so. Not anymore.'' She tossed the apple up in the air and caught it again. ''Here's what you want, Mr. Vaughn.'' She tossed the crystal object once more and caught it easily. Beyond the door Adrian did not move. He was as still as midnight waiting to descend. She couldn't see his eyes but she knew they would be quite colorless.

''I think,'' Vaughn said abruptly, ''that I've had enough of your games, bitch.''

''Ah, but I'm so good at them,'' she protested gently. ''What you want is right out here in front of your very eyes, Mr. Vaughn. As clear as crystal. Just the sort of trick my uncle would pull, don't you think?'' With sudden decision she hurled the apple toward the window.

''What the hell…I've had it with you, lady. I'm going to kill you for this!'' Without warning, Vaughn's patience snapped. He surged out of the chair, his gun trained on Sara but his eyes following the apple as it crashed against the tempered glass.

The sound of the crystal striking the window and falling to the floor was lost beneath Brady Vaughn's scream of pain and rage as Adrian floated through the doorway and brought the base of the gun down in the direction of the other man's skull. In the split second before the butt of the gun would have made contact with his head, however, some instinct must have warned Vaughn. He threw himself to one side, tumbling across the desk. Adrian's gun struck him violently on the shoulder but it didn't stun him. The weapon Vaughn had been holding, however, fell to the floor and skidded along the hardwood surface until it struck the edge of a rug.

On the other side of the desk, Sara screamed. She was trapped against the wall as the momentum of Vaughn's panicked, sliding rush across the desk threw him toward her. An instant later he seized her even as he stumbled wildly to his feet. Sharp steel blossomed in his hand. He held the knife to Sara's throat, his arm locking her against his body.

"Hold it right there, Saville. Come one step closer and I swear I'll kill her."

Sara couldn't take her eyes off Adrian. The temperature in the study seemed to have suddenly dropped by about twenty degrees.

His face was utterly without emotion. It reminded her of the way he had watched the fish dying at his feet the other morning on the pier but it was a thousand times more remote. He didn't look at Sara. His whole attention was on the heavily breathing man who was holding the knife to her throat.

"Let her go, Vaughn."

"You think I'm crazy? She's my ticket out of here. Drop the gun." He jerked his arm more tightly around Sara's neck. "I said, drop it, damn you! Think I'm playing games?"

"No, I don't think you're playing games." Moving slowly and deliberately, Adrian took a step forward and set his handgun down on the floor at his feet. The blue steel gleamed savagely in the light of the desk lamp.

"Come on, you bitch." Vaughn tugged Sara around the edge of the desk, clearly heading toward the spot where his own weapon had landed when it had been jolted from his hand. "Move, damn you!"

Sara tried to make her body as limp and heavy as possible but the feel of the steel at the base of her throat kept her from refusing to cooperate entirely. Vaughn would use that knife, she knew. Just as he would use the gun when he got his hands on it.

Across the room Adrian stood balanced a step away from his own weapon. If push came to shove, Sara didn't doubt but that he'd make a grab for it. He watched Vaughn the way a wolf might watch a circling hyena.

"Your best bet is to make a run for it, Vaughn. Hanging on to Sara will only slow you down."

Sara felt the tension in her captor's body as he pulled her

toward his gun. ''I've come too far in search of that gold, Saville. I'm not leaving without getting what I want.''

''Sara doesn't know where it is.''

''Maybe. Maybe not. I can't quite figure sweet Sara. But Kincaid knows where it is, and when he finds out I've got his niece, he'll bargain.''

''You think so? I've never known Kincaid to bargain for anything without coming out on top,'' Adrian said thoughtfully.

''You don't know him as well as I do,'' Vaughn assured the other man. He stopped beside the gun on the floor and his fingers bit abruptly into Sara's shoulder. ''Bend down very slowly, Sara, and pick up the gun, muzzle first. And keep in mind that I'll have this knife at the nape of your neck.''

Sara realized that it would be dangerously awkward for him to try scooping up the gun while still retaining a stranglehold on her. The action might give Adrian the opening for which he was clearly waiting. So Vaughn was going to make her pick up the lethal chunk of steel and hand it over politely to replace the knife.

Sara glanced down at the gun and then up at Adrian's still, unreadable face. If she gave the gun to Vaughn, he would surely use it against the one thing that stood between him and the door: Adrian.

''Do as I say!''

Slowly Sara knelt, aware of the tip of the knife following her nape. Adrian didn't move, his eyes never leaving Vaughn's face. She went all the way down on her knees and reached out reluctantly for the muzzle of the gun.

''Hurry up,'' Vaughn snarled, forced to bend over slightly in order to keep the knife within striking distance of her neck. ''Pick it up and give it to me!''

She wasn't going to get a better opportunity, Sara realized. It was now or never. Handing the gun to Vaughn was the equivalent of signing Adrian's death warrant. She took a deep breath.

Then she threw herself full-length on the floor and rolled to one side, straight into Vaughn's legs. Her falling body covered the gun.

''Damn you!''

The knife flashed as Vaughn was forced to step backward in order to regain his balance. The blade arced downward, scoring Sara's shoulder. She felt the icy sting of the steel even as she struck his left leg. The pain brought a startled cry to her lips.

''Sara!''

Her name was the only sound Adrian made. In the next instant he launched himself across the room in a deadly rush.

But Vaughn was already moving. He hurled the blade straight at Adrian, who must have guessed what was going to happen next. Sara opened her eyes in time to see Adrian throw himself to one side. The blade whipped harmlessly past and imbedded itself deep into the far wall. The rushing assault had served to draw the snake's fangs.

In the small space of time he had bought for himself, Vaughn glanced down and seemed to realize he didn't stand a chance if he took another moment to push Sara off his gun. He raced for the door even as Adrian dived for his own gun.

Sara gasped in pain, her fingers going to the wound on her shoulder just as Adrian leaped for the door. Her cry of anguish stopped him as effectively as a steel cable. He whirled and came back to her even as the sound of Vaughn's running footsteps disappeared down the hall.

''My God, Sara.'' Adrian went down on his knees beside her. ''How bad is it? Let me see.'' Carefully he guided her to a sitting position, pulling her face into his shoulder as he pushed aside her shirt.

''I…I don't think it's all that bad,'' she managed, inhaling sharply as she leaned into him. She was trembling. ''It just hurts.''

''I know, Sara,'' he soothed in a soft growl as he examined the shoulder. ''I know. But you're right. It isn't very deep. Do you think you can handle it yourself?''

''Myself?'' She lifted her head in astonishment and then realized what he meant. ''Adrian, you're not going after him!''

''I've got to, Sara. You know that.''

''No, I do *not* know that,'' she retorted. ''Let the police worry about him. It's not your job—''

''Sara, it is my job.'' Adrian's face was a cold mask, his light eyes frozen, crystal pools. ''After what he's done to you, I don't have any choice.''

''No, damn it!'' she raged, grabbing at him as he rose to his feet. ''You'll never catch him, anyway. He'll take my car. He's got the keys.'' But even as she argued she realized there was no sound of a car leaving the drive.

''I took care of the car before I came into the house. A precaution.'' Adrian moved away from her, scooping up the gun and started for the door. ''He'll be on foot and unarmed. This is easy hunting, Sara. Don't worry about it.''

''I don't want you going hunting! Please, Adrian, wait....''

But she was calling to no one. Adrian had already disappeared down the hall after his quarry.

Easy hunting. Sara's eyes filled with tears. She didn't want Adrian going hunting. In that moment she would have given her soul to keep him from pursuing Vaughn.

Once again she remembered the way Adrian had watched the fish dying on the pier.

Outside the house Adrian paused briefly on the porch, listening. He shoved the gun back into the leather holster he wore at the base of his spine. The rain was coming down heavily now, obscuring visibility. Sara's car stood silently in the drive, unable to function since he'd clipped two strategic wires.

He'd really made a mess of this, Adrian told himself grimly as he started down the porch steps at a long, loping run. Everything was coming apart in his hands, and to top it all off, he'd nearly gotten Sara killed. The fury and fear he had felt when he'd realized what was happening inside the study were unlike anything he'd ever experienced in his life. The combination of the two had risen up to choke him, causing him to mishandle the situation badly.

But Sara was safe now. The knife had drawn blood but it hadn't gone deep. She had been too close to the floor, depriving Vaughn of an easy target.

Vaughn. Adrian shook his head as his sense of logic returned. There were only two ways off the island, the ferry from Winslow and the bridge at the far end of Bainbridge. Vaughn would head for the highway and try to commandeer a car to go for the bridge. The ferry was already pulling out of its slip on the return run to Seattle. There would be no chance for Vaughn to catch it.

His hunting instincts told Adrian that Vaughn would stick as much as possible to the wooded terrain until he spotted a car that could be hailed. And he would want to keep moving in the general direction of his goal, the bridge. Panicked quarry didn't think to backtrack or race off along a route that would seem to be in the opposite direction. When you were trying to escape, the sense of urgency effectively destroyed a good portion of natural logic.

With grave certainty, Adrian started toward the woods that bounded the road. He moved silently on the wet ground, oblivious to the rain that was soaking his hair and clothing. He knew he was heading in the right direction when he found the scrap of cloth Vaughn had apparently lost when he'd blundered into a thick cluster of blackberry bushes. After that, the trail became increasingly easy to follow.

Just like old times, Adrian thought with a chill that did not come from the rain. Maybe you could never really leave the past behind. Maybe it stayed with you forever.

He had told himself a year ago that a good, solid, iron-tight cover was the answer. A good cover had saved his life often enough in the past. Logically it should be able to provide him with a new life in the future. He'd had it all worked out, every detail in place, every aspect of his new world under control. He was a writer now, a slightly eccentric vegetarian, a man who could fall in love and marry just as other men did. If asked, he could have supplied a complete life history that would have satisfied any inquiring reporter.

The cover had been letter perfect until this afternoon when he'd walked into his study and seen the truth in Sara's eyes. That's when Adrian had learned that there was no such thing as a perfect cover.

She knew who he was. He'd blown it all when he'd stood in the hall with a gun in his hand.

A good cover, it seemed, couldn't quite cover up the past.

Vaughn was moving with increasing carelessness. Probably because there hadn't been any traffic on the quiet road. Maybe he was beginning to realize that making his way to the other end of the island was going to be very difficult.

Not difficult, Adrian thought savagely. Impossible. Vaughn wasn't going to drive, walk or fly off Bainbridge Island. At least not under his own power. Adrian quickened his pace, gliding silently through the rain-wet trees, skirting the berry bushes and listening with every nerve in his body.

In another couple of minutes he heard the first faint sounds of his quarry. Vaughn might be good but he obviously didn't know much about this kind of fieldwork. He was probably more accustomed to the streets of foreign cities. Most likely he'd never done a lot of real fieldwork in Vietnam or South America. An office spy. A man who worked embassies and cocktail parties.

Easy hunting.

Adrian could hear him clearly now. Vaughn wasn't far ahead of him. What lead he'd had had been chewed into by berry bushes, a driving rain and a woodsy terrain with which he wasn't familiar.

Adrian, on the other hand, knew every inch of the woods around his house. He'd walked them often enough, head bent against a cold drizzle, hands stuffed into his jacket. He'd thought about *Phantom* during those long walks. And he'd thought about the mysterious Sara.

Sara. My passionate, impulsive, loving Sara. Sara, from whom he would have done anything to keep the truth. Too late now. The cover was blown.

A rough, hastily bitten-off oath from the man ahead blended with the steady beat of the rain but Adrian heard it. He slipped forward, starting to reach for the gun in his holster at his back. And then he caught sight of the muted, striped shirt Vaughn was wearing. Vaughn was having to swerve in order to go around another thicket of blackberry bushes. Adrian changed his mind about the gun. *Easy hunting. Easy prey.*

You should never have touched her, Vaughn. You should never have gone near Sara. It's going to cost you everything.

Vaughn trotted to the left, searching for a way around the thorny bushes. He heard nothing as Adrian made his silent rush through the trees. In the last second, though, Vaughn felt the movement behind him. He whirled, clawing at his pocket to withdraw a switchblade.

But he was too late. Adrian's body catapulted into his quarry's, bearing both men to the soggy ground. Adrian had his hands locked around the fist that held the knife. He crushed with all his strength, hearing something snap. Vaughn yelled. The knife fell into a pile of leaves.

It was all over in less than a minute. Adrian had the advantage and he used it. With brutal efficiency he used his hands to stun his opponent. In a startlingly short period of time Vaughn lay limp and dazed beneath his attacker.

Ten

Sara adjusted the bandage on her shoulder for the twentieth time, using the bathroom mirror to guide her. It had been exceedingly awkward trying to bandage the wound without help but at last she'd gotten the bleeding stopped. She had been right. It hurt like hell, but the slicing cut wasn't all that deep. Her gaze went to the watch on her wrist. It had been over two hours since Adrian had left the house in pursuit of Vaughn.

Too much time. She was growing increasingly frightened as the minutes ticked past. But she felt incredibly helpless. Not because she thought for a moment that Vaughn would succeed in ambushing Adrian, though. Her mouth twisted in response to another stab of pain from her shoulder. No, Adrian would get his man. The wolf was on the hunt and he always did what had to be done.

Just as Phantom always did what must be done.

What truly frightened her was the thought of Adrian being thrown back into the life he had left behind. She would have given anything to keep him from having to resurrect the past. Because now she knew just how hard he had worked to put it behind him. But there was nothing she could do.

Adrian was the man they had once called Wolf, the legend who had been only too real. She had been coming slowly to that conclusion all day as bits and pieces of evidence came together in her mind.

When she had realized that her only hope of escaping Vaughn lay with Adrian, Sara had acknowledged the truth. Her life had depended on the man code-named Wolf, the man she had once imagined was a renegade killer.

And she had known on some instinctive level that Adrian would save her. That was why she had lured Vaughn back to the island house.

It was her love for Adrian that had enabled her to view the evidence of his past with different eyes. That love had begun from almost the first moment she had turned to find him watching her going through his study. She had known in that first glimpse that this man was different. He was her uncle's friend. The kind of man you could count on when the chips were down.

She had known for certain she was in love last night when she'd lain in Adrian's arms and prayed he wouldn't leave in the morning.

It was all so clear now. Crystal-clear, in fact. She probably should have been suspicious from the start about his identity. He was a man who needed to control his environment, to maintain a cover. It was the way he had built a new life.

Sara shuddered and tears filmed her eyes as she wondered how Adrian had felt when he'd realized his carefully structured world was crumbling around him. She ached to be able to comfort him but she was terribly afraid he wouldn't want the comfort. He had depended on no one but himself for too long.

The knock on the door shocked her into dropping the roll of tape she had been using. Sara frowned into the mirror. Adrian wouldn't knock on his own door, surely. Nervously she held a square of gauze to her shoulder and adjusted her shirt as best she could. Then she went cautiously down the hall to the front door. Standing on tiptoe, she peered through the tiny viewing port.

A man dressed in a wildly patterned aloha shirt and holding a festive-striped umbrella stood on the porch.

"Uncle Lowell!" Sara flung open the door and rushed into his arms. "My God, Uncle Lowell, are you all right? We've been so worried. Adrian's gone after Vaughn and it's been over two hours! I've been going out of my mind. How did you get here? Where have you been?"

"Easy, Sara," Kincaid said, smiling down at her. "One question at a time. Where did you say Adrian was?"

Sara stepped back into the house and held the door. "He's gone after Vaughn." She shook her head, trying to sort it all out for him. "Vaughn was holding me prisoner. He was going to trade me to you for information about that damned gold. Adrian rescued me but in the process Vaughn got away."

Kincaid arched shaggy eyebrows. "He did?" He followed his niece through the door, shaking out the umbrella as he did so. "That doesn't sound like Adrian."

"Well, it was all very chaotic, believe me." Sara sighed. "Vaughn was holding a knife at my throat and he'd made Adrian throw down his gun. Oh, it's a long story. But the end result is that Vaughn got clear and Adrian went after him. I've been worrying myself sick, Uncle Lowell."

"What's wrong with your shoulder?" Kincaid leaned forward, thick brows drawing into a solid line.

"Vaughn scratched it with the knife." She turned her head, trying to look at the gauze-covered wound. "It's not really that bad but it hurts so."

"Knife wounds generally feel like fire. Here, let me see if you've got it properly bandaged."

"The wound is all right, Uncle Lowell. It's Adrian I'm getting frantic about." But she stood still while Lowell glanced at the slice in her shoulder and then taped down the gauze.

"Adrian can take care of himself."

"You two keep saying that about each other but, personally, I'm having severe doubts! And I didn't want Adrian having to...to go back to his old business!"

Lowell tilted his head to one side, studying her speculatively. "So you've figured out what the old business was?"

Sara nodded grimly. "And I mean to have a heart-to-heart chat with you about that. But we can do it later. I've got other things on my mind just now."

"So have I. Got any coffee? After a few days in sunny Hawaii, it's a bit of a shock to come back to Seattle.'' Lowell started in the direction of the kitchen.

''But what about Adrian?'' Helplessly Sara followed in her uncle's wake.

Lowell Kincaid was the same as ever, she decided. You'd never know that behind the laughing blue eyes was a brain that could function in the most convoluted patterns. He was nearing seventy now and had gone quite bald except for a fringe of well-trimmed gray hair. Kincaid had never gone to fat; his body was still whipcord lean. In addition to the aloha shirt, he was wearing sandals and a pair of white cotton slacks that were spotted with rain. On his wrist was a gold watch. It went nicely with the thin gold chain around his neck. Sara knew the gold was real. Her uncle never wore fake gold.

''Adrian will be back when he's taken care of things.'' With the familiarity of a man who has frequently been a guest in the house, Lowell began making coffee. ''Damn sorry he had to clean up my mess, though.''

''Uncle Lowell,'' Sara said with forced patience. ''Why don't you tell me what the hell has been happening?''

Lowell stretched and lifted a hand to rub the point between his shoulder blades. ''Well, to put it in simple terms, I've just spent the last few days following a false trail in Hawaii. Came back today when I realized it was a dead end. Vaughn really had me running around the countryside,'' he added ruefully. ''I feel like an idiot.''

''Who is Vaughn, anyway?''

''Old business.''

''Oh, yes.'' She nodded, remembering the taped message. ''You said something about taking care of old business.''

''Look, when Adrian gets back, he's going to want some explanations, too. Why don't we wait until we're all sitting cozily around a nice warm fire. And what about dinner?''

''Dinner,'' Sara said vengefully, ''is the last thing on my mind at the moment. What are we going to do about Adrian?''

''Absolutely nothing. Never was much anyone could do

about Adrian,'' her uncle said reflectively as he poured boiling water over instant coffee. ''Just aim him and pull the trigger.''

Sara felt sick to her stomach.

SARA KNEW who he was. *She knew who he was.* Adrian couldn't forget the memory of her description of the man she knew as Wolf. Her words still rang in his head. A renegade killer or something equally picturesque. A man who, when he walked into a room, chilled everything and everyone. He'd seen the expression in her eyes when he'd stood in the hall just outside the study early this evening. She had looked up from the manuscript and he'd known that for her the room had grown very cold.

It was all over.

He drove back to the cabin with a sense of deep foreboding. There was a good chance she wouldn't even be there. Then what? When he pulled into the drive and saw the familiar green Toyota, he felt some sense of relief. Lowell was back. And that meant Sara was probably still around. Her car was still there but that didn't mean much since he'd disabled it earlier.

It was nice that Kincaid was home safe and sound, of course, Adrian told himself as he opened the car door. But the real benefit to his return was that it meant Adrian wouldn't have to face Sara alone. He still hadn't figured out what to say to her and he was beginning to accept the fact that he might never figure it out. He'd never been very good with words around Sara. In any event, she would probably be gone from his life soon, anyway.

She wouldn't want to hang around a wolf.

He walked slowly up the porch steps. The wet night had descended completely now and the warm lights of the house beckoned. But Adrian wasn't fooled. He knew the warmth was an illusion. Without Sara, there could be no real warmth in his life. He tried to dredge up some polite greetings, the sort of thing a man might say in this situation. He should be a gentleman about it. Give her an out. But deep inside he wasn't sure he could do it. He wanted her so and he'd begun to believe lately that he could have her. The thought of letting her walk out now filled him with a tight, gnawing tension.

There were a lot of things a man could take in this world but a woman's love was not among them. It had to be given willingly and it had to be for real. He had spent the last few days realizing the truth of that. The wonder of having Sara for himself couldn't be pushed back into the corners of his mind where he now kept other things that were better forgotten. He couldn't give her up.

But she hated and feared the man called Wolf.

The mechanical-sounding words Adrian had been practicing as he climbed the steps were wiped out of his head as the front door was thrown open.

''It's about time you got back!'' Sara cried as she flew across the porch. ''Adrian, it's been hours!''

He felt the soft impact as she hurled herself against him. Automatically his arms went around her. He was dazed by the greeting.

''Sara?''

''You said you'd be back on the five-fifty-five ferry,'' she whispered into his wet shirt. ''I knew you'd get back on time. I knew all I had to do was have Vaughn here and you'd take care of everything.''

He held her fiercely, absorbing the warmth of her. ''Yes.'' He stroked her hair wonderingly. ''I got the readout from the house alarm system right after I drove off the ferry.'' His fingers tightened abruptly in her hair. ''I've never been so scared in my life, Sara.''

''Hi, Adrian, sorry about all this. Everything okay?''

Adrian gazed over Sara's head, his eyes meeting those of his friend. ''Everything's taken care of.'' He felt Sara shiver in his arms.

Kincaid nodded. ''Figured it would be.''

''You may have a few questions to answer from your old pals at the agency in the morning, though.''

Kincaid's eyes gleamed. "How's that?"

"I left Vaughn tied up in a neat package a few yards off I-90. Then I called the West Coast agency office and left a message telling them where they could find him. When the guy who took the call demanded to know who was leaving the message—"

"You gave him my name." Kincaid grinned ruefully. "Thanks a lot, pal. Well, I guess I can't complain. I deserved it. Lord knows I owe you for taking care of Sara. Besides, maybe Gilkirk and his boys will be so delighted to have their hands on Vaughn they won't want to ask too many questions."

Sara lifted her head, her hands moving upward to frame Adrian's face. "You didn't kill him."

"No."

She smiled. "Of course not. Supper's ready. Go and take a hot shower. I'll pour you a glass of wine." She pulled free and disappeared back into the house.

Adrian stared after her, aware of a gnawing uncertainty. The uncertainty was painful but it was better than the cold, dead certainty of loss he'd been feeling earlier. Uncertainty contained hope. He followed Lowell into the house and headed for the bathroom, stripping off the wet Windbreaker as he moved.

ADRIAN HAD BEEN WATCHING Sara since he'd emerged from the shower, trying to second-guess her thoughts. She'd chattered about the gold while she'd prepared a hearty rice and vegetable salad, making a joke out of her uncle's idea of a wedding gift. She'd poured him and Lowell a glass of wine and put the sourdough rolls in the oven while discussing Lowell's unplanned vacation in Hawaii. Then she'd kept up a running monologue on Kincaid's new aloha shirt and how typical it was of him to bring something like that back from Hawaii.

Lowell had talked easily, too, leaning against the kitchen counter while responding to her teasing about his new shirt.

"Glad you like it. Got three more in the suitcase. Picked 'em up while I waited for the flight back this morning." He'd glanced down at the front of the splashy shirt with obvious pleasure.

Adrian had felt left out of the conversation but he hadn't known how to get into it. Sara and her uncle kept up a bright dialogue that covered everything under the sun except the subject of the man called Wolf. Adrian told himself morosely that it was probably because they were both too polite to talk about someone when the object of the conversation was within hearing distance brooding over a glass of wine.

During dinner Sara finally pounced on her uncle, demanding answers. Adrian surreptitiously kept an eye on her lively hazel eyes while she quizzed Lowell Kincaid. He searched for signs of disgust or fear or rejection in her expressive features. The stranger inner anxiety was eating him alive, demanding assurances and explanations and at the same time preparing him for the worst. Surely, after everything she had believed about the man named Wolf, she couldn't possibly be this warm and nonchalant now.

Adrian's fingers crumpled the napkin in his lap and he glanced down, vaguely astonished at the outward show of tension.

''All right, Uncle Lowell, let's have it,'' Sara demanded as the meal came to a close. She leaned back in her chair, her fingertips steepled beneath her chin as she regarded Kincaid with a gleaming gaze.

''Well,'' Lowell began with an easy grin, ''I had to go to about three shops before I found just the right selection of shirts but when I saw this one with the pineapples on it, I knew—''

''Lowell Kincaid, I am not talking about the aloha shirts and you know it. I want to know about the gold.''

''Ah, the gold,'' he echoed softly. ''I figure that you may not be able to get at it until sometime around your twenty-fifth wedding anniversary, or you may have let your children inherit the treasure map, but either way it makes an interesting wedding present, don't you think? Even if you never actually see the gold itself, you'll have it to talk about and laugh about and tell stories about. I can just hear the tales you'll be telling your kids.''

''I think,'' Sara interrupted firmly, ''that we're getting a little ahead of ourselves. I'm not interested in what I may be telling my kids, especially since I don't have any.''

''Yet,'' Lowell interjected wisely.

Sara raised her eyebrows but Adrian noticed she didn't look at him. She kept her attention on Kincaid. ''I'm more concerned with the past at the moment. Did you or did you not steal CIA gold and stash it near the Cambodian border?''

Kincaid grinned at Adrian. ''She's rather aggressively direct when she wants an answer.''

''Umm.'' Adrian sipped the last of his wine and wondered why Sara hadn't been aggressively direct in pinning him down about Wolf. Maybe she didn't want to know the full truth. He set down the wineglass with grim care.

''Okay, Sara, here's the story,'' Kincaid began. ''For starters, it wasn't CIA gold. It wasn't U.S. gold in any sense of the word, really. It belonged to some very astute gentlemen who were doing an active drug business under the guise of working in a civilian capacity for the U.S. government. I accidentally stumbled across them while working with some friends of mine.''

''Friends?''

Lowell nodded. ''I had spent a lot of time with the people of a particular village. They had been very useful during the war, supplying information and some very brave young men and women. At any rate, I was in the village when rumors came of the two drug runners being killed. The business career of a drug runner is precarious, to say the least. I was near the scene of the killing and, through a series of, uh, arranged coincidences, managed to get my hands on the gold.''

''Uh-huh.'' Sara sounded distinctly skeptical. '''Arranged' being the operative word, I imagine.''

''I then had myself a problem. I knew things were deteriorating rapidly. Saigon was about to go under, and everyone who had any sense was aware of it. I was several miles away and there was no way I could make it back to the embassy with the gold. I would have been lucky to make it back with my life. So I decided on another route out of the situation.''

''A route that would allow you to take some of the gold with you?''

Kincaid chuckled. ''You know me and gold, Sara. I couldn't bring myself to just toss it away.''

''Vaughn said he uncovered a file that indicated you left some of it behind with your friends in that village.''

Kincaid's shaggy brows lifted. ''A file, hmm? I wondered how he got curious enough about the gold after all these years to make a try for it. Well, Sara, let me tell you a fact of life. There's nothing quite as useful as gold when you're trying to survive in a country that's recently been overrun by a conquering army. And I owed those villagers. As for myself, I'd been making some friends near the Cambodian border and decided to call in a few favors. I loaded my share of the gold on a jeep and drove to the border. There was no way I could get it out of the country, so I buried it, made a map and then rendezvoused with my contacts. They got me out of the country.''

''Where does Brady Vaughn fit into all this?'' Sara demanded.

''Vaughn has been a thorn in the agency's side for some time. We all knew he was working both sides of the street.''

''He said something about working two jobs,'' Sara said dryly. ''Was that what he meant? He was selling information to the other side?''

''Information we wanted him to sell, although he didn't know it. We used him after we'd learned he'd been turned.'' Lowell smiled. ''But his usefulness was becoming limited from what my former associates have told me. Apparently the other side felt the same. Vaughn was smart enough to sense that something was going wrong and wisely decided to disappear.

Apparently he wanted a little nest egg to cushion his sudden retirement.''

''And he chose your cache of gold.''

''He'd been assigned to Saigon during that last six months. We'd worked together on a couple of jobs. But I never did fully trust the man. I tried to plant my own rumors about the gold whenever I heard it mentioned after the war. I knew it would be almost impossible to keep the whole thing absolutely secret. There were all those villagers who knew about it, for one thing. And Lord knows who the drug dealers knew. But I made sure most of the gossip about the missing gold implied the stuff was government material kept at the embassy and used for clandestine operations. I sort of left the impression that the two drug dealers were really agents. And of course I kept my own name out of it. You never know. I didn't want to implicate myself. If someone knew the drug story or got too friendly with the villagers, he might be able to track down more of the tale.''

''Apparently some journalist did get friendly with the villagers,'' Sara said. ''And his notes somehow ended up in an old file that Vaughn came across.''

Lowell sighed. ''I thought after all these years the story of the gold really had become nothing more than a legend.''

''Vaughn said he deliberately planted a rumor about him being in Hawaii recruiting mercenaries to help him get your treasure,'' Sara said.

Kincaid shook his head. ''I'm embarrassed to admit it worked. I got wind of the plan and did exactly as he anticipated. I took off for Hawaii.'' He glanced at Adrian. ''I honestly thought I'd have everything taken care of within forty-eight hours or so. Didn't think you'd be bothered with cleaning up my mess.''

Adrian couldn't think of anything to say. He just nodded austerely and continued to watch Sara's face through narrowed eyes. Why didn't she say something about what had happened that afternoon. The suspense was going to shred him. A part of him wanted to get the confrontation over and done with. Another part wanted to pretend nothing devastating had occurred. Abruptly he pushed his chair away from the table and went over to where he kept the brandy.

"Can I pour you some, Lowell?" His voice felt thick and scratchy in his throat.

"Sounds great." The older man beamed.

Sara focused on her uncle again. "Vaughn is definitely out of the way? He won't be bothering us again?"

Lowell Kincaid smiled. "You don't have to worry about him. I'll talk to Gilkirk in the morning. But from what I hear the agency's tired of using him, anyway. Even if he got turned loose tomorrow, he realizes everyone knows who he is and what he's been doing. He'd disappear in a hurry."

"He had plans, you know," Sara mused.

Adrian could feel her watching him as he poured the brandy. "What plans?" he managed to ask, although he couldn't have cared less. Vaughn, as Kincaid had just said, was no longer an issue. He'd made sure of that when he'd left the sullen man bound and gagged in the rain beside the freeway. Vaughn was smart enough to know that everything had fallen apart. Vaughn, too, knew what it meant to have his cover completely blown.

"He thought that, given the map and a few carefully selected mercenaries, he could get into Cambodia and get at the gold. He told me all about his scheme," she finished blithely. "Aren't you going to pour me some brandy, too?"

Adrian turned back to the counter and poured another glass. "Sorry," he muttered shortly. When he handed it to her, she raised it cheerfully.

"Here's to finally getting some answers." She downed a healthy swallow.

Lowell grinned. "Haven't I always told you that answers are always crystal-clear once you know where to look?"

With a snap, Sara set down the brandy snifter. "Speaking of crystal-clear answers," she began. And then she was on her feet, hurrying down the hall toward the study.

Kincaid traded glances with Adrian. It was the first time

they'd been alone together without Sara in the room. "Everything's under control?"

Adrian nodded. "Yeah. The agency will handle it. I really did lead them to believe you were the one who'd wrapped Vaughn up for Christmas. I guess if Vaughn says too much, though, Gilkirk may figure out I'm still around."

Kincaid chuckled. "Even if he does, you'll be all right. You're old news now, I'm afraid. The last time I talked to Gilkirk I casually brought up your name just to see what he'd say. He wasn't terribly interested, frankly. You'd be a minor curiosity and that's it. Gilkirk won't push it. He owes you and he knows it. He's a good man. Pays his debts."

"I like being old news." Adrian thought about that. "But Sara…"

"Don't worry about Sara," Kincaid said softly. "She's my niece. I know her."

"She's a woman," Adrian countered. "And she had a wild image of Wolf built up in her mind. What did you tell her about me, Kincaid?"

"Only bits and pieces. I was very concerned about you a year ago, my friend. I wasn't sure if this book was going to be the therapy you needed. I guess I had a few drinks with Sara one evening and talked. More than I should have, probably. She took the information and embroidered it a bit with her rather active imagination."

"Did you really give her some idiotic story about the temperature, uh, dropping in a room when I walked in?" Adrian demanded.

Kincaid blinked. "I suppose I did. There are times when it's perfectly true."

Adrian winced. "No wonder I don't get many invitations to cocktail parties."

Lowell Kincaid howled with laughter. "Don't worry. The description only applies when you're working. If you're not getting party invitations, it's because people suspect you're not the party type. Not because they don't need an extra ice bucket.''

''What about telling her I was a...a renegade?''

Kincaid looked surprised. ''I never said that. I'm afraid she came to that conclusion on her own. I told her that I had trained a man who wound up with the code name of Wolf and that I was now worried about him. I guess she assumed—'' He was about to say something else and stopped as Sara trotted back down the hall, tossing the crystal apple in her hands. ''Ah, the apple.''

''Yes, the apple.'' She pinned him with a mock-ferocious glance. ''This is where the answer is, right Uncle Lowell? Clear as crystal?''

He nodded genially. ''It's a microdot masquerading as one of the bubbles captured in the crystal. Pretty little apple, isn't it? I had one made especially for both you and Adrian. You each have half of the map. That's the wedding present, you see. Not the gold itself but the adventure of having a treasure map of your very own. And someday, someone in your family will be able to go after the gold. Maybe twenty years from now, when the politics and violence in that part of the world have changed. Maybe the next generation will get it. Who knows? In the meantime you'll have the fantasy.''

''It was a brilliant gift idea,'' Sara said with a warm smile.

''I thought so. Just the thing for a woman with an overactive imagination. When did you figure out that the apple was the key?''

''While I was talking to Vaughn. I knew the answer wasn't in the manuscript.'' She slid a quick glance at Adrian. ''*Phantom* answers some other questions, but it doesn't tell where the gold is hidden. I just used that as an excuse to get Vaughn back here to the house. I figured out the role of the apple, though, when I put everything I knew together. The gold, you implied, was a wedding gift. Something to be shared. And you had given both Adrian and me an apple. It was a link between us. The key. Then there was your penchant for hiding things out in the open, the way you always say answers are crystal-clear. The apple itself has a gold stem and leaf and that was another clue. The gold on the apple was meant to be a connection to the gold in Southeast Asia, right? And you'd given us the basic clue when you told Adrian the legend. Last but not least, I knew you always like to cover your bases. You would have wanted the information available to both Adrian and me just in case something ever happened to you. It made sense that you had given us the answers. And you would have given them to us jointly. All we had to do was look around.''

''And you realized that the only thing I had given both of you was the apple.'' Kincaid nodded. ''Not bad, Sara. Not bad at all.''

''Games,'' Adrian heard himself mutter.

''Better get used to them if you're going to marry into the family,'' Lowell advised lightly.

''I've played enough for one day. If you both will excuse me, I'm going to go to bed. Lowell, you can have the couch. Your niece has the spare bedroom.'' Adrian got to his feet.

Sara's head came up quickly. ''Adrian...''

He stood still, looking down at her. ''What is it, Sara?''

''I...I just wondered about your trip this morning.'' She chewed on her lower lip, obviously searching for the right words. ''I mean, Vaughn seemed to think you'd gone to Mexico.''

''That's what I wanted him to think.''

''But...''

''I bought the ticket. But the plane made a few stops between here and Mexico City. I got off in L.A.''

''I see,'' she said quietly. ''You planned it that way to make Vaughn think you'd left the country to go after the gold yourself.''

''I thought my leaving would draw him out into the open,'' Adrian explained very patiently. ''I figured he'd make his try at night, thinking you'd be alone. I'd planned to circle back and be waiting for him. I had it all worked out. But you rewrote the rules.''

''He tricked me,'' she protested. ''I had a phone call from Uncle Lowell. Or at least I thought it was from him. Vaughn made a tape from the answering-machine recordings in Lowell's cottage and mixed up the words into whole new sentences.''

''I know,'' Adrian said. ''Vaughn told me.''

Sara eyed him curiously. ''Did he?''

''He told me a great many things,'' Adrian said. ''Good night, Lowell. Sara.'' He left the room.

Sara watched him go, the smile fading from her eyes and being replaced by a wistful yearning. Slowly she lowered the apple into her lap as she sat down beside her uncle.

''He has a nerve accusing us of playing games,'' she whispered. ''What does he think he was doing today when he fed me that song and dance about going off to find a mysterious contact who might know where you were?''

Kincaid swirled the brandy in his glass. ''He wasn't playing games. Adrian never plays games. He simply didn't want you to know the truth.''

''What truth?''

''That he didn't have any magic man to contact. The only one around he could depend on to protect you was himself. He had to make Vaughn believe he had really left town and the only way to do that was to actually get on the plane. Mexico City was the logical choice because it has a reputation in the industry. Vaughn made all the assumptions he was supposed to make when he discovered that was Adrian's destination.''

''But why didn't Adrian tell me?'' She sighed.

''He wanted to keep you from finding out the truth about him. In the end there was no way he could accomplish that. Not and save your life, too.''

''What did you mean about Adrian never playing games?''

''Just that.'' Lowell took a long swallow of brandy and gazed up at the beamed ceiling for a moment. ''You and I, Sara, we have a capacity for stepping back emotionally from a situation we don't like. You did it all the time in the corporate world. You treated it as a game when it threatened to get too serious or intense. I saw you do it in the academic world and when you played at being an artist. It was a survival mechanism for you. It works very well. I should know. I've used it myself. I could frequently put my work into that kind of perspective when things got too grim. I would detach myself and instinctively try to see all the moves and countermoves as just part of a great big chess game.''

''And Adrian couldn't do that?''

''No. For him it was very real. He gave everything he had to his work and it finally took its toll.''

''*Phantom.*'' Sara stared down at the crystal-and-gold apple. ''The real truth in the manuscript isn't the hint about the gold that you put in, is it? It's the part Adrian put into the story. The reality of what he faced.''

''When he finally realized the job would eventually break him, he turned in his resignation. It wasn't accepted. They told him there was one last mission.''

''And he went on it.'' Sara shuddered. ''I think he just barely survived, Uncle Lowell.''

''He did what he had to do. Adrian always does what has to be done. He was quite lethally serious about his work and that attitude made him the best there was in the industry.''

''Better than you, Uncle Lowell?''

''Better than me. But the violence and the frustration of that last job were the end for him. When it was over he simply disappeared. He showed up on my doorstep three months later, calling himself Adrian Saville.''

''That's not his real name?'' Sara asked in astonishment.

Lowell Kincaid smiled. ''It is now. I told you, Adrian doesn't play games. Everything is for real. He took another name and started a new life. He would have done anything to keep it real.''

''Well, it is real,'' Sara protested. ''Nothing's changed.''

''Now you know the truth about him,'' her uncle pointed out quietly.

''But I don't feel any differently about him,'' she breathed. ''How could he think—''

''Apparently you gave him quite a horror story about Wolf.''

''That was all your fault. You're the one who told me the tale!''

''I was a little drunk that night as I recall. And I was genuinely worried about Adrian. I wasn't certain writing the book was going to work for him.''

''That's no excuse. You told me things—''

''They were all true,'' Lowell Kincaid said, giving her a level glance. ''But I will not assume responsibility for what you did to the facts with your imagination.''

Sara grimaced. ''When I found myself realizing this afternoon that my only chance for surviving lay with Adrian, I knew who he was. I also knew that whatever he had been, he was now the man I loved. You were right about him. He's the kind of man you can count on when the chips are down. Why did you sketch that wolf's head on the manuscript?''

''I was just doodling. It was natural that I'd be thinking about Wolf when I read the tale of Phantom.''

''I suppose so. It put me on the wrong track altogether, though. I thought it was Wolf you had gone after.'' Sara fell silent for a moment. ''I guess I'll go to bed, too.''

''You do that,'' her uncle murmured blandly.

She shot him a half-humorous, half-rueful glance. ''Going to throw your favorite niece to the wolf?''

''Wolves take care of their own.'' Lowell got up and headed across the room to the brandy bottle. ''Good night, Sara.''

She went over to him and hugged him affectionately. ''Good night, Uncle Lowell. I'm so glad you're safe.''

''Not half as glad as I am that you're okay. Guess I owe Adrian for that.''

Sara said nothing. She merely smiled and walked down the hall toward Adrian's bedroom with a deep sense of certainty.

Lying in bed, his arms folded behind his head, Adrian stared into the darkness and listened to the sound of Sara's footsteps. He waited for them to stop outside her bedroom door, and when she didn't even pause he tensed.

It would be best if she stayed in her own room, he told himself. Quickly, silently, he ran down a list of why she shouldn't open his door tonight. Too much had happened today and she was inclined to be emotional. She was also inclined to be impulsive. She needed time to sort out her feelings. He didn't want her coming to him without having had time to absorb the full implications of what she had learned about him today. She might be feeling sorry for him. She might have convinced herself he needed her and she was too compassionate to deny him comfort. He didn't want her pity.

So many reasons, he thought savagely. So many excellent reasons why he should send her back to her own room if she dared to open the door.

She turned the doorknob and stepped inside. Adrian looked at her as she stood silhouetted against the light and knew that he could never find the willpower to send her back. He needed her warmth too badly tonight. It had been so cold today.

''Asleep, Adrian?'' she asked softly, shutting the door and coming forward into the shadowed room.

''No.''

''You must be exhausted.''

''Umm.''

There was a rustle of clothing as she undressed. He saw the pale gleam of her bare shoulder and then the lighter area of her hip as she stepped out of the jeans.

''I'm a little tired myself,'' she admitted softly as she walked naked to the bed.

''Sara...'' He tried to say the words that should be said, tried to explain why she shouldn't be there. But she was pulling back the comforter and slipping in beside him and the logical phrases disintegrated in his throat. The warmth and softness of her as she reached out to hold him were a temptation and that was far more difficult to resist than all the gold in Southeast Asia.

"Don't worry," she whispered huskily. "I won't be making any demands on you tonight. We've both had a hard day." She stroked her fingers through his hair, soothing the nape of his neck.

"Sara, it's not that, it's just... Oh, Sara, hold me. Put your arms around me and hold me."

She did, cradling him even as he pulled her tightly into the curve of his body. Adrian inhaled the familiar, enticing scent that was uniquely hers, knew the incredible comfort of her touch, felt the shape of her locked securely in his arms and relaxed for the first time since the day had dawned. Now he would be able to sleep.

Hours later he awoke to the light of dawn and the knowledge of what he must do. A part of him resisted the knowledge even though another side of him realized it was the only sure way. It was best to do things the sure way, he reminded himself. Careful, cautious, certain. He had spent the past year carefully, cautiously, certainly pulling himself back together. He knew about patience. He knew about being sure.

It would be tricky trying to teach those skills to the warm, frequently impulsive woman who lay curled so contentedly in his arms. But it was the only way. Above all else he wanted her to know exactly how she felt about him.

No games. Not even the kind played out of pity or compassion. Especially not those.

Adrian didn't move as he lay beside Sara. He was almost afraid of disturbing her because once she came awake he would have to explain his decision. He preferred to steal these last few minutes of closeness and warmth, make them last as long as possible. A wolf, he thought wryly, took whatever he could get.

Sara opened her eyes slowly, aware of Adrian's arm around her, his hand resting possessively on her breast. She lay still for a moment, letting herself realize fully just how good it felt to lie next to him. It felt right. A sense of deep certainty settled on her. It was unlike any emotion she had ever known. She was in love with Adrian Saville. She had known it since yesterday.

It didn't surprise her that love would arrive like this. Such an emotion, when it finally came into her life, was bound to happen in just this manner. For someone like her there was no other way. Quick, impulsive, but absolutely right. She knew real gold when she found it. Lazily she stretched, a serene, confident expression in her eyes as she turned to meet Adrian's steady gaze.

"Good morning," she murmured, touching her mouth lightly to his. "How did you sleep?"

He blinked, his features holding a trace of surprise as he thought about the question. "Solidly." His hand moved on her, following the curve of her thigh. "Thanks to you."

"Good." Feeling vastly pleased with herself, Sara stretched again, this time bringing her body quite deliberately against his. "I'm glad I'm useful for something. I felt like such a fool yesterday when I walked straight into Vaughn's hands."

Adrian didn't respond to the invitation of her languid stretch. In fact, she decided, he seemed almost tense. Not at all like a man who'd had a good night's sleep.

"It wasn't your fault," he told her. "Anyone would have been fooled by the recording. I've heard tapes scrambled from other tapes. They can sound very real. But you kept your head. You got him back here."

"I knew you would be coming back and that you could handle everything," she said.

"How long have you known?" He watched her with cool eyes.

Sara knew the coolness was deceptive. She also knew the real question he was asking. She knew him very well now, Sara decided. Reading *Phantom* had filled in many of the blanks a person normally encountered when learning about another human being. Her heart ached to replace what had originally occupied those blanks in his life.

"How long have I known that you were the man they used to call Wolf?" There was no point in not being totally honest. "Since yesterday for certain. When Vaughn told me that Wolf had been a legend at one time but had not made it back from his last assignment—"

"Because I'd cracked," Adrian put in bluntly.

Sara refused to acknowledge his interruption. "I began to think about Phantom. About a man who had been to the brink and hung on instead of going completely over the edge. A man who had forced himself to survive when by all logic he should have been crushed. And then I thought about the way I feel safe around you..."

"Safe?"

She nodded. "I realized it that day at the Pike Place Market when you showed up just as Vaughn was about to coerce me into his car. And yesterday when I found myself trying to think of a way to deal with Vaughn. Something told me I only had to get him back here. When you arrived I knew I would be safe again. There were lots of other little clues, of course. Your concern with the security of this house. The way you move. That sketch of my uncle's. Even the way you play checkers. So intense and cool. Then there was your recent conversion to vegetarianism. Somehow that seemed symbolic. Something a carnivore might do if he were trying to put aside that aspect of his life. It all fit. Especially once I knew for certain that Vaughn wasn't Wolf."

"You had such a terrible image of Wolf," Adrian began heavily.

"By the time I realized you had once been Wolf, I was ready to throw the image out the window. I knew the real you by then." She smiled dreamily, loving him with her eyes.

Adrian's face became remote. "I'm not so sure, Sara."

"Not so sure of what?"

"That you know the real me." He stilled the protest that

rose instantly to her lips by putting his fingers against her mouth. "Listen to me, Sara. I rushed you into bed that first time. The second time was too intense, too emotional because you knew I was leaving and you weren't sure what was going to happen. We've been living in the eye of a storm ever since I walked into this house and found you in my study. There's been no chance for you to get to know me in a normal fashion."

Alarm flickered into life. Sara watched him intently. "Are you trying to tell me you aren't sure how you feel about me, after all?"

He shook his head once, a quick, violent negative movement. "I know how I feel about you. I've been wanting you for months. You've been growing in my mind every day, taking shape, tantalizing me, until I knew I had to have you. But your uncle was right. There was something else I needed to do first."

"Write *Phantom.*"

"That book was a final step in freeing myself, Sara."

"I understand." And she did. Completely now.

"You were a goal, a treasure waiting for me after I had put the past behind me. I feel as though I've been getting to know you for months. Your uncle saw to that. But it didn't work that way for you. You've only known me a few days and that time has been too intense, too dangerous and too emotional."

"Falling in love is bound to be emotional!" she put in quickly.

"Are you saying you think you're in love with me?" He searched her face.

"Yes." She spoke the single word with gentle assurance.

"Sara, you can't know that!"

"You told me once that you would like me to love you," she reminded him.

His fingers tightened on her. "I want that very badly. But you have to be certain. You have to be sure. No games, Sara."

"I've never played games with you."

"How about with your own mind? Honey, it's just too soon. You can't possibly know how you feel. Not yet. Hell, up until yesterday, you've been thinking of Wolf as some kind of psychotic killer. Now you've learned that Wolf and I are one and the same. You can't tell me you've managed to adjust to that kind of news overnight!''

''I get the feeling I can't tell you much of anything,'' she tossed back. ''You're not ready to listen to me. You've already decided the way things have to be, haven't you?'' The alarm was coiling tightly in her as she began to see where his words were leading.

''Sara, I want you to have time to get to know me,'' he told her urgently. ''This time around we'll do it right.''

''I don't understand!'' But she did and the realization panicked her.

Adrian continued forcefully, his certainty clear in every word. ''Yes, you do, honey. We're going to do it right. I want you to have a chance to make absolutely certain of your feelings. The next time you tell me you love me I want you to have had plenty of opportunity to think through just what you're saying.''

Sara pulled free of him, sitting up with the sheet held to her breast. Her hair swung in a soft tangle around her shoulders as she stared at him. ''Are you sending me away?'' Her voice sounded odd. She was clinging to more than the sheet. She was hanging on to her control with both hands.

Slowly Adrian sat up beside her, his eyes almost colorless. He was committed to finishing what he had started, Sara realized. She would not be able to reason with him this morning.

''We're going to start a normal relationship,'' he said.

''What's normal? Adrian, you of all people should know by now that life is short and highly uncertain. We've found something wonderful together. Why should we waste time? Please don't do this.'' The plea was all wrong, she thought. She was letting her emotions rule her tongue. Adrian wouldn't trust her to know her own feelings if she did that. He didn't trust emotions.

''I'm not sending you to Outer Mongolia,'' he said.

"No? Then where are you sending me?"

"I think it would be best if you went back to San Diego."

"San Diego! But I don't even have a job there!"

"You've got your apartment, don't you? It's still your home."

She groped for an argument. "What about you? Are you just going to sit around here until you figure I've had enough time to know my own mind? Adrian, that doesn't make any sense. I'm an adult. I already know how I feel."

"I'm going to come and see you. Call you. Sara, I'm going to court you, don't you understand? I'm going to give you plenty of time—"

"How much?" she challenged.

He looked blank. "How much what?"

"How much time, damn it!"

"I don't know." He frowned. "However long it takes, I suppose."

"That's not fair, Adrian. If you're going to sentence me to exile, you have to at least put a time limit on it. Give me a date. One week? One year? I want a date."

"Sara, you're getting hysterical."

The worst part was that she knew he was right. She was losing her self-control. It was the shock, Sara decided. The shock of waking up in love and being told by Adrian that he wasn't ready for her love. Sara gulped air, swallowing sobs of anger and panic. The more emotional she became, the less Adrian would trust her to know what she really wanted. For the sake of their future, she had to get hold of herself.

"Yes," she whispered, sliding off the edge of the bed. She looked around a little frantically for something to wear and finally saw her shirt on the floor where she had left it last night. "Yes, you're quite right. I'm getting emotional." Her fingers fumbled with the buttons but she managed to get the shirt on. Then she picked up her jeans with hands that still trembled. Adrian never took his eyes off of her.

"Sara, honey, listen to me."

She shook her head. ''No, no, I'm all right. I understand. You don't fully trust intense emotions because you learned once that they can take you to the edge of the disaster. I should have realized that after reading *Phantom.* That was the lesson you learned when you went through with that last mission and then disappeared, wasn't it? Your emotional response to your work nearly got you killed. You kept yourself so tightly leashed and under such control for so long that in the end you almost came apart when the explosion occurred. That's why you talk in terms of appreciating life's pleasures. Anything stronger than pleasure might be dangerous.''

Adrian got slowly to his feet, completely unconcerned with his nakedness. ''I just want you to be sure of how you feel,'' he repeated stubbornly.

She got her jeans zipped and lifted her head to meet his eyes. ''You want to be sure of everything. Sure of the security of your house, sure of me, sure of your own self-control. Well, go ahead and make sure, Adrian. Being absolutely sure of things seems to be one of the few *pleasures* you get out of life. Who am I to deny you?''

Whirling, Sara fled from the room.

Eleven

Adrian's version of a courtship, Sara decided a month later, was going to drive her slowly insane.

Over and over again she told herself that he was the one who needed the time. Time to be sure of her. She would give him that. After all, she loved him; she would give him anything he asked. But how long would the farce continue, she wondered dismally.

''Farce'' was hardly the most respectful term for Adrian's courtship, but it was the one that came to Sara's mind most often during the torturous, contrived, carefully choreographed weekends. True to his word Adrian flew down to San Diego every Friday evening. He spent Saturday and Sunday with her and then flew home to his island.

Sara's hopes for the first weekend were dashed when he checked into a motel near her apartment and continued to retreat to it every evening of his stay. The other weekends were no different. He took her to dinner, shows, the zoo and the beach. But he never took her to bed.

In fact, he rarely touched her with any intimacy at all. That was the part that was beginning to drive her out of her mind, Sara realized. She was left with a feeling of genuine panic every Sunday evening when she saw him off at the airport. Perhaps he wasn't capable of making the final step of total commitment. She knew he wanted her, knew he took pleasure in her company but he had convinced himself that she didn't understand her own feelings.

What she really feared, Sara decided, was that he didn't understand the depths of his own feelings for her. He was afraid to surrender completely to the force of his emotions.

They would be fierce and intense, the emotions of a strong man who had much to give once he had accepted the power of his own nature. But he had learned the hard way that there was a risk in losing some of his self-control. She yearned to set him completely free, to urge him to take a risk both on her and on himself but there was no way to break through the controlled facade. On Monday morning after the fourth weekend Sara acknowledged that Adrian had established the rules and he was going to force her to play by them.

Bad analogy, she told herself wryly as she fixed coffee with her imported Italian espresso machine. Adrian didn't like anything that smacked of game playing. She stared morosely out at the palm tree in front of her kitchen window and thought of the carefully restrained kiss she had received at the airport the previous evening.

Uneasily she tried to brush aside the worry that perhaps Adrian would never be able to relax and let himself trust both of them completely.

He did love her, she told herself with some violence. He hadn't said the words but that was all right. She knew him, understood him. She had complete confidence in his love. Her only fear was that he would never have the same confidence.

Somehow he had to learn that the iron control he held over himself wasn't necessary any longer. He was a whole human being now. He'd healed himself. He must learn to have faith in the health of his emotions and in those of the woman who loved him. He could live safely now without a perfect cover.

And she did love him, Sara knew. With every fiber of her being. One month of the stilted courtship hadn't changed that. Nothing on earth could change it. She had never been so certain of anything in her life.

She was at home that evening when he called. She was always at home these days. Not because she didn't have friends or invitations but because she was terrified that Adrian might phone and find her out. She wanted nothing to upset him or alarm him. She wanted him to know that she was simply waiting for him.

The conversation followed by its now predictable path.

"How was the flight back to Seattle?" she asked politely.

"Fine." He hesitated. "Have you eaten?"

"Oh, yes. I fixed myself a salad." Sara searched mentally for something to add to the careful conversation. "And I had a glass of wine."

"I went down to the tavern and had a beer."

At least you got to get out of the house, Sara thought irritably. *I'm forced to sit here from five o'clock on because I can't be sure when you'll call. And I'm terrified you'd use the evidence of my not being at home as an indication that you were right not to trust me.* "Sounds good," she said brightly. "How's the plotting going on the new book?"

"Okay. I'm trying to figure out how to untwist some things in chapter four without giving away too much information. This book is going to be a lot easier to write, though, than *Phantom* was."

Not surprising, Sara thought. This second book wouldn't be nearly so autobiographical. *Phantom* had been a form of catharsis. The next book would truly be fiction. She didn't have any doubt that it would be as good in its own way as its predecessor, however. The bottom line was that Adrian really could write. "Speaking of giving away information, Adrian," Sara heard herself begin quite firmly.

He paused before inquiring cautiously, "Yes?"

She floundered. "Well, I was wondering. I mean, it's been a month now and I was just thinking that you might have come to some, er, decision."

"About what?"

Sara very nearly lost her temper. "About us!"

"Oh. You still want a date when everything's going to be settled, don't you?"

''Adrian,'' she tried reasonably, ''this is getting us nowhere. I've tried to be patient—''

''You don't know much about patience, honey.''

''Don't be condescending. Just because people like you know all about patience, doesn't meant the rest of us—''

''What do you mean, people like me?''

Sara wanted to cry for having used all the wrong words. The forbidding cold was back in his voice. ''I just meant that you seem to have developed a great deal of patience during your life. I, uh, I haven't been quite that fortunate, Adrian, I'm trying to give you the time you need, but—''

''I'm not the one who needs the time,'' he interrupted quietly.

''Well, I sure as hell don't need it! I know what I want. I'm in love with you, and this past month has been awful. I feel like I've been in exile. You don't touch me, you're so polite I could spit, and you won't tell me how long it's going to go on. There are times when I really begin to wonder if you—'' She halted the flow of words abruptly.

True to form, Adrian refused to be left hanging. ''You wonder if I what?''

''Nothing,'' she mumbled.

''Sara, tell me what you were about to say.''

She sighed. ''I wonder if you will ever really trust yourself or me enough to love me.'' There. It was said. She hadn't dared anything that intimate before and she wasn't at all certain how he would react. She had been assuming a great deal, Sara thought bleakly.

Silence on the other end of the line greeted her statement. Then Adrian's voice came with rock-hard certainty.

''I love you, Sara.''

She caught her breath, her fingers clutching the receiver. ''You do?''

''You've been a part of me for months. I can't imagine life without you.''

The simple words were devastating to her. ''You never said

anything quite that explicit before,'' she finally got out rather weakly.

''I don't think I've thought it out quite that explicitly until now,'' he admitted slowly. ''You've just been there, a part of me.''

She closed her eyes in relief. It was finally over. It must be over. ''Oh, Adrian, Adrian, thank you. I love you so much and I've been going crazy down here waiting for you to be sure.''

''I've been sure all along.'' He sounded vaguely surprised. ''It's you who needed the time.''

Sara's eyes narrowed as she picked up the first inkling that her waiting might not be ended after all. ''I don't need any more time, Adrian. Please. I've been very patient. I could wait forever if there was a real need, but there isn't. There's no need for us to be apart.''

His voice hardened. ''I want you to have more time.''

She heard the finality in his words and fury mingled with despair. ''You think I'm playing a game with you.''

''No, Sara, it's not that. I just—''

She didn't let him finish. ''Adrian Saville, you don't know what real game playing is!'' Quite precisely and quite definitely, Sara hung up the phone. Then she walked to the hall closet and found her shoulder bag. There was a chic, cheerful little tavern down the street and around the corner. If Adrian could have a beer in the evenings, so could she. Come to think of it, she needed it a lot more than he did tonight.

The phone rang insistently behind her but Sara ignored it. She walked to the door, opened it as the phone continued to ring, and then she stepped outside. It was a wonderful, balmy Southern California evening. The scent of the sea hovered in the air and the row of palm trees lining her street rustled lazily in the evening breeze. Sara walked briskly down the sidewalk, wondering what the trees looked like in Southeast Asia.

The tavern was only half full, with a crowd of people in their late twenties and early thirties. The women, with their cleverly casual hairstyles, their silk shirts and jeans, chatted vivaciously with men in equally expensive hairstyles and designer jeans. Several heads nodded familiarly as Sara took a lone seat in the shadows at the back of the room. She ordered an imported beer and sipped it thoughtfully when it arrived.

The trees in Southeast Asia. Images of menacing jungles and treacherous swamps came to mind. Not really her kind of place. Adrian had learned caution the hard way in such places around the world. Caution and patience.

But there was a time and place for caution and patience. Surely they shouldn't be allowed to stand in the way of a loving commitment. Love was so rare and so valuable it was a shame to make it wait on caution and patience. Sara took another taste of the expensive import and thought about Adrian's reluctance to release himself completely from the reins of his self-control.

He had let those reins slip on a couple of occasions, she reminded herself. The first time he had made love to her, for example. The second time as well. Of course, on those occasions he had been assuming that he could keep his past hidden from her. He'd had no need to fear her reactions to learning his full identity because he'd assumed she never would know of it.

But even that last night at his home he had been unable to send her away although he had already made up his mind to give her time. He had needed her that night, not in a sexual way, but in the way a man sometimes needs comfort from a woman. He'd let her comfort him to some extent, she reminded herself on a note of hope. He'd held her very tightly that night, even in his sleep. She'd been aware of the tension gradually leaving him. She seriously doubted that Adrian had ever risked taking much comfort from others.

Sara turned the matter over in her mind. He loved her and she loved him. And as she had told him, life could be short and precarious. Love was too important to risk losing because of too much caution and patience. She needed to find a way to make Adrian understand that. She needed to yank him out of his cautious, patient, controlled world.

An hour later she walked home alone, opened the door and saw the gleam of the crystal apple as it sat reflecting the light of her desk lamp. She stared at it for a long moment, thinking of Vaughn's plans to retrieve the gold. Then, very slowly and very thoughtfully, she closed her door.

The phone rang just as she was about to get into bed an hour later.

"Hello, Adrian."

"Have you calmed down?"

"I've calmed down."

"I love you," he said quietly.

"I know. I love you."

"Just give it a little more time, sweetheart," he urged. "The waiting isn't easy for me, either."

"I think it's easier for you than it is for me," she told him.

"No," he said in a raw tone. "It isn't. Good night, Sara. Sleep well."

"Good night, Adrian."

She hung up the phone and trailed slowly out into the living room. Once more her eyes fell on the crystal apple. There must be a way to break the impasse. The apple held the key to the gold. Perhaps it held the key to unlocking Adrian's emotions.

Again she wondered what the trees looked like in Southeast Asia.

ADRIAN ANSWERED his phone on Friday morning with a sense of anticipation that he couldn't deny. Very few people in the world had his unlisted number. Sara was one of those people.

"Hello?"

"She's gone crazy, Adrian. I warned you this would happen. Don't say I didn't warn you!" Lowell Kincaid was one of the few other people who had the number.

"You didn't warn me," Adrian said patiently. Determinedly he squelched his disappointment that the caller wasn't Sara. After all, he would be seeing her this evening. He could wait. "Calm down and tell me what you're talking about, Lowell."

''You think it's a joke, but I can tell you from past experience, it isn't.''

''Okay, it's not a joke. Now tell me what it is that isn't a joke.''

Kincaid spoke grimly. ''She's applied for a passport.''

Adrian paused, absorbing that. ''A passport?''

''And she called me up to see what I knew about getting in and out of Cambodia.''

''That is a joke, right? You and she both have a very strange sense of humor, Kincaid. I've told you that on previous occasions.'' But Adrian's hand was like a vise on the telephone receiver.

''Believe me, I'm not finding this funny. Applying for a passport isn't the end of it, either.''

Adrian sucked in his breath. ''All right. Let me have it.''

''She asked me for a second copy of your half of the map and she's put an ad in the L.A. *Times*. Want to hear it?''

''No. But I think I'd better.''

''Listen to this.'' There was a rustle of newspaper on the other end of the line and then Lowell began to read: '''Danger, adventure, financial reward for the right person. Applicant must be willing to travel out of the country, able to take care of himself and willing to follow employer's orders. Personal interviews only, no phone. Three o'clock on Friday.' That's today, Adrian.''

''I know it's today.''

''She goes on to name the hotel down in San Diego where she'll be interviewing applicants. You know as well as I do that every California bozo who's into fantasy violence is likely to show up. Adrian, this is all your fault. I'm holding you personally responsible.''

''My fault? You're the one who gave her half a map and a legend, for pete's sake!''

''And then I gave her and the map to you, damn it! I thought you would now how to take care of both!'' Lowell hung up the phone with a crashing noise that made his listener's ear hurt.

Adrian stood silently staring at the receiver for a very long moment. The lady was playing games again. In her usual impulsive, off-the-wall style she was issuing a full-blown challenge.

She appeared to have absolutely no fear of him. Sara must know that he would be furious when he found out what she had planned. Everything she had done was quite deliberate, of course. She'd notified her uncle just to make certain Adrian would find out immediately what was happening.

A challenge, Adrian thought as he yanked his canvas overnight bag down from the closet shelf. She had one hell of a nerve. He recalled the way he had walked into his home that first night and found her casually searching his study. She'd had no fear of him then, not after she'd found the apple. And she obviously had no fear of him now.

But she had shuddered and gone cold whenever she had mentioned the man called Wolf. And she knew he had been Wolf.

He had wanted to give her plenty of time to accept him completely once she'd learned the whole truth. He'd wanted to be certain she could handle the idea of what he had once been. He loved her. It would tear him apart if deep down she was unable to accept him and his past. A few more weeks or months and he would have been more certain she knew what she was doing.

But Sara had no patience for strategy. She had applied for a passport and put an ad in the papers. She was going to force his hand.

Adrian zipped the bag closed, checked for his keys and set the house alarms. It would take him several hours to get to San Diego and he didn't want to waste any time. There was a midmorning flight that he just might make if he moved quickly.

He was astonished to find himself suddenly very impatient.

THE LINE BEGAN FORMING outside the hotel room at two o'clock. Sara watched in growing trepidation from the lobby, trying not to be obvious. If any of the wildly varied assortment of men in the line realized that the potential employer was the lady in jeans who was hanging around the front desk, she would be mobbed.

She had never dreamed so many people would show up in response to that ad. What really alarmed her was that Adrian was not among the thirty-plus males lounging in line. Nervously Sara wiped her hands on her denim pants. In a few minutes she was going to have to start dealing with that motley crew. Several of them looked rather tough. One or two appeared to be ex-bikers. A few were probably ex-military and some appeared merely curious. None of them was an ex-wolf.

Reaching for a pad of hotel paper and a pen Sara tried to jot down a few interview-type questions. What did one ask a mercenary? Especially when one had absolutely no intention of hiring him? She needed a question or two that would definitely exclude everyone in that line. Desperately she searched her brain for something that would make each of the waiting men ineligible.

At five minutes to three Sara steeled herself for the task ahead. Adrian was nowhere in sight. She was going to have to start the interviews or risk a very discontented line of applicants. The hotel management would not thank her for starting a riot.

Chin high, she took hold of her jangled nerves and swept down the line of rather scrungy-looking males. Without glancing at any of them she opened the hotel-room door and said over her shoulder, ''I'll see the first man in line now.''

Five seconds later she found herself alone in the room with a swaggering young man who was wearing a much-abused military fatigue shirt. He took one look at her and grinned arrogantly.

''You the lady who wants to hire me?''

''I'm the lady who is looking for the right man,'' Sara said coolly. ''Now, if you don't mind, I'm going to ask you a few pertinent questions.''

"Go right ahead, ma'am," he retorted with mock courtesy. "I'm at your service."

The swaggering young man's grin was gone when he stomped out of the room five minutes later. He was grumbling fiercely under his breath. Sara beckoned for the next applicant.

She had sent fifteen of the men packing when there was a loud commotion in the hallway outside the room. Angry voices rose in protest and a second later the door was shoved violently open. Sara looked up from interviewing candidate number sixteen and saw Adrian filling the doorway. Anger, a seething impatience and a vast masculine annoyance burned in his eyes when he looked at her.

But the room didn't go cold.

Adrian pinned her for an instant, then his gaze flicked to candidate number sixteen, a middle-aged ex-military type running to fat.

"Out."

The ex-military type examined the newcomer for a few taut seconds, then shrugged and got to his feet. "I was just leaving. Seems I don't fit the profile of the successful applicant," he drawled. He used the words Sara had just spoken a second before the door had been flung open. He sauntered past Adrian, a flicker of amusement in his expression. "A very interesting lady. Good luck, buddy. I think you're going to have your hands full."

Adrian ignored him and turned to confront the remaining candidates. "Everyone can go home. Interview time is over. The lady has already hired a man. Me."

"Now wait just a damn minute, pal...."

Adrian glanced over his shoulder at Sara. "Tell them, Sara."

She got to her feet and realized her knees were slightly shaky. She had seen Adrian in a lot of different moods, including the one that could chill a room. She had never seen him thoroughly annoyed. She summoned a polite smile as she nodded at the men in the hall.

"I'm afraid he's right. Mr. Saville is the perfect candidate. Thank you all for showing up today."

There were a few growls of protest but the cluster of men dissolved. A moment later the hall was empty and Sara was left to face Adrian alone.

He leaned back against the doorjamb, his arms folded across his chest. "What the hell kind of game do you think you're playing, Sara Frazer?"

She sighed and sat down again. It was easier than standing. "I didn't know so many people would actually answer an ad like that."

"This is California, remember? Put an ad like that in the paper and you're bound to lure a lot of nuts out into the open." He came away from the wall and stalked over to the desk, flattening his palms on its surface as he leaned down to glare at her. "Did you think I'd let you get away with a stunt like this?"

She smiled tremulously. "No."

He narrowed his eyes. "I'd have been here earlier but the flight was delayed. I've been amusing myself for the past several hours thinking of what I was going to do to you when I finally did get to San Diego."

"I can imagine."

"I ought to take a belt to your sweet backside."

"Sounds kinky."

"Damn it, Sara, what the devil do you think you're doing?" He straightened away from the desk and paced to the window. "I'm furious with you."

"Yes. I'm sorry about that part, but I—"

"Sorry about it!" He whipped around to stare at her. "Sorry about it!"

"I couldn't think of any other way to force you into realizing that this stupid courtship has to end. It's driving me crazy, Adrian." She sprang to her feet to confront him. "We're wasting time and love, and everyone knows those are commodities that are too valuable to waste."

"What makes you think you've achieved anything other than annoying the hell out of me?"

She faced him determinedly. "There's only one way you can keep me from going to Southeast Asia."

"Really?" he asked with soft menace. "And what's that?"

"You're going to have to marry me. If you don't, I'll be on my way as soon as my passport arrives."

He looked dumbfounded. "Marry you!"

"This is blackmail, Adrian. Pure and simple. I'm giving you an ultimatum. Marry me or I'll go off on my own in search of that gold."

Adrian continued to stare at her as if she'd taken leave of her senses. "You're serious, aren't you?"

"I'm serious. This isn't a game, Adrian. I don't play games with the really important things in life."

"And I'm one of those things?"

"Adrian, you are the most important thing in my life," she said with simple honesty.

There was a moment of profound tension as he regarded her with an unwavering gaze. Sara had the impression he was seeking the proper words to express his feelings. She waited in an agony of suspense.

"Sara," he finally said carefully, "I'm very angry. I can't ever remember being quite this angry."

"I know," she whispered. "And I regret that, but—"

"But you're not afraid of me, are you?" he finished.

"Are you kidding? I've crossed all my fingers and toes." Her mouth curved in wry humor.

"But you're not terrified, are you?" he pressed.

"Not the way you mean, Adrian. The room hasn't gone cold. The only time it ever did was the time you rescued me from Vaughn. And I knew at the time that the chill was my protection, not something I had to fear. I love you and you love me. How could I be truly terrified of you?"

He ran a hand through his hair and turned back to the window. "I've been scared to death," Adrian admitted starkly.

"Of loving me?"

He shook his head. "Of worrying that you couldn't really love me knowing who I am."

Sara stepped around the desk and walked slowly toward him. "I love you, Adrian. I love you so much that I'll do whatever I have to do to stay with you. I know all the important things about you. I read *Phantom,* remember? I told you after I read it that I'd fallen in love with the hero."

"And I told you that I'd rather you fell in love with me."

"You thought it would be pleasant." She nodded.

"I think," Adrian said huskily as he turned toward her, "that it would be more than pleasant. I think it's absolutely essential."

"Oh, Adrian," she breathed, throwing herself into his arms. "I love you so much. Don't send me away again. I couldn't bear it." She buried her face against his shirt, clinging to him.

"You do tend to dramatize, don't you? I never sent you away. This past month was supposed to be a courtship."

"It was a test and I hate tests. I trust you, Adrian. All I want is for you to trust me."

"Or else you'll blackmail me into marriage?"

Her nails bit into the muscled back beneath his shirt. "I've told you, I'll do whatever I have to do in order to keep you."

He stroked her hair, tangling his fingers possessively in the golden-brown strands. "I believe you, honey. After this fiasco today, how could I not believe you? I have to admit you're not exactly looking for a way out of our relationship. But I thought I had to offer you that escape if you wanted it."

"So that you could be sure of me. Well, I'm not looking for an escape, Adrian Saville."

"I love you, Sara."

She lifted her head, eyes shimmering with emotion. "I love you."

He smiled and wrapped her close. "Can we go home now?" Adrian asked.

"Yes."

"We can stop in Vegas on the way back to Washington," he went on thoughtfully.

"You really are going to marry me?"

"I thought I didn't have a choice."

"You don't," she assured him.

Adrian thought about being wanted so badly by Sara that she'd do anything to keep him. It was a novel idea. He discovered he liked it. He was suddenly very sure she wasn't playing games.

The phone was ringing in Sara's apartment when they walked in the door a few minutes later. Adrian reached for it.

"It'll be your uncle," he explained as Sara glanced at him in surprise. Then he spoke into the receiver. "Hello, Lowell. You can stop panicking."

"I knew you'd handle things once you got there," Lowell said in tones of great satisfaction. "What happens now?"

"We're going to get married in Vegas on the way up to Washington."

"The hell you are! Whose idea was that?"

"Sara is blackmailing me into it," Adrian explained, watching her as he talked.

"Blackmail, hmm? I always knew the two of you had a lot in common. You both know what's important in life and you'll both do whatever it takes to get the job done. You just approach things in a slightly different style, that's all."

"Umm."

"But that doesn't mean I'm going to let you two get away with a Las Vegas wedding. I've been waiting for years for Sara to find the right man. I demand a real wedding. With me there." Lowell paused and then said in tones of satisfaction. "I won't have to worry about shopping, will I? I've already given you your gift. That reminds me, I'll be expecting a thank-you note." Lowell Kincaid hung up the phone.

Adrian stood looking at Sara. "Your uncle wants a thank-you note."

"Don't worry, I'll write one."

''He's also demanding what he calls a real wedding. He doesn't approve of the Vegas idea.''

Sara grinned. ''He just wants an excuse to wear one of those dumb aloha shirts.''

''Lowell always did like parties.''

Sara smiled. ''Well, much as I hate to admit it, we may have to accommodate him. I'm extremely grateful to him. But not for the map.''

''I know what you mean. I feel the same way.'' Adrian moved, sweeping her up into his arms. ''You're the real treasure. I will take very good care of you, my sweet Sara.''

She nestled trustingly against him. ''I know. And I will take very, very good care of you.''

It was a long time later that Adrian stirred in the depths of the tangled sheets of Sara's bed and remembered the question he had wanted to ask earlier. He drew a hand playfully down her spine until he arrived at her derriere.

''Sara?''

''Umm?'' She was rapidly adopting his characteristic response.

''What did you tell all those candidates before I arrived at the hotel? How did you get rid of them?''

''I told them that there was one important requirement the successful candidate had to meet.''

''What requirement?''

''The successful applicant had to be a vegetarian.''

There were a few seconds of startled silence. Sara turned over onto her back in time to see the laughter dawn in Adrian's eyes. A moment later it consumed him completely and she was left to marvel at the first full-throated laugh she had ever heard from him.

She decided that a laughing wolf was a very enthralling sight. She would make certain Adrian laughed a lot more in the years ahead.

THE WEDDING RECEPTION, held on the ocean-front terrace of the home of Sara's parents, was a loud and exuberant success.

Mr. and Mrs. Frazer were pleased with their new son-in-law. For them, Adrian's cover was still nicely intact. They thought he would have a steadying influence on their beloved but often unpredictable daughter. They had several qualms about allowing Lowell Kincaid to act as best man, however.

"I knew he'd wear something ridiculous," Mrs. Frazer said with a resigned groan as she stood with her daughter near the punch bowl. "Just look at him in that silly shirt. Everyone else is in formal wear! I should have put my foot down right at the beginning and made it clear he would not be allowed to participate in this wedding unless he was willing to conform!"

"You wouldn't have had much to say about it, Mom." Sara laughed at her attractive, worried mother. "The best man was the groom's choice, not yours."

"It's not that I don't love my brother dearly, it's just that he's so...so..." Mrs. Frazer waved her hand helplessly.

"Have some more punch, Mother." Sara leaned over to pick up a fresh glass of the frothy red concoction.

"And that's another thing," her mother went on a little grimly. "Does this punch taste funny to you?"

"Spiked to the hilt, I'm afraid," Sara admitted cheerfully. She was watching her new husband as he stood talking to her father. The two men appeared to be involved in a very serious discussion.

"I knew it," Mrs. Frazer exclaimed. "I thought I saw Lowell fooling around near the punch bowl an hour ago! The champagne wasn't enough for him, I suppose!"

"Excuse me, Mom, I think I'd better go rescue Adrian before Dad sells him on the idea of investing all his royalties in long-term certificates of deposit."

"Adrian is a very stable, very intelligent man, dear. I'm sure he'll want to hear your father's advice. He's a man who will want to plan for the future."

"Adrian has me to help him plan his future." Sara swept up

another glass of punch for herself and went off to join her husband.

The look in Adrian's eyes as she went to stand beside him warmed her from head to toe. He loved her. Above all else, he loved her. His was a total commitment. Just as hers was to him.

''Your father's been telling me about the advantages of long-term investments,'' Adrian said, putting his arm around his wife's waist.

''I'll just bet he has.'' Sara smiled at her father.

''I'll go over some more details with you later, Adrian. So glad Sara found herself a man who has his feet on the ground,'' Frazer said easily. He nodded in a friendly fashion, leaned down to kiss his daughter and went off to have some more of the heavily spiked punch.

''Feet on the ground, hmm?'' Sara tipped her head up so that Adrian could brush his mouth against hers.

''That's not where they're going to be in a couple of hours,'' he warned.

''No?''

''Nope. Unless we decide to try something really unusual in the way of wedding nights, I plan to spend the evening horizontally.''

''Adrian, I must tell you that lately you've begun to develop an odd sense of humor.''

''Any sense of humor is better than none,'' Lowell Kincaid declared jovially as he sauntered up to join them. He was holding a glass of champagne in one hand and a glass of punch in the other. ''Nice party, Sara. Your mother can throw a decent bash when she sets her mind to it.'' He took a sip out of each glass.

''Glad you're enjoying yourself, Uncle Lowell.''

''I always enjoy parties. Say, I'm glad I finally caught the two of you alone. I've been wanting to talk to you all day.''

Adrian looked at him warily. ''Is that right?''

''Yeah, you know, I've been thinking.''

''I'm getting nervous already.''

Lowell shook his head. "No, no, this is serious. I've been giving some thought to Vaughn's little plan for getting the gold out through Cambodia. After Sara put that ad in the paper—"

"Don't remind me of that ad," Adrian warned.

"I'm telling you, Adrian, it's given me pause. There just might be a way to do it." Lowell leaned forward conspiratorially. "If we put together the right team—and you know we've got some good contacts—we could slip in and out of the country without anyone even knowing we were there."

"Uncle Lowell!" Sara's eyes widened excitedly. "Do you really think so?"

"Well, it would be risky, of course. But it just might be feasible."

Adrian's gaze narrowed. "The only reason it sounds feasible to you, Kincaid, is because you've been drinking too much of that damn punch. Forget it."

Sara turned to him eagerly. "But, Adrian, just think. What an adventure it would be!"

"I said forget it and I meant it." Adrian lifted his champagne glass and swallowed deeply.

"But, Adrian, darling…"

"Don't 'Adrian, darling' me. I said no. That's the end of it."

Lowell chuckled. "How about this. Your first marital quarrel."

"And you started it," Adrian shot back.

"You know what I think?" Sara demanded, glaring up at her husband. "I think Adrian is taking his new sense of husbandly duties a little too seriously. He's starting to lay down the law and we haven't even left the reception."

"Start as you mean to go on," Adrian quoted blandly. "And speaking of going on, I think it's time we said good-bye to all these nice folks. We've got a wedding night waiting for us. Are you ready to leave, Mrs. Saville?"

"Yes, Adrian."

"I've never seen her quite so amenable," Lowell marveled.

Adrian grinned suddenly. "It won't last. I intend to take advantage of it while I can. Let's go, honey."

Sara caught her uncle's eye as she obediently turned to leave on her husband's arm. Kincaid winked. Sara laughed silently back at him. The gold could wait for a while. After all, legends lasted a long time.

Lowell Kincaid's sister drifted up to stand beside him. She smiled maternally after her daughter. "Well, Lowell, in spite of that idiotic shirt you're wearing, I have to admit that this time you really came through. I was beginning to wonder if my daughter was ever going to fall in love. But you seem to have found just the right man for her."

Kincaid raised one of the glasses he was holding and grinned. "The best. A legend in his own time."

JAYNE ANN KRENTZ

LEGACY

One

He hadn't planned to move in on her this quickly, but Honor Mayfield was making it so easy he knew he would be a fool to waste the opening. Spinning a web was a delicate task, and one of the most important aspects of the job was selecting the beginning point. It looked as though Honor was going to provide the perfect beginning herself.

Constantine Landry sat alone in a private box fronting the Santa Anita Racetrack. One booted foot lazily braced against the partition, an expensive set of Japanese-crafted field glasses resting on the empty seat beside him, he could have been any one of a number of the more affluent racing enthusiasts who occupied the row of private boxes.

But his attention wasn't on the results of the second race that were being posted on the lighted board below. Instead, he watched with calculating eyes as a woman with golden-brown hair walked quickly along an aisle in the grandstand behind him. She had a very serious expression on her face and was obviously intent on following a flashily dressed man several yards away from her.

Might as well make it a parade, Landry thought as he got to his feet with an easy, coordinated movement. The first strand of the web was waiting to be strung, and unless he missed his guess it was going to be a very strong anchor thread. Honor Mayfield, it appeared, was headed for trouble. Keeping her out of it would give him exactly the kind of opening he needed.

Landry was accustomed to waiting and watching for openings. Trained hunters learned those necessary skills quickly or remained singularly unsuccessful. Landry had been very successful in his profession. He had been dealing with two-legged prey a long time. One brightly dressed, unprotected female who had no idea she was being pursued presented no real problem. What was definitely out of the ordinary was this strange restless excitement that was suddenly pervading his bloodstream.

It wasn't the cool intensity of the hunt as he might have expected. It was a deep, thrumming sense of anticipation. And it was all wrong. He knew instinctively that it was not the right sort of emotion for this kind of thing, but he didn't seem to be able to repress it.

The warmth of the Southern California sun beat down on Landry and his quarry with pleasant warmth. Hard to believe it was only January, he thought vaguely. He'd forgotten that on days when the smog factor was low and the California sun was living up to its promise, the towns that sprawled out from the heart of Los Angeles could still remind one of just how beautiful the countryside had once been. The San Gabriel Mountains formed a magnificent backdrop for the picturesque racetrack. If one concentrated on the scenery one could ignore the huge, modern shopping center that, in true California style, stood nearby. Southern Californians never felt entirely comfortable unless they were close to one of the many luxurious enclosed shopping malls.

Landry stalked Honor Mayfield at a discreet distance, questions without clear answers circling in his head as he moved through the crowd. He didn't understand the questions any more than he understood the unexpected sense of anticipation. He knew what he was doing, had planned the contact carefully. So why was he questioning his own motives at this late juncture? Around him people were hurrying to make their bets on the next race, crowding the aisles en route to the windows where cashiers waited patiently to accept what seemed to be an endless river of money.

It was a little difficult keeping Honor in sight without closing in on her. She was only about five feet four inches tall, easily lost amid the crowd. But the watermelon-pink of her shirt helped identify her as she slipped through the crush of bettors. One of the things Conn Landry had learned about her these past few months was that Honor had a passion for brilliantly-hued clothes.

He'd acquired a variety of such small tidbits of information about her and he still couldn't quite explain why he found each little detail so fascinating.

He increased his pace enough to close some of the distance between himself and his quarry as she, in turn, hurried after the man in the avant-garde safari suit. Landry knew whom she was following. His name was Granger and the abundance of rings he wore in addition to his clothes made him an easily recognized figure. Once again Landry wondered why Honor Mayfield was interested in him. Granger was dangerous.

But, then, so was Constantine Landry. And as far as Honor Mayfield was concerned, Landry decided objectively, she had more to fear from him than from Granger. She just didn't know it yet.

There were a lot of things she didn't know yet, and Landry made a decision. He would not tell her everything until he understood exactly why he was experiencing such a strange sense of ambivalence about what he was doing. It was the quarry who should remain uncertain and off-balance, not the hunter. He would approach her as a stranger, he told himself.

Months of hunting came to an end as Landry shortened the distance between himself and Honor.

Leaving the grandstands behind, Honor experienced a surge of nervous tension that almost broke her resolve. *Face it,* she told herself grimly, *you don't really know what the hell you're doing.* Not knowing, however, didn't solve any problems. She had no choice but to keep pushing blindly along the course she had set for herself.

The crowd thinned out as she followed Granger toward the

barns. Grooms soothing high-strung Thoroughbreds and maintenance people carrying tools and equipment replaced the betting enthusiasts. Soon she would come up against the impenetrable barrier of the gates that protected the stables. Without a pass she would be unable to get past the uniformed guard. If Granger was going beyond that boundary she would be out of luck.

It was with mixed emotions that she saw him turn off to head toward the parking lot area that was reserved for people whose business was connected directly with racing. Owners, racetrack employees, trainers and similar types were entitled to use the lot toward which Granger was now moving. She knew he hadn't parked there, because she'd seen him come through the front entrance of the track grounds an hour earlier. She suddenly realized that following Granger through a crowded grandstand was one thing. Following him away from the relative safety of the crowd was quite another. Granger moved in a different world, one that existed beyond the legal fringe of racing. People in that world tended to make their own rules.

Honor took a deep, steadying breath and her fingers tightened on the strap of her turquoise-blue shoulder bag. Perhaps she should have hired a professional, she told herself. A private detective, for instance. Someone who knew the people and rules of Granger's world. How did one approach a loan shark, anyway? The idea of dashing up to him and catching hold of the sleeve of his off-white safari suit was rather intimidating. Honor was trying to formulate a list of other possible approaches when a man's hand closed around her upper arm.

"What the—? No! Let go of me!" The words came out in a frightened gasp as she spun around to confront the stranger who was laying claim to her arm. Instantly she pulled herself back under control. Panic wasn't going to get her anywhere. She was still within shouting distance of help.

"Ladies intent on tailing people like Granger should take

care not to wear shirts the color of the inside of a ripe watermelon,'' the man said in a cool, dark, gritty voice that ruffled her already agitated nerves. ''It makes you a little too visible, you see.''

Honor struggled to keep the raging fear-inspired adrenaline under control. ''I beg your pardon,'' she snapped icily, ''but I have no idea what you're talking about. Kindly let go of my arm before I'm forced to scream for help.''

The man gave her a curiously twisted smile that didn't have any impact on his gunmetal-gray eyes at all. ''You've already got help. I'm it.''

She stared up at him, conscious of feeling very vulnerable as she sensed the strength in his grip on her arm. He wasn't quite six feet in height but there was a chilling power in his lean, hard frame that made itself felt on several levels. A bodyguard, she wondered fleetingly. She'd always thought of professional bodyguards as being big and burly, men whose threat lay in their massive, rocklike bodies. But this man made her think of the elegantly lethal qualities found in a stiletto or a coiled whip. Infinitely more dangerous.

''Do you—do you work for Mr. Granger?'' she heard herself ask uneasily and then realized how much information she had provided just by admitting to knowing Granger's name.

''No.'' The strangely bleak smile stayed in place. ''I only work for myself.''

Which made perfect sense, Honor realized abruptly. Men such as this one did not take orders from slick loan sharks like Granger. But that only made her present situation even more confusing.

''Then I really can't see that we have anything to discuss,'' she began bravely. ''If you'll excuse me, I must be going. I have to take care of some business.''

''So do I, lady. So do I.''

The grip on her arm tightened just enough to remind her that she couldn't possibly escape it, and then Honor found herself being led back toward the barn area.

"Wait a minute! What do you think you're doing? I don't even know your name."

"Constantine Landry. Call me Conn."

"Mr. Landry, I demand that you release me. I have something I must do," Honor said with soft urgency. Granger was even now disappearing from view behind a large building. She struggled in Landry's grip and seriously considered yelling for help. There were plenty of people around. Surely this man wouldn't do anything drastic to her in front of so many witnesses.

"If you're talking about your little plan to tail Granger, I'm afraid you're going to have to think of a more pleasant way to spend the afternoon."

"You are working for that bastard!"

He slanted a wry glance down at her as he pulled her toward the guarded stable gate. "I've told you. I don't work for anyone except myself. Not anymore."

"Then why are you interfering with me now? And how do you know who Granger is?" Honor asked grittily.

"A lot of people around here know who Granger is. He's been involved in everything from loan sharking to drug dealing. Not a nice man. I can't help being curious about why a nice lady such as yourself is following him. Believe me, unless you're feeling masochistic, you don't want to go where Granger's going right now."

Honor stared up at Conn Landry's savagely carved profile. "Just where is Granger going?"

"Straight into a police trap. He's been set up. Granger believes he's about to connect with one of his drug couriers. And he is, in a sense. But the courier has been working undercover for the past six months. Today the cops pull the plug. It wasn't an easy trap to set, you know. Granger's big enough to employ others to take his risks for him. But this time he was convinced that the deal was too big to leave in the hands of employees." Landry shook his head ruefully. "Some people just can't learn to delegate when they should."

Honor dug in the high heels of her turquoise leather sandals. ''How do you know all this? Who are you, Conn Landry?''

He politely allowed her to drag him to a halt, turning to confront her questioning hazel eyes. ''That's simple. I'm the man who's saving your sweet tail from the rather unpleasant surprise awaiting Granger. Just how would you explain your presence to the cops when they closed in on him and found you wriggling in the net, too?''

''I don't understand any of this!''

''That's obvious. And that's why you should have the sense to stay clear. Come along, lady in the watermelon shirt. I want to introduce you to a friend of mine.''

Confused and wary, Honor again found herself being led toward the stable yard. At the guarded gate Constantine Landry flashed an owner's pass, and the next thing she knew she was inside the perimeter that protected the expensive animals. Rows of barns, horse trailers and small cottages for the grooms were scattered around the grounds. The pleasant, earthy scent of well-cared-for horses filled the air. In the grandstands all was excitement, disgust, urgency and despair, depending on the outcome of the current race. Here there was a subdued, businesslike bustle of activity.

''Mr. Landry, this is ridiculous. Please let go of my arm!''

''I told you to call me Conn. And I think this is about the safest place for you until Granger's been taken out of commission. From what I could tell you were hell-bent on following him right into trouble.''

''Why should you care?'' she snapped furiously.

His mouth kicked up briefly at the corner in that odd little smile that didn't go anywhere. ''A good question.''

She waited for the answer and when it didn't come, Honor pursued her arguments for freedom. ''Look, if you're a police undercover agent or something and I've gotten in your way, I'm sorry. I didn't mean to interfere in any sort of operation designed to take Granger off the streets! Believe me, no one wants him in jail more than I do!''

Landry nodded. ''Mind telling me why?''

''I can't see that it's any of your business. You haven't shown me a badge or any identification.'' Immediately wary, Honor backed off from being pushed into an explanation. ''I still don't have any idea of who you really are, do I?''

''The situation is mutual. You haven't introduced yourself, either.''

''I don't intend to do so. You seem to know far too much already.'' There was a certain satisfaction in being able to deny him something, at least, Honor discovered. Constantine Landry was almost frighteningly sure of himself. The rigorously austere planes and angles of his features held no trace of softness or warmth.

''I think,'' Landry said too quietly, ''that it's time you told me who you are.''

''Are you asking in an official capacity?'' she demanded with a show of bravado that was only skin-deep. With a flash of intuition she sensed that introducing herself would be a small act but a crucial one. It was as though he were asking that she commit herself somehow, demanding that she acknowledge the tenuous acquaintance, insisting that she take a potentially dangerous first step. Oddly enough she could have sworn in that moment that he already knew who she was and that he was only asking to maintain an illusion. She brushed aside the uneasy thought. Of course there was no way he could know her identity.

''I'm asking. Period. No official reasons.''

Honor felt the lapping waves of his will and knew that the full force of an ocean of strength lay behind them. They halted in the shade of a long barn and she looked up at him searchingly. Quite suddenly she knew that in the end he would have his answer. She had the feeling he'd gotten answers from people before; he was that kind of man. There was no point resisting the soft command in his voice.

''As I said before, I think you know too much already,'' she observed quietly. ''But for the record, my name is Honor Mayfield.''

''Yes.'' He took her arm again and led her into the barn. There had been satisfaction in the single word.

Just yes. Simple and certain. As if she were merely confirming something he already knew. What was going on here? she wondered.

''Mr. Landry, I've answered your question. Now tell me what your role is in all this. You owe me that much.''

''Do I?'' He had halted in front of a roomy stall. There was a soft rustling sound from within, and a few seconds later an inquisitive equine head emerged to investigate. ''Hello, Legacy. I hope you feel like running today.''

''Legacy?'' Honor stepped forward, putting out a hand to touch the nose of the horse who watched her with avid interest. ''This is Legacy?'' For a moment Granger and all the related problems were forgotten as she stared at the beautiful bay colt.

Landry's chilled eyes studied her reaction to the horse. ''I own him.''

''I see.'' Honor couldn't think of anything to say. She was looking at a tiny piece of her past and for a moment the impact was unsettling. ''I didn't realize,'' she went on weakly. ''That you owned him, I mean. I saw his name on the program. He's running in the fifth, isn't he?''

''That's right.''

Honor withdrew her hand and the sleek Thoroughbred extended his nose to follow the movement. ''He's very beautiful.''

''Very.''

''He's favored to win today, isn't he?'' She couldn't take her eyes off the animal.

''Slightly. This is only his second race and he still has a ways to go to prove himself.''

Honor stepped back out of range of the questing mouth that

was beginning to nip interestedly at her silk shirtsleeve. "I'm sure he'll do well."

"He comes from good stock," Landry said deliberately.

"One of Stylish Legacy's descendants." Honor didn't realize she'd whispered the words aloud until Landry responded.

"You seem to know something about the line."

She shook her head. "Not very much, really. I don't follow the details of the racing world closely. Once in a while I come to the track when I can find the time. When I was a kid I had the usual female hang-up on horses."

"But you know about Stylish Legacy?"

Honor sighed. There was no harm in admitting the truth. "My father once owned him. He and another man, that is. Is Stylish Legacy still at stud?"

"Yes. He's eighteen years old now. But still producing winners." Landry stroked the warm bay neck, and Legacy nuzzled his chest, inhaling the man's scent through the fabric of the coffee-colored shirt. The horse clearly enjoyed being the center of attention. "So your father once owned Stylish Legacy?"

"It was a long time ago. He and a partner—" Honor broke off quickly. "Look, Mr. Landry, I think this has gone far enough. Please tell me what your connection is with Granger. Is he really walking into a trap out there in the parking lot?"

"Most of us walk into a trap at some point in our lives."

"I am not in the mood for cryptic comments!"

Legacy reacted to the sharp tone of her voice, his sensitive ears flicking in irritation. Landry soothed him.

"Take it easy, boy. She's just a little nervous, that's all."

"I have a right to be nervous," Honor muttered, glancing down the row of stalls. Several curious muzzles were appearing and a half-dozen pairs of interested brown eyes were examining the scene at the far end of the long, shaded barn.

"You'd have a lot more reason to be nervous now if you

were out there in the parking lot taking the fall along with Granger,'' Landry told her.

Honor shifted restlessly. ''If what you say is true, then I suppose I should be grateful to you for stopping me.''

Landry inclined his head. ''Yes, you should be. Feeling grateful, Honor?''

''I'm not sure yet. Basically because I'm not sure how you're involved.''

''A bystander. Nothing more. But I'd heard rumors around the track about what was being planned for Granger today. Racetracks thrive on rumors. When I saw you following the man, I decided to pull you out of the action. Somehow you just didn't look like the type to be up to your neck in loan sharking and drug dealing.''

Honor shuddered, utterly repelled. ''I'm not.''

''But you were following him,'' Landry pointed out coolly.

''It's a private matter, Mr. Landry,'' she told him stiffly.

''Will Granger's arrest take care of this private little matter for you?''

''With any luck, yes,'' she answered fervently.

''Then I think, on the whole, that you really should feel grateful to me, Honor Mayfield.''

Her gaze narrowed. ''Are you the type to hold that sort of thing over my head?''

He looked at her, gray eyes unreadable and unyielding. ''I keep track of what I owe in this life, Honor. And even closer track of what's owed to me.''

For a long moment she couldn't drag her gaze free of the invisible bonds Constantine Landry was using to chain her full attention. She had never met a man like this. A part of her was genuinely apprehensive and cautious. But another part of her was deeply aware of him, and that disturbed her even more than the understandable wariness she was experiencing.

''I believe you, Mr. Landry.'' And she did. Completely. ''You aren't a cop, are you?''

''No.''

"And you do own Legacy?"

"Oh, yes," Landry told her with great sureness. "I own him." For a moment a genuine expression of emotion flickered in the gray eyes. A mixture of pride and pleasure and enthusiasm.

Scenes from the past flashed briefly through Honor's mind. She remembered a similar expression in the eyes of her father when he had talked about Stylish Legacy. People who owned racehorses were infected with a certain kind of fever, even when they tried to pretend that the horses were purely financial investments or tax shelters. Getting involved in the racing world almost always meant getting involved on an emotional level. It wasn't just a realm of numbers and big financial transactions. It was an arena that involved the emotions. It struck Honor as strange that Constantine Landry should be interested in such a world. He looked like the kind of man who kept the emotional side of his nature under rigid control. In fact, a person could be pardoned for questioning whether or not Conn Landry would even be capable of a strong emotional response, Honor decided dryly.

"You really did just happen to hear about the police's plans for Granger and decided to rescue me when you saw me headed for the ambush?"

"Yes."

"Just because I didn't look like the type to be involved with a man like Granger?" she persisted. Her hand twisted the leather strap of her shoulder bag as she remembered the feeling she'd had that he already knew her name before he asked her to introduce herself.

"I had my reasons. That was one of them."

Honor drew a breath. "Well, then, I *am* grateful to you. To tell you the truth, I was not anxious to confront him, anyway. If the cops have him now that certainly will take a problem off my hands." For the first time since the whole mess had started, Honor permitted herself to give in to a feeling of relief. Overwhelming relief. A tentative smile lightened her eyes.

Landry saw the incipient relaxation and the hint of warmth in her and congratulated himself. The first strand of the web was in place. Honor Mayfield did not yet understand that she would have been better off taking her chances out in the parking lot along with Granger. Explaining herself to the cops probably would have been simpler and safer in the long run than explaining herself to him, Landry decided. But, then, she didn't have any choice.

Come into my parlor, pretty fly.

Actually, he admitted, she wasn't exactly pretty. But there was a compelling quality about her that seemed to fascinate him. The hazel eyes were expressive and serenely intelligent. Here in the shade the subtle golden highlights of her hair were hidden, but the style suited her. It was a smooth, casual curve that just touched her shoulders. A soft mouth and a slightly aggressive nose blended pleasantly enough with the wide, faintly tilted eyes, but taken independently the features would never be labeled beautiful.

Still, Landry realized, he found himself studying Honor's face, searching for whatever it was that intrigued him. Perhaps it was the hint of feminine strength in the way she carried herself. Or perhaps it was the shuttered, cautious warmth he saw in her eyes. She was not a superficial woman. Pride and intelligence and gentleness hovered just beneath the surface. Landry had spent a good many years learning to make accurate judgments of other people. His life had sometimes depended on that ability. Yes, there would be rewards in store for the man who slipped past her barriers.

The rest of her was proving unexpectedly interesting, too. A pair of pleated khaki pants that tapered to the ankles emphasized the curve of a nicely rounded derriere. The watermelon shirt was loose but didn't conceal the fact that her waist was small and so were her pert breasts.

In bed she would be sleek and responsive, Landry decided

abruptly. He wasn't certain how he knew that but he was convinced of it. His whole body was convinced of it. The unexpected surge of a very ancient kind of awareness took him vaguely by surprise. It also put a piquant focus on his plans for Honor Mayfield. Once again he was forced to confront the wavering image of the goals that should have been crystal clear in his head. Determinedly he ignored the sense of ambivalence.

"Honor," he murmured, tasting her name aloud.

She looked up at him curiously. "Yes?"

"It's an interesting name."

"My father's choice," she informed him flatly.

"And do you live up to it?"

She didn't care for the direction of the conversation. "Since I'm not playing poker with you, I can't see that it matters."

"Is your father pleased with your efforts?"

"My father is dead, Mr. Landry."

Silence greeted her repressive remark. Landry didn't make the usual "I'm sorry" murmur. He merely accepted the information as if he already knew the answer. She didn't like the way he seemed to anticipate her. It made Honor nervous. She was already uneasy enough as it was today.

On the other hand, she would have been feeling distinctly more anxious right now if Conn Landry hadn't intercepted her en route to the parking lot. Her mouth relaxed into a warm smile.

"What are you thinking, Honor?"

"That I owe you one if you really did save me from getting involved in the setup meant for Granger."

"I agree."

Her smile tilted into a sardonic curve. "A more gallant approach would be to shrug and tell me your assistance was nothing, that I shouldn't feel obligated because of it."

He was silent.

"But you're not going to take the gallant approach, are you?" Quizzically she examined his hard face.

''No. Why should I? I prefer to keep the scales balanced.''

He looked slightly puzzled that she should even suggest another way of operating than the one he was using. Honor knew in that moment that the words were a fundamental tenet for him, a doctrine by which he lived. He might be a harsh man in many respects, she decided, but he had his own code. Here in Southern California, where so many people ignored such archaic things as personal codes of behavior in favor of convenience and indulgence, there was something deeply intriguing about a man who lived by his own rules.

''Then you may have to write off this particular debt, Mr. Landry. I don't see how I can repay you,'' Honor said coolly.

''You can watch Legacy win in the fifth with me,'' he tossed back smoothly. ''I'm using the trainer's box. I'd like you to join me. Especially since you have some connection with his sire.''

Relief flared in her as she realized he wasn't going to ask too much after all. ''I never actually saw Stylish Legacy run. My parents were in the process of getting a divorce during those years and there was a lot of…unpleasantness between Mom and Dad. I didn't get to spend a lot of time with my father. It was all a long time ago.'' Which didn't mean she hadn't been thrilled at the idea of her father's actually owning a racehorse, Honor remembered.

''You'll join me in Humphrey's box?''

''Well, if you insist,'' she agreed doubtfully, trying to hide her budding excitement.

''Having just saved your neck from the long arm of the law, granting me the favor is the least you can do, isn't it?'' Conn said laconically.

''You have a remarkably undiplomatic way of putting things, Conn.'' Her words were tinged with some of the asperity she was feeling. Damn it, she did owe him some repayment for his fortuitous interference. But she didn't like the way he was using that obligation for his own purposes. Conn Landry, Honor decided, tended to be more than a little ruthless. Some of her initial excitement faded. ''I can't see why you'd particularly want my company to watch Legacy run, but—''

''I do. So that settles it.''

''Mr. Landry,'' she began fiercely, only to be interrupted by a new voice. It was a man's voice and it held a deep Southern drawl.

She turned to see a large, balding man with a paunch and an easy smile approaching. He was wearing a beige Stetson with what appeared to be a genuine snakeskin band. The rest of the outfit from the Western-cut shirt and flared trousers to the hand-tooled cowboy boots harmonized nicely with the hat. He was probably in his sixties, she estimated. The crinkles around his eyes when he smiled made her want to respond in kind.

''Have a heart, ma'am, Conn's only in town for the races. He's all alone and it seems perfectly logical to me that he might want to share Legacy's big race with a pretty little thing like you.''

Landry nodded toward the newcomer. ''Honor, this is Ethan Bailey. He's got a couple of horses with the same trainer I use, Toby Humphrey. Ethan, meet Honor Mayfield.''

''How do you do?'' she said politely, extending her hand. Her fingers were immediately crushed in a warm paw.

''Just fine, Miss Honor, just fine. It is Miss, isn't it?'' He made a show of examining her ring finger. ''Out here in California a man can't always be sure. You folks have a rather interesting approach to life.''

''Don't let Ethan put you on,'' Conn advised dryly. ''He may have been born in Texas, but he spends a hell of a lot of time in California.''

''Only because Toby Humphrey's the best trainer around and he works here in California.'' Ethan Bailey sighed. ''And I like to be close to my horses as much as possible.''

''Just a good old ranch boy at heart,'' Conn said, but there was an easiness in his tone that told Honor he liked the other man. ''You'd never know he made his living wheeling and dealing in West Coast real estate, would you?''

''Now, Landry, old buddy, you know damn well that my calling is every bit as legitimate and inspirational as your own. Some objective folk might say even more so.'' Ethan Bailey grinned, reaching out to pat Legacy's neck. ''He's looking good today, aren't you, Legacy? Going to leave the rest of those clodhoppers behind in the dust.''

There was a rustle of movement from the far end of the stable and a small, wiry man who appeared to be somewhere on the far side of sixty-five came striding toward them at a brisk pace. He was accompanied by two young grooms.

''Afternoon, miss.'' The small man tipped his battered cap politely to Honor as he came to a halt in front of Legacy's stall. ''Hello, Conn, Ethan. Time to take Legacy down to the saddling ring.'' He stepped aside, and so did everyone else as one of the grooms, a young woman, moved forward to take charge of Legacy.

''Toby, I'd like you to meet a friend of Landry's.'' Ethan Bailey introduced the trainer, whose attention was divided between Legacy and the man who paid him to train the animal.

''He's in good shape, Conn,'' Humphrey pronounced. ''Real good shape.''

The horse strode out of the stall with an energy that spoke of his breeding and fitness. Honor found herself entranced by the beautifully built creature. The muscles of Legacy's strong hindquarters moved sleekly beneath a coat that had been burnished by hours of hand grooming. The center of attention now, and well aware of it, he tossed his head and pranced.

''Let's go,'' Landry said softly. He took Honor's arm and guided her after the small procession formed by the trainer, the grooms and the dancing horse.

''He's so beautiful,'' Honor breathed, no longer even thinking about getting out of her commitment to watch the horse race. She was getting caught up in the behind-the-scenes excitement and knew it.

''You've got a stake in him, you know,'' Landry pointed out, watching her changing expression. ''A family connection.''

''Maybe I'll splurge and put a couple of dollars down on him,'' Honor decided. She ignored the subtle emphasis he put on the words ''family connection.''

''We'll go place our bets after we've seen him saddled.''

They followed Legacy and his attendants to the stalls near the grandstands where the horses were saddled and the jockeys mounted.

''Who have you got on top of Legacy today?'' Ethan Bailey asked conversationally as they watched the postage-stamp-size saddle put in place.

Landry hooked one booted foot over the bottom rung of the metal barricade and leaned forward on his elbows to watch the prerace activity. ''Humphrey picked Milton. Says he'll have enough sense to let Legacy alone when the time comes.''

Bailey nodded. ''He's putting Milton on Cavalier in the eighth, too. Can't complain about the boy. Did real good by me last time he was on Cavalier.''

Honor listened to the racing talk flowing around her and felt her pulse begin to quicken. At least the excitement in her system now wasn't from fear, she thought with a burst of gratitude for the taciturn man beside her. Hoping devoutly that whatever had taken place in the parking lot would result in her never having to worry about Granger again, she allowed herself to be swept up in the unique thrill of being connected, however distantly, to a real, live racehorse once again.

She was barely able to contain herself as they watched Legacy and his competitors being led out of the saddling area. Milton, the jockey, was tossed on board and then the restless animals headed toward the tunnel that opened onto the track.

''Come on, Honor. Let's get our bets down. See you around, Bailey.'' Landry nodded at the other man as he propelled his willing captive in the direction of the stands.

''He's going to win,'' Honor declared as she stood in line to place the bet. ''I just know it.''

''If you're sure of it, why are you only putting a couple of bucks on him?'' There was a brief, teasing light in Conn's eyes.

''If you knew me better, you'd realize that's as big a risk as I ever take,'' she retorted.

''You were taking quite a risk this afternoon by following Granger.'' The hint of indulgent humor disappeared.

Some of Honor's new bubbling mood evaporated. ''That was different.'' She was saved from explaining just why it was different because her turn came at the window. Hastily she put down her two dollars and accepted the ticket.

Two hundred on his own horse wasn't overly ostentatious, Honor decided a few minutes later as she watched Landry place his own bet at a different window. Of course, the real money for the owner would be in the winning purse and in the prestige. Landry took her arm very firmly once more and led her into the stands.

Seated in the private box Toby Humphrey maintained for the use of his clients, Landry settled back to watch Legacy being edged into the gate. Out of the corner of his eye he could also watch the excitement on Honor's features.

She was caught up in it all now, he thought with satisfaction. She'd had no intention of getting involved with him this afternoon, yet here she was beside him, thoroughly engrossed in the coming race. He knew damn well that she was very grateful for his intervention earlier. He also knew she had been almost as wary of him as she was of Granger. But here she was, right where he wanted her.

It had all worked out very neatly. The first strand of the web was in place. There would be no escape for Honor Mayfield. He had counted on Legacy as a lure and it had worked. He'd assumed she'd have some interest in the horse because of the fact that her father had once owned the sire. Keeping her free of Granger was an added plus and she was bound to be grateful. Conn knew the starting point of the web was firmly attached. From now on he would move more and more surely into her life, taking advantage of every opportunity to get closer to this woman who was a link to the mystery of the past. He wanted her gratitude, her trust, her confidence, and he also wanted her to sense that he was the one in control.

Remaining in control was critical, Conn reminded himself. The last thing he wanted to risk was being tugged into the heart of the web right along with his victim.

Two

Legacy breezed in three lengths ahead of everything else in the field. Milton, the jockey, sat politely on the horse's back as though he'd just been invited along for the ride. Honor found herself on her feet and shouting along with everyone else. The excitement of horse racing was highly contagious.

''He won! He won! Conn, he did it!''

She thought she saw a brief sign of satisfaction in his expression, and then it changed to an arrogantly aloof interest in the fact. He appeared far more curious about her bubbling reaction to the win.

''Yes, he did.''

''You're going to clean up on your bet and so am I. Come on, let's go. We've got to hurry. They'll be taking the photos in the winner's circle.'' Honor impulsively reached out to grasp his hand and hustle him out of the box.

''What's the rush?'' But Conn got slowly to his feet. He sounded slightly perplexed.

''The rush is that they'll take the photo regardless of whether or not the owner is there. And you want to be in the picture, don't you? You can hang it on the wall in your bathroom or something. Didn't you get your picture taken the last time you watched him race?''

''No,'' he admitted. ''I've only watched him race once before, and I'm not all that familiar with the track formalities. I was sitting in the stands and no one sent for me or told me how to get into the picture.''

She laughed up at him, finding the trace of genuine disappointment in his voice rather endearing. ''No one sends for you. You get into the picture by running. Come on, Conn, let's go!''

Swept up in the thrill of being connected to a winning racehorse, Honor was only vaguely aware of how hard she had to work to get Landry down into the winner's circle where a head-tossing, sweat-soaked Legacy was waiting to have his picture taken.

Everyone in the vicinity, it seemed, except Landry was eager to participate in the little ritual. Conn seemed almost embarrassed by the activity going on around his horse. It occurred to Honor that he wasn't accustomed to being in the limelight. A man of the shadows, she thought fleetingly and wondered vaguely what he'd done during his life. By the time Honor had pushed Conn into position near Legacy's head and the track officials had taken their customary places, a few other totally unrelated faces were already standing near the horse.

At the last moment Landry looked around and saw Honor waiting behind the barrier. Suddenly he held out his hand in a cool, commanding fashion.

''Come here, Honor. You might as well be in this shot, too.''

''Oh, no, I had nothing to do with him winning,'' she protested. But there was more than politeness in his eyes; there was a strangely intense insistence. He wanted her to join him, she realized, and in those hectic moments Honor's instinct was to obey. Besides, how often would she have a chance to be photographed with a winning racehorse, she asked herself cheerfully. She hurried forward to take her place beside him.

It was all over in a moment. The track officials did this sort of thing after every race and had the routine down pat. Four photos of winning horses and their beaming owners had already been taken this afternoon and there were several more to go. The crowd around Legacy broke up quickly as Humphrey took charge and led the horse away toward the stables. Landry still retained his remotely satisfied look, but he didn't completely fool Honor. The deep pleasure in Legacy's win was there. Intuitively, she sensed it.

''A winner has a lot of friends,'' Honor observed as the strangers who had managed to push their way into the photo drifted off, laughing.

''A fact of life. Losers, on the other hand, fare a little differently,'' Conn Landry said dryly as he guided Honor back into the stands.

That thought sobered her. ''I wonder how many friends Granger will have, now that he's been arrested. If he was arrested. What if he's out on bail within a few hours, Conn? Or what if the trap didn't close properly?''

''Since I don't know why you're worried, I can't be very reassuring, can I?''

Honor flushed and firmly changed the subject. ''We'd better go collect our winnings.''

He hesitated as she made to hurry toward the betting windows. ''Honor?''

''What is it, Conn?''

''I think you ought to tell me what's going on.''

''Why?'' she asked starkly, her mood fading rapidly. The momentary excitement of being carried along with the thrill of the racing world was almost entirely gone.

''Because you owe me an explanation,'' he said simply.

''You said I only owed you my company while we watched Legacy win.''

''That's just a part of what you owe me.''

She saw the unreadable chill in his eyes and suppressed a shiver. Around them the crowd ebbed and flowed, ignoring the small confrontation as if it wasn't taking place. Honor felt alone and isolated, forced to deal with a predator on his own terms.

''Perhaps it would have been better if you hadn't interfered earlier,'' she said quietly.

''But I did interfere, and now it's too late.''

''Too late for what, Mr. Landry?''

He smiled weakly. "You were calling me by my first name a few minutes ago."

"Just tell me what you want from me," she exploded tightly. The turquoise leather strap of her bag was damp with moisture from her palm.

"Dinner tomorrow evening?" he suggested gently.

Her eyes widened. "Dinner!"

"As Ethan told you, I'm only in town to check on Legacy's progress. I don't know anyone else except Ethan and Humphrey and a couple of other people who have horses in Humphrey's stables. Is it so strange that I'd want to have dinner with an attractive woman whose father owned Legacy's sire?"

"I don't know, Conn. Is it strange? There's something about you that confuses me and I think you know it."

"Bailey and Humphrey can vouch for me," he pointed out calmly. "If you don't trust me, ask them for a reference."

"It's not that exactly—" She broke off, floundering. "It's this other business with Granger. I still don't understand how you knew what was going on this afternoon."

"I told you. Racetrack rumors. They're rampant."

"Apparently they didn't reach Granger's ears in time!"

"Probably because most people around here would just as soon see him removed from the scene. He's lowlife."

"I'll agree with you on that point."

"I'd like to know how you got involved with his sort."

"And if I don't feel like telling you?" she challenged.

"I'd still like to take you out to dinner."

But it wasn't a simple invitation. If it had been, Honor knew she would probably have accepted without much hesitation. There was something about Conn Landry that intrigued and compelled her. But the way he was asking her out to dinner made her wary. His request contained the same sort of insistence and urgency she'd sensed when he'd demanded that she be in the photograph a few minutes ago. On the other hand, she owed him a great deal, probably more than she knew, for his interference earlier in the afternoon. And then there was the fact that Ethan Bailey and Toby Humphrey seemed to like him, for whatever that was worth.

He must have seen the flickering uncertainty in her eyes, because Conn gave her his strangely sardonic smile and pushed her lightly in the direction of the pay windows. ''Give me your address and I'll pick you up at seven.''

''I don't think—''

''Where's your ticket?'' he asked as they reached the window.

''Here.'' Her fingers moved nervously in her purse, searching for her winning two-dollar ticket. A small plastic envelope fell to the floor during the awkward shuffling. Honor stifled a small sigh as Conn reached down to pick up the business card case and read:

Mayfield Interiors

Designs for Commercial and Residential Space

After noting the title of her business, Landry calmly pocketed one of the cards and then handed the case back to her. ''I'll give you a call tomorrow when I find out Granger's status.''

Honor shook her head once in silent acceptance of fate. Conn now knew her business address and her phone number. It would be a simple matter for him to get in touch any time he wished. Her last hope of retaining some anonymity and therefore some protection from him evaporated. The disconcerting part of it all was that she wasn't sure but she was glad the matter had been taken out of her hands.

Half an hour later, after watching a proud Legacy being given his cool-down walk by a groom, Honor finally made her escape from the Santa Anita racetrack. The afternoon had proved a total surprise, she decided as she drove back to Pasadena. On the one hand she had been saved from that tricky business with Granger. But the other side of the coin had revealed a situation that, in its own way, was fraught with just as much risk.

So many questions surrounded Constantine Landry. How would he know Granger's status by tomorrow? Was he really in town just to watch his horse run? What had that vague crack of Ethan Bailey's meant? The one about real estate being a bit more legitimate than Landry's occupation. Perhaps she should have done as Conn had dryly suggested and asked Bailey and the trainer for a reference. No, that would have made her feel ridiculous. Obviously they would say reassuring things about him, or Landry would never have made the suggestion in the first place. Besides, Landry was a good client of Humphrey's. It was unlikely the trainer would have said anything negative, anyway. And as for Bailey, well, the older man had seemed to like Landry.

And then there was the little matter of Landry having saved her from having to deal with Granger.

That alone put her deeply into his debt, Honor decided. There was no way around the issue. When it came to paying her debts, Honor made a point of living up to her name. The family's reputation had been tarnished enough fifteen years ago to last more than a generation. Yes, she would meet Conn Landry for dinner if that's what he thought she owed him.

The phone was ringing as Honor turned the key in the lock of her apartment door. She didn't rush to answer it because she was almost certain she knew who was on the other end. She was right.

"Hello, Adena."

"You're back!" her younger sister exclaimed in frantic tones. Adena rarely spoke in mild or neutral tones. Everything was exaggerated, dramatic, excited or outrageous. Adena fit very well into the Southern California life-style. "What happened? Did you see Granger? Talk to him? Oh, Honor, I've been so scared."

"Yes and no, respectively." Honor tossed her blue bag

down on the kitchen counter, aware of the irritation behind the act. She was very fond of Adena but lately the bonds of sisterly affection and family loyalty had been pushed a bit far.

"Yes and no! What on earth does that mean? Did you work something out with the man or not?"

"Calm down, Adena. Things didn't go exactly as planned. But it may all be for the best. You'll be glad to know that Granger is currently in police custody."

There was a stunned silence on the other end. "The police have him?" Adena finally asked in confusion. "But how? When? I don't understand."

"Apparently a trap had been planned for him today," Honor explained steadily and then gave her sister the few details she had.

"But a man like that will be out on bail in a few hours," Adena cried.

Honor said nothing. She was well aware of that possibility.

"And who is this Landry person?"

"Beats me. Owns a beautiful horse, though. A colt sired by Stylish Legacy."

"Stylish Legacy?" There was a questioning note in Adena's voice. "Wasn't that the horse Dad used to own?"

"That's right." Adena had been only eight years old when Nicholas Mayfield had been killed. She remembered the horse only because of some of the mementos that had been left behind. Honor, at thirteen, had been fascinated with the idea of having a horse in the family, even though she had never gotten to watch him run. Stylish Legacy had only been in a handful of races before the two men who owned him had both died in a bloody scandal that had traumatized Honor more than anyone else in the family. Adena had been too young to understand fully what had happened, and Mrs. Mayfield, who had been in the midst of messy divorce proceedings, had been almost relieved to have everything ended.

"Well, I don't see what this has to do with anything. Where does Landry fit into all this?" Adena asked anxiously.

''He kept me out of the trap that had been set for Granger. And when he found out I had some distant connection to his horse, he, uh, invited me to watch the race.'' ''Invited'' was something of a euphemism for the command Landry had issued, but Honor didn't feel up to explaining her own wariness of the man.

''And he's going to tell you what happens to Granger?''

''He said he'd find out tomorrow.''

''Honor, this is getting messier and messier. Why couldn't you just have paid off Granger and put an end to it all?''

Honor closed her eyes, momentarily seeking patience. ''Because by the time I was about to catch up with him, the police were waiting.''

''So this Constantine Landry says. What if he was wrong? Or playing some weird game? This doesn't solve anything! I'm in the same mess I was in before. What are we going to do now?''

''Adena, I don't know. I have no way of knowing what was happening out there this afternoon,'' Honor said flatly. ''You'll have to forgive me if I'm not handling this in the proper manner, but I haven't had a whole lot of experience dealing with sharks such as Granger!''

''Meaning I have?''

''You're the one who owes him five thousand dollars, not I!''

Adena broke into tears and, as usual, Honor felt guilty.

''Forget it, Adena,'' she soothed wearily. ''I'll take care of everything. I'm seeing Landry tomorrow and he'll tell me whether or not we still have to worry about Granger.''

''Are you sure you can trust this Landry person?'' Adena demanded through sobs.

''No.'' The initial response had been immediate. But then Honor thought about the man with the gunmetal-gray eyes. ''Well, maybe,'' she temporized.

''What kind of an answer is that?''

''The truth is, I just don't know yet. But there's something about him, Adena. I think he might be quite ruthless on occasion but I also have a feeling that he's, well, concerned with keeping the books balanced.''

''What books?''

''Never mind. I'll call you tomorrow after I find out more. Goodbye, Adena.'' Honor put down the phone before her sister could get in another question.

Then she moved deliberately across the living room with its red, black and yellow furnishings on a white carpet and into the red-and-black-tiled kitchen. It had been a rough day in several ways, and she deserved some compensation. Pouring herself a glass of cool Napa Valley Riesling, Honor went back into the living room. She sank down into a black-webbed rocking chair and propped her feet on the red hassock. Silently she toasted the palm tree outside her window.

''Here's to you, Constantine Landry, whoever you are. I'm not sure yet whether I should be thanking you or running as fast as I can in the opposite direction. But one thing's for sure. You aren't going to make my life dull.''

By the time Conn showed up at her door the following evening, Honor had decided that running really wasn't necessary. In fact, she told herself as she took in the sight of him standing on her doorstep, she was beginning to look forward to the evening.

He wore an immaculately cut gray linen jacket that had a subtle slub weave. Charcoal trousers that ended above handsewn calfskin shoes emphasized the coiled strength of his body. The crisply striped shirt and silk tie completed the quiet look of expensive power.

The only factor that bothered Honor was that she couldn't identify the type of power that emanated from Conn Landry. It wasn't, for example, the muted ritualized power associated with the corporate world. Nor was it the flashy, tacky, heavy-handed power of the Southern California film crowd. It crossed her mind briefly that what she was seeing was the cool arrogance of a professional gangster, but she dismissed the idea at once. Instead, the strength in Landry seemed to be uniquely his own. And she had the sense to know it was, therefore, more dangerous in some ways than the more easily recognized sources of power. It was always simpler to deal with a factor that could be labeled and understood.

But for some reason, although she was warily respectful of the potential danger in him, Honor didn't fear Conn. That knowledge gave her the poise to smile warmly at him.

Landry saw the confidence in her and told himself he was amused. Yet a part of him knew a sense of reluctant admiration. The lady had guts. Having just recently finished with a rather blunt heart-to-heart chat with Granger, he now knew just how much nerve she must have buried beneath that bright, stylish exterior.

She was wearing a yellow-gold chemise that was sashed low on the hips with a crisp, wide band of black. The effect was both rakish and self-confident without being outrageous. The black sandals and the ebony bracelet on her small wrist completed the outfit. Her hair swung in a sleek curtain around her shoulders and as he stood there on the threshold, Landry had an almost overpowering urge to run his fingers through the golden-brown stuff. He wanted to touch her with the familiar intimacy of a lover. She'd look good a little mussed from his touch, he decided.

Once again he realized he should be questioning his own reactions. It was reasonably safe to admit he found himself responding physically to Honor. Conn decided that he understood that part and could deal with it. But it definitely was not on the program to uncover this vein of whimsically indulgent tenderness.

"The desk clerk at my hotel recommended a little restaurant downtown," Landry said as he walked her toward the silver-gray Porsche that waited at the curb. He told her the name. "Know it?"

Honor nodded. "It's an excellent choice." She allowed him

to slip her into the front seat and then had to wait impatiently while he circled the front of the car and slid in beside her. ''Well?'' she invited cheerfully. ''When are you going to tell me all the details?''

His promised phone call that afternoon had been brief, disappointingly so, Honor had discovered after she'd replaced the receiver. Landry had only asked for her home address and then said quite calmly that Granger was no longer a problem. He'd refused to tell her more at that point.

''I'll give you the full story over dinner,'' Landry promised now as he pulled away from the curb. The quiet, tree-lined streets near the California Institute of Technology campus were relatively empty at this hour, and he made his way through them with an ease that told Honor he didn't need directions.

She wondered briefly how he happened to be so familiar with the Pasadena streets, and then promptly forgot the matter as her mind went back to Granger.

''He really is out of the way, though?''

''He won't bother you or your sister again.''

Her head snapped around. ''How did you know about my sister's involvement in all this?''

''I'll tell you that over dinner, too.'' He threw her a sidelong glance. ''Relax, Honor. I've taken care of everything.''

Some of her breezy confidence faded. ''*You've* taken care of everything? I thought it was the police who had handled Granger.''

''Whether or not they do doesn't affect you anymore.''

''Do you know, Conn Landry, you have a remarkable talent for the cryptic comment?''

''Since my talents are rather limited, I try to perfect the few I have.''

''I get the feeling your sense of humor may not be numbered among your few perfected abilities.''

''Probably not,'' he admitted without any show of concern.

''Pity,'' she said dryly, trying to sound just as cryptic as Conn.

Driving ability was, apparently, one of his limited number of talents, Honor observed as he parked the Porsche with neat precision in front of the casually elegant little restaurant. When Conn opened her car door and took her arm to escort her across the sidewalk she decided that he had another talent: He had the ability to make her feel safe.

It was an odd sensation on her part, she reflected as she was seated. Honor had never been aware of needing or desiring a man's protection. Whatever protection a man offered his women had disappeared when she was thirteen, and she hadn't depended on any since then.

Containing her curiosity until after she'd obediently ordered her meal of broccoli salad and scallops, Honor waited for an opportune opening. When the Sonoma County Chardonnay arrived at the table after much deliberation between the wine steward and Conn, she decided she had waited long enough. Smiling expectantly, she sipped the beautiful white wine and repeated her question.

''Tell me what they did to Granger.''

Landry shrugged, reaching for his own glass. ''He's out on bail. Eventually he might wind up in jail on a more or less permanent basis, but probably not this time.''

Honor's expectant smile disappeared. ''You said everything was all right now, that Granger has been dealt with and was no longer a problem. I was afraid of this,'' she went on morosely. ''As long as he's running around loose, I'm going to have to find him.''

''You're not going anywhere near that scum. I told you the situation is under control.'' There was cool command in Conn's gaze again.

''I haven't got much choice,'' Honor shot back.

''You're right. You don't have much choice. You're going to do as I say in the matter.''

''You don't have any conception of what's going on!''

''No?'' Broodingly he studied her set face. ''I know your sister owed him five thousand dollars because of that loan he gave her to pay off her gambling debts. And I know she didn't have the money. Apparently she went to you for it.''

''How do you know all this?'' Honor demanded fiercely.

''Some of it I learned from Granger and some of it I figured out for myself,'' Conn explained easily.

''You've actually talked to Granger today?'' She was stunned by the news. ''You saw him?''

''He headed for the racetrack as soon as they released him. He's a real racing addict. But, then, you must know that, or you wouldn't have been there yourself yesterday looking for him.''

''Adena told me she thought that was the most likely place to find him,'' Honor admitted slowly. ''But I don't understand why you approached him.''

''Don't you?''

''Well, no. None of this is any of your business.''

''It is now.''

''Conn, this is ridiculous. You can't just choose to involve yourself in my personal life!''

He watched her intently for a long moment and then reached across the small table to draw a thumb along the back of her wrist. His hand, Honor realized uneasily, was as strong-looking as the rest of him. Large, square, powerful. At first glance a woman wouldn't guess that those blunt fingers could be so amazingly sensitive. Yet the small pattern he traced on her wrist sent a tremor of awareness through her.

''I've already involved myself in your affairs, Honor. I paid Granger off and told him not to go near your sister again.''

Honor's gaze reflected her shock. ''You paid him off! You gave him five thousand dollars?''

''That's what your sister owed.''

''Yes, but—''

''Honor, it's all over,'' Conn told her with a surprising

twist of gentleness in his voice. ''You don't have to deal with Granger. I've already handled him for you.''

Confused and alarmed at the implications of having this man take charge of such a personal and dangerous matter, Honor found herself fumbling for words of anger and protest. ''You have no right! You should have consulted me. Now I owe you the five thousand dollars. That's assuming you're telling me the truth in the first place. Maybe this is all some sort of scam to take me for another five thousand. How do I know that you're any less dangerous than Granger?''

''You don't.''

''Damn you and your cryptic comments!'' She tossed her napkin on the table and prepared to get to her feet. The large, square hand that had only moments ago been tantalizing the back of her wrist suddenly closed around it like a manacle.

''Sit down, Honor,'' Conn ordered quietly.

''Why should I?'' she hissed in response.

His mouth lifted in the now familiar faint smile. ''Because you owe me five thousand dollars?'' he suggested smoothly.

Honor went very still. She couldn't have gotten out of her chair now even if the room were on fire. Her eyes met Conn's unreadable gaze. ''My checkbook is at home. Take me back to the apartment and I'll give you your money. The same money I was going to give Granger. I get the feeling it doesn't much matter which of the two of you I pay. You seem to have a lot in common, you and Granger.''

For a split second she was certain she'd gone much too far. The fingers shackling her wrist were now tight bands of steel and the cold of Conn's eyes could only have its source in the farthest reaches of the universe. In that taut instant of time Honor's instinctive wariness of the man made the transition to genuine fear.

And then, quite suddenly, she was free. Landry released her hand and sat back in his chair, reaching for his wineglass. He took a long swallow before he spoke. When he looked at her again, the frightening ice of his eyes had disappeared, leaving only his usual, remote expression. The wry tone of his words dissipated most of the remaining tendrils of alarm that curled through Honor's body. He inclined his head once, very formally.

''Congratulations, lady, you nearly managed to push me over the edge with that last crack. Not many people have the power to do that to me.''

She swallowed awkwardly. ''My guess is not many people care to make the attempt.''

''Did I frighten you?''

''I don't know how to take you, Conn,'' she said honestly. ''Yes, you frightened me for a moment. After all, I don't know much about you, do I? And now I owe you five thousand dollars.''

''Wouldn't you rather owe it to me than to Granger?''

''I don't know yet. At least I have a fair idea of where Granger fits into the grand scheme of life. He's a loan shark. Once I'd paid him off he would have been out of the way. You're not so easy to classify.''

''I'll take that as a compliment. A minute ago you were pointing out how much I had in common with Granger. Apparently my status isn't really that low in your eyes.''

''Why did you do it?'' she asked starkly.

He didn't pretend to misunderstand. ''Because I didn't want you going near that man,'' he declared with absolute conviction. ''You don't know anything about dealing with people like him. How did your sister get involved?''

Honor sighed, relaxing a little now that Conn seemed under control. ''For a while this fall she was dating a man who, among other things, gambled heavily. I guess he made it all look so easy and so much fun. He took her to Vegas and to the races and encouraged her to try her luck. At Santa Anita he introduced her to Granger. I gather he often used Granger as a banker. Granger made the money so readily available that my sister couldn't resist. She wanted to keep up with the high-rolling crowd she was moving with and eventually got run over, instead. She luckily came to her senses and dropped the boyfriend.''

''But by that time she was already into Granger for the five thousand?''

''Actually, she only borrowed three thousand,'' Honor said bluntly. ''But the government doesn't regulate interest rates in Granger's world.''

''Two thousand dollars in interest on a three-thousand-dollar loan. Yes, Granger is a step ahead of most banks. Well, if it's any consolation, he won't be approaching your sister again, even if she shows up at the track.''

Honor considered that. ''Because you told him to stay clear?''

''That's right.''

''Why is Granger so willing to take orders from you?''

''Maybe I make him nervous the same way I make you nervous,'' Conn offered laconically as the broccoli salads arrived.

Honor ignored her food. Leaning forward intently she said, ''Conn, I will repay you tonight. I have the money.''

''It's not necessary.''

Honor shook her head violently. ''It is most definitely necessary. I will give you the money tonight.''

He watched her expressive face for a moment as if trying to make up his mind about something. Then he nodded. ''All right. If it will make you feel more comfort-able.''

''It will!''

He smiled faintly. ''Yes, I can see that it will. And I do want you to feel comfortable around me, Honor.''

''Do you?'' she asked skeptically.

''It's a priority of mine,'' he assured her calmly.

Honor had to admit that by the conclusion of the meal, Conn had achieved at least a portion of his goal. Her sense of caution around him was still very much alive, but the compelling attraction he held for her was stronger than ever. There had been no argument over the matter of her giving him the money, so he obviously didn't intend to hold it over her head in any way. His main objective, apparently, had been to protect her from having to face Granger.

Strangely enough his protectiveness left her feeling in some ways more deeply in his debt than she would have felt if she'd simply owed Conn five thousand dollars. It was an odd bit of irony, she reflected as she gave him the key to open her front door.

"Would you like some brandy while I write out the check?" she offered politely as she stepped inside the apartment.

"Thank you, I'd appreciate that," he murmured, prowling through her strikingly decorated living room. "Just tell me where it is. I'll get it."

"In that red lacquered cabinet by the window."

He nodded and paced across the white carpet. He was taking in every detail, Honor thought fleetingly as she went quickly down the hall to her bedroom to get her checkbook. How much could that man read from the design details of her living room? Probably far too much.

It was as she stepped into her Japanese-inspired bedroom that Honor experienced her first sense of something being subtly wrong. For an instant she stood poised in the doorway, frowning as she looked into every corner of the room.

A moment later she shook her head in self-annoyance. Everything was in order. The red-and-black gilt-trimmed drawers of her dressing table were closed, just as they should have been, and her bed was dramatically neat, with its embroidered quilt in place. The room was a visual interpretation of subtle, sophisticated serenity. The only jarring note was the television set, and it was discreetly concealed behind a folding screen.

Honor nibbled on her lower lip for a few seconds, trying to shake off the feeling that there was a new element in the room. Then, half-disgusted with herself, she strode over to the closet and yanked open the shoji-screen doors. Inside, her brilliantly colored clothing hung in place above the array of equally bright shoes. Everything was as it should be.

"You're turning into a nervous little old spinster, my girl," she told herself bitingly. Determinedly she bent over the dresser and scrawled out the five-thousand-dollar check. After signing it she straightened, aware that the eerie trickle of uneasiness was still thrumming in her veins.

The only place in the room she hadn't checked was under the bed. Surely she wouldn't give in to the impulse, she chided herself.

"Oh, nuts!" She went to her knees on the white carpet and peered beneath the bed. Conn's blandly interested voice from the doorway sent a jolt through her.

"Well, I'll be damned. I've heard tales of single ladies who reach the point where they start looking under the bed before they go to sleep at night, but I didn't imagine you were one of them."

"I was right earlier this evening when I decided your sense of humor was not among your limited selection of talents, Mr. Landry." Awkward with embarrassment, Honor got to her feet and turned to pick up the check that lay on the dressing table. Aware that her cheeks were stained with a strong shade of pink, she spent an extra moment studying the check so that she wouldn't have to meet his mocking gaze.

But when Honor swung around with a flippant remark ready on her lips she suddenly found herself in Conn's arms. He had crossed the white carpet without making a sound, coming up behind her as stealthily as any predator.

"Conn?"

"There's no need to go looking under your bed, Honor. I'm right here."

Standing very still in his arms, Honor watched with fascination as he lowered his mouth to hers. He was there, all right, filling up every inch of her beautifully designed bedroom with his own brand of strength and presence. All thoughts of a vague wrongness in the atmosphere went out of her head as he took her lips. Conn Landry felt very, very right.

It was not the sort of kiss she normally expected and received the first time she kissed a new date. Landry's mouth did not move on hers with the tentative, questioning approach a man generally used in the beginning.

Instead he took her mouth as though he had been anticipating the action for a long while. The hunger in him was blunt and dangerously near the surface. What should have bothered her was that her body seemed to respond with the same feeling of being suddenly on the verge of discovery and release. It was an exciting, exhilarating sensation.

Her arms came up to wind slowly around his neck as he coaxed apart her lips. She shuddered a little as his tongue swept behind the barrier of her teeth. His response was to tighten his hands on her waist. Conn pulled her into his heat with irresistible pressure, gently forcing her into total awareness of the tautness of his thighs. And all the while he explored her mouth, drinking hungrily from the intimate, moist depths.

Honor's lashes closed slumberously and her body was invaded with a sweet lethargy that was shot through with red threads of anticipation.

''Honor, honey, you taste so good,'' Conn murmured in a husky growl as he reluctantly freed her mouth. He sampled the hidden skin behind the curve of her hair, his teeth nibbling with exquisite gentleness. ''Spicy, sweet and sexy. I knew you'd taste this way.''

Reflexively her nails kneaded his shoulders, the coral tips sinking deeply into the gray fabric of his jacket. He groaned and raised his hands slowly along her rib cage until his thumbs rested just beneath the curve of her unconfined breasts.

''Oh, Conn.''

''We're going to be good in bed together, you and I,'' he interrupted with soft satisfaction. He grazed the pad of his thumb across the crest of one breast and felt it flower to life beneath the yellow-gold silk.

His absolute certainty got through the sensual haze that seemed to be clouding her senses. "No," she whispered. "Not bed. Not yet." And, if she had an ounce of genuine intelligence, she added silently, not ever. She should know better than to play with fire at her age.

"I won't rush you," he vowed soothingly as he continued to glide the flat of his thumb across her silk-sheathed nipple.

Questioningly she lifted her head to meet his intent gaze and found herself staring into gray, bottomless seas that swirled with masculine desire. The depths of his hunger startled her even as it called to her.

"I think," she began carefully, "that you'll do things exactly as you want to do them, regardless of whether or not it means rushing me."

"Don't be afraid of me, Honor," he rasped against her ear. "There's no need."

"What's that supposed to mean?" she asked urgently, a strange panic sizzling through her.

"Nothing. Just relax. I want you, but I can wait." He used his strong hands on the nape of her neck, gentling her tense body until she did as he asked and relaxed against him. "I can wait," he repeated half under his breath.

There was something about the way he touched her, the way his hardness felt against her softness that was undermining all her defenses, Honor realized vaguely. The attraction between them was so unexpectedly strong, so out of the ordinary, that she wasn't fully prepared to handle it. Time was the key. She sensed that much.

Apparently Landry did, too. Slowly he eased himself away from her, mouth crooked just a bit at the edge. "I'll give you a little time, Honor." He brushed his mouth lightly across her parted lips. "But I think I'd better get myself out of your bedroom or I won't be able to keep my promise."

Without a word she followed him out into the living room,

the check clutched in her hand. He finished his brandy while standing by the window gazing out into the darkness. They spoke little during those few minutes but the atmosphere was heavy with unsatisfied male desire. When at last he turned to leave, Honor thrust the check at him. Conn took it without glancing at it, stuffing it into his jacket pocket.

''Feel better now that you've paid the debt?'' he asked softly.

''Yes.'' But she didn't feel she had paid the debt, Honor decided as she said good-night to him at the door. He had protected her from having to deal with Granger. She didn't have any way to repay that part of the obligation and the knowledge caused a faint tingle of unease.

It wasn't until she had turned out all the lights in the living room and walked slowly back down the hall to the bedroom that the sensation of wrongness returned. Once again she found herself standing in the doorway, trying to understand what it was that bothered her.

This time she finally focused on the cause. The large, folding screen with delicate Japanese artwork wasn't standing in quite the same place it had been earlier this evening when she had left the house. It didn't quite hide the television behind it.

The designer instincts in her had always insisted on using the screen to hide the brash, high-tech look of the portable TV. The twentieth-century technology had seemed to clash with the elegant serenity of the room.

Curious, Honor walked over to where the screen stood and examined the flattened areas of carpet where the legs of the screen had once pressed it down. She knew she hadn't moved that screen in two weeks. It had been that long since she'd used the television.

It was such a small thing, she told herself nervously. But designers were trained to notice small details in a room. It was often the little things that made the difference between a room with dynamic, personal impact and a simple showplace that had no warmth. The little things could also destroy the image. People in her profession soon learned to recognize odd little details that could produce great effects or ruin beautifully planned projects.

Someone had been in her bedroom that night.

Three

"She's a nice young lady, Conn," Ethan Bailey said. He was focusing a set of field glasses, watching a fast filly go through her morning workout on the track.

"Your horse or Honor Mayfield?" Landry leaned against the railing, his eyes following Bailey's expensive filly.

"Both, I reckon. But to tell you the truth it was that sweet little Honor I had in mind."

"You trying to tell me something, Ethan?" The odd little smile flickered at the edges of Landry's mouth.

Still gazing through the glasses, Bailey shrugged. "None of my business, of course, but, well, she doesn't seem quite your type, son."

"I agree. It's none of your business and she's probably not my type." But Conn kept his tone easy, not wanting to offend his friend. "On the other hand, I've never been really sure exactly what my type is. And Honor is turning out to be… interesting."

Ethan's brow held a trace of a disapproving frown. "You planning on playing games with Miss Honor?"

"You're certainly concerned about her."

"Like I said, I like her. Back where I come from a man's not supposed to play games with a lady like her."

"She can handle them." Conn relented. "Look, Ethan, don't worry about her. And don't worry about me, either. I know what I'm doing."

"You always seem to be in control of things, I'll grant you that." Ethan grinned abruptly. "Forget I tried to give you the dose of fatherly advice. A man my age sometimes takes a few liberties he's got no right to take. Besides, if you scratch deep enough, you'd probably find out my motivations weren't exactly pure as the new driven snow.''

''Meaning you're jealous?''

''You bet,'' Ethan acknowledged fervently. ''The reason a man my age starts offering fatherly advice is precisely because he's a mite envious of a man your age. It's our way of getting even with you young folks. Spiteful. Downright spiteful.''

Landry's eyes lightened with fleeting humor. ''That showgirl I saw hanging on your arm last month in Vegas didn't seem interested in finding anyone younger than you!''

Ethan sighed grandly and shook his head. ''Sad to say, I'm afraid my main attraction for that little gal was my bank account. Unfortunately I doubt that Miss Honor would be similarly impressed.''

''You don't think so?'' Landry asked thoughtfully.

''Well,'' Ethan drawled lightly, ''I suppose it might be worth a try.''

Landry was startled by the sudden, unexpected tension that flashed through him as he pictured Ethan Bailey or anyone else trying to impress Honor Mayfield. He must be crazy, he told himself. Ethan was only teasing him. Deliberately he summoned up a determined casualness. ''Hands off, Ethan, old buddy, I saw her first.''

''And when do you plan on seeing her next?''

Landry glanced around at the quiet grounds. ''This morning. I invited her to come watch the workouts.'' His eyes narrowed faintly as he glanced at his watch. ''She said she'd try to make it.''

''Maybe something came up,'' Ethan said. ''The lady's got a business to run, didn't you say? Some kind of decorating work?''

''Interior designs for offices. Homes, too, I think,'' Conn answered absently, beginning to wonder if Honor might be going to stand him up after all. He'd called her yesterday, the morning after their dinner date, and issued the invitation to join him at the track today. The lure was an attractive one, he'd told himself. He had a hunch she'd enjoy watching the horses working out. She had seemed initially hesitant and then in a little rush of enthusiasm, she'd said she'd try to make it.

He'd been certain she'd show. Everything seemed to be falling into place quite neatly. When he'd accepted the check the other night they'd both known it didn't erase the debt between them. He'd seen the gratitude in her eyes. It had been coupled with caution, but it had been genuine.

She'd been frightened of Granger and he'd assumed the task of dealing with the man on her behalf. In addition, he'd kept her from getting mixed up with the police trap that had been set in the parking lot. A real knight in shining armor, Landry told himself sardonically. Then he wondered why the image bothered him.

There were a lot of things bothering him that shouldn't have been making him uneasy. He didn't understand it. Everything had seemed so simple and straightforward when he'd originally decided to track her down. The decision had been based on an intuitive, gut-level feeling that there were questions to be asked and that the only one left who might have some answers was Honor Mayfield. It wasn't that he thought she would really know what had happened all those years ago, but she was a Mayfield. Through her he might be able to satisfy the uncertainties, the *wrongness,* the sense of injustice that had haunted him so long. But she would run if she found out who he was. In fact, she would probably be wise to run. So he had to ensnare her firmly before he revealed himself.

And now that he'd kissed her, Landry knew the first strands of the web were securely locked in place. The response from her had been unmistakable. His body still remembered it, along with the seething frustration of knowing that the time was not yet right to push her into bed.

Yes, she'd show up this morning, he told himself, aware of a sense of satisfaction. The bonds of gratitude and sexual attraction were in place. The combination was a strong one—with any luck at all, an irresistible one.

"Here she is." Ethan Bailey interrupted Conn's thoughts to wave cheerfully at Honor, who was walking toward them with a foam cup of coffee in her hand. "Over here, Miss Honor."

Conn turned his head to look at her, aware of a certain possessive pleasure. She looked good this morning, her hair brushed back behind one ear and held with a clip. An indigo-blue chambray shirt was belted over a pair of snug-fitting jeans. Something about the way she moved as she walked toward him sent a flare of anticipation through him. Conn got to his feet.

Honor saw the hunter looking out at her from Conn Landry's eyes as she came up to the railing. It sent a tiny jolt through her, even as she acknowledged the sense of pleasure she felt in his presence. Perhaps she had been right early this morning when she'd told herself it might be better to forgo the invitation. Every time she was with Conn she risked deepening an involvement that she sensed was dangerous. Yet here she was, unable to stay away.

"I was beginning to think you might not make it," Conn said quietly after the greetings had been exchanged. His gaze moved over her, seeming to take in every detail.

"I wasn't sure myself." She smiled politely and sipped her coffee, refusing to elaborate. "Is that one of your horses, Ethan?"

"Yes, ma'am," Bailey declared proudly as he set a stopwatch to time the filly. "Paid a handsome sum for that little lady. Expect great things from her."

"Ethan expects great things from all his horses," Conn remarked.

"I want more than tax shelters, I want a winner," Ethan said firmly. "All the tax sheltering in the world ain't as satisfying as one good win."

''How long have you owned racehorses?'' Honor asked curiously.

''Oh, years. More than I care to count. Gets in a man's blood.''

''Is it in your blood, Conn?'' she asked, looking directly at him.

''I don't know yet. Legacy is the first horse I've owned,'' he told her flatly. The gray eyes were very cool as he returned her questioning glance. ''A lot of things besides racing can get in a man's blood.''

Honor felt a prickle of alarm. ''Such as?'' she challenged with false lightness.

''A woman.''

''Or hot coffee,'' Ethan Bailey inserted suddenly, as if sensing the new tension in the air. ''That cup of java sure looks good, Honor.''

''I got it at a concession stand. They've opened one to serve people who are attending the workout session this morning. If I'd known you didn't have any I would have picked up an extra couple of cups.'' She felt oddly grateful to the older man for having dispelled the momentary uneasiness caused by Conn's words.

''What say we get ourselves some, Conn?'' Ethan suggested promptly.

Landry got to his feet. ''I'll get the coffee.'' He turned and paced toward the concession stand.

Honor watched him, conscious of the smooth coordination of his stride. He was wearing jeans today and an open-throated khaki shirt that suited the hunter she had seen in his eyes a few moments earlier. Honor shifted restlessly and took another sip of her coffee.

For the hundredth time since he had left her the night before last, she told herself she would be wise to ease out of the rclationship that was developing between herself and Conn Landry. And for the hundredth time she decided she'd wait just a little longer before making a firm decision in the matter.

''He's an interesting man, Honor.'' Ethan spoke quite gently as he picked up the field glasses and focused them on his filly.

''Have you known him long, Ethan?'' She wasn't quite sure how to ask all the questions she wanted answered about Conn.

''Just since he bought Legacy. He's new to the racing world.''

It seemed to Honor that Ethan was about to say more and then changed his mind. She felt an overpowering urge to push a little further. ''Do you know what, uh, kind of business he's in?''

Ethan lifted one shoulder indifferently. ''Well, I believe he's made a few substantial investments.''

''In what?''

Ethan lowered the field glasses and gave her a vaguely troubled look. ''Business investments. You know, a bit of this and a bit of that.''

''Where are these investments?'' she tried to ask casually, deeply aware of the older man's hesitation.

Ethan cleared his throat. ''I think he mentioned Tahoe at one point.'' Then his face brightened. ''Lots of lovely land up around Lake Tahoe.''

''Lots of lovely gambling casinos, too,'' Honor noted dryly. ''Is Conn involved in gambling, Ethan?''

''Don't you think you should be asking Landry these questions, Honor?'' the older man asked with obvious unease. It was clear he was feeling awkward.

She felt a wave of embarrassment. ''You're probably right. Sorry. It's just that he's a difficult man to get to know. Doesn't talk about himself much.''

''There's usually a good reason why a man doesn't want to talk about himself,'' Ethan said very soberly. ''Sometimes it's best to respect that privacy.''

Honor considered her next comment but went ahead and made it anyway. ''He did me a big favor yesterday, Ethan.''

''Handling Granger for you? Yeah, he said something about that. Everyone knows Granger's bad news.'' There was a meaningful pause. ''But a lady probably ought to be careful about taking favors from Conn Landry.''

She went still, aware of more than just a subtle hint of warning in Ethan Bailey's words. Impulsively she put out a hand and touched his arm. ''Ethan, please. Is there something I should know about Conn?''

Bailey exhaled deeply. ''Honor, I like Conn Landry. I like him a lot. But the plain truth is, I'm not sure he's the sort of man a woman such as yourself should be getting mixed up with, if you take my meaning.''

''I'm not sure that I do,'' she said quietly.

''Oh, hell, listen to me,'' Ethan growled with what sounded like forced humor, ''I've been sounding like someone's Dutch uncle all morning. I surely didn't mean to go and make you nervous. You're a big girl. Last thing you need is advice from an old goat like me.''

Honor smiled warmly at him, knowing he wanted to be off the hook. ''You're hardly an old goat, Ethan Bailey.''

He slanted her a quick glance. ''Are you kidding? I'm old enough to be your father. Or Landry's father, come to that.''

''Don't you know that owning horses makes you fascinating to most females?'' She chuckled as she spotted Conn on his way back with the coffee. ''Women love horses.''

''Is that a fact?''

''Is what a fact?'' Landry asked as he handed Ethan a cup.

''Honor, here, was just telling me that women love horses, and that men like me who own them are *fascinating*.'' He seemed vastly pleased with the word.

''Let's not forget I own one, too,'' Conn said blandly, his gaze raking Honor's features. ''Does that mean I'm in the fascinating category?''

Honor was saved from having to answer because at that moment Bailey's beautiful filly came thundering past. Immediately all attention went to the horse. Morning workouts were, after all, a serious business.

An hour later, when Honor finally decided she ought to be getting back to work, Conn walked her to her red Fiat. It was the first time they'd been alone that morning. As they halted beside the car, he turned her to face him, his strong hands settling on her waist.

"Did you miss me the other night after I left?"

It was difficult to lie to a man with eyes the color of gunmetal, Honor discovered. She compromised. "Actually, I had other things on my mind," she informed him flippantly.

"Another man?"

She didn't like the way he said that. "Not quite. A little matter of a folding screen that wasn't where it should have been."

He frowned. "What are you talking about?"

Honor sighed. "Remember when you came into my bedroom and found me checking under the bed?"

"I remember."

"Well, I was doing that because I had a funny feeling that something wasn't quite right. I know it sounds ridiculous, but a designer develops an unconscious eye for the details of a room. And I know my own place so well that when the least little item isn't in the right location, I'm aware of it."

"A screen wasn't in the right place?"

"I use it to hide my television set," she explained, feeling vaguely silly. "It had been moved a few inches. Figuring out why and when kept me busy for a while."

He tilted his head to one side, studying her. "And what kind of answers did you come up with?"

"The most logical one is that my younger sister visited the apartment while we were out that evening. She has a set of keys, and she's been known to make raids on my wardrobe."

"Had she visited your place?" Conn persisted.

Honor shook her head, remembering the phone call she had made the next morning to Adena. "She said she hadn't, but to tell you the truth she was so busy singing your praises for having handled Granger that I'm not sure she was paying much attention to my question! You've got a real fan in Adena.''

He ignored that last comment. ''So what about the screen?''

''Well, another possibility is that the apartment manager let herself in for some reason or another. Unfortunately she went out of town yesterday morning and won't be back until tomorrow. I won't be able to ask her until then. And then there's the last possible reason.''

''Which is?''

Honor smiled humorously. ''That my so-called trained designer eye isn't quite as good as I assumed. All in all, the whole incident doesn't amount to much.''

''Nothing was missing?''

''Nothing.''

''Then it wasn't a robbery attempt.''

''Fortunately I was saved that bit of melodrama,'' Honor said feelingly. ''One of my friends got hit six months ago. The thieves cleaned out everything except the carpet. Don't look so concerned, Conn. Obviously there's some perfectly logical explanation for the screen having been shifted a few inches. I've stopped worrying about it.''

''But it kept you from thinking about me that night,'' he murmured, rubbing the edge of his thumb along the line of her jaw.

No, it hadn't kept her from thinking about him but Honor decided it was best to let his assumption stand. Instinct warned her that it would be risky to let Conn know just how much he filled her mind. What was it Ethan had said? *I'm not sure he's the sort of man a woman such as yourself should be getting mixed up with.* She wasn't at all sure, either.

''Will six o'clock be okay for dinner tonight?'' Conn asked softly, his thumb caressing her chin now.

Almost violently aware of the small, intimate touch, Honor

reminded herself of her own uncertainties regarding this man. The way he asked told her he had no doubts at all but that she'd be free for him tonight. His confidence scared her.

"I'm sorry, Conn, but I have a business engagement tonight."

The gray eyes chilled. "A date?"

"You could call it that." She owed him no explanations, she assured herself.

His thumb stopped its gentle stroking and she felt his fingers as he lightly touched her throat. "Cancel it, Honor."

She swallowed, a frisson of fear flickering through her. "I can't do that. I have a business to run, Conn. Don't you know anything about the pressures of business?"

"I know about business pressures. I also know something about nervous fillies. Relax, Honor. Cancel your other engagement and come to dinner with me." His voice was rough and persuasive, a lover's voice.

Honor reacted to it, hovered on the brink of surrender and then retreated barely in time. "No, no, I can't do that, Conn. I'm sorry but I really do have to be going. Thank you for inviting me to the workouts this morning. I enjoyed them. How much longer will you be in town?" She made the question casual, subtly emphasizing the short-term nature of their association.

He watched her slide quickly into the front seat of the Fiat, closing the door as if it were a locked gate behind which she would be safe.

"It all depends."

Honor frowned up at him, eyes narrowed against the sun. "Depends on what?" she asked as she turned the key in the ignition.

"On some business matters I'm handling."

"I thought you were only here to see Legacy run."

"I'm taking the opportunity of tying up a few loose ends," he said coolly.

She hated it when he was so damn cryptic. "Well, I certainly wouldn't want to keep you from attending to business.'' Honor put the car in gear and drove off without glancing back.

She had been undecided about whether to attend the private party being held to celebrate the opening of a new restaurant that evening. The interior had been designed by a friend, however, and Honor knew Susan Mallory would appreciate having her show up. A finished project gave a designer the same sense of pleasure and satisfaction as a finished painting gave an artist. By the very nature of the business, neither could retain possession of the creations. There was only a limited period of time for the creator to enjoy it and show it off.

Honor didn't try to kid herself as she dressed for the event. She had made the decision to attend based almost entirely on an instinctive desire to put some distance between herself and Conn Landry.

Ethan Bailey's awkward but well-meant warnings had only served to crystallize her own uncertainties concerning Conn. He was getting too close, too fast.

Honor checked the sweep of the magenta-colored blouson dress she had chosen to wear and then brushed her hair back into a neat twist at the nape of her neck. It was difficult to get excited about the evening ahead. All she could think of was how much anticipation she would be feeling now if she were waiting for Conn Landry to collect her.

The festivities were in full swung by the time Honor arrived. She drifted through the crowd of fellow designers, reporters, friends of the proud new owner and local restaurateurs, idly searching for Susan. En route she helped herself to the unlimited quantities of exotic cheeses that had been set out. When the crush of people maneuvered her close to the bar, she ended up with a plastic cup of a low-budget Italian wine that helped wash down the cheese. She wondered what Conn was doing at that moment.

''Honor! You made it! I'm so glad. Tell me, what do you think?'' Susan Mallory, attired in the latest of oddly layered

Japanese fashions, pushed through the crowd toward her. In one hand she held a plastic glass of wine and with the other she waved at the art deco interiors she had designed.

Honor smiled at her attractive dark-haired friend. "It's wonderful, Susan. Absolutely wonderful. It's just too bad that it's not customary to put up a little plaque saying who designed the space."

"I know." Susan sighed theatrically. "No one ever thinks to credit the designer." She brightened. "But I have gotten some good referrals out of it."

"Good. How are the wedding plans going?" Honor helped herself to a chunk of imported Camembert.

"Perfectly," Susan enthused. "As a matter of fact I was going to call you next week and ask if the beach cottage was going to be available."

"Second week in June?" Honor tried to reconstruct the rental schedule in her head. "I think so. The agent said he'd booked it for the month of August, but part of June was still free. What made you decide to honeymoon in Ventura? Isn't that a bit ordinary? I thought you were going to Hawaii or Puerto Vallarta?"

"Everyone goes to Hawaii," Susan informed her blithely. "And those who don't, go to Puerto Vallarta. Richard and I discussed the matter the other night, and when I told him that you owned a charming, secluded place right on the beach just up the coast, we decided to ask if it was available. Going to use the house yourself this year?"

"I rarely use it," Honor said quietly, thinking of the beach cottage that had been her only inheritance from her father, other than a small trust fund that had helped see her through college. "Once in a while during the winter when it's not being rented out I spend a weekend there, but that's about it."

"I don't see why you don't use it more often. I love the marvelous country retreat look you achieved with all that lovely rustic furniture and those horse-racing photos scattered on the walls. I had a great time there last summer.''

Honor thought of the pictures of Stylish Legacy that had belonged to her father and that she had left in place at the cottage, along with a variety of other racing mementos and paraphernalia. It was difficult to explain that she had always found visits to the cottage vaguely depressing. Memories of that traumatic year when she was thirteen seemed to be waiting for her there. It was easier to give a more rational explanation for her failure to use the beach house.

''I'd lose the rental tax advantages if I spent too much time there,'' she said easily.

''Oh, of course,'' Susan said. Being a Californian, she understood the implications of tax-advantaged investments immediately. People in California worried a lot about such investments. ''Does your sister use it?''

''Rarely. My mother used to go there occasionally before she remarried and moved back east. Basically I'm just hanging on to the place for the appreciation and for tax purposes. And if it's free that second week in June, you're welcome to use it.''

''Great, I'll tell Richard. Come along, I want to introduce you to my client.''

''The gentleman in the mauve suit?''

''That's him.''

By ten o'clock Honor decided she'd had enough cheese to supply her calcium needs for a month. She was tired of the party and tired of the endless cocktail chatter. It was time to leave. It was with a feeling of relief that she headed out into the parking lot to find her Fiat.

She didn't notice the headlights in her rearview mirror until she was only a few blocks from her apartment. Honor didn't know when it occurred to her that the same pair of headlights seemed to have been behind her for quite some distance, but when the thought finally did strike home she felt her palms grow damp on the steering wheel.

It was not unheard-of for a lone woman driver to find herself being followed, forced off the road and assaulted. Honor had read that one technique for dealing with the situation was to drive to the nearest police station. On no account were you supposed to lead the trailing car to your home.

But she was only a block away from the apartment house now and she couldn't be absolutely certain she was being followed.

The headlights edged in closer behind her as she turned onto her quiet street. If she was being followed the vehicle could probably close in so quickly that it would slip through the automatic gate of the apartment garage when she opened it to let herself inside. Honor could easily find herself trapped inside the locked garage with whoever was driving the other car.

Then, again, it could be her imagination at work. The same vivid imagination that had insisted on believing someone had moved the screen in her room the other night.

Honor considered her options and decided to drive on past her apartment. She would circle the block and see if the other car followed. If it did, then she would lose no time racing back out onto a more crowded thoroughfare and heading toward the nearest police station.

The other vehicle was suddenly very close behind her, its headlights on high beam so that she could see nothing in the mirror except a blinding glare. She was about to accelerate past the apartment complex when her own lights picked out the silver-gray Porsche parked at the curb. There was a dark figure in the driver's seat.

Quite suddenly Conn Landry's presence seemed the most reassuring sight she'd seen in a long time. Without pausing to think, Honor pulled in to the curb behind him, aware that the car behind her was slowing, too.

Switching off the ignition, she was out of the Fiat and running toward the Porsche before the tailing vehicle could edge in to the curb.

She saw the door of the Porsche swing open and then Landry was in front of her. In that moment his quiet power offered precisely the comfort and safety she wanted. Honor threw herself into his arms.

"Honor? What the hell—?"

The angry roar of a pickup truck motor cut off his startled demands. A second later the black truck accelerated past and disappeared around the corner.

Honor glanced up briefly to get a quick look at the vehicle but she made no effort to pull free of the iron-hard embrace in which she was wrapped.

"I think...I think that truck was following me," she managed as relief surged through her. "It had been behind me for blocks. I've heard of weirdos who do that, you know, follow a woman home and then attack her. I was going to drive on past when I saw your car. Oh, Conn, I've never been so glad to see anyone before in my life! What on earth are you doing here, anyway?"

"Guess," he growled succinctly. When she looked up at him with puzzled eyes, he sighed and loosened his grip on her long enough to close his car door. "I was waiting for you, naturally. Why else would I be sitting out here in front of your apartment building at this hour of the night?"

Honor's racing pulse slowed to a more normal level as the full implications of his presence hit her. "I'll assume that last crack is a rhetorical question." She pulled free of his encircling arm, smoothing her dress. "Don't get me wrong, Conn, I really was glad to see you, but I think it would be interesting to know exactly what you thought you were going to accomplish sitting out here in the first place."

"Let's go inside and I'll explain it all in great detail," he murmured, taking her arm. "But first of all tell me about that truck."

"I honestly don't know any more than I just told you. A California crazy who gets his kicks following single women, I suppose. I should report him to the cops."

''Report what? That truck didn't even have a license plate on it.''

''Well, he's gone now, thank heavens.''

Conn propelled her lightly through the gate and up one flight of stairs to her apartment. It was as he took her key to open her front door that Honor realized she still didn't know what he was doing here.

''Conn, about this business of you waiting for me,'' she began with what she hoped was a suitably imperious air, ''I'd like to know just what you thought you were going to accomplish.''

He slanted her an unreadable glance as he stepped around her and headed for the red lacquered cabinet that contained the brandy.

''Priority number one was to see who would be bringing you home.'' He poured a shot of brandy into a glass. Then he raised the glass in a faint salute. ''Priority number two was to make sure you didn't take him upstairs.''

Honor heard the quiet arrogance in his words and swallowed uneasily. ''As you can see, I'm really not into truck drivers.'' She decided to go on the offensive. ''Did it occur to you that I might object to your making yourself right at home with my brandy?''

He stalked toward her with cool, masculine grace. ''It seems to me that offering me a drink is the least you could do under the circumstances.''

''What circumstances?'' she flared.

''I've been around when you needed me lately, haven't I?''

She licked her lower lip. ''No one asked you to be around, Conn.''

''But you've been grateful, nevertheless, haven't you?'' He took a large swallow of the brandy and regarded her with his gunmetal eyes. ''How was your *business* engagement, Honor? Have a good time?''

''Reasonably so,'' she said, mustering her composure. ''Until that truck picked me up on the way home.''

He nodded, taking another sip of brandy. Conn was wearing the jeans and the khaki shirt he'd had on earlier that day, Honor realized vaguely. The dark clothing combined with his somber, dangerous mood made him a formidable force in her living room.

"I think it's time for a little honesty from you, Honor Mayfield," he told her consideringly.

"What, exactly, do you want me to be honest about?"

"The reason you wouldn't have dinner with me tonight will do for a start."

"I told you, I had a business engagement."

"A very convenient one."

"Are you accusing me of something, Conn?"

"Yes. Avoiding me. And I'd like to know why."

Honor tried to move around him and found he was somehow blocking her path. She lifted her chin with cool hauteur. "Because there's too much I don't know about you. You frighten me a little, Conn, and I think you realize it."

The gray eyes flickered. "Yes."

"Then why put me through the third degree about this evening?" she challenged tightly. "Unless you really want to scare me for some reason."

She had the oddest feeling that he was forced to stop and think about the answer to that question. There was a tension in the room that wasn't doing much to dry her already damp palms. This evening was turning into a full-scale disaster.

"You have a point, Honor," Conn said finally. "I don't have any right to dictate how you spend your nights, do I?"

"No," she got out in a thin whisper.

"The problem is that I'd like that right," he continued.

"Conn, please..."

"I'd like you to know that I'll be there when things turn nasty the way they did with Granger and the way they did tonight when that truck followed you. I'd like you to trust me, Honor. I want you to know you don't have to get nervous and make up excuses for not seeing me."

His words poured over her in a rough, sensual cascade that caught at Honor's senses. But they weren't simply smooth lover's lies. There was an underlying urgency in them that forced her to accept their sincerity. In that moment she wasn't even sure Conn himself realized the intensity with which he was speaking.

Honor watched him as he moved toward her, aware of the swirl of male hunger in his gaze. She remembered the reassuring feeling of his arms going around her earlier out on the street and realized she wanted to know that sensation again.

"Conn, there's so much we don't know about each other," she tried with a touch of desperation.

He set down the brandy glass and touched the base of her throat with a remarkably sensitive fingertip. The desire in his eyes was an endless gray sea.

"I agree. There is much we don't know about each other. But I think tonight would be a good time to discover some basic truths."

Whatever her answer would have been, it was swallowed up in the depths of his kiss.

Four

It came as a shock to Conn to discover that he didn't want her to be afraid of him, that, instead, he wanted her to trust him. It was a further surprise to find out just how protective he now felt toward her. The image of himself wearing a suit of polished armor should have made him laugh but it didn't. He was beginning to experience a possessiveness that should have made him uneasy.

When he'd found himself sitting in the car out in front of her apartment, waiting to see who would bring her home, Conn had finally acknowledged that he had a problem, one he hadn't counted on having to handle.

He'd planned on being the one who spun the web; he hadn't anticipated the danger of getting tangled up in the delicate, sticky strands himself. He would never remain objective enough to sort out the truth if he lost control of himself and the situation.

Now, tonight, it seemed very important that he regain control over events and in the process satisfy this dangerous desire that was threatening to undermine his original goals.

Yes, Conn told himself as he felt the trembling re-sponse on Honor's lips, that's what he was doing tonight. He was simply regaining control.

Her mouth was soft and warm. He wanted to crush it beneath his own, just as he wanted to crush her body into the embroidered quilt on her bed. The uncertainty in her was turning rapidly into passion. He was holding a woman who wanted him, even if she wasn't sure she ought to want him. Sensing her desire, his own soared.

''It's all right, sweetheart,'' he breathed as he freed her mouth to taste the warm sweetness of her throat. ''Just let go. Just let it happen. I'll be right there with you and I'll take care of everything.''

''Conn,'' she whispered shakily, ''I wanted time. I'm not sure of anything right now.''

He wrapped his fingers lightly around the nape of her neck and used his thumbs to lift her chin so that she had to meet his eyes. Her gaze was half-drugged with a combination of desire and wariness.

''I'm the man who's there when you need him, remember?'' he reminded her softly. ''And you need me tonight. We need each other. I don't make a habit of sitting in front of a woman's apartment waiting to see who will bring her home. I was there for nearly two hours, trying to imagine how I would handle the other guy.''

''What…what would you have done if I'd been with someone else?''

He groaned and pulled her fiercely against him. ''Don't ask. Finding out you'd been followed by some punk in a pickup truck was even more of a shock, though. I don't like your living alone. It's dangerous.''

''Yes, I know.'' She made the comment into his dark shirt, and Conn knew she meant it to cover him as well as stray hoodlums in black trucks.

''Don't be afraid of me, Honor.''

He didn't know how to counter her caution with words, but Conn did know that he needed to touch her more intimately. The scent of her was tantalizing, beckoning, full of womanly promise.

''I couldn't resist you tonight even if I wanted to try. And the last thing I want to do is try,'' he grated. He slid his palms down her back to the rounded curve of her hips. She murmured something into his shirt as he pulled her lower body against his own. Conn knew from the way she tensed and then softened that she was now fully aware of his arousal.

"Conn, we should talk..." Her voice trailed off beneath his mouth.

"In the morning," he promised when he released her lips. "We'll talk in the morning. We'll settle everything in the morning."

"Will we?" Her eyes were questioning, luminous pools in which a man could get lost.

"Please trust me tonight, Honor." Was that him pleading for a woman's trust, Conn wondered vaguely. Tomorrow when he was more rational he would probably be shocked at the husky words. But tonight he longed only for an affirmative response.

"Can I trust you, Conn Landry?"

He moved abruptly, lifting her up into his arms.

"Yes, you can trust me!" The vow was ground out with a force that amazed him. She seemed to accept the rough promise. Her arms wound around his neck and surrender flickered through her body, making her even warmer and gentler than he had imagined.

Conn left the lights off in her bedroom as he carried her through the door. The pale glow from the hall provided all the illumination he needed. Standing her carefully on her feet he fumbled for the fastenings of her bright-magenta dress. When she leaned against him, her head nestled on his shoulder, he wondered what the hell had happened to his normally coordinated hands. His fingers never trembled like this.

It seemed to take forever before the silky garment obligingly gave way and fell into a frothy heap around her feet.

"Honor," he murmured wonderingly, drawing his hands lightly around her shoulders and down to the curve of her breasts. He touched the lacy edge of her bra, sliding one finger underneath to find the peaking tip of her nipple. "Honor, I want you so much."

She said his name into his shoulder, her nails sinking into the fabric of his shirt. "You make it impossible for me to even think tonight. Why is it like this with you, Conn?"

With a small, impatient gesture he unsnapped the front hook of her bra. His palms slipped over her breasts. ''I don't know,'' he heard himself say with unexpected honesty. ''I could ask you the same question. Why do I feel like this with you? I never meant—''

''Never meant what?'' She raised her head to look up at him through her lashes.

''Never mind. Don't think about anything other than tonight, sweetheart. Heaven knows you're all I can think about at the moment.'' He framed her face with his hands and kissed her druggingly, glorying in the vibrant response he received. ''Take off my shirt. Let me feel your hands on my body,'' he ordered thickly.

She obeyed willingly, her fingers shaking faintly as she struggled with the buttons of his shirt. But in a moment she had it off and then she tugged awkwardly with the buckle of his leather belt.

Trying not to hurry, but knowing he could barely contain his need, Conn finished undressing her. He slid his hands down the length of her, dragging off the satiny underpants and the gossamer panty hose. When she pushed at his snug-fitting jeans, he stepped back and tugged at them himself.

A moment later his jockey shorts fell to his feet and he heard Honor's sharp intake of breath as she saw the evidence of his rising desire.

''I told you I wanted you, sweetheart. Did you doubt me?'' he said in a husky voice, aware that he needed some sign of her acceptance of him as a lover. Why it mattered he couldn't have said. He only knew that he wanted her to affirm her desire for him. He wanted her to need him as much as he needed her. ''Are you still afraid of me?''

She shook her head, stepping close so that she could feel his excitement pressing hungrily against the smooth skin of her stomach. She cupped him gently with her hands and Conn thought he would lose all control.

''I want you, Conn.'' There was a mesmerizing sincerity

in her throaty voice. ''I don't completely understand all of my feelings tonight, but I know I want you.''

''Honor, I'll make it good for you, I swear it.''

Her mouth curved gently in an age-old smile of feminine promise and provocation. ''What if I'm the one who doesn't make it good for you?''

''Little cat,'' he murmured, determined to kiss the sensual teasing out of her. ''You couldn't be anything but perfect for me.'' He lowered his head and parted her lips with his mouth, forcing his tongue deep inside. Then he shaped her buttocks in his hands, letting his fingers graze tantalizingly over her flesh. When he heard her gasp of anticipation he stroked around to the front of her body and touched her intimately between her thighs.

Honor moaned, and his own pulse beat heavily as he felt the dampening heat of her. When she seemed to lose her balance and collapse lightly against him, Conn knew a primitive sense of masculine satisfaction. Leaning down he yanked back the quilt on her bed and then he lifted Honor and settled her gently into the depths of the bedclothes.

She fell back sensuously, her hair fanning out on the pillow, hazel eyes gleaming up at him through her lashes. ''Have you hypnotized me, Conn Landry? It's either that or I must be slightly out of my head tonight.''

He felt the fire in his veins as he stood staring down at her. If he'd experienced a feeling of possessiveness earlier it was nothing compared to this inferno leaping through him now.

''I'm glad you're feeling disoriented,'' he muttered as he came down beside her in a heavy rush. ''This is just the way I want you, warm and welcoming and all mine. I don't want you to be able to think straight. Not tonight.''

He buried his mouth against the base of her throat, stroking his palm down her stomach to the treasures below. She whispered his name in aching desire and he felt the readiness in her. When she arched her hips against him in silent demand he told himself he'd make her wait a little longer. He wanted her so hot and passionate that she would not be able to imagine living the rest of the night without having him inside her. It was, after all, exactly the way he himself was feeling.

"Tell me about it, Honor, honey. Tell me how much you want me." He made the demands in a husky tone in between stringing kisses across her breasts.

"So much, Conn, I want you so very much. I've never felt like this." She lifted her hips again, grasping his shoulders to urge him to her.

He pushed one knee between her legs and felt her open immediately for him. The invitation jerked a rough cry of passion from him and he knew he couldn't wait any longer. Conn settled himself between her thighs, aware of her fiery need teasing him.

"Take me inside, sweetheart. I have to be inside you or I'll go crazy!" He moved his hand down to touch the folds of exquisitely sensitive feminine flesh, assuring himself once again that she was ready. She murmured in passionate response.

"Please, Conn. Please, *now!*"

He couldn't hold back any longer. Catching her shoulders, he thrust deeply, embedding himself in her pulsating, clinging warmth. He felt the shudder go through her as her body adjusted to the masculine invasion. Instantly he stopped.

"Honor?"

She didn't open her eyes but her legs moved slowly to wrap his lean hips. He felt her nails in his back and the small pain sent another ripple of excitement through him.

"Love me, Conn. Please make love to me."

"Honor, I couldn't do anything else!" He began to move within her, feeling her body growing increasingly tense around him.

"Conn, *Conn!*"

He sensed the uncertainty in the breathless way she called his name and dimly realized she wasn't quite sure of what was happening to her body.

''Let go, sweetheart,'' he rasped against her breast. ''Just let go. I'll catch you.''

She cried out as the heightening tension suddenly unleashed itself in one shattering conclusion. Conn lifted his head to cover her mouth, drinking the passionate sounds she made far back in her throat, and then he felt his body arching heavily as it sought its own release.

For long, timeless seconds he rode the storm with the woman in his arms, holding on to her more tightly than he'd ever held on to anything or anyone in his life.

Honor came slowly out of the hazy world into which she had drifted. She was aware of Conn's heavy frame sprawled along hers, felt the weight of his thigh chaining her leg. She was still wrapped securely in his arms, and the knowledge filled her with deep pleasure. Languidly she toyed with the silver-shot blackness of his hair, studying the dark lashes that were the only hint of softness in his face. Then he opened his eyes.

Like a cat, he was fully alert instantly, no hint of sleepiness or sensual lethargy in his gaze. But there was a strong element of satisfaction there, Honor realized—sure, arrogant, masculine satisfaction. She found it somewhat amusing until he spoke.

''No more nights like tonight,'' he said bluntly.

''No? You didn't enjoy tonight?'' she teased lightly, knowing he couldn't possibly be referring to what had just happened between them.

Conn shook his head once, impatiently, and then lifted himself off her body with obvious reluctance. ''I meant no more nights where I sit in front of your apartment and wait to see who's bringing you home.'' He cradled her possessively in the crook of his arm. The musky scent of him filled her nostrils as she burrowed willingly against his shoulder.

''How many more nights will there be to worry about, Conn? Soon you'll be going back to Tahoe and you won't be terribly interested in how I spend my evenings.''

The wave of unhappiness that washed over her as she listened to her own words occupied her for several seconds. Then she noticed in astonishment that Conn had gone dangerously still.

''Who told you about Tahoe?'' he asked, his voice low and harsh.

Honor stirred uneasily. ''Ethan said something about your having business interests there.'' She turned her head to meet his eyes.

''That's all I have there. I don't make my home in Tahoe,'' he said in clipped tones. ''I just own some real estate there.''

''I see.'' Honor wasn't certain what to say next. Clearly he didn't want to talk about Tahoe or where he actually did live. And she didn't want to spoil the magic intimacy of the moment. There would be time enough in the morning for discovering all the facts that mattered. ''It's all right, Conn. I didn't mean to pry. And you don't owe me any promises or commitments. I understand that.''

The information didn't seem to please him. ''The hell I don't,'' he growled, twisting to pin her gently back against the pillow. ''Honor, you and I are bound together now. Don't you understand that? You just gave yourself to me.''

''Do you realize what you're saying, Conn?'' she asked carefully, afraid to let herself hope for too much from him.

''I know exactly what I'm saying,'' he told her evenly. ''I couldn't walk away from what we've started. And I won't let you walk, either.''

She smiled tremulously. ''Do I look as though I'm trying to get away?''

''You tried to avoid me this evening,'' he pointed out gruffly. He sounded as if the fact had hurt him in some fashion.

Her fingers moved in delicate patterns on his broad shoulders. Unintimidated by the harsh lines of his face, she looked up at him with the soft eyes of a woman who knows she's falling in love.

"That was earlier. This is now," she explained as if it were obvious.

"You're not frightened of me any longer?"

"I don't think I was ever really scared, just wary," she said dismissingly.

"And you're not still wary?" he pressed.

"Should I be?" she countered lightly, not understanding why he was so insistent.

"No," he rasped, lowering his mouth once more to hers. "There's no need any longer."

A part of her wanted to ask what that meant, but he was already restoking the fires it seemed only he could ignite. Honor felt the throbbing intensity in him and had no wish to resist.

The commitment between them was new and untried, fragile and unexplored, but it had been established. Conn was right. Neither of them could walk away from it now.

Hours later Honor came slowly awake, aware that the man beside her was not asleep. She snuggled against his side.

"Conn? Is something wrong? Can't you sleep?"

"I'm just doing some thinking, honey."

"What about?"

"About that pickup truck that followed you home tonight. Among other things." The last three words were tacked on in an almost inaudible tone.

"What about the truck?" she pressed, yawning.

"I don't like the fact that somebody tried to get at you tonight."

She frowned slightly in the darkness. "You don't suppose there's a chance Granger sent someone after me?"

Conn shook his head once. "No, he'd have no reason to go after you. It would be your sister he'd try to terrorize and she—" He broke off as Honor suddenly sat bolt upright.

"My sister! Conn, what if he's going to do something to Adena?"

Conn reached up to pull her down. "Relax. As I was about

to say, she's paid her debt. Granger wouldn't go after her now.''

''You sound awfully sure of that.''

''I am sure.''

For some reason Honor believed him. The quiet strength in his words spoke volumes. She relaxed. ''Then the incident tonight was just another crazy Southern California event.''

''Unless you add it to that business of your screen being moved the other night,'' he said thoughtfully.

Honor was silent for a moment. ''I'm sure that was just a mistake on my part.''

''Positive?''

Lying there in the darkness with Conn's easy, masculine strength to cling to, it was easy to be positive. Honor nibbled invitingly at his lower lip.

''Positive.''

Honor awoke early the next morning with the feeling that her whole life had changed overnight. When she turned her head to gaze down on Conn's magnificently sprawled form, she knew the intuition was right. Even if he walked out on her today her life would never be quite the same because she would never be able to put him completely out of her head.

His body was lean and tan against the tangled white sheets. The intriguing darkness of his hair on the pillow made Honor want to reach out and run her fingers through it as she had last night.

Weren't harsh-faced men supposed to appear more relaxed and even gentler in sleep, she wondered idly as she studied the grim planes and angles of his face. If that was true, Conn didn't fit the mold. His strength and determination were too much a part of him to disappear temporarily while he slept. In the fresh light of a sunny morning he still looked like the kind of man only a fool would want for an enemy, the kind of man a woman would not risk pushing too far.

The realization sent a wave of restlessness through her that drove Honor out of bed. Barefoot, she padded into the black-

and-white-tiled bath. The full-length mirror threw her nude image back at her, revealing a mussed halo of golden-brown hair and eyes that reflected a deep, feminine wonder.

Conn had made love to her last night in the most satisfying way possible. He had not played sophisticated games, trying to dazzle her with technique and style. Instead he had lost himself in her, at the same time possessing her completely.

Admittedly her experience was limited, but Honor instinctively knew that the kind of passion she had experienced last night could not be a common thing.

Stepping into the shower, she let her pleasantly sore body soak beneath the hot spray. Every time she moved today she was going to be reminded of Conn's elemental style of lovemaking, she thought wryly.

She heard the bathroom door open and close. A moment later Conn appeared on the other side of the glass shower door, smiling lazily. One thing had changed about him, Honor realized suddenly. The smile was a full-fledged one this morning, not that strange, grim twist of his mouth with which she had become so familiar. That knowledge pleased her deeply.

He opened the shower and stepped inside, reaching for her. "Mmm," he murmured through a long, luxurious kiss, "you taste good in the morning."

"Considering the amount of goat cheese I sampled last night, that's saying something." She grinned, winding her arms around his neck.

"I consider it a part of the earthy side of your nature." He slicked his hands down her wet body to her hips, squeezing gently.

"I'm a Southern Californian. I'm not supposed to have an earthy side to my nature. I'm supposed to be all gloss and cutting-edge glitter," she complained.

"Then you're a failure as a Southern Californian. But I knew that the moment I met you."

She tilted her head. "You did?"

To her surprise he gave her a sober, intent look. "The last

thing you are is superficial, Honor. Even if your apartment does resemble a picture in a design magazine. I knew when I realized why you were going to confront Granger that you had guts. And your enthusiasm for Legacy's big win the other day was genuine, even though you only had two dollars on him. Last night you gave yourself completely to me. No games. I could list a lot of other reasons why I know you aren't the kind who flits along on the surface of life."

"But?" she prompted, a little shaken by his blunt observations and determined to lighten the atmosphere a little.

"But all my glowing compliments would probably go to your head and spoil the basic sweetness of your nature." He chuckled, slapping her affectionately on the rear and turning to pick up the soap.

"Beast. I was just getting to like the compliments. I'd rather hear them than listen to you yelling at me for daring to have another engagement last night."

"I didn't yell at you." He stuck his head under the full force of the water, eyes closed. "I simply explained a few facts of life."

She went still as she listened to the possessiveness in his voice. "Conn?"

"Hmm?"

"It works both ways, you know."

He pulled his head out from under the shower and opened his eyes. He looked down at her searchingly. "Both ways?"

"I won't be involved in a one-sided relationship," she said with quiet insistence. "I have to know that you'll live by the same rules you're imposing on me."

"You think I won't?" There was soft challenge in the words.

Honor studied him for a moment longer, thinking over what she knew of this man. It wasn't all that much in some respects. Yet a part of her longed to trust him implicitly. "I think you will." She finally smiled tremulously. Hadn't she sensed from the start that he was a man who lived by a code? He kept the scales balanced.

Conn moved, wrapping her close against his warm, wet chest. ‘‘Does that mean you trust me, finally?’’

Her fingers splayed through the damp, curling hair that covered him in a sexy pelt. ‘‘Yes.’’

‘‘Thank you, Honor. I’m glad,’’ he said simply.

So am I, she thought, *because I’m in love with you.*

An hour later Honor was slicing papaya and sprinkling it with lime while Conn made coffee. The doorbell chimed just as she was putting the fresh fruit on the table. Wiping her hands on a red kitchen towel, Honor went to answer it.

‘‘Adena!’’ she exclaimed. ‘‘What are you doing here?’’

‘‘Just dropped by on my way to work to see if I could borrow that great chunky leather belt you bought the other day. Hey, is that an extra slice of papaya? Great, I didn’t have time for breakfast this morning.’’

With her usual impulsive approach to everything, Adena whipped around the edge of the door and came to a halt, staring at Conn. Conn stared back, politely examining the flashy little gamine in front of him.

Adena’s bright blond hair was cut in an eye-catching wedge that framed her outrageously made-up hazel eyes. While Honor’s tastes in clothing were stylish, her sister’s were definitely trendy. A less charitable observer might have termed them outrageous. This morning Adena was wearing knee-high cavalry boots, tight-fitting red pants and a huge, boxy, loosely woven cropped top. She carried it off with her usual enthusiastic panache.

‘‘Good grief,’’ Adena said in obvious astonishment, ‘‘who are you? Honor *never* has men stay for breakfast.’’

‘‘I insisted, I’m afraid. You’re Adena?’’

‘‘That’s right.’’ Adena swung around with a grin. ‘‘Where did you dig him up, Honor? He’s much more interesting than those designer types you usually hang out with. Good grief! This one’s not even wearing mauve!’’

''This is Constantine Landry,'' Honor said very firmly. She could feel the faint flush on her cheeks as her inquisitive sister began to pry for information. ''I believe I mentioned him,'' she continued sardonically.

''Landry! The guy who handled Granger for me. Of course.'' Adena almost pounced on a somewhat startled Conn. ''You're an absolute jewel, you know.'' She kissed him noisily before he realized what was happening and then she released him to leap for the coffeepot. ''Can't tell you how much I appreciate your help. Took a terrible load off my mind. Granger gives me the creeps. And if I was worried, that's nothing to what poor Honor felt!'' Adena shivered theatrically as she helped herself to coffee.

''Then I trust you will stay away from him and others like him in the future. I don't expect to have to handle that kind of situation again, and if I find out you've tried to coerce Honor into doing it for you, I will be very displeased,'' Conn said flatly as he picked up the coffeepot and set it down on the table.

Honor heard the cold, lecturing tone and saw that Adena had heard it, too. Her volatile sister was not accustomed to having men lecture her.

''Hey, what's with the big brother attitude?'' Adena demanded, plunking herself down at the table. ''It's too early in the morning for that sort of thing. Any more papaya, Honor?''

''There's another one in the refrigerator, if you want to cut it.''

''Too much work. I'll share yours.'' Adena leaned forward to scoop out a sizable chunk of the deliciously colored fruit.

Stifling a sigh of resignation, Honor quickly began to eat the rest of the papaya, knowing that if she didn't she would lose most of it to Adena.

''I'm not your brother, big or otherwise,'' Conn pointed out grimly. ''My only interest is in your sister. I will therefore hold you responsible for anything you do that gets her into a difficult situation. Do I make myself clear?''

''Conn, there's no need to come down on her like a ton of bricks,'' Honor said a bit stiffly as she saw the uncomprehending expression on Adena's face. ''It was all a mistake and Adena knows it. She won't be getting into that kind of trouble again, will you, Adena?''

''Golly, I feel as if I'm sitting in the middle of a scene from 'Father Knows Best.' Doesn't it strike either of you that it's too nice a morning for lectures?'' Adena complained.

''What kind of a morning was it the day you first started borrowing from Granger?'' Conn calmly ate his papaya, oblivious of Honor's frowning glance.

''I get the point,'' Adena said disgustedly, shooting to her feet with lively grace. ''If you'll excuse me I think I'll be on my way. Something about the atmosphere around here is depressing. How about the belt, Honor? Okay if I take it?''

''Help yourself,'' Honor agreed, as she nearly always did. ''Oh, and Adena…?''

''What?'' Adena was halfway down the hall.

''Are you sure you weren't in here the other evening?''

''Positive. I went with Gary to see that new slasher movie I told you about.'' She disappeared into the bedroom and reappeared a moment later carrying the prized belt. ''My goodness, you two certainly did something energetic on that bed. Well, see you guys later.'' She was gone before either Conn or Honor could respond.

For a moment after the whirlwind left, silence hung over the table. Then Conn said very thoughtfully, ''I can see that she's been something of a handful for you. Your mother…?''

''My mother remarried a few years ago and moved to the East Coast. Adena wanted to stay out here with me. There are times when I'm afraid I may not have handled her all that well, but she's basically a good person.''

''Perhaps,'' Conn suggested carefully, ''she needed a firmer hand while she was growing up.''

"She was only eight when Dad was killed." Honor tried to put a lot of finality into the sentence.

"How old were you?"

"Thirteen. Conn, I don't really like to talk about the past," she explained quietly.

He stared at her for a moment. "You can't pretend it doesn't exist."

"I don't pretend it doesn't exist," she said coolly. "I just prefer not to discuss it. The circumstances surrounding my father's death were, well, traumatic for all of us. It nearly devastated me. Thirteen-year-olds tend to take things very seriously, I'm afraid."

"What happened, Honor?"

She looked at him over the rim of her coffee cup. "Why do you want to know?"

"Because I want to know everything about you."

Honor closed her eyes. "Believe me, you don't want to know about that aspect of my life."

"Yes, I do," he countered in a soft but steely voice. "And I won't stop asking until I get all the answers."

She slammed her cup down into the saucer, growing annoyed with his insistence. "All right, I'll tell you. I'm the daughter of a man who was killed, along with his partner, while running an illegal shipment of guns into the Middle East. Does that answer your question? It was tacky, embarrassing and traumatic. The papers had a field day with it. They called my father a traitor and a criminal. The general implication was that in the end he got what he deserved."

"Along with his partner," Conn said slowly.

"If you want my opinion," Honor said bitterly, "I've always thought that the real criminal probably was his partner. I'll bet my father caught him with the shipment and his good buddy pulled a gun. In the end they both died. My father was apparently armed, too." Honor swallowed some of her childhood anger. "They were supposed to be respectable oil executives." She sighed.

Conn's eyes narrowed and the fingers around the handle of his coffee cup tightened as he regarded her tense face. "You've always assumed that your father's partner was the guilty one?"

"No one will ever know. The authorities said they were both in on the gunrunning." Honor shook her head, striving to return to normal. "And I guess it no longer really matters, does it? It was all a long time ago."

"Some people aren't satisfied until they've tied up all the loose ends," Conn Landry said so softly that Honor wasn't certain she'd heard him.

Her head came up quickly as she scanned his face with her growing knowledge of him. "You're one of those people, aren't you?" she hazarded. "The kind who ties up loose ends. You like things balanced."

"Yes."

Honor absorbed the loaded sound of the single affirmative word. It had all the impact of a poised knife. Constantine Landry was being honest, straightforward and utterly truthful, she decided. He wasn't telling her anything she hadn't already guessed, but by reinforcing the knowledge he reinforced the sensation she had of danger hovering like an aura around him.

Memories of the night tangled in her mind with the trickle of unease Conn seemed to generate in her. Adena had been right in saying this man was unlike the other men in Honor's world. Honor reflected for a moment on the wisdom of terminating the relationship and knew in her heart of hearts that she would not be able to do it. Not yet. Conn had claimed there was a bond between them now and a part of Honor recognized it. There was a hunger in her to follow the dangerous path that might lead past Conn Landry's emotional barriers. For a few minutes last night she had been allowed through the gates. She wanted more opportunities to discover the man behind the seemingly impervious walls of cool control.

Honor made a decision in the warm light of a new day. She would take the risks inherent in becoming involved with Constantine Landry. She had no real choice.

Five

It couldn't be love, Honor told herself at least fifteen times several days later on a Friday as she worked on some space-planning arrangements in her office. She'd only known the man for approximately two weeks, and if she were truthful with herself she actually knew very little about him.

But Conn was making a habit of staying for breakfast, and she realized she wanted him at her table tomorrow morning, too.

Idly she pushed around the little cutouts that represented various sizes and shapes of office furniture, but it was hard to keep her mind on the floor plan in front of her. All she could think about was the fragile new relationship she had begun with Constantine Landry.

It shouldn't be love, not so soon and not when there were so many unanswered questions, but she was very much afraid that it was. She'd never felt so vulnerable before in her life. Only love left a woman of twenty-eight feeling so precariously poised on the brink. Why was she fighting it, she wondered.

But she knew the answer. Conn Landry didn't fit any mental image or preconceptions she'd had about the man to whom she would one day give herself so completely. His background was still exceedingly vague, for example. He'd alluded briefly to various investments and mentioned that he'd spent a great deal of time overseas until two years ago. Something to do with being a go-between for corporations. Whatever that meant. And he'd told her he lived in the San Francisco area.

Honor sighed and reached for another cutout of a table that could be used for large meetings. It was oval and would be far more interesting in the office space she was designing than the square one she'd been trying. She could see it now in rich gray slate on a black steel pedestal. It would give an impression of solid reliability to the clients of the securities brokerage house for which she was doing the design.

When you got right down to it, Honor told herself, what she knew about Conn revolved around impressions of him as a man rather than knowledge of the realities of his life. As a man he appealed to her senses on every level. She knew it was far more than a physical attraction. It had been from the first, even when she'd been so wary of him.

Some of her initial caution still existed, she had to admit, but she had shoved it far to the back of her thoughts. Instead, she now focused on ways of gently penetrating the emotionally controlled exterior that surrounded Conn. So far her only real success in that area seemed to take place in bed. Honor grimaced ruefully. She didn't like the idea that the only way she could really reach him was with sex.

Honor glanced up from her desk as the front door opened. Ethan Bailey smiled genially as he stepped inside the sleekly furnished room. He glanced around with interest.

"This is right nice," he observed, touching the finely-grained beige leather of a chrome-and-leather chair. "Is that real marble?" He indicated her desk top.

"Absolutely." She smiled, motioning him to one of the chrome-and-leather chairs. "Nothing like a sheet of black marble to impress potential clients. What can I do for you, Ethan? Don't tell me you need some design work!"

He chuckled, lounging back comfortably in the chair. His hand-tooled boots were revealed as he extended his legs and steepled his fingers. "To tell you the truth, I hadn't thought much about it until now." He glanced around at some of the photos on the walls. "Looks to me like you know your business. I like that one there."

Honor followed the direction of his glance. "Ah, my one shot at the Southwestern look. I can see why that would appeal to you." She smiled at him. "What on earth made you decide to stop by and see me, Ethan? I would think you'd be out at Santa Anita."

"Already watched the morning workouts," he said easily. "Conn was there, too."

She nodded composedly. "Yes, he said he wanted to discuss Legacy's future with Toby Humphrey."

"Well," Ethan said as if he weren't quite certain how to continue. "He did. He also talked a bit about Legacy's past."

Honor's gaze was quizzical. "Is something wrong, Ethan?" she finally asked gently.

The older man shifted uncomfortably. "To tell you the truth, I don't rightly know. But I've been around a long time, Miss Mayfield. Maybe too long. A man can get cynical in his sunset years."

"You're hardly in your sunset years. I don't think you'll be the type to ever hit them." Honor grinned.

He returned her smile but there was a measure of seriousness in his normally cheerful eyes. "Honor, I wonder if I could speak quite frankly."

"Of course."

"What I'm going to say is probably none of my business. But I feel obliged to say it, anyway. You're such a nice young lady. And seeing you off and on with Conn at the track I've come to think of you as a friend."

A trickle of warning went down Honor's spine. "What's wrong, Ethan? Why are you here?"

He sighed, glancing up at the photo of the Southwestern-style office. "Your last name is Mayfield."

She blinked in astonishment. "Well, yes."

"Conn said this morning that your father had once owned Legacy's sire, an animal called Stylish Legacy."

"That's right."

Ethan closed his eyes briefly and when he opened them his

gaze was very level. ''Your father's full name would have been Nick Mayfield?''

The warning sensation was stronger now. ''Did you know him, Ethan?''

The older man shook his head. ''I've been in racing a long time, Honor. It's kind of a small world. When I heard your last name was Mayfield, I just brushed the whole thing off as a coincidence. After all, it's been a long time...''

''It's been fifteen years since my father died, if that's what you're trying to say.''

Ethan cleared his throat. ''Not exactly. That is, I remember the newspapers really played it up big.''

''Yes.'' The residual anger of a helpless thirteen-year-old girl still simmered. ''Everyone seems rather interested in ancient history these days. Did you know my father?''

''Not well. But I was certainly aware of the horse he owned. Stylish Legacy was the most promising colt on the West Coast fifteen years ago. Since he was sold to that syndicate he's lived up to that promise. Legacy cost Conn a fair-size fortune.''

''Ethan, I still don't understand what you're trying to say.''

''I'm making a mess of this,'' he grumbled. ''Honor, this is real tough on me. Lord knows I don't want to get involved in anything personal between you and Conn, but I don't want to see you hurt, either. Conn, well, he can take care of himself, but you're just a little thing and you don't know what's going on behind the scenes. I didn't know myself, or rather, I didn't want to admit I knew until this morning when Conn mentioned that your father was the Mayfield that had owned Stylish Legacy.''

''Please get to the point, Ethan,'' Honor said tensely. ''It's obvious you're trying to tell me something.''

He inhaled deeply. ''Honor, you probably know your dad had a partner.''

''I'm aware of it.''

''The man the newspapers said was with him in that nasty

business in the Middle East,'' Ethan went on doggedly. ''Do you remember that man's name?''

''Vaguely. I think it began with an *S*. Stone or Stanton or something. Why?'' Honor realized she was tapping the tip of a pencil against her floor plans and leaving small black marks. Annoyed, she forced her hand to remain still.

''His name was Stoner. Richard Stoner,'' Ethan said flatly.

''So? I'm afraid I don't understand where all this is leading.''

''All right. I don't know how else to give this to you except straight. Landry is Conn's middle name. He's used it for years because he was working overseas for a lot of fancy corporations that might have been nervous about dealing with Richard Stoner's son.''

The pencil in Honor's hand snapped in two. Blindly she stared down at the broken halves. Slowly she raised her head to meet Ethan's unhappy expression. ''Conn Landry is the son of my father's partner?'' she whispered uncomprehendingly. ''But why didn't he tell me?''

Ethan leaned forward anxiously. ''Honor, you were only a kid when your father and Stoner killed each other during that quarrel. Conn was twenty-three, just out of college and starting his first job with the oil company for which his dad and your father had worked. Leastways, that's what I recall. The scandal hit him pretty hard, I gather. It's not something he talks about, but I heard rumors around the track when the story hit the papers. Racing people talk. Too much sometimes.''

''Racetrack rumors,'' Honor echoed huskily.

''They said—'' Ethan halted abruptly, as if searching for the right words and then tried again. ''They said Conn was convinced your father had betrayed his. People said he swore vengeance on your family fifteen years ago.''

''Vengeance!'' A man who liked to tie up loose ends. A man who kept the books balanced. The words went through her head in staccato fashion.

''It's the kind of thing an angry, hurt twenty-three-year-old man would say,'' Ethan pointed out gently.

''The kind of thing a twenty-three-year-old Conn Landry would say, I suppose,'' Honor said bleakly.

Ethan was silent for a moment before continuing.

''Fifteen years have gone by. I expect most everyone's forgotten now. I hadn't thought of the story in ages. When Landry bought Legacy and his horse and mine wound up in Humphrey's training stables, somebody remembered that Richard Stoner had had a son who used the name Landry. I kept my questions to myself. Didn't seem like any of my business, after all. Not until you showed up in the picture.''

''I see.'' Honor's eyes narrowed. ''And then you started wondering?''

He nodded forlornly. ''It was the coincidence of the whole thing that worried me. It didn't seem strange that Conn might have returned to the States after several years and decided to buy a colt sired by the stallion his father had once owned. But when he picked you up at Santa Anita the other day, I started remembering all those stories about how he'd vowed to make your family pay for what your father did to his.''

''My father didn't do anything to Richard Stoner! Certainly he didn't betray him,'' Honor hissed, the old anger welling higher within her. ''I always thought there was a damn good chance that Stoner was the one who was smuggling weapons and that my father had the bad luck to discover him doing it.''

Ethan held up his hands in a placating gesture. ''Please, Honor. I don't know anything more about that end of things than anyone else who was reading the papers at the time. From what little I knew of your father personally, I have to say he always seemed a decent man. He never spent much time around the track, so I really didn't get too well acquainted, but I was under the impression that folks respected him.''

''Really?'' There was a scathing tone in her voice as Honor

remembered the humiliation that her mother had been forced to endure as so-called friends turned their backs on her after the scandal hit the papers. The fact that her mother had been filing for divorce hadn't lessened the humiliation Mrs. Mayfield had to handle. And nothing could have mitigated the pain Honor had gone through.

''I knew I shouldn't have come here today,'' Ethan growled in embarrassment. ''But I just couldn't stand by and not tell you who Landry really was. You have to make your own decision about the man, but I thought you ought to know that his interest in you might be based on something besides... besides...''

''I think you're trying to tell me that he might have some motivation other than love at first sight,'' Honor observed coolly.

Ethan stared at her for a moment. ''I tried to tell you that the other day. Men like Conn Landry don't know much about love, Honor. But that was just an old man trying to pass along a little advice to a young woman who was in danger of getting swept off her feet. I knew then that you weren't his usual kind of date. But I also figured you were old enough to make your own judgments. This morning, though, when Landry mentioned your father as having been the Mayfield who owned Stylish Legacy, I got rather worried.''

''Why would Conn bring up the subject?''

Ethan shrugged. ''I don't know. He doesn't realize I know who he is. I suppose he didn't think I'd make any connection. Or maybe he wouldn't care if I did.''

''You've never told him you're aware he's Richard Stoner's son?'' she asked in amazement.

Ethan's mouth firmed. ''You have to understand how it is in the racing world, Honor,'' he said gently. ''For the most part a man's past is his own business. As long as he's honorable in his dealings, sees to it that his horses are well cared for, tips his jockeys properly when they win, no one really questions his past. At least they wouldn't do so to his face.

People around the track might gossip about it, but that's as far as it goes. A fellow owner wouldn't dream of confronting another owner and demanding explanations. Our only association is through racing. I don't generally pry into matters that don't concern me.''

Poor Ethan, Honor thought distractedly. He was very upset at having taken on the responsibility of warning her. She could see he was already regretting his involvement.

Her own mood was precarious, she realized. In all honesty, Honor wasn't sure how she felt as she absorbed the implications of the news of Landry's identity.

But it explained so many things, she thought grimly. Looking back over the past several days she began to see the pattern of his actions, and it was almost frightening. He had kept her from getting involved in the trap meant for Granger. Then he'd handled the business of Adena's debts to the man so that Honor wouldn't have to deal with him. It was after that that Honor had begun to experience the odd sensation of being in Conn Landry's debt. Conn had done nothing to ease that sensation.

Then there had been that incident the other night when his presence had scared off the punk in the pickup truck. Following that, Conn had made fiercely passionate love to her, placing bonds on her that chained her senses.

Honor was appalled, seeing herself as a small female animal that had been neatly driven into a strange sort of trap. What was Conn Landry Stoner planning on doing next, she wondered in frozen pain. What was the point of the trap?

''I suppose I ought to thank you for telling me all this,'' she managed distantly.

''Not hardly!'' Ethan exploded in self-disgust. ''If I were you I'd kick me out of this office. I probably had no business coming to see you about all this. But I swear, Honor, I just didn't know quite what to do. If you'd been anyone else except the daughter of the man Conn blamed for betraying his father, I wouldn't have opened my mouth any more than I did the other morning when you started asking questions about his, uh, investments. I figured I'd overstepped myself then. Now I've really put a foot in it, haven't I?''

''I know you meant well, Ethan.''

''Meant well! Hell, Landry's a friend of mine. I felt torn apart, not knowing which way my duty lay. Heaven knows what he'll say when he finds out I'm the one who told you who he really is.'' Ethan sighed.

''He couldn't have expected to keep it a secret forever,'' she pointed out.

''That's true,'' Ethan agreed. ''But what if I've got this all botched up? What if it's all perfectly innocent? A genuine coincidence? He meets you by accident at Santa Anita, takes to you and decides to keep his identity quiet because he knows you might be nervous about seeing him if you know who he really is.''

''Do you believe that, Ethan?'' she asked soberly.

''I might. If it weren't for one thing,'' Ethan admitted slowly.

She frowned. ''What's that?''

''That business about Granger being about to walk into a police trap the other day?''

''What about it?''

''Well, I got to thinking about it. I hadn't heard any rumors about that ambush. So I checked with some folks I know. Granger wasn't arrested that day, Honor. Best anyone can figure out, he didn't walk into a police setup. He wasn't set free on bail, either. Just been running around loose as usual.''

Two hours after Ethan Bailey had left her office, Honor finally accepted the fact that she wasn't going to get any productive work done that day. She locked her door and walked out onto the busy thoroughfare that fronted the building in which her office was located. It was another of the days for which Southern California was famous: temperatures in the mid-seventies and reasonably clear of smog. A good day to go to the beach, she thought. The water would still be uncomfortably cold for anyone except surfers, but it would be pleasant to take off her shoes and walk in the sand.

This wasn't the first time since Ethan had left that she had thought of the beach and of the cottage her father had bequeathed to her. She rarely used the house, as she had told her friend the other evening at the party. But quite suddenly she had begun to see it as a place to which she could escape. Honor had a strong need to lick some very raw wounds and she wanted to do so in private.

How did one confront the Conn Landrys of this world and demand explanations, she asked herself as she sat down at a table in an outdoor café. The menu wouldn't come into focus long enough for her to concentrate on the special of the day, so she ordered her usual avocado-and-sprouts sandwich. When it arrived she barely tasted it.

Her fingers trembled as she sat beneath the huge umbrella that shaded her table and tried to picture Conn's face. Such a harshly carved face, with eyes that reminded her of the color of a lethal weapon.

Dangerous. She had known from the beginning that he was dangerous. He had told her he was a man who kept the score even. But she'd had no way of knowing then that he had a score to settle with her family.

Honor didn't finish the sandwich. She paid for it and walked to the parking lot where her Fiat waited. Slowly she drove home, her mind in a turmoil. By the time Ethan Bailey had left she was feeling sorry for the older man. It was obvious he had been in a terrible quandary about whether to come to her with his information. Now he was no doubt consumed with guilt for having warned her about a man he considered a friend.

Looking back, Honor was sickened by the easy way she had allowed Conn Landry to get close to her. What a fool she had been to fall in love with a man who was driven by some twisted notion of revenge.

Assuming, of course, that revenge really did lie behind his actions, Honor reminded herself without a great deal of hope. She knew the odds were against it all being some horrendous coincidence, and there was that business of Conn's having lied about Granger. But what if there was some viable explanation for everything, she asked herself over and over again as she parked her car in front of her apartment.

The only thing she could do was confront Conn and ask him. She had to know the truth and she had to hear it from him. Nothing else was going to kill the love that had begun to grow within her.

It was impossible to concentrate on anything that afternoon as she waited for Conn. He had said that morning that he would be at her door at six this evening. As the day dragged on Honor realized how much she was beginning to cling to the hope that he would have explanations for everything.

It was ridiculous to allow herself that hope. She was setting herself up for a fall. But there was no real alternative. Nothing would convince her completely that she had been manipulated for some bizarre reason of revenge until she heard the damning words from Conn himself. The catch, of course, was that in all probability he would simply lie to her.

''Surely I'll know if he's lying. We've become so close in the past few days,'' she said half under her breath as she paced the white carpet. Another illusion. What made her think she would know if he was telling her the truth, she thought. After all, if everything had been a lie until now and she had believed it, there was no reason things would be any different tonight.

Close. That was another illusion. The only true closeness they had achieved had been in bed, and for all she knew, that feeling had been entirely one-sided. There was no reason to believe their mutual passion had been more than a good toss in the hay from his point of view.

Pausing by the window, Honor stared sightlessly out at the palm tree and wondered what kind of revenge Conn Landry

Stoner would go after from a woman. She wasn't wealthy. She wasn't married, so there was no relationship for him to spoil with insinuations or threats. She had inherited nothing from the partnership formed by their respective fathers, so there was nothing of value to demand from her, at least nothing she knew of except that beach cottage up the coast. As far as Honor knew, it had belonged only to her father. It had never been a part of the partnership. Stylish Legacy, the most valuable remainder of that business arrangement, had long since been sold and the profits evenly split between Nick Mayfield's widow and whoever had inherited Richard Stoner's estate.

But there was no denying that some way, somehow, Conn would want to even the score. She had to accept the fact that he seemed to have chosen her as the one who would pay for that betrayal fifteen years in the past.

The old resentment washed through her. As a young girl who had loved her father, she would never have been willing to believe that he had betrayed his friend. The evidence of that bloody night was fated to be forever vague and uncertain. The killings had taken place in a far-off land, and those who had been in charge of the investigation had been more concerned with dealing with the embarrassment the incident had caused a huge oil corporation than with getting at the truth. The main goal of the company for which Richard Stoner and Nick Mayfield worked had been to hush up the whole mess. Both men had been working for the company until just prior to the discovery of the gunrunning. Stoner and Mayfield had formed their own firm, but still had ties and contacts in the larger corporation they had just left. The huge conglomerate had its image to consider.

By rights, Honor told herself violently, she had as much reason to want revenge as Constantine Landry Stoner. She ought to be thinking of a way to turn the tables.

But all she could think of this afternoon was how she had

fallen in love with a man who apparently wanted only vengeance.

Honor was in a pair of old jeans and an emerald-green dolman-sleeved top when she went to answer the door at six o'clock. She had pulled her hair back into a strict knot at the nape of her neck. It must have been obvious immediately that she was not dressed for an evening out. Conn took one look at her unsmiling face and stepped inside.

"I take it we're staying in this evening?" he said coolly as he shrugged out of his impeccably tailored dark linen jacket.

"I think we need to talk, Conn." Honor was remotely pleased that her voice was calm. She watched him toss the jacket over a chair and marveled at his easy familiarity with her apartment. He hadn't hesitated to move right in on her private space, she realized.

He slanted her an assessing glance and sank easily into a chair. "Something wrong, Honor?"

She drew in a deep breath and walked back to the window to stare into the darkness. "That's what I want to ask you, Conn."

"You're the one who's being cryptic now."

She heard the hard-edged caution in him and wondered at it. He knew enough about her to realize that matters were serious, she thought bleakly.

"You never bothered to mention that your last name was Stoner," she said quietly.

There was a second of dead silence behind her. Honor was almost afraid to move.

"Stoner never has been my last name."

Startled, the wild hope leaping up within her in spite of her efforts to quell it, Honor spun around. "You're not Richard Stoner's son?"

"I'm his son."

Hope died. "I see."

"In all the ways that count, Richard Stoner was my father.

I was twelve years old when my mother married him. My biological father was killed when I was a baby, but she never wanted me to deny his existence. Stoner agreed with her, so there was never a formal adoption. But I grew up thinking Richard Stoner was the kind of man I wanted to become.''

Honor stared at the granite-hard expression on the face of the man she loved and knew there was no more reason to hope. Some perverse element in her nature insisted on spelling it all out, however, and she found herself asking the next question.

''You knew who I was before you met me?''

He leaned his head back in the chair, watching her through narrowed eyes. ''You've been busy today.''

''Just answer the question,'' she pleaded.

''I knew. I've known for several months.''

She closed her eyes briefly and turned back to the window, her hands clasped tightly in front of her. ''Other than making me feel like a fool, what did you plan to accomplish, Conn?'' she asked steadily.

He came up out of the chair without making a sound. Honor didn't know he was so close until he spoke from only inches behind her. ''The flat truth is that I didn't really know what I wanted from you in the beginning. I only knew there was something to be settled between my family and yours.''

''You wanted revenge. You believe my father betrayed yours,'' she whispered starkly.

''The official investigation of what happened that night concluded there had been a quarrel between partners, that Nick Mayfield had planned to kill my father and finalize the sale of the guns himself. Something went wrong. Richard Stoner had managed to get off a couple of shots before he died and neither man came out of it alive. Personally, I think my father discovered yours was using his cover as a respected executive to smuggle those arms shipments and confronted him.''

''And in the ensuing fight, they killed each other,'' Honor finished distantly.

''Something like that.''

''Either way, you're convinced my father was guilty of betraying yours.''

''I've had no reason to think otherwise for fifteen years,'' Conn said levelly. ''I knew Richard Stoner well. He wouldn't have been involved in anything like gunrunning.''

''My God,'' she breathed. ''Fifteen years. Fifteen years of plotting your revenge. It must have eaten away your soul.''

She sensed a slight movement, and then his fingers touched her shoulder. Honor froze.

''It wasn't like that, Honor. If it had been, I would have done something drastic long ago. Are you willing to listen to me tonight?''

''I don't have much choice.''

''No,'' he agreed grimly, ''you don't. You're the one who brought up the subject.''

She wished he would take his hand off her shoulder. His touch made her want to turn around, bury her face against his chest and cry out all the anger and pain. ''How long would it have been before you bothered to bring up the real reason you've been sleeping in my bed, Conn?''

His fingers tightened dangerously, and she sensed the tension in him. ''Listen to me, Honor, and listen well. This isn't going to be easy to explain. I've had a hard time comprehending it myself.''

''It seems quite simple to me.''

''That's because you don't know what the hell it's all about! I haven't been hidden away in some dark hole plotting vengeance for the past fifteen years, for heaven's sake. I've been working overseas just as I explained to you. It was a good job, a high-paying position. I was busy and I was always on the move. What's more, I was very good at what I did.''

''You never got around to explaining just what a go-between does, Conn,'' she pointed out dryly.

He bit off an exclamation of impatience. "I was a sort of troubleshooter. I got sent in when a company was having problems on a foreign job site."

"What sort of problems?" she pressed dismally. "Don't tell me you handled labor disputes."

"No," he said, gritting his teeth, "my specialty was security problems. Honor, my former job hasn't got anything to do with this. I only mentioned it because I was trying to show you that I haven't been exactly brooding for the past fifteen years."

"But you haven't exactly forgotten the night our fathers shot each other, either, have you?" she flung back.

"Neither have you."

She inclined her head once in aloof acknowledgment of that truth. "No, neither have I."

He applied pressure to her shoulder, turning her easily under his strong hand. She found herself forced to face the full intensity of those gunmetal eyes. The implacable hardness in him was almost overpowering.

"Honor, I'm a man who believes in tying up loose ends. I've told you that."

"Yes."

"When I decided to resign from my job and return to the States two years ago, a part of me started thinking about the unfinished business between my family and yours. I remembered my father's interest in horse racing, too, and something made me decide to find out what had happened to Stylish Legacy. Discovering what had happened to the horse seemed like a place to begin the search for the truth about what had happened between our fathers that night. The next thing I knew I was buying one of the colts. It seemed the right thing to do. Perhaps I absorbed some of Richard Stoner's fascination with Thoroughbreds. Or maybe I find the horse a link to the past. Buying Legacy was a mistake in some ways, though."

"Because every time you looked at him you thought of his

sire and of our fathers' partnership,'' Honor guessed unhappily.

''Honor, I have a thing about betrayal. Perhaps I've seen too much of it in my line of work. Perhaps it all stems from the way my stepfather died. I don't know. Maybe it's just built into me. Whatever the reason, once I'd bought Legacy, my need to settle the past became more and more important. I told myself I would at least find out what had happened to Nick Mayfield's kids. It wasn't hard to track you down. Once I had located you, I decided to keep going. Something kept pushing me.''

''A need for revenge.'' She met his eyes with a level gaze of her own, refusing to flinch from the grimness in him.

''All right,'' Conn replied, ''maybe that's what it was. Call it what you want. But I think it was something else. I had this feeling, you see, that if I found out what Nick Mayfield's eldest daughter was really like I might learn something about what Mayfield himself was like. I might be able to decide once and for all if he was the kind of man who would have killed his partner in cold blood. I'd be able to put the past to rest. And once I'd bought Legacy, I couldn't seem to stop the search for the truth. One thing led to another. For the past three months I've known where you lived, where you worked, whom you dated and that you occasionally went to the track.''

''You had me followed!'' She was appalled.

''Only for a week. Long enough to find out the critical details. Then I took over the job myself. It's the sort of thing I've been trained to do.'' His mouth tightened.

''You must hate me very much, Conn Landry,'' she whispered.

''No, damn it, I don't hate you! That's what I'm trying to explain,'' he snapped furiously. ''After I bought Legacy I had to keep going. Don't you understand? One thing led to another. After I had discovered the whereabouts of Mayfield's elder daughter I had to find out what she was like.''

''Why?'' she cried. ''Because of some criminal theory out

of the Middle Ages that states the tendency toward betrayal runs in a family?''

''Maybe I just wanted to see if she'd turned out like her father. I don't know exactly why I had to track you down and meet you. You were another link, like Legacy. I only knew that it was important.''

''Because there was unfinished business to settle,'' she finished savagely. ''Why the trap, Conn?''

''What trap?'' But she saw the wariness shimmer in his gaze.

''Come on, there's no need to pretend. From the first moment I met you, you've been boxing me into some kind of cage. There was that incident with Granger, for example.''

There was rough-edged steel in his response. ''You want the truth? I'll tell you. In the beginning I wanted to make certain that when I made contact, I would be the one in control. The best way to manage that, I decided, would be by spinning a web around you. I wanted you in my debt at first and later—'' He stopped suddenly.

Honor already knew what he'd been going to say.

''And later you decided that seducing me would add to your sense of control. You're a very thorough man, Conn.''

''It's the reason I was successful in my job while I worked overseas. And it's the reason I've been successful in my investments during the past two years. Being thorough is part of the way I do things, Honor.''

''I still don't understand what you want from me,'' she said stonily, all hope dead within her now. ''You seduced me. Believe me, that's about all I have to give. There's a little money, I suppose—''

''I don't want your money, damn it!''

''My father left me a beach cottage up the coast,'' Honor went on doggedly, her gaze never wavering. ''It's worth something. You've met Adena. You must realize there's not much to be had from her. She's still just a kid in a lot of ways. I imagine you could successfully seduce her, too, if you put your mind to it, but that seems a bit tacky, doesn't it?''

''Will you shut up? You're not even trying to understand!''

''What exactly am I failing to comprehend?''

He released her, removing his hand so quickly she wondered if he'd been afraid of losing control and actually hurting her. It was so hard to imagine Conn losing control in any situation. Stepping around her he reached inside the red lacquered liquor cabinet and found a bottle of Scotch. Honor watched as he splashed some of the amber liquor into a glass. He swirled the liquid once and then took a swallow.

''It's hard to explain what I've been feeling for the past couple of months, let alone the past few days. I only know that my feelings toward you were, well, ambivalent. You were the elder daughter of the man who had betrayed my father. Something in me has always wanted to put to rest what happened between our parents fifteen years ago. There was nothing I could do at the time. I was a twenty-three-year-old kid, and none of the honchos in the corporation would give me any real help in finding out exactly what had happened that night. I had to piece it all together for myself between what I knew of Richard Stoner and what the newspapers told me. It's never felt right, never felt finished.'' He ran his fingers restlessly through his hair.

''Did seducing me somehow put an end to it for you?'' Honor asked coldly.

Conn looked at her. ''Seducing you changed everything.''

She caught her breath. ''Is this the part where you tell me you've fallen madly in love? That since meeting me you've given up all notion of revenge? That the past doesn't matter any longer?''

The gunmetal-gray eyes were colder than the landscape of the moon. ''Look, Honor, I'm trying to be completely honest with you.''

''That's a change.''

''You little—'' He took a step forward and halted abruptly,

visibly restraining himself. The poised-to-spring tension in him now was very evident. "Honor, I don't know much about love. It's an undefined, vague concept that usually doesn't sustain itself for long from what I've seen. And I won't tell you that I've completely forgotten what happened between Richard Stoner and Nick Mayfield fifteen years ago. But something very basic has changed in this equation and that's the way I feel toward you. My feelings about you are no longer in the least ambivalent. I want you. And I have some first-hand evidence that you want me. I'm prepared to start over on that basis."

"Start over!" She couldn't believe what she was hearing. "Are you out of your mind?"

His face was a set mask. "I've been asking myself that question for the past few days. No, I'm not out of my mind. At least I don't think so," he added wryly. "There are bonds between us, Honor, and I suspect you realize that as much as I do. There are ties, factors that link us. Factors that brought us together and that we can't shake off very easily. Whatever the initial cause and effect was, the result exists. You and I are together now."

"I would never have guessed you were a believer in fate!" she stormed.

He shrugged. "Maybe I've spent too much of my life in parts of the world where people believe in things such as fate and destiny."

"Well, I'm from Southern California," Honor flung back fiercely, "and here we shape our own future. I was a fool to get involved with you, Conn Landry, but I can assure you I'm not going to stay involved. Please get out of my apartment. Now!"

He set down the half-finished glass of Scotch. "You know it isn't going to end this simply."

"Get out."

"I'll be back. We'll talk this over when you've calmed down. There is too much between us." His mouth lifted in the faint cynical smile. ''Murder and betrayal fifteen years ago between our fathers, passion and *obligation* between you and me. Don't forget that last bit, honey. You owe me. We're all tangled up together in this now.''

He turned and walked out the door before Honor could find an answer.

Six

He would give her twenty-four hours, Conn decided. Hell, who was he kidding? He needed the time just as much as she did. Conn piloted the Porsche to his hotel, parked the car in the lot and stalked inside to the English-pub-style bar. It wasn't until he ordered the Scotch that he realized just how much of his tightly controlled sense of frustration and anger must be visible. The bartender acted as though he were serving a shark who had casually wandered into the comfortable lounge. From across the room Conn recognized a couple of men who had horses at Santa Anita. They were staying at the same hotel, but neither of them made any move to invite Conn to join them. His dark mood must have been evident even from this distance.

Landry downed a long swallow of the Scotch after it was placed gingerly in front of him and then sat glowering at his reflection in the back-bar mirror. A grim-faced man with eyes that were sheets of frozen metal stared back.

Twenty-four hours. That should be long enough, he thought. She was shaken and upset right now, but twenty-four hours hence she would have calmed down enough to listen to reason. With any luck he would have calmed down a little himself.

He hadn't expected it to happen this way, hadn't thought she would learn the truth on her own. He'd intended to give her the facts carefully so that she wouldn't be alarmed. He would have told her eventually, when he judged the time was right and when he'd sorted it all out in his own mind.

That was the most complicated part, he realized. Sorting it

all out in his own head was taking some work. Faced with having to put his strange initial ambivalence toward Honor into words, he'd fumbled badly and he knew it. He hadn't done a good job at all of soothing her fears or of explaining something he barely understood himself. If only he'd had some time to prepare.

But his feelings toward Honor had been crystallizing slowly and in fragments. He hadn't yet put them together into a complete whole that would be comprehended. It was as if he'd started fitting together the various glittering shards of a broken mirror. Some things were clear already, Conn realized. He knew beyond a shadow of a doubt that he wanted her. He'd accepted his need to protect her. And he no longer struggled to ignore the strange possessiveness he felt.

But other images in the mirror were still jagged and out of focus. He wasn't sure of Honor's feelings, for example, other than a certainty that he could make her respond magnificently in bed. When he'd told her that seducing her had changed everything, he hadn't been lying. It had. What she might not have realized was that matters hadn't been fundamentally changed just for him. They had altered just as completely for her.

At least, Conn admitted in a flash of clearheaded honesty, he wanted very badly to think they had changed for her. The possibility that the lovemaking hadn't been as intense and meaningful for Honor as it had been for him created a sick dread in the pit of his stomach. He drank some more Scotch to mask it.

There were other fragments of certainty, he assured himself. He sensed a basic integrity in her that he hadn't expected to find in Nick Mayfield's daughter. When she was with him he had a feeling of rightness that he couldn't explain. He liked the expressiveness of her hazel eyes and he liked the way she had run to him the other night when the guy in the pickup truck had frightened her. He'd liked the feeling of playing hero and protector, Conn decided. He appreciated the courage it had taken for her to try to deal with Granger on behalf of her sister. So many things about her seemed to draw him.

For those reasons and a thousand more he had told himself that he needed time while he reevaluated the situation. But something had happened today to steal that factor from him. How the hell had she found out that he was Richard Stoner's son? For the record, he'd have to clear that up the next time he saw her. Racetrack gossip, probably.

His mouth thinning dangerously, Conn ordered another Scotch and considered the lonely dinner that lay ahead. Maybe he'd just stay here until it was time to go upstairs and face an even lonelier bed. Plenty of nutrition in good Scotch.

Several blocks away from the hotel, Honor locked the door of her apartment and picked up the red leather suitcase at her feet. She'd left a message for Adena on her sister's answering machine. Adena could handle anything that came up that affected the apartment. Honor carried the bag down to the garage and stuffed it into the Fiat's trunk. Then she slipped into the driver's seat and shoved the key into the ignition. It was going to be a long drive, but she would have plenty of time to think en route.

She was so wrapped up in her churning thoughts that she didn't notice the black pickup behind her until she was on the on-ramp of the freeway. When a casual glance in her rearview mirror picked it up, Honor's stomach twisted into a sudden knot of fear.

You can't be sure it's the same truck, she told herself. But she couldn't see any license plate, and Conn had mentioned the other night that the black pickup that had followed her home hadn't had plates. It was dark now, however, and she couldn't be certain of the image in her rearview mirror.

The tension in her doubled as she considered the possibility that she'd been singled out by a genuine lunatic. Perhaps some crazy had decided to follow her around terrorizing her.

She could try driving to a police station to see what happened, Honor thought as her knuckles went white on the wheel.

Just as she was deciding which off-ramp might take her to a station, however, the truck dropped back several car lengths. Two other vehicles filled the space between herself and the pickup, and Honor began to relax. Perhaps it had been just a coincidence or her imagination. The potential perils of freeway driving claimed her attention for the next several miles as the lanes became crowded. The freeways around Los Angeles were packed at this hour on Friday evenings. She lost sight of the pickup completely and told herself it had been nothing to worry about. There were a heck of a lot of pickups on the roads these days.

The temporary nervousness quelled, Honor's mind went back to the festering emotions that had driven her into leaving town. The pain of discovering that Conn Landry had lied to her wasn't diminishing. If anything, it was far stronger now that she'd had his deception confirmed from his own lips. There was no denying that she'd been secretly hoping there would be some logical explanation for everything.

And, of course, there had been a logical explanation, she thought bitterly. What Ethan Bailey had told her was the truth. Explanations couldn't get much more logical than that.

She'd fallen in love with Richard Stoner's son. She had been so very stupid. Landry had manipulated her from the moment they had met. No, he'd begun setting her up long before that. He'd admitted he'd been stalking her for months.

She was being pursued by a dangerous man, all right, but not the one in the pickup truck. Her nemesis drove a Porsche and harbored a taste for revenge that was more than old-fashioned; it was primitive. Her only choice was to escape the vicinity while she tried to deal with the traumatic turn of events.

Honor fled up Highway 101 as if she were being chased by demons.

* * *

Conn had good reason to remember his decision to drink his dinner the previous evening when the phone in his hotel room rang shrilly at seven-thirty the next morning. The simple act of trying to answer it kick-started a throbbing headache that had apparently been waiting in the wings.

"Hell," he groaned as he fumbled for the receiver. "I didn't leave a wake-up call," he grumbled before the person on the other end could greet him.

"Conn? Is that you, Landry?"

Conn sprawled back against the headboard, one hand on his throbbing temple. His stomach was definitely unsteady, he realized. "Who is this? Ethan? What the hell are you doing calling me in the middle of the night?"

"Sorry to wake you. I'm at Santa Anita. Came to watch the morning workouts." There was a pause.

"I plan to skip them this morning," Conn muttered, closing his eyes and inhaling carefully. "I've got some other things on my mind." He thought he could handle the stomach. It was his head that would be the death of him.

"Yeah. Listen, Conn, I'm not calling about that. There's something else. Something strange. I think you ought to get out here."

"Give me one good reason."

"It has to do with Legacy," Ethan said levelly.

Conn opened his eyes and immediately regretted the violent exercise. "Legacy? What's wrong with him? Is he okay?"

"Well, yes, but—"

"Where's Humphrey?" Conn sat up in bed, ignoring his head with a fierce act of willpower. "If there's anything wrong, get Humphrey to look at the horse. I'll be out there as soon as I can."

"Legacy's all right, Conn. But this has something to do with him, and frankly, I'd rather not talk about it. This is a public phone."

Through the pain in his temples, Conn heard the man's

concern. ''Okay, okay. I'll be right out. You're sure the horse is all right, though?''

''He's fine, Conn,'' Ethan said wearily.

Landry slammed down the receiver and swung his feet to the carpeted floor. It took guts just to get out of bed, but he made it to the bathroom. Unzipping the shaving kit, he found a bottle of aspirin and gulped down a few tablets. Then he turned on the shower and stood under the spray for several minutes brooding about how long it had been since he'd gotten drunk because of a woman. He couldn't even remember if he'd ever deliberately set out to get stoned because of a female. A first for Honor.

He'd have to tell her just what she'd done to him. He'd put it on the list of grievances he planned to present to her when the twenty-four hours were up.

His head had settled down a bit by the time he located the Porsche in the hotel parking lot and started out to Santa Anita, but Conn was still moving with a bit of care as he walked through the track parking lot toward the barns.

Ethan Bailey met him just outside the guard gate. One glance at the older man's face and Conn knew there was a truly major headache waiting. Bailey's normally laid-back, easygoing manner was nonexistent this morning.

''You'd better tell me the worst and get it over with,'' Conn said, sighing.

''Let's go out to my car,'' Ethan suggested gently. He didn't wait to see if Conn would follow, but started toward the parking lot.

''What the hell are you being so mysterious about this morning? I'm really not up to this sort of thing today. If something terrible has happened to Legacy, just tell me.'' Conn paced beside his friend, his unsettled temper bubbling just below the surface. He felt angry at the whole world this morning. The past, the present, Honor Mayfield, Scotch, the whole world. And now Bailey was playing games.

No, that was unfair. Bailey was very concerned. He wasn't

playing games. In fact, in the couple of years he'd known the man he'd never seen Ethan Bailey this upset.

"You look worse than you did the time that real estate deal in Orange County went sour," Conn grumbled.

"That was business. This is personal," Ethan told him in a troubled tone. He paused beside his big white Mercedes and turned to look at Landry. "Maybe too personal. Maybe I handled this all wrong." He wrenched open the door and reached inside to pull out a bundle wrapped in burlap. "You can tell me where to get off if I screwed this up, Conn. But I wanted you to see this before I did anything too dramatic."

"What is it?" Frowning, Conn glanced down at the harmless-looking bundle.

"I found these inside Legacy's stall this morning. I went past it while he was out having his morning gallop and I just happened to glance inside." Slowly Ethan unwound the burlap and revealed two green apples. Conn stared at the fruit in mild surprise. "A couple of apples. So? One of the grooms probably brought them in for him."

Ethan shook his head. "You know how strict Humphrey is about the horses' diet. None of his grooms would dare bring in anything special for Legacy or any of the others. Humphrey's got all his animals on scientifically formulated feed. Conn, someone brought these in for Legacy and put them in his feed while he was out getting his morning workout. Look at this." Ethan turned over one of the apples, revealing that it had been cored.

The carefully honed instincts of several years spent in the security business finally emerged. Conn reached for one of the apples and examined the hole in the base of it. Without a word he moved his hand to the pocket of his blue denim work shirt and removed a small star-shaped metal object.

Ethan's brows came together in a thick shaggy line. "What the heck's that widget?"

"Something I picked up a few years back," Conn explained absently as he used one of the sharp points of the star to neatly slice the apple in two. ''Kind of a good-luck piece, I guess you could say.''

''Didn't know you were the superstitious sort,'' Ethan observed.

Conn cleaned the star on his jeans and dropped it back into his pocket, his attention completely on separating the two halves of the apple. ''A man picks up some odd habits when he works in some of the places I've worked. Well, what do you know?'' he concluded in a whisper as the large capsule hidden in the apple was revealed.

Ethan stared at the powder-filled capsule. ''I was afraid there wasn't going to be any real good explanation for those apples being in Legacy's stall.''

Landry lifted chilled eyes to meet the other man's dismal stare. ''I wonder if Granger decided he didn't like being told to lay off Adena Mayfield.''

Ethan looked back at him steadily. ''Conn, Granger's from the bottom of the barrel, but he's sort of old-fashioned.''

''Spell it out, Ethan.''

''From all accounts he's what the women's movement would call a genuine, dyed-in-the-wool male chauvinist pig. He doesn't hire females.''

Conn went very still. ''What the devil are you talking about, Bailey?''

Ethan made a visible effort to steel himself to deliver the rest of his news. ''When I found those apples this morning, I casually asked the guard if there'd been a lot of strangers coming into the stable area. He said no.''

''Granger could have bribed someone who works here,'' Conn interrupted irritably.

''That was my next thought.'' Ethan heaved a sigh and glanced at the wall of mountains in the distance. ''But the guard went on to say there had been one person through thc gate on a visitor's pass. A woman. A lady with light-brown hair who wore a pair of yellow pants and a blue windbreaker. She didn't stay long.''

Conn didn't move for a timeless instant, images of Honor's bright-brown hair and vivid wardrobe flashing into his aching head. Honor, who saw herself as a woman who had been used, the victim of a man who had tracked her down out of revenge. Honor, the daughter of a man who had once betrayed and killed his best friend.

Like father, like daughter? "No," he whispered under his breath.

"You all right, Conn?" Ethan squinted at him worriedly.

"I'll live." Maybe. He suddenly wasn't sure. There was a strange, painful tightness in him, a nausea that had nothing to do with his hangover.

"Do we go to the track authorities with these apples?"

Conn forced himself to deal with one thing at a time, although his mind was racing in a hundred meaning-less directions. "No." Damn it, why couldn't he think straight?

"I don't know," Ethan said uneasily, "maybe we ought to get the contents of that capsule analyzed before you make any decisions. After all, we don't know for sure just what's in there."

"How many reasons can you think of for stuffing a capsule inside an apple and feeding it to a hundred-thousand-dollar racehorse?" Conn asked sardonically as he rewrapped the apples. He was amazed at how much effort the small task required until he looked down at his hands and realized they were shaking.

"I can't rightly think of any good reasons. Unless Toby Humphrey was trying to trick Legacy into taking some medication?" he added hopefully.

"I had a long talk with Toby yesterday about Legacy's health and future. The horse isn't on any medication." Conn spoke flatly, without any emotion. "Whatever's in this capsule was meant to poison Legacy."

"The authorities—"

"No!" The denial was much too harsh, too loud. He brought himself under control with savage willpower. If he wasn't very careful his voice would soon be shaking as badly as his fingers. ''I'll handle this on my own.'' Conn held the wrapped apples in one hand and looked at his friend. ''You knew I'd want to deal with this myself, didn't you? That's why you called me first instead of the track authorities.''

Ethan nodded gloomily. ''When the guard said something about a woman, well, I...'' He didn't finish the sentence.

''You knew who the description fit.''

''Conn, this is just about the most goddamned miserable mess I've ever seen. What did you do to that little lady to make her want to do something like this?''

Conn glanced down at the bundle in his hand. ''Made her mad, I guess.'' He turned and started toward his Porsche. ''But that's nothing compared to what she just did to me.''

That was the truth, he added silently, as he flung himself into the Porsche and tossed the burlap bundle onto the floor of the car. He probably shouldn't even be behind the wheel of a car right now. If he had any sense he would go somewhere and calm down before confronting Honor.

Then, again, if he had any intelligence he wouldn't be in this situation. Everything he'd learned about human nature during all those years working security for multinationals around the world seemed to have evaporated around Honor Mayfield. What the hell had happened to his normal, realistic approach to people, he wondered.

He ought to have expected something like this, Conn thought in disgust, glancing at the incriminating bundle. She was the daughter of a man who had betrayed and killed his best friend. Did that sort of inclination run in the blood? There were places in the world where people believed it did. Even if the instinct wasn't hereditary, there were other factors he should have taken into account last night, such as the fact that he hardly qualified as her best friend.

Honor had been infuriated yesterday when she'd learned the truth. He knew she was capable of passion. It stood to reason that such a fundamental capacity would affect other areas of her life in addition to her responses in bed.

Reason. He couldn't seem to reason clearly at all this morning and not just because of the effects of his hangover. It took Conn almost the entire distance of the drive from Santa Anita Racetrack to Honor's apartment house to acknowledge that his own passions were running dangerously close to being out of control. Between the throbbing ache in his head and the twisting pain in his gut he was incapable of calming himself.

It was the pain he didn't fully understand. It should have been the cold, hard tension of fury. Instead it was something else, something he wouldn't have guessed himself capable of feeling anymore. He *hurt,* not just physically but on a primitive emotional level that hadn't been touched since the day they'd told him Richard Stoner had been murdered.

As he slammed the Porsche to a halt at the curb in front of the apartment complex the simmering caldron of his emotions threatened to explode. He was actually having to fight for self-control, and the knowledge only served to increase the level of explosive tension. He'd never had this kind of problem. He was always the one in command of himself and any given situation. Such talents had been a necessary skill in his job and he had come by those abilities naturally. For years he'd taken his chilled, controlled, efficiently ruthless approach to life for granted. The fact that this particular woman had pushed him beyond those boundaries was almost stunning in its impact.

Conn took the stairs to the second floor, loping up them two at a time, and came to a halt in front of Honor's front door. There he drew a couple of deep breaths in a useless bid to pick up the leash on his anger. Then he pounded brutally on the door.

It took several minutes of pounding and the frowning inquiries of a couple of Honor's neighbors to convince Conn that his quarry had fled.

"Look, mister," a man damp with sweat he'd worked up

jogging said, "I just came up through the garage. Her car isn't down there. Take my word for it. She's gone for the weekend." Wiping the perspiration off his forehead, the jogger dug out the key to his own apartment.

"Do you know where?"

The knife blade buried in Conn's tone brought the man's head up just as he unlocked the door. "Sorry," he said crisply. "I don't." Rather hurriedly he stepped inside and slammed the door behind him. Conn heard the bolt being shot home.

Terrifying Honor's neighbors wasn't going to achieve much. Time to track down Adena. He had the younger woman's address in that pile of information he'd garnered during the past few months. Driving back to the hotel and digging through the data took time and chewed at his insides, but it was the only approach. He was about to walk out of the room with the piece of paper in his hand when he remembered the aspirin. He could use a few more. His head was not improving at all. At least his stomach was staying under control. Pausing to gulp a couple more tablets, Conn wasted no more time. Ten minutes later he was pounding on Adena Mayfield's door. This time he got an answer.

"Good heavens, what do you want? It's only eight-thirty and it's Saturday. If you're here to give me another lecture about Granger, kindly skip it. I have an excellent memory." Adena glared at her visitor, clutching at the red-and-purple kimono-style bathrobe she'd apparently slung on to answer the door. Her stylish haircut had not yet been blow-dried into its proper wedge shape and her blond hair was in a tangle. Without her normal outrageous makeup she looked much younger, Conn realized.

"I'm looking for your sister," he spat out.

"Honor?" Adena blinked vaguely. "How should I know where she is? You're the one who's been spending so much time with her lately. You've probably got a better idea of her whereabouts than I do."

''She's not at her apartment.'' It was taking a savage effort to keep his voice even remotely level.

''Don't blame me if you've managed to misplace her,'' Adena grumbled. ''Hey, what is this?'' she added in a gasp as Conn suddenly pushed open the door and stalked into the entry hall. ''Look, she's not here, if that's what you're thinking.'' Something about his mood finally hit her still-sleepy brain. ''What's wrong, Conn? Is Honor okay?''

''I have to find her.''

''Why?'' There was a sudden, wary concern in her voice.

Conn heard the change in her tone and forced himself to contain his fury. If he alarmed Adena too much it would be tough to get information out of her. ''We argued last night. She's apparently left town. I'm trying to locate her.''

''Ah,'' Adena said, her face clearing. ''You want to do a little groveling, is that it?''

Conn stared at her. ''I hadn't thought of it quite that way.''

''Well, don't worry. Honor is a very forgiving, tolerant soul. Heaven knows she's put up with a lot from me during the past few years. Let me see if she left any messages for me on the machine. She usually tells me when she's leaving town.'' Stifling a yawn, Adena padded into the kitchen and switched on the telephone-answering machine.

Conn listened to two calls from young men begging Adena to go to the same punk rock concert and a call from a young woman wanting to know if Adena cared to go to the mall to check out the latest fashion scene before Honor's tense voice was heard. Unconsciously Conn's hand clenched so tightly the knuckles went white.

''Adena? This is Honor. I'm going out of town for a couple of days. Thought I'd get some use out of Dad's cottage before the season starts. I'll call you when I decide to return. Please don't tell...'' There was a pause before Honor's voice continued. ''I'd appreciate it if you wouldn't let anyone know where I am. I need some time alone.''

''Uh-oh.'' Adena grinned wryly as she switched off the

machine. ''Looks like I should have vetted that call before letting you listen, hmm? Then again, I expect Honor's ready to hear your abject and humble apologies. Are you going to the cottage?''

''I'll need directions.''

''Sure.'' Quickly Adena rattled them off and then she eyed her visitor keenly. ''What did you and Honor fight about?''

''It's a private matter,'' Conn said stiffly, heading for the door.

''Oh. Well, as I said, I'm sure Honor will take you back,'' Adena assured him cheerfully. ''I've never seen her this way about a man before. Of course, I've never seen her with a man like you, either. You're not her standard fare.''

Conn halted halfway through the door. ''Because I don't own a pair of designer loafers and wear mauve ties?''

''Somehow,'' Adena said dryly, ''I think there's more to it than that. Goodbye, Conn. Don't forget to practice your groveling technique while you're driving. I think it needs work.''

Conn left before he gave in to the impulse to explain to Adena that groveling wasn't exactly what he planned to do when he finally tracked down Honor.

He made one more stop at the hotel to pick up his shaving kit and a couple of other items and then climbed back into the Porsche. An hour out on the freeway he still couldn't detect any change in his unstable mood. Maybe he should have had something to eat. Taking all that aspirin on an empty stomach probably wasn't such a bright idea. On the other hand, the thought of eating didn't do much for his seething temper, either. He only had to glance at the burlap bundle on the floor of the car to rekindle the simmering pain and its accompanying rage.

Betrayal shouldn't hurt this much, he decided. It was, after all, just another fact of life. Why was it that a woman's act of betrayal could slice a man to the bone? The image was apt. He felt as though he were, indeed, bleeding.

* * *

When she arrived at the cottage late the previous evening, Honor had experienced the sense of unease and distant, unhappy resentment that she always felt when she opened the door of the beachfront house. The feelings had lessened with time. They weren't nearly as strong as they had once been, but they had remained forceful enough through the years to keep her visits to a minimum.

Saturday morning she rose after a restless night's sleep and prepared a breakfast of dry cereal and coffee. As she ate she glanced around the walls, absently noting the framed photos of Stylish Legacy in various winner's circles. Honor rarely studied the pictures closely. It hurt to see the face of her father smiling back at the world as if the future looked good to him.

There were other mementos of her father's interest in racing scattered about the room. A bridle hung on the wall beside a small racing saddle that had been left over after the sale of Stylish Legacy. In one corner stood an old wood-and-iron chest containing various racing memorabilia. One of Stylish Legacy's blankets was folded on top. Locked in a drawer in the bedroom were copies of the *Daily Racing Form* from fifteen years ago, containing glowing accounts of the promising colt. There were also some copies of the horse's pedigree and other papers that had once held meaning to her father. Honor kept those locked away, too.

Perhaps she'd made a mistake coming here after all, Honor thought. The cottage depressed her. But she had been running the way a wounded animal runs, and this was where she instinctively headed. It was either this or check into some anonymous motel. Somehow that alternative seemed even more depressing. Maybe a walk on the beach this morning would lighten her mood.

Honor changed into a pair of jeans and some tennis shoes and pulled a heavy peach-colored velour top out of the suitcase. It was turning chilly. By the evening the coastal fog would no doubt be rolling in and blanketing this stretch of beach. The promising warmth in Pasadena did not extend this far north today.

The empty sandy beach didn't prove as therapeutic as she had hoped. It stretched for a distance of a couple of hundred yards before terminating in a rocky outcropping. At the foot of the rocks the water foamed dangerously, driven by a current that made swimming unsafe. It helped to walk, and the crisp wind from the sea was invigorating, but nothing eased Honor's pain. She found herself going over and over the sequence of events surrounding her relationship with Conn Landry, looking for the point at which she should have seen what he was doing to her. It appalled her to realize that she had been so incredibly vulnerable.

It was even more appalling trying to deal with the turbulent mix of emotions that shook her to the center of her being. She had fallen in love with the man. *In love!* Remembering all her initial wariness of Conn, Honor wondered how she could have been so stupid.

Giving up on the walking therapy after forty minutes or so, Honor turned reluctantly back toward the house. It really was turning cold, and the fog would be arriving earlier than she had originally anticipated. She could feel it in the air.

Her father's cottage stood isolated and alone on the bluff overlooking the beach. There were a couple of other cottages nearby but they were both empty at this time of year. The region had remained underdeveloped because it was just a little too far from Santa Barbara to become chic. Someday, Honor had told herself, when development caught up with this area of the coast, her inheritance would be a gold mine. She had used that rationalization whenever logic had dictated that she sell the cottage.

The truth was that a part of her never wanted to sell. Although the place depressed her and made her strangely uneasy, she couldn't bring herself to get rid of it. It was as if too many questions remained unanswered about the past, questions that should have been settled fifteen years ago.

Honor had been unable to settle the questions or let go of the things in the cottage that raised those questions in the first place.

She was pondering the vagaries of her own nature when she heard the roar of the Porsche engine as the sleek black-and-silver vehicle pulled into the cottage driveway. Honor halted abruptly, all her swirling emotions threatening to consume her.

Conn Landry had come after her.

In stunned silence she watched as he thrust open the car door and strode to the cottage. She was several feet away, standing in the shadow of the house, but she could see the implacable expression on his harsh face. Honor let him raise his hand to pound on the door before she stepped around the corner, her head high, hands shoved into the pockets of her velour top. The breeze caught her hair, whipping it around her shoulders.

''Hello, Conn. Still looking for your revenge? I should think you'd have had your fill by now. Even if you haven't, it's all you're going to get.''

He spun around to face her, his lithe, strong body dangerously balanced. The cold gray eyes raked her with a simmering emotion she couldn't name. It couldn't possibly be pain, she thought.

''Lady, you could teach me a few things about revenge,'' he retorted softly. ''You surprised me, do you know that? I would never have guessed you'd try to get at me through the horse. God only knows why, but I would have staked my life on the belief that you weren't the type.''

Honor felt a jolt of fear. ''What are you talking about?''

''Your little scheme to poison Legacy.''

''Are you out of your mind?'' she gasped out.

He inclined his head once, in brutal mockery. ''That possibility exists. I've been asking myself the same question for the past couple of hours. I must have been crazy to think you were a different breed from your father.''

''Don't bring my father into this!'' she flared furiously.

''Why not? It all started with him. But it's going to end here, Honor Mayfield. I swear, it's going to end here between you and me.''

''Don't touch me,'' she breathed, truly frightened now. At the same time her own fury wouldn't allow her to turn and run, as all her instincts dictated.

''I've got to,'' he told her roughly as he came toward her. ''I have to find a way to get you out of my system. You've pushed me over some edge I haven't come close to since the night they told me Richard Stoner had been killed. That was the last time I felt this wild, Honor. But fifteen years ago there was no one who could be made to pay for what had happened. This time it's different. This time I've got my hands on you.''

Seven

Honor turned and ran, not because she had some misconception that she might actually be faster than Conn or that he wouldn't come after her. She ran because one glimpse of the rage in his normally remote gray eyes convinced her she was dealing one hundred percent with the avenging, predatory side of his nature. And when you were the potential victim in a situation like that, you ran.

She fled around the corner of the house, heading for the beach simply because there was nowhere else to go. She knew he was right behind her even though the sound of his movement was inaudible above the slap of the surf and the rising rush of the sea breeze. Honor also knew that fleeing was hopeless. She had yearned to get past the barriers of Conn's self-control but she had never dreamed of doing it this way.

He didn't call out to her or order her to stop. Conn simply bore down on her with the silent intensity of a large hunting cat intent on bringing a gazelle to the ground. Running across the sand was like running through snow. It dragged at her feet, making Honor think of those odd nightmares in which the sleeper found herself being pursued but was unable to escape. She sucked in the cold air, her heart pounding from exertion and fear, and as she reached the water's edge Honor felt Conn's hand on her waist.

''No!'' she shrieked, spinning around to strike at him in desperation. ''Let me go, damn you!''

''Did you think you could run from me? There's no place on this planet you could hide.'' He pulled her against the hard length of his body, trying to control her struggles.

But as far as Honor was concerned at that moment, she was fighting for her life. She lashed at him with her nails, kicked at him with her feet, twisted relentlessly in his grasp and tried to use her teeth on his arm.

''You little—'' Conn's words were muffled as Honor's constant struggling threw both victim and pursuer off balance. They landed in a sprawl on the cold, wet packed sand. ''I'll teach you to betray me,'' Conn rasped, throwing his thigh heavily across her legs to still their thrashing movement.

''I didn't betray you!'' The words were torn from her as she pushed uselessly at his descending weight. ''I don't know what you're talking about, but you can't do this to me. You have no right to hurt me!''

''I haven't even begun to hurt you. After the way you've hurt me—''

He broke off abruptly, but not before Honor had heard the startling rawness in his voice. She wondered at it, trying to make that evidence of pain mesh with the rage she was certain was governing his actions. Breathlessly she pushed at him.

He pinned her relentlessly to the damp sand, using his weight to crush her beneath him until her struggles finally stilled. For a long moment Conn stared down into her blazing eyes. He held her wrists above her head as he lay on top of her.

''You bastard.'' The anger and fear were still warring within her. There was no time to analyze the flash of emotional agony she thought she'd detected in his gaze. She had her own pain to deal with. Honor felt Conn's strength overwhelming her, leaving her physically helpless.

''You've got a hell of a nerve calling *me* names.''

Her head moved on the sand. ''I never even knew you, did I? I never had a chance. You lied to me about yourself from the beginning.''

His face was a harsh composition of hard lines and flaring eyes. As she stared up at him Honor was vaguely aware of the twin red marks that coursed down the side of his cheek.

She was vaguely shocked at the wound she had inflicted. He would carry the sign of her struggle for a few days, she knew. Yet other than holding her helpless, Conn hadn't physically hurt her.

"I wasn't the one who lied," he gasped. "You lied to me every time I took you to bed. All that softness and warmth, it was all an illusion, wasn't it? I had begun to think you were different."

"Different from what?" she flung back, stricken that he could believe she had somehow faked her reaction in bed.

"Different from other women. And different from your father!"

"Leave my father out of this!"

"I can't. What he did is at the middle of this whole damn thing. I should have realized that. Should have known that his daughter wasn't likely to be any different. She's just as capable of betrayal."

"I haven't betrayed you!"

"Then why hide? Tell me why you ran, Honor."

"I'm not hiding. I just wanted to get out of the vicinity of the man who had been using me for his own warped notions of revenge. Is that so strange? Damn you, Conn Landry, who gave you the right to inflict your warped sense of justice on me? And who says I have to let you do it?"

"I wasn't inflicting any punishment on you," he exploded. "I haven't done a thing except take you to bed, come in handy when you were being followed by a punk in a pickup, and rescue your sister from the mess she was in with Granger, remember? I never hurt you! I never wanted to hurt you!"

"You tracked me down just so you could 'tie up loose ends,'" she hissed. "You wanted to settle old scores. You admitted it! Taking me to bed was part of your twisted idea of getting even. And now you have the nerve to accuse me of betraying you!"

"You tried to poison Legacy!"

She gasped in amazement and then her eyes slitted in fury.

"Never. I would never hurt your horse. Or any other horse, for that matter!"

"It was the only way you could get back at me after I told you I hadn't simply been swept off my feet by you, wasn't it? After you found out that I had other reasons for meeting you than because I'd fallen in love at first sight or some such idiocy, your feminine ego was enraged, wasn't it?"

"I was upset that you didn't feel the same way toward me as I felt toward you! Yes, I was angry. I had a right!"

"You were the one who wanted to punish someone, Honor. You wanted to get back at me and you chose Legacy as the means to do it."

"That's not true," she cried, appalled. "Do you really believe I would do such a thing? Is that how little trust you have in me, Landry? I admit we haven't spent a lot of time together and I'll also admit that you told me lies for most of that time, but everything I said or did was real. I meant everything. *Everything!*"

"Then why did you try to feed those apples to Legacy this morning?" he almost shouted.

Honor stilled as she heard the agonized plea for an explanation in his words. If she was feeling torn apart, Conn was also in shreds. "I've been here at the cottage since late last night. I haven't gone near Legacy." The cold from the sand seemed to be seeping into her. She was chilled emotionally and physically. The only warmth in the world right now was the heat from Conn's hard frame.

"You were seen at the stables this morning. A bright pair of yellow pants and light-brown hair. The only visitor through at that hour. It had to be you."

"If you believe that, then why don't you go ahead and finish whatever it is you're going to do to me? What are you planning to do, Conn? Strangle me? Beat me? Call the cops? Make up your mind. I'm getting cold out here on the sand."

"Damn you!"

For an instant she thought he really was going to strangle

her. The frustrated fury in his eyes was terrifying. But before Honor's instinctive scream could leave her lips her mouth was crushed ruthlessly beneath his.

It was not a kiss of either passion or gentleness. There was nothing but naked despair and masculine outrage involved. Conn tore through her mouth, annihilating resistance as he went until she stopped fighting altogether and went passive beneath him. There were no other options for her, Honor thought. It was the despair she sensed in him that made it impossible for her to struggle. Some fundamental part of her wanted to offer comfort and warmth, even though she was putting herself at risk.

It seemed forever before some of the emotion began to drain out of the marauding assault. When Conn finally raised his head, Honor risked lifting her lashes just far enough to examine his features. Her mouth felt bruised and her body felt as if it were trapped under a granite boulder but she knew that Conn wasn't going to strangle her. That realization went deep, and she could not have said just why she was so certain. But the relief she felt was in her eyes.

''Don't get the impression that it's all over, Honor,'' Conn snarled softly. ''It's hardly begun.'' He rolled off her, uncoiling to his feet and reaching down to pull her roughly up beside him. Without a word he started back toward the cottage, his hand locked around her wrist.

Honor stumbled along behind him, confused and still frightened. She pushed her sandy hair out of her face as the wind caught it. ''What now, Conn? How are you going to take your revenge?'' she challenged.

''I haven't decided.'' He slanted her a cold sidelong glance. ''Believe me, when I do, you'll be the first to know.''

''You think I'm going to be dumb enough to hang around and wait for your bizarre brain to come up with something suitably satisfying for you?''

''You're going to hang around, all right. You're not going anywhere, Honor. Not until I've had my fill of you. I'm going to work you out of my system and then I'm going to get as far away from you as possible.''

She heard the ruthless promise in his words and shivered violently. The cold within her worked deeper into her body. ''Not a chance, Conn. I'm no masochist.''

''You don't have any choice. You owe me, lady. More than you can ever repay. Somehow I'm going to collect. I swear it. I won't let you rip me to pieces and then walk away!''

He shoved open the door of the unlocked cottage, tugging Honor in behind him. Then he kicked the door shut and released his victim. His gray eyes raked her. ''Go take a hot shower and change your clothes. You're a mess.''

Honor didn't argue. She fled to the single bedroom and locked herself inside. On the other side of the door she took several deep breaths, fighting to get herself back under control. So many emotions roiled within her—anger, shock, pain and a sense of loss. Unsteadily she began to undress. Conn was right. She needed that hot shower and dry clothing. She had never felt so cold in her life.

When she emerged from the shower sometime later and tugged on a fresh pair of jeans and a bulky knit sweater, Honor felt more in command of herself. She stood in front of the mirror blow-drying her hair and wondered why she didn't look as bruised and battered as she felt. Only her eyes reflected the pain she had suffered. But even as she stared at her reflection Honor saw the courage return to her gaze.

The man she had been stupid enough to love was dangerous, but he was back in control of himself. She finished pulling a brush through her hair, clipping the soft tendrils at the nape of her neck. Then she turned and walked out of the bedroom with a determination to hold her own with the man who waited for her.

Conn was in the kitchen, running water into the coffeepot. For a moment Honor stood in the doorway watching him in taut silence. He didn't look up, but she knew he was aware of her presence. The set of his face was as grim as ever and there was a tension in him that communicated itself across the room.

"By all means, feel free to make yourself at home," Honor muttered.

He ignored the small piece of sarcasm, concentrating on the task of getting the coffee going as if it took all his attention. "Sit down, Honor. We have to talk."

"About what? Your mind is apparently made up, and I don't recall your asking for any input from me." She sank wearily into one of the white wicker chairs at the table. "I've been tried and convicted, haven't I?"

"The evidence is pretty conclusive. And then there's motive." He threw himself into a chair across from her, regarding her with a deep, brooding expression. "We both know you think you had a motive, don't we?"

Her hand curved into a fist. "I had a motive, all right. I was the one who felt betrayed. But I'll tell you this, Landry. If I had set out to get even I wouldn't have used poor Legacy to achieve my ends. I'd have gone after you directly. I wouldn't have involved an innocent animal." She shook her head in despairing wonder. "You must think I'm as low and filthy as…as that loan shark, Granger."

Conn shifted restlessly. "No. I think you were furious. A woman scorned. Isn't that how you saw yourself? They say a woman who feels that way is capable of just about anything. True?"

"It doesn't matter." She stared at him. "It just doesn't matter."

Conn was about to say something else and then thought better of it, apparently. He got to his feet and stalked across the kitchen to pour the coffee. With his back to her he stood for a moment staring out the window, watching the sea. Slowly he sipped the piping-hot black brew.

"Maybe it does matter," he finally growled. "You're a passionate woman. In a moment of rage and hurt you might have lost your head and—"

''I didn't do anything to your horse, so don't bother searching for excuses for me to use. I can't imagine why you'd want to find reasons, anyway.''

''Believe me, I'm asking myself the same question. I'm going to get you out of my system and then I'm going to leave.''

Honor felt the renewed tension but she didn't move. ''Why should you need to get me out of your system? How could you possibly let a woman you think so little of get so close?''

''I was a fool.'' He didn't turn around.

''Well, that makes two of us, doesn't it?''

''Yes.''

Honor blinked back the tears, refusing to give in to them. ''At least we aren't trying to shoot each other the way our fathers did when things went wrong in their business relationship. Although I wasn't altogether certain just what you had planned out there on the beach. I suppose it's lucky for me you don't pack a gun, isn't it?''

He swung around with controlled violence. ''This isn't a joke.''

''Do I look as though I'm joking? Conn, this is the end of it and you know it. Unless you're going to physically hurt me, you might as well leave. You hate me, and the sooner I'm out of your sight, the better,'' she whispered.

He slammed down the coffee cup. ''I'm not leaving. Not yet. I told you yesterday that I want you and I'm going to have you. On my terms.''

''I thought I made it clear that I'm not a masochist. I won't play victim for you, Conn, not anymore.'' She got slowly to her feet, one hand on the edge of the table for support. Her gaze was unwavering.

''And I thought I'd made it clear you don't have any choice.'' He started forward with a cool, measured stride.

Honor stepped back. He wasn't enraged this time, but she knew she was in just as much danger. She edged backward until she was in the main room of the cottage, standing beside an end table that held a lamp. "I won't let you do this to me, Conn."

"From what I remember about the way you respond in my arms, you want me as much as I want you!"

"Damn you! I went to bed with you because I fell in love with you!" For an instant she regretted letting the truth emerge, but a moment later her pride surfaced. What did it matter if he knew she had gone so far as to fall in love? He already despised her.

Conn halted, his eyes blazing. "Love? You expect me to believe that? After what you've done?"

"Believe what you like," she replied steadily. "It's the truth, I only went to bed with you because I cared. Because I was in love."

"Prove it," he taunted coolly.

Her eyes narrowed. "What are you talking about? There's no way I can prove a thing like that. How should I prove my love? Go out and throw myself off a cliff into the ocean? I doubt that you'd believe me even if I did. I don't think you know how to trust anyone, Conn Landry. That's probably why you're so hot to settle old scores and collect all outstanding debts. Life is safer that way, isn't it? You don't have to worry about taking a risk."

"Skip the psychoanalysis. If you loved me a couple of days ago, you must still love me now, right? By all accounts true love isn't an emotion that dies easily."

"How would you know?" she flung back tightly. "You don't even believe in it!"

He came another step forward. "So why don't you try to convince me?" Conn taunted.

"How?" She eyed him with renewed wariness, uncertain of his mood now.

"Tonight when we go to bed you can give yourself to me without any arguments or recriminations. Just the way you did last week. Let me have all that warmth and sweet passion as if they were for real! Maybe you can convince me that it was unrequited love that made you try to poison Legacy!''

''Prove my love for you by going to bed with you? Conn, you're supposed to stop using that line the day you graduate from high school!''

''I take it you're not still in love?'' he mocked cruelly. ''A somewhat short-lived emotion, wasn't it?''

''It didn't die a natural death. You murdered it.''

''Then it wasn't a very sturdy emotion, either, was it?''

''Stop goading me,'' Honor hissed. She reached out and scooped up the small brass table lamp. Her hands were trembling.

Conn glared at her. ''Put that down, Honor.''

''Not until you get away from me.''

''You really think you'd use that on my skull?''

''Anyone who would deliberately try to poison a horse would be capable of cracking a man like you over the head,'' she warned half-hysterically.

For some reason that halted him in his tracks. He stood staring at her in stunned amazement. ''Are you saying you did put those apples in Legacy's feed?''

''I don't know anything about any apples. But I do know I'm not going to let you touch me as long as you hate and distrust me so much,'' Honor vowed. Her grip on the lamp base tightened.

The passionate fury that sparked between them seemed to flicker and then, very slowly, it began to fade. Conn didn't move for a long moment and then he asked softly, ''Is my trust so important?''

''It's the most I could have hoped for from you, isn't it? You don't know the meaning of love.'' Honor heard the raw truth in her own words as she slowly lowered the lamp.

Conn hesitated. Then quite coolly he stepped forward and removed the lamp from her unresisting fingers. ''You'd come to me without any guarantees of love?''

''I haven't had any guarantees for the past week, have I?''

She stood very straight, hazel eyes brilliant. ''But I was under the illusion that there was at least some mutual trust and respect between us.''

''And that's enough for you?'' he pressed deliberately.

''I was fool enough to think so,'' she admitted, knowing deep down that she had been banking on the wealth of her own love for him to fill in the gaps.

''If I said I believed you, was willing to accept the possibility that it wasn't you who put the apples in Legacy's feed, would you let the situation between us go back to the way it was before...before yesterday?''

Honor caught her breath at the implications of what he was saying. He was going to back her into a corner from which there would be no escape except into his arms. It took her a moment to comprehend why he was doing it. Then the truth hit her in a cold shower of realization.

''That's the only way you'll feel safe with me, isn't it? The only way you'll be able to handle an affair with me now. I'm to tell you that I love you and give myself to you without any reservations. In turn you'll tell me you believe I might not have been the one to poison your horse.''

''It sounds like a fair split to me.'' He shrugged carelessly. ''Both of us take a risk.''

''What risk are you taking?'' she demanded tightly.

''That I might wake up one morning to find you've tried to crush my skull with a handy object such as that lamp,'' he said dryly.

''And in turn I get to love a man who doesn't know how to love me and who might still be using me to satisfy his need for revenge. That's a hell of a bargain, Landry. You must have been playing in some rough leagues for the past few years to learn that kind of wheeling and dealing,'' she told him scathingly.

He ignored that. ''As I said, we both take a few risks. Does this famous love of yours give you enough guts to make the deal?''

He was walking on ice he couldn't measure, Honor realized sadly. Conn Landry was terrified of having it crack beneath him and finding himself in water that was way over his head. He wanted her, perhaps so much so that he was even willing to believe she might not have tried to poison his horse. But he was afraid to risk loving her.

The other side of the coin showed her wanting him. But she wasn't nearly so adept at bargaining with emotions. The only way she could give herself to him was if she simultaneously took the risk of loving him.

"A few minutes ago there wasn't any doubt at all in your mind but that I was the one who had tried to poison Legacy. Why are you willing to consider other possibilities now, Conn?"

He looked at her, silent for a long moment. Then he said softly, "You're wrong, you know. During the past few years I have learned how to take a few risks. I don't like them. I do my best to minimize them whenever I can, and I prefer to plan matters so that there are as few chances as possible. But that doesn't mean I don't know how to take them. What about you, Honor? Can you take them?"

Honor drew a long breath and then she sank wearily into the chair beside the end table. She clasped her hands in her lap, not looking at him. "I might. For the right man. But you're not that man, are you, Conn? The right man for me would never have believed me capable of trying to avenge myself by poisoning a horse. The right man for me wouldn't have threatened violence. The right man would have trusted me when the chips were down."

She sensed his restless movement, but he didn't try to touch her.

"The chips are down," he bit out huskily. "And I'm willing to…to consider your side of the story. I could almost believe that even if you did it, you might have thought you had a reason."

The awkward, uncertain way he said it infuriated Honor.

Her head snapped toward him. "Oh, golly gee, thanks. You don't know how terrific that makes me feel. Your generosity of spirit overwhelms me, Landry."

He glowered at her, shoving a hand through his tousled hair. "You don't know what I've been through last night and this morning. I woke up with a hangover that would have constituted a reasonable excuse for turning myself in to a hospital emergency room. Then I get a phone call telling me to come down to the track, where I'm shown some very convincing evidence that the woman I've been sleeping with has tried to take some revenge by poisoning my horse. I haven't had a thing to eat since yesterday and I can't think of anything except the fact that the woman I'd decided was different from her father has probably made a fool of me. She tells me she loves me in one breath and then turns around and deliberately taunts me when I give a little ground and admit I'm willing to look at her side of the matter. Is it any wonder I'm not feeling extremely charitable?"

"What about me? I've been through the wringer myself. I discover that the man I've fallen in love with has only been playing some kind of strange game with me. I come to the beach for a little peace and quiet and find out he's followed me, intending to punish me for a crime I didn't commit. He succeeds in terrifying me and then announces he's willing to make a deal. I'm going to be allowed to go to bed with him a few more times so that he can work me out of his system. In exchange, he's willing to concede I might not have tried to injure his horse. No guarantees, no nonsense about falling in love, no promises for tomorrow. Heck of a deal you're offering, Landry."

He moved then, reaching down to haul her abruptly to her feet. "Believe me," he muttered, his face very close to hers, his eyes ablaze with a strange light, "it's better than the deals I usually offer." Conn's arms locked around her as he brought his mouth down on hers.

But this time the kiss was different. Honor sensed the

change at once and knew that this time she didn't have to fight back. She relaxed faintly, letting his frustrated, demanding need wash over her in waves.

She shouldn't have had even a vestige of concern for his emotional state. It was her own she ought to have been worrying about. But she was a woman in love, and in spite of what she had told him earlier, nothing could alter that. Her palms stroked slowly down his back in a gentling fashion.

"Honor," Conn growled softly. "Honor, don't fight me. I want you the way you've been since our first night together. Warm and sweet and welcoming."

She wondered vaguely if he'd even realized what he'd just said and decided that he probably didn't. Not entirely. Regardless of what had happened between them, she was coming to understand this complicated man. He needed love whether he knew it or not. And a part of him was trying to reach out and take it even though another aspect of his nature was warning him that she was capable of betrayal. The conflict within him was almost palpable.

Slowly she pulled free of his embrace and he let her go reluctantly.

"Honor?"

"You said you hadn't eaten since yesterday," she murmured, starting back toward the kitchen without meeting his eyes. "It's almost lunchtime."

He hesitated and then followed her. "Are you going to feed me?" Conn asked with deliberate mockery.

"I'm going to feed myself. I can make an extra sandwich for you, if you'd like." Honor opened the refrigerator door.

"Yes," he said so quietly she wasn't sure she heard him. "I'd like." He sat down at the kitchen table, watching her intently as she went about the business of slicing bread for sandwiches. He didn't say a word as she finished slathering the chutney-and-cream-cheese mixture on the bread and set a plate down in front of him. When she sat down on the other side of the table, Conn finally spoke again. "You were right about one thing."

"What's that?"

"At least we're not at each other's throats the way our fathers ended up all those years ago." He picked up a sandwich half and took a large, healthy bite.

"Could have fooled me," Honor said bluntly. "I could have sworn you were at my throat."

Conn's gaze narrowed as he munched his sandwich. "You don't know me all that well, Honor. If I'd really gone for your throat..." He let the sentence die, turning back to his food with a vengeance as though he didn't want to finish his words.

Honor swallowed and stared at him for a long moment. "Yes, I know. If you'd really gone for my throat you'd have torn it out by now. What's been holding you back, Conn?" For the first time she allowed herself to think about the full ramifications of his behavior. Intuitively she knew she was right. If Conn Landry had been intent on tearing her apart, he'd have done it by now. Men like Landry didn't compromise.

Yet Conn was willing to compromise with her.

He looked at her, considering. "Beats me," he finally said, shrugging.

Honor sighed. "I like a man who knows his own mind."

"I'll admit that right now I'm not entirely sure of myself or of you. I don't like the feeling, but I'm stuck with it."

"You prefer everything cut-and-dried, don't you?"

"I prefer everything clear and comprehensible," he drawled. "There are a lot of things going on between us that aren't either clear or comprehensible. They make me—" he hesitated and then concluded "—uneasy."

"Did you really have a hangover this morning?" Honor asked suddenly.

His glance was mildly savage. "I went to bed very drunk last night."

''Because of what had happened between us?'' she pressed.

''I was annoyed. Irritated. Disgusted. Impatient. I decided to medicate my emotions with an old-fashioned remedy. What the hell's so amusing about that?''

Honor's faint flicker of humor disappeared at once. Indeed, she wasn't even sure from where it had sprung. ''Nothing. I guess it's just, well, *interesting* to think of you deliberately getting drunk because of a quarrel with a woman. Somehow it doesn't sound like something you'd do.''

''You're such an expert on what I'm likely to do in any given situation?'' he challenged roughly.

''I'm learning fast,'' she shot back. ''Do you want another sandwich?''

He chewed for a moment before answering, his gaze reflective. Then he nodded briskly. ''Yes, please. I think I'm going to live.''

''Poor Landry,'' Honor said with surprisingly gentle mockery. ''You really have had a hard day, haven't you?'' She got to her feet and went over to the counter to construct another cream-cheese-and-chutney sandwich. Then she poured some more coffee.

Carrying both over to the table, Honor sat down again and silently asked herself the question she couldn't decide how to ask aloud. *What now?*

''This cabin belonged to your father?'' Conn asked after a moment, glancing around at the rustic interior.

Honor had the distinct impression he was searching for a topic that, while it might not be completely neutral, because nothing was neutral between them right now, was at least less emotional.

''Yes.'' Compelled to further his efforts at nonlethal communication, Honor sought for something else to add. ''He used to bring Adena and me and Mother here whenever possible. I don't use it much anymore. Generally I keep it rented out, but this time of year it's often empty.''

''That's Stylish Legacy?'' Conn nodded toward one of the

winner's circle photos. A framed clipping cut out of a fifteen-year-old issue of the *Daily Racing Form* hung beside it.

"Yes." Again Honor struggled for neutral words. "All the photos are of Stylish Legacy."

Conn finished his sandwich and picked up his coffee cup. Then he got to his feet and wandered over to the nearest photograph. The picture showed the stallion, head high, jockey still perched on his back, posing for the camera with the usual assortment of people crowded around. Nearly twenty people had squeezed into the photo, most of whom were total strangers who had dashed in front of the photographer just for fun.

Richard Stoner and Nick Mayfield stood nearest the groom, who held Stylish Legacy's head. Conn studied the fifteen-year-old photo of his father and his father's best friend for a silent moment and then he turned away.

"You've kept all your father's records and mementos of Stylish Legacy?" he asked, wandering out into the living room to glance at some more of the pictures.

"I couldn't bring myself to throw them away, but I didn't want them in my apartment, either. Too many memories," Honor confessed.

"Too many unanswered questions, you mean." Conn fingered the small racing saddle.

"Perhaps."

"They look very pleased with themselves, don't they?" Conn stopped again in front of another winner's circle photo.

"Dad and Richard Stoner? Yes, they do," Honor agreed, getting up to go stand in the kitchen doorway. She watched Conn as he studied the picture. "Proud and excited by the win."

"They trusted each other at that point."

"Yes." She waited, uncertain what to say next. "They were partners and they owned a winner."

"Apparently that wasn't enough to hold the partnership together.'' Conn swung around, pinning her with his eyes. ''I wonder what it takes.''

''To hold a partnership together?''

''To hold two people together. A man and a woman, for instance,'' he said deliberately.

''I don't know,'' Honor retorted carefully. ''I suppose it depends on the particular man and woman involved.''

''There would have to be trust,'' Conn suggested too quietly.

''At a minimum.'' She decided to ask the question she hadn't dared ask earlier. ''What now, Conn?''

He set down his coffee cup and looked at her. ''A walk on the beach?''

''I've already been for a walk on the beach.''

''I could use the fresh air.''

It was an overture, Honor realized. Tentative, cautious, uncertain, but an overture nonetheless. ''All right.''

Eight

Honor lay alone in bed that night and wondered for the hundredth time what was going through Conn Landry's head. He was out there in the living room, supposedly sleeping on the couch. He'd accepted the arrangement without a murmur of protest, as if he couldn't have cared less where he slept. She had been very calm, very deliberate, about fetching pillows and a quilt from the closet and setting them out on the sofa. He'd simply watched her, sitting by the fire, his head back against the cushion of the chair.

She'd been deeply aware of his intent stare all evening, aware of dark, unspoken questions hovering in his mind, aware of the tightly restrained desire in him. All of Honor's feminine instincts warned her that the smoldering caldron of emotions tormenting Conn tonight constituted real danger for her. But a part of her was resonating in response to the mixture of sensations emanating from him.

Honor turned on her side, twisting restlessly amid the sheets and blankets. She hadn't slept at all since going to bed an hour and a half earlier. Dinner had been a quiet affair. Neither Conn nor Honor seemed able to make casual conversation under the tense circumstances. Honor had considered various ways of telling Conn that he couldn't stay the night, but all the phrases of rejection had died on her lips.

It wasn't just that she was afraid he wouldn't leave; it was that, deep down, she didn't want him to leave. A tentative truce had been established out there on the beach that afternoon. She wanted time to pursue it, time to rebuild some basis for trust.

She was a fool to want to reestablish something that had never really existed in the first place, Honor told herself again and again as she lay listening to the insistent pulse of the sea. There was nothing to be salvaged between herself and Conn. He had been using her from the beginning to work out a warped notion of revenge, and now that someone had menaced his extremely valuable racehorse he would probably never trust Honor, even if she could somehow prove her innocence.

And how could she prove her innocence? Someone had apparently seen a visitor at the barns who looked like her. Given the shaky situation between herself and Conn, that was more than enough to damn her in his eyes. Furthermore, he was convinced she'd had a motive.

He'd arrived at the cottage in a fury, full of threats and retaliation. But somehow none of those promises of menace had really materialized. There had been moments of genuine danger; Honor was well aware of them, but Conn hadn't actually carried any of them to the ultimate conclusion. He hadn't hurt her, and tonight he was sleeping on her sofa, not forcing his way into her bed.

Honor tried to think logically, to analyze Conn Landry's actions since his arrival at the cottage. There was no doubt in her mind that he was coiled like a whip, poised to strike. But this evening he seemed uncertain of his target, even though she had been within range all day. She wondered what was holding him back.

Perhaps the part of him that seemed to need her was stronger than the side of him that couldn't trust her. The need in him would involve much more than physical desire, Honor realized. A man like Conn Landry would not be at the mercy of his hormones. He was too self-contained, too controlled. If he was in a turmoil because of a woman it was because he wanted or needed something from her more than physical satisfaction. By the same token, Honor decided, it would be difficult for him to accept that he needed more from a relationship. It would force him to acknowledge a certain vulnerability and that would be hard on Landry.

It was all very confusing, deeply troubling, and it was definitely making it impossible to sleep. Honor moved uneasily, adjusting the covers with a futile gesture. She wished she wasn't so pulsatingly aware of Constantine Landry's presence in the next room. It was as though his own turbulent emotions were reaching out to tangle with hers. Lying there alone she couldn't be certain how much of the tightly-wound sensation she was feeling was due to her own jumbled thoughts or to her awareness of his. The sensation of commingling was strange, adding to her restlessness.

Surmounting all the questions, anger, doubts and fears, however, was a gradually strengthening desire to ease the pain she had seen in his eyes. The tension that had been flowing back and forth between herself and Conn all evening had taken its toll on him as well as on her. She wanted to ease the fierce intensity she sensed in him and in so doing, ease the uncertainty within herself.

But she would be a total idiot to go out into the other room and make any such efforts. There was enough of the predator in Landry to make such a move dangerous in the extreme. True, he had himself under control now, but if she wandered out there dressed in her nightgown, her hair tumbling around her shoulders, her feet bare, he was liable to read an open invitation in her actions. And who could blame him?

Still, she wasn't going to get to sleep tonight at this rate, and the turbulent state of her emotions demanded some positive action. The knowledge that Conn was experiencing his own heightened tension was enough to push Honor into doing something decisive, even if it was reckless.

With a surge of determination she pushed aside the covers and reached for her robe. When she stepped off the small rug beside the bed, her toes curled in response to the cold hardwood floor. But Honor ignored the chilly sensation and walked to her bedroom door. She opened it slowly, softly, and found the living room illuminated only with the faintly smoldering ruins of the fire.

Standing there in the doorway, her fingers clutching the lapels of the robe, Honor swept the shadows with her gaze. She was seeking the man whose unsettled state seemed to have been tangling with her own. When her eyes found his lean form still sprawled in the overstuffed chair in front of the hearth, some of her initial determination faltered. She stood very still in the doorway, not certain what to say now that the moment was upon her.

"Conn?"

"Go back to bed, Honor." The words were spoken in a flat, inflexible tone of warning. Conn didn't move.

Honor took a step forward, the robe flaring gently around her ankles. "I want to talk to you," she said.

"I don't think that's such a good idea right now." He kept his brooding gaze on the fire.

Honor took another step and then a third. She kept going until she was standing beside his chair. "I can't sleep, and it doesn't look as though you've been doing much sleeping, either. We need to talk, Conn."

"About what?" he asked roughly. The pale flicker of the remnants of the fire highlighted the harsh lines of his face as he continued to gaze down into the embers. "We've had trouble talking all evening, in case you haven't noticed. Why should we try it again now? I think it would be much more intelligent on your part if you went back into that bedroom and closed the door."

Honor caught her breath and sank down onto her knees beside the chair so that she could meet his eyes. Her movement finally forced him to look at her, and when he did, she saw the turmoil of frustration and pain and hunger in his gaze.

"Maybe you're right," she said softly. "Maybe now isn't the time to talk."

"Get out of here, Honor. Believe me, it would be best if you went back to your room. I'm not—" He broke off, searching for words and then continued evenly, "I'm not sure of myself right now. I'm not sure that I'm in complete control."

He sounded vaguely dazed by the admission and the words released much of the restraint Honor had tried to put on her own emotions. She reached out and touched his fingers as they lay curling tightly into the arm of the chair. "It's all right, Conn. I'm not in complete control, either. But, then, I never am around you." She risked a tentative smile.

He stared at her. "Woman, do you know what you're doing?"

"Yes. No. Not completely. I only know I can't go back into that bedroom alone. There is too much going on between us. Too much that is unsettled."

The hand she had been lightly touching moved, shifting abruptly to catch her questing fingers in a grip of iron. "Unsettled questions are dangerous, Honor. Don't you know that?"

"I'm learning."

He drew in a deep breath and she could see the decision in his burning eyes. "Why are you so willing to take risks tonight?" he demanded softly.

"I don't seem to have any choice."

Conn gave her a strange look. "You may be right." For a moment longer he simply gripped her hand, not moving as he continued to search her face. "No more choice than I've got in the matter. We're trapped in this web together, you and I. It's been like that from the beginning. I should have realized how it would be. But how could I have guessed?"

"Conn? I don't understand—"

But he didn't allow her to finish the question. Instead, he uncoiled to his feet, retaining his hold on her and drawing her up to stand in front of him. Honor felt the fine trembling in his touch as he pulled her slowly, inevitably, against the length of his body. The heat in him seemed to reach out, engulfing her, and she responded with a soft cry. Her arms went around his waist and she let her head sink down on his shoulder.

"Neither of us can find the words right now," he grated hoarsely. "There's no point trying. You've come to me when you could have stayed safely in your room."

"Yes."

"Then there's nothing else to talk about." He lifted her face with the edge of his palm. For a few intense, vital seconds he stared down into her soft eyes and then he muttered something incomprehensible. Whatever it was got swallowed up in the kiss that followed.

Honor gave herself over to the drugging emotion of the embrace. It seemed to her now that only the flaring passion that ignited so quickly between them could bridge the chasm that stretched between herself and Conn. A part of her would pay any price to cross that abyss tonight. Even if the bridge was made of rainbows and fire and would disintegrate before morning, she would build it because the need to reach him was so overwhelming.

Conn's mouth was a furnace of damp heat that communicated his passion without any restraint. His hands slid down her back to her hips, moving possessively on her. The fierce urgency in him sought to overtake her and bring her to the ground. The predatory quality in Conn that Honor had sensed from the beginning was fully alive tonight, but she understood it because there was an echo of it in herself. Her own need to communicate, even though the communication was on the sensual level, approached the violent in its intensity.

"Honor, I have to have you now. I couldn't stop even if I wanted to try. Woman, you don't know how it is with me tonight, what I feel like inside. I'm burning." Conn's mouth moved heavily on hers, staking a claim before moving to the curve of her shoulder.

Honor gasped as she felt the light touch of his teeth on her bare skin. Then her robe was being loosened, pulled free of her body and discarded at her feet. She shivered as his hands shaped the curves of her breasts, the heat of his palms sinking into her through the soft nightgown. And then the interior of the cottage spun around her as Conn abruptly swept her up into his arms.

She closed her eyes and drew her fingers lightly along the nape of his neck as he carried her into the bedroom. The strength in him made her feel secure, even though a small voice whispered that perhaps she should fear it.

Conn settled her into the depths of the tousled bed and stood for a moment looking down at her. His eyes never left hers as he unbuttoned his shirt and unfastened his belt. When at last he stood naked, his maleness an aggressive force dominating the room, Honor moved. She put out a hand to draw him down to her.

''Honor, honey. Oh, *Honor!*''

He came to her, stripping off her nightgown in a swift, impatient movement that left the material crumpled in a heap at the foot of the bed. Then Conn moved across her body with the power of a wave breaking on a reef. Honor felt herself responding vibrantly, her body achingly alive and aware. The emotional tension that had been tightening within her all day was transmuted into a physical tension. It sang through her nerve endings and throbbed deep in her lower body.

She traced the outline of Conn's hard, muscled frame with soft fingers that held a woman's demands. He groaned in response to her touch, pushing himself into her palm when she drew her hand down his thighs.

''Conn,'' she whispered as the driving power in him throbbed under her touch.

''I want you, Honor. I can't stop wanting you,'' he rasped. His lips roved from one nipple to the other, exciting and challenging. When Honor lifted her hips instinctively, moving against him with unconscious need, he traced a sensuous path down her body to the apex of her legs. ''Open for me, sweetheart. Let me feel the passion in you.''

She writhed beneath him, obeying the command. His husky

words of encouragement and demand were dark and heavy in her ears. Then she felt his fingers working exotic magic amid the secrets of her body and she cried out again.

"You want me," he growled, pushing his strong legs between her soft thighs. "Say it. Say you want me!"

"Yes, darling. I want you. With everything that's in me. I've never needed anyone the way I need you."

Her words seemed to thrust him over the edge. Conn muttered her name between clenched teeth, and then he was forging into her warmth, claiming her fire for his own with relentless force.

"Hold me," he ordered with an aching harshness. "Hold me, Honor. Wrap yourself around me and don't let go!"

Honor had the fleeting but vivid impression that Conn wasn't even aware of his own rough command but she reacted to it with everything that was in her. With all her strength she clung to him, riding the whirlwind. The final burst of unraveling excitement sent shivers through her that generated a powerful reaction in Conn. His fingers sank into the skin of her shoulders and he arched heavily into her softness. There was a thick muffled, wholly male cry of release and satisfaction from far back in his throat and then he was collapsing damply along her body.

For a long while Honor lay quietly beneath Conn's muscled weight, recovering her energy and her senses. She was beginning to think he might have gone to sleep when he finally stirred and opened his eyes to look down at her flushed face.

"I wonder," Conn murmured at last, "if you have any idea of what you've done."

"They say that in reality it doesn't work," she whispered soberly.

"What doesn't work?"

"Going to bed with a man in order to achieve some sense of communication. The conventional wisdom has it that in the end all you get is a few moments of illusion. In the morning everything's the same."

His lashes lowered until she couldn't read the expression in the gray eyes. ''Is that what you were doing? Trying to communicate?''

''I suppose. I couldn't stand the distance between us any longer. I guess a part of me thought that if we...if I...''

''A part of you thought that if you seduced me the distance between us would disappear?'' He toyed with a tendril of her hair as it lay along her bare shoulder. ''You took a big risk.''

''Did I?''

He paused a few beats as if thinking it over. ''Yes. I could use you now. Let you think that you were achieving your mystical, nonverbal communication for a few days.''

''While you worked me out of your system?'' she dared.

''Umm. And when I've had enough I could simply walk out the door.'' He twisted the tendril of hair between his fingers and tugged slightly, his mouth tightening.

''Yes,'' she agreed. ''You could do that.''

''There's just one problem,'' Conn continued thoughtfully.

''What's that?''

''I don't think I could ever get enough of you to work you out of my system. I'd be deluding myself if I decided to try that route.''

Honor closed her eyes briefly, aware of the precarious balance between them. ''I was deluding myself when I decided to try going to bed with you in order to communicate more effectively.''

He went still. ''Were you?''

''I went to bed with you because I love you,'' she admitted softly. ''I suppose communication is a part of love, but the truth is that I would have walked out into that living room tonight even if I knew that I'd never see you again afterward.''

''Honor,'' he breathed, lowering his head to brush his mouth against hers, ''I'm glad.''

''You probably are,'' she agreed wistfully. ''The way it stands now, I get to take all the risks, don't I?''

"Loving me is a risk?" He frowned.

"A big one. I never dreamed I'd fall in love with a man who couldn't give me his trust. But, then, I never thought I'd be foolish enough to fall in love with a man I couldn't trust, either."

Conn's frown metamorphosed into cold anger, but he didn't move. "You're saying you love me but you don't trust me? I don't believe you, Honor. I've never given you any reason not to trust me."

"You didn't tell me you were Richard Stoner's son," she reminded him.

"That's different," he flared, visibly offended by her interpretation of his silence on that score. "I never lied to you about it. I simply decided not to mention it until...until I got to know you better."

"Until you'd decided how you'd take your revenge?"

He shook his head once with savage impatience. "No. I knew it would introduce a problem into our relationship and I didn't want to do that. Not when everything between us was so new and fragile. I wanted to move cautiously until I knew you understood how things were between us."

She stared up at him. "And how are things between us?" Honor whispered.

Conn's head lifted with faint masculine challenge. "I want you and you love me. That pretty well sums it all up, don't you think?"

"I think I'm getting the short end of the deal," she tossed back. "Other than that—"

"No," Conn interrupted grittily. "You're not getting the short end of the deal. You're getting everything I have to give."

Dumbfounded, Honor looked up at him. "All you have to give? I don't understand."

His hands framed her face, holding her still. "I want you," he said evenly, "more than I've ever wanted any woman in my life. It goes beyond wanting in a physical sense. I could handle that if it only involved a desire to take you to bed. But it's more than that. I need you in some way I can't explain. And because I have to have you in order to stay sane I'm prepared to take a risk. More of a risk than I have ever taken with another human being. I've been thinking about it all afternoon. It's what was going through my head out there in front of the fire. It's been eating at me since I got here this morning. I have to trust you. I don't seem to have any choice. Tell me again that you didn't try to poison Legacy.''

''I didn't try to hurt Legacy in any way,'' she answered in a low but very steady voice.

He sighed and she felt something in him relax. ''I've met a lot of people who can lie while they smile and look you straight in the eye. Enough of them to know you're probably not one of them. It's taken me a few hours to work it out because everything hit me like a ton of bricks this morning.''

''And you instinctively expected the worst from me because I'm Nick Mayfield's daughter, right?'' she asked with resigned bitterness.

''I'm accustomed to expecting the worst from people in general,'' he admitted calmly. ''Life is safer and simpler that way. That philosophy has been responsible for keeping me alive on occasion.''

''I can imagine.'' But she knew he missed the note of irony. Conn was too busy finishing what he had to say.

''But there's a softness in you that wouldn't mesh very well with a woman who would try to get revenge on a man by poisoning a horse. You give yourself too completely when you give yourself to me. You don't hold back. Even tonight when you thought you were only seducing me in order to reestablish communication you weren't careful or cautious. There is no restraint in you when you take me in your arms. You wrap yourself around me and make it very clear that you want me and need me. You're *vulnerable* to me, aren't you?''

''Not by choice.''

A cool, laconic smile flickered briefly at the edge of his

mouth. ''No, not by choice. In spite of yourself. You know you should be wary of me. You're smart enough to realize I could be dangerous. From the very beginning you've tried to be careful around me, put some distance between us. But it didn't work, did it?''

''No.''

He nodded in deep satisfaction. ''When you opened the door and walked out into the living room tonight, I knew for certain.''

Honor moved her head uneasily on the pillow. His palms slid down to her throat. ''Knew what for certain?''

''That you couldn't stand the space between us. The knowledge that what we had together was teetering on the brink was eating at you, wasn't it? You couldn't bear to let it all fall apart. When you came out into that room to find me, I realized you couldn't let me go any more than I could allow you to walk away from me.''

''You make it sound as though we're trapped together.''

''We are. Caught up in a web from which neither of us can escape. We need each other. You label your emotion love and I call mine wanting, but it amounts to the same thing.''

Desperately Honor tried to think it all through. ''You believe I didn't try to get at you through Legacy?''

''I believe you didn't try to poison the colt,'' Conn stated quietly.

The breath Honor had been holding escaped in a long sigh. ''Thank you, Conn.''

His thumb moved slowly along the base of her throat. ''It's your turn. Do you believe I didn't deliberately seduce you in order to get revenge for what happened between our parents?''

''I think,'' Honor said very honestly, ''that you would use some other method if you were really out to punish me for what you think happened fifteen years ago. As I said earlier, if you ever went for my throat, you'd be quick and brutal about it. You wouldn't make love to me the way you do.''

The smile reappeared fleetingly. ''And just how do I make love to you?''

''Completely. Overwhelmingly. I can't believe that you're playing bedroom games with me. There's too much of...of *you* in the way you make love.'' It was the truth, Honor realized. There was a quality of blatant, fundamental honesty in the way Conn staked his claim of passion and possession. No games, no fancy techniques such as another man might employ to achieve a woman's surrender. Just rock-solid desire that carried its own kind of reassurance and established its own integrity. She, too, had had a chance to do some thinking this afternoon and evening, Honor decided with sudden insight.

''I think we both needed the breathing space we got this afternoon,'' Conn said, his eyes intent.

''Did you mean what you said a minute ago? That your idea of wanting and my notion of love amount to the same thing?'' She wasn't certain why she risked the question. There was too much riding on it, too much hope. It was reckless to ask questions like that, but she needed to know exactly how he felt about her. If he chose to label his love for her ''wanting'' and ''needing,'' she could live with that. So long as underneath she knew that what he really felt was equivalent to what she felt.

The gray eyes softened indulgently. ''Why do women always want to dress it up by calling it love?''

''It's not a matter of dressing it up. Love is what it is. Why not call it by its proper name?'' It was Honor's turn to be indulgent. ''I think you're the one who's searching for labels. Do you love me, Conn? Are you playing it safe again by hiding behind more acceptable macho words like *want* and *need?*''

His eyes narrowed faintly. ''I'm not trying to play it safe. I'm trying to be honest with you. I want nothing but honesty between us from here on in, Honor. We have to establish that if we're to have a basis for a future.''

"I agree," she whispered tremulously. "We need honesty. But if we're to have a future, we also need love. I thought—that is, I was beginning to think—that maybe you were falling in love with me and that you just weren't sure of the words yet. But that's not the case, is it?"

"I know the words don't mean much. Do you want me to say them even though I don't believe in them?" he challenged roughly.

"No." She shook her head quickly. "No, I don't want you to lie to me. Not ever."

"I won't, honey," he soothed, stroking her cheek with infinite care. "You can believe anything I tell you."

"What about the things you don't tell me?"

He shrugged, his sleek shoulders moving easily in the shadows. "The things I don't tell you aren't important for you to know. They don't impact us."

She swallowed, a little stunned. "You're so incredibly arrogant at times. And the most arrogant thing of all is that I don't think you even realize it. You just take your own assurance for granted. Will you take me for granted, I wonder?"

He moved his head in a gesture of absolute denial. "Never. I'll take care of you, Honor. I'll protect you. I'll take you to bed as often as possible and I'll always tell you the truth. But I swear I'll never take you for granted. How could I? I've been around long enough to realize that some things are unique in the universe."

"But you don't love me," she concluded sadly.

Anger flashed quickly across his face. "What I feel for you hasn't got anything to do with something as rosy and soft and ephemeral as love. It's a hell of a lot more certain and more real. I'm making a commitment to you, lady. And I'm asking for a commitment in return. Something we can both count on, something solid and sure. If I'm going to get tangled up in this web with you, I'm going to pull all the strands as tight as possible."

''Because you always tie up loose ends,'' she finished for him.

''Always.'' He relaxed again. ''Why do you keep pushing, sweetheart? You know it's settled now, don't you?''

''I think it is. For you.''

''It works both ways. Whatever chance you had of freeing yourself from the trap in which we're caught disappeared when you came out into the living room to find me tonight.'' He lowered his head to seal the words against her mouth. ''I don't want to talk anymore for a while, Honor.'' His palm slid meaningfully down her arm until his fingers twined with hers. Then he raised her hand to a level with her ear and turned it so that he could kiss the vulnerable inside of her wrist.

Honor hesitated for a moment, trying to hold back long enough to force him to continue the dialogue that had just been established. Then she gave up the effort. What was the point? She'd accomplished so much. She would make herself be content with what she had achieved tonight. After all, she had known from the beginning that Conn Landry did not understand love. She could hardly expect the revelation to hit him on top of everything else that had happened today. At the moment she would be grateful that the relationship between herself and the man she loved had not fallen over the brink on which it had been so precariously balanced. Together she and Conn had rescued it.

Love would come eventually, Honor reassured herself as she surrendered to the insistence of Conn's touch. For him the trust was the hard part and she hoped that tonight his belief in her integrity had been established. There was time to work on building the rest.

Honor awoke a long time later, vaguely aware that she was lying alone in bed. It took a moment to reorient herself, and when she did, she sat up with a sudden, panicked jerk.

''Conn?''

''I'm in the kitchen. Be back in a minute. I just wanted a glass of water.''

''Oh.'' In relief Honor glanced at the clock beside the bed. It was two-thirty in the morning. Now that she was awake, she felt a little thirsty herself. Sleepily she pushed aside the quilt and padded barefoot into the kitchen. Conn was standing near the sink, drinking his glass of water while he studied yet another shot of Stylish Legacy.

''Hey, it's cold out here,'' he murmured as Honor reached into the cupboard to get a glass for herself. ''You should have put on your robe.''

''You're a fine one to talk,'' she grumbled, eyeing his attire, which consisted solely of a pair of white briefs. ''You've got on a lot less than I have.'' She yawned as she filled the glass.

''I was planning on using you to warm myself up as soon as I got back into bed,'' Conn informed her absently as he bent a little closer to Stylish Legacy's photo. ''You know, I think Legacy inherited his sire's basic conformation, especially the strong hindquarters.''

Honor gave him a small, amused smile. ''You've got it bad, Conn.''

''What?'' He turned his head to glance at her in surprise.

''Racing. I can see it's really getting a hold on you. My father was that way about it. He tried to keep Stylish Legacy just a business deal, a tax shelter. But the truth was that he was hooked on the whole racing scene.''

Conn watched her drink her water. ''So was my father. Just look at the two of them in this photo. You'd think they'd won the Kentucky Derby instead of just another stakes race.''

Automatically Honor's gaze followed his. She rarely looked at the photos closely. Whenever she saw the pictures of her father and his partner, the old, unsettled sensation swept over her. As a result she had gotten into the habit of never really studying the photos.

But for some reason Conn's deep interest in the pictures of

Stylish Legacy intrigued her. For the first time in years she found herself looking at the jumble of people around the winning horse. Conn was right. Regardless of what had happened between them later, at the time this picture was taken Richard Stoner and Nick Mayfield were two very happy, very satisfied racehorse owners.

"They do look quite pleased with themselves," she acknowledged softly.

"So does everyone else in the photo. How do all those strangers always manage to crowd into the picture?"

"I expect it's kind of a game. Like getting yourself on TV when a television film crew shows up." Honor realized that she wasn't feeling the usual uncomfortable sadness she remembered experiencing in the past whenever she'd looked at these pictures. Out of curiosity she moved across the kitchen to glance at another. Her trained eye began to pick out details, automatically recording the color of the riding silks the jockey wore, the fifteen-year-old suit her father had on and the cowboy hat on the head of the man standing directly behind Richard Stoner.

Honor blinked and leaned closer.

"What is it?" Conn asked, moving across to stand beside her.

"I think this guy in the hat behind your stepfather is also in that other photo."

"The trainer, probably."

"No, I don't think so. There's something familiar about that hat, Conn." Thoughtfully Honor went back to stare at the other picture. "Same hat. I can't really see his face, but I'd swear there was something about him...." Honor moved to yet another picture, and in this one the face beneath the brim of the cowboy hat was much clearer. "Conn! It's Ethan Bailey. A lot slimmer than he is now and fifteen years younger, but I'd swear it's Ethan."

Conn leaned over her shoulder to stare at the man in the hat. "You're right. But Ethan barely knew either of our fathers. Why would he show up in three winner's circle photos with Dad and Mayfield?''

''At three different tracks, too. He's hardly the type to run down into the circle to get into the picture just for kicks. That sort of activity is for kids and pranksters.''

Conn straightened, shaking his head. ''We'll have to ask him about it sometime.'' He reached for Honor's hand. ''Come on, honey, let's go back to bed. My feet are getting cold. Along with a few other parts of my anatomy.''

''You expect me to warm all of those parts?''

''It would be a nice, considerate gesture.''

A wifely gesture, Honor thought wistfully. But she kept the comment to herself.

''You know,'' Conn observed lazily as he snuggled Honor down into the covers a moment later, ''I feel as though I'm finally able to think normally again. I spent most of the day feeling bruised, battered, hung over and furious. Now at last everything's begun to settle down.''

''That must be a relief,'' Honor murmured, running her fingers through his hair. ''I have a hunch you're not used to being shaken up and confused, are you?''

''No,'' he growled. ''I'm not.'' He curled Honor closer into his body, luxuriating in the warmth of her.

''Well, if it's any consolation, neither am I,'' she told him gently.

It was then that Conn's new clearheadedness reminded him of the question he had intended to ask Honor. He paused, his mouth hovering just over hers.

''How did you find out I was Richard Stoner's son?''

Honor was quiet for a moment and then she said calmly, ''Ethan Bailey told me.''

Landry swore very softly and sat up in bed. ''Why is it that every time I turn around lately, Ethan Bailey seems to be nearby?''

Nine

"Didn't you realize that Ethan Bailey knew who you were?" Honor asked. She lay propped up on the pillows, watching Conn as he swung his feet over the edge of the bed and turned on the lamp.

"The subject never came up with Ethan."

"You've said yourself that racetrack rumors are prevalent. And Ethan's been around racetracks for years. Other than using your own name instead of Stoner, did you ever make any effort to hide your connection with Stylish Legacy and his original owners?"

"No." The answer was clipped, impatient, as if Conn's mind was busy tracing a pattern and didn't want to be bothered with side issues. Conn stared unseeingly at the wall for several tense minutes, his face set in familiar, harsh lines.

Uneasily Honor leaned forward to touch his shoulder. "Conn?"

"Ethan was the one who found the apples in Legacy's feed this morning. The one who told me you'd been seen around the barns very early today."

"Oh." She didn't quite know what to say in response. Her hand dropped from his shoulder.

Conn twisted around to meet her eyes, his gaze cold and intent. "When did he tell you who I was?"

"Yesterday. He came downtown to my office and said he felt obliged to warn me that you might not be telling me the whole truth about yourself," Honor said in a low voice. Conn's mouth became even grimmer. "It wasn't the first time he'd tried to warn me about you."

Conn caught her chin on the edge of his hand and held her still. The gunmetal-gray of his eyes was almost lethal in the soft light. "What else did he tell you about me?"

Honor licked her suddenly dry lower lip. From out of nowhere the fear of Constantine Landry resurfaced. A knot of tension began tightening in her stomach as she felt the power in his hand. He wasn't hurting her, merely anchoring her in place for the moment, but the leashed savagery in his eyes was more than enough to trigger elemental alarms all over again. Forcibly she fought down the doubts and uncertainties. Conn's violence was not aimed at her.

"He implied at one point that you might be mixed up in gambling up at Tahoe. I wondered if that was why you knew how to bring pressure to bear on Granger," she admitted unsteadily.

"That bastard," Conn said far too calmly. He didn't release her.

Honor wasn't certain if he was referring to Ethan Bailey or Granger. Taking a grip on her nerves she continued more firmly. "He told me that I wasn't your usual type."

"As if he'd know."

"Yes. Well, then yesterday he said he'd realized who both of us were and he wanted to warn me that you'd once sworn revenge on my family. He implied you were playing some kind of cat-and-mouse game with me." With a touch of anger Honor wrenched herself free of Conn's grasp and drew her knees up under the sheet. She balanced an elbow on each knee, folded her arms and rested her chin on them. "Which you were, in a way."

Conn exhaled slowly. "Which I was, in a way," he agreed coolly.

He made no immediate move to touch her, but Honor could feel the implacable intensity of his eyes. "For the record," she asked softly, "just how do you make a living that allows you to buy expensive racehorses and gives you the free time to hang around Pasadena looking up old family acquaintances?''

There was a measure of silence before Conn retorted, ''Does it matter?''

She slid him a sidelong glance and then returned to her contemplation of the foot of the bed. *Did it matter?* She could practically feel the challenge in him. He was deliberately pushing her, she thought, and wondered why. There were two possible causes: arrogance and insecurity.

The idea of Conn Landry feeling insecure and needing reassurance was laughable. But even Landry's arrogance had its limits. She took another risk.

''Do you mean, does it matter in terms of how it affects our relationship? No, it doesn't. But I guess I'd like to know whether or not I'm going to be expected to entertain business acquaintances like Mr. Granger on a frequent basis.''

''Relax, Honor,'' he murmured, his voice softening with a combination of amusement and satisfaction, ''I don't make a living by investing in Granger's kind of business. The investments I've made are mostly in real estate. I was paid far too much for the kind of work I did overseas, and since I had no one to spend it on and was too busy to use it myself, I just kept funneling it into stateside property. By the time I came back to the States, there was a nice nest egg waiting for me.''

The way he said it was just a little too smooth, Honor decided, not without a trace of amusement. She lifted her chin off her arms and looked at him. ''How is it you were able to deal so effectively with Granger? Or was he just intimidated by your, uh, forceful personality?''

Honor could have sworn that a red stain appeared momentarily along Conn's cheekbones. She found it almost endearing.

''I occasionally do some consulting work,'' Landry admitted with great care. ''You get to know people that way. Make certain contacts.''

''Consulting work for whom?'' She pressed more out of curiosity now than uneasiness.

''Businesses,'' he said very easily. ''It was my field of expertise, you know. People hired me to analyze security procedures and come up with ways to minimize risks overseas. The same needs exist here in the States.''

''Go on,'' she encouraged, intrigued now.

''Well,'' Conn continued cautiously, ''one of my first jobs when I got back to the States was to analyze the security arrangements around a certain, er, businessman who deals heavily with some of the rougher elements of society.''

''You did consulting work for a gangster.'' Honor nodded in sudden comprehension.

Conn's expression turned distant and forbidding. ''He was a friend of mine. Someone I met a long time ago. He and I had a lot in common at one time but he chose to take a slightly different route to success. When I got back to the States he got in touch. Said I was the only man he could trust to set up a security system for him. I owed him, Honor. He saved my life once when we worked together briefly several years ago. I always pay my debts. At any rate I used my connection with my former, uh, client, when I confronted Granger. Clout, you might say.''

''It's all right, Conn. I trust you,'' Honor said with a smile. ''No more questions about how you managed to intimidate Granger.''

He frowned. ''Are you sure?''

''I'm sure.''

''That still leaves us with the current problem,'' he remarked, clearly relieved to be able to put the other aside.

''Ethan Bailey.''

Conn nodded, saying nothing.

''Ethan did more than tell me you were looking for revenge,'' Honor offered offhandedly. ''He also told me you lied about Granger.''

''Lied about Granger! What did he say?'' Conn demanded.

"That Granger had never been picked up that day at the track. That he hadn't walked into any trap."

"The implication being, of course, that I hadn't saved you from getting mixed up in the mess. That the whole story had been a fabrication designed to establish a link between you and me. A link I could use." Conn sounded coldly bitter.

"You've implied more than once that I was under some sort of obligation to you," she reminded him gently.

"Damn right," he shot back. "You were. But it was a legitimate obligation. I didn't fake it."

Honor shook her head, another flash of amusement lighting her eyes. "So arrogant."

Conn's mouth curved wryly. "I must seem that way to you at times."

"So Granger really did walk into a trap set by the authorities that day?" she queried.

"Oh, yes. And he was released on bail shortly thereafter."

"What would you have done if I hadn't conveniently needed rescuing?" Honor asked, accepting his version of the truth.

"Found another way to approach you. When I realized you were following Granger, I decided to wait and see what was happening. It raised a lot of questions. Brought up the possibility that you were in trouble."

"So you decided to take advantage of the situation."

Conn shrugged. "That's the way I am, Honor. I take advantage of my opportunities. I wanted a solid approach to take with you, and that business with Granger gave it to me. I would have been a fool to let it slide."

"I can see why you've been financially successful," she said dryly. The predator in him would never be far below the surface.

"I suggest we get back to Ethan Bailey," Conn said harshly. "It seems very clear that he's the reason we're both here instead of having dinner in Pasadena. He warned you off of me."

''Perhaps out of genuine concern,'' Honor pointed out.

Conn brushed that aside. ''He did more than warn you, he lied to you about Granger. Implied I had lied to you.''

Honor heard the emphasis on his last words. ''That really bothers you, doesn't it? That he made it sound as though you'd been less than truthful with me.''

''I told you earlier tonight that I've never lied to you,'' he said grittily.

Honor nodded quickly, aware of the simmering fury in him. ''All right. We've got a situation in which Ethan Bailey keeps cropping up, apparently with the goal of making each of us distrust the other.''

''He sure as hell implied that it had to be you who tried to give the poison to Legacy,'' Conn said. ''But why? It makes no sense.''

''I know. No sense at all. Why should Ethan care about you and me getting together?''

''There's another name that keeps recurring, too—Granger.'' Conn became thoughtful for a long moment. ''It seems to me we've found ourselves talking about him almost as often as we've talked about Bailey.''

Honor put her chin back down on her arms. ''Remember the evening that guy in the pickup truck hassled me?''

''Yes.'' He looked at her sharply.

''Well, I could have sworn a similar sort of pickup followed me when I left Pasadena yesterday evening.''

Conn was suddenly tense. He leaned forward and caught her shoulder, pulling her around to face him. ''You're sure?''

''No. No, I'm not sure,'' she said honestly. ''Traffic was heavy and I could have been mistaken. There are a million pickups on the road these days. You know that. I didn't notice it after a while. Just for a time there, after I got on the freeway. It made me nervous. Then it disappeared. It was probably just my imagination.''

''Right now I'm not willing to write anything off to imagination,'' Conn said bluntly. ''This is getting screwy.''

''We've got so little to go on. Ethan in those photos with Dad and your stepfather. The guy in the pickup truck. Granger.''

''The guy in the pickup truck could be associated with Granger,'' Conn said slowly. ''But I don't know why. Granger and I did business together. When it was concluded I thought each side was reasonably satisfied with the results.''

''Maybe he didn't like the way you got involved in the affair,'' Honor suggested. ''After all, it was between him and Adena.''

Conn shook his head. ''I guess he might have decided to teach me a lesson.'' He sounded as though he thought it was highly unlikely.

''If he did would he have been capable of hurting Legacy in order to punish you?''

Conn gave her a pitying glance. ''Granger has been successfully collecting money from his loan shark operations for years. Believe me, he's resorted to more exotic techniques than poisoning a horse.''

''So I'm a little naive,'' she mumbled. ''I just can't see someone deliberately poisoning a beautiful animal like Legacy.''

''You're right. You're a little naive.'' There was affection in his tone as Conn threaded his fingers through her tangled hair.

''You know, we're forgetting something here,'' she went on musingly. ''Legacy never was actually poisoned. You said Ethan showed you the evidence?''

''That's right. Claimed he got it out of Legacy's stall.''

''And then he told you I'd been seen around the barns.''

''Yes.'' The affection disappeared from Conn's voice.

Honor shook her head. ''You must have hated me for a while.''

He hesitated. ''I felt betrayed,'' he finally acknowledged.

''Like father, like daughter?''

He winced. ''I'll admit the thought went through my head.

But you must have felt the same way after Ethan told you his tales.''

''I did. Betrayed.''

There was another moment of silence before Conn said softly, ''Ironic, isn't it?''

''Because of the betrayal that occurred between your father and mine? Maybe it was inevitable once you and I made contact.''

''No, it was not inevitable,'' Conn muttered tightly. ''The sense of betrayal you and I experienced was deliberately fostered by a third party.''

''Ethan Bailey. But he had the material with which to work, didn't he? And he was right, in a way,'' Honor added.

''Right about what?''

''I'm probably not your usual type,'' she explained lightly.

''Am I yours?'' he retorted.

''Well, no, you're not. Adena was right about that fact, I'm afraid.''

''Lady, are you teasing me?'' Conn moved abruptly, pushing her back against the pillows and pinning her there. He searched her face, daring her to admit it.

''Maybe. A little.''

Conn groaned and then gave her a quick, hard kiss before sitting upright again. ''If it matters, I don't think I have a usual type. There haven't been a lot of women in my life, Honor.'' He looked down at his hands.

''I'm not surprised,'' she said calmly.

He slid her a startled glance. ''Why do you say that? Am I that poor a catch?''

''You wouldn't make a poor catch, just an extremely difficult one to land,'' she drawled thoughtfully. ''A woman would need a very carefully built net.''

His eyes narrowed. ''It's academic now, isn't it? You and I wound up in the net together. We're both caught.''

No, Honor thought, *not quite. I don't have you, not completely. But you do have me. A little unfair, but that's the way the world works, I guess.* Aloud she said, "As you say, it's academic. Especially tonight."

"Especially tonight. Tonight we've got to think a little more about Ethan Bailey."

"And Granger," she added.

Conn suddenly surged to his feet, reaching out for his jeans and pulling them on quickly. "Maybe I can get a few answers about Granger at least."

"Right now?" Honor asked. "In the middle of the night?"

"Some of the people who would know about Granger tend to work the night shift," Conn informed her, buttoning his shirt. "In my line of work I tend to make just as many contacts on the right side of the fence as I do on the wrong side."

"What are you going to do?" Honor slid out of bed and tugged on her robe.

"Make a few phone calls." He started out into the living room with a purposeful stride. "Good thing you keep a phone here."

"Have to. The people I rent to usually can't afford to be without access to a telephone, even when they're on vacation. They're always wheeling and dealing or pretending that they are. Part of the L.A. image." Honor followed him, stepping into her slippers en route. She reached the bedroom doorway just as Conn reached for the phone.

She saw the sudden hardening of his expression even before he started to dial.

"Damn," he muttered, tossing the receiver back into its cradle.

"What's wrong?"

"Phone's out of order." He stood staring at her, gaze unreadable.

"Are you sure? There hasn't been a storm or anything recently."

"No, there hasn't, has there? Get dressed, Honor."

"Dressed! But it's three o'clock in the morning."

"I'm aware of that. It's three o'clock in the morning, the

phone's out of order, and we're miles from town. Add to that a short list of rather pithy questions that remain unanswered and the fact that I'm finally starting to think clearly again—and you've got a very messy situation. I want us both out of here. Now. Go get dressed and don't waste any time on the job.'' He started toward her.

''All right, all right, I'm going,'' she said quickly. Honor spun around and headed back into the bedroom, spurred on by the cool command in his words. ''Are you always like this when you're working?''

He was busy stuffing a few of her things into her suitcase. ''Like what?''

''Overbearing and intimidating. You sound like you've had a lot of experience giving orders.'' She yanked on the jeans and a vividly striped cotton sweater.

''Maybe. Frankly, I've never thought about it.'' He snapped the case shut. ''Ready?''

''No.''

''Too bad. Let's get going.'' He took her arm and towed her toward the door.

''Do you think it's possible you're overreacting to a dead telephone?'' Honor inquired dryly.

''Possible. Even probable.''

''But that's not going to slow us down, is it?''

''Not a bit.'' He opened the front door, slamming it behind them and fishing the Porsche keys out of his pocket in one movement. ''Get into the car, Honor.''

She was beginning to absorb some of his strange sense of urgency, Honor realized, as she hurried around the front of the Porsche and opened the passenger door. He was inside, twisting the key in the ignition even as she dropped into the seat beside him. The normally responsive engine came alive briefly, shuddered and died.

Conn swore and tried again. This time there was even less reaction. He didn't bother to try a third time. Instead he drummed his fingers lightly on the steering wheel and stared out into the darkness.

''We,'' he announced mildly, ''have very big trouble.''

''We could try my car,'' she volunteered tentatively, sensing his deadly serious concern.

''We could, but I have a strange hunch it wouldn't do any good.'' He shoved open the car door. ''Come on, Honor, let's go.''

''Where are we going this time? And what do you mean about my car being dead, too?'' Anxiously she leaped out of the Porsche, wresting her own keys out of her purse.

Conn glanced around, sweeping the night-dark scene around the cottage. He seemed to make a decision. ''Okay, let me have the keys. We'll give it a try.''

When her car didn't start on the first attempt, Conn didn't bother with a second. He was out of the seat, grabbing Honor's wrist and yanking her along behind him before the car door had swung shut.

''You think someone sabotaged the cars?'' she gasped in amazement, stumbling a little as he pulled her back toward the cottage.

It wasn't Conn who answered her. Another voice responded to the question. ''If he does think that, he'd be right,'' drawled the man who had last been seen driving a black pickup truck. He stepped around the corner of the cottage, allowing the weak moonlight to illuminate the gun he held.

Honor was so startled that she stumbled heavily against Conn. He automatically reached out to steady her but somehow managed to pull her even more thoroughly off balance. In the next instant they both tumbled to the ground with Honor landing in an undignified sprawl across Conn's body.

''Golly, lady. You got a problem or something?'' demanded the man with the gun. ''Get up. Both of you. Mr. Granger don't want no delays.''

''Granger!'' The astonishment as well as the anger in Conn's tone was real. Slowly he got to his feet, using his left hand to steady Honor. She was trembling, he realized, but there was little he could do at the moment to reassure her. "Granger sent you?"

"I guess you must have made Mr. Granger mad, moving in on his turf and all." The young punk motioned with the nose of the Saturday night special. "Let's go. Don't got all night."

Conn kept his hold on Honor's arm, pulling her with him as he slowly obeyed the gunman's orders.

"Conn?" Honor spoke his name softly, questioningly, but she followed the urging of his grip as they set out toward the beach.

"Do as he says, honey. He's wired," Conn said in a low voice. The sound of the surf covered his last words but they were dangerously true. The guy with the gun was probably only eighteen or nineteen, street-tough, but riding some kind of high. Perhaps it was just the tense excitement of holding a gun on two people or the rush of power that undoubtedly was coursing through him. Perhaps he'd indulged in a few chemicals to work up his nerve for the task. Whatever it was, the man was lethally high-strung and therefore very unpredictable. Conn had seen the syndrome before. The only way to deal with it at this point was to keep him talking. Conn needed an opening.

"I thought Granger and I had a deal," Conn said, projecting his voice over the increasing noise of the surf. "I was under the impression Mr. Granger stuck by his deals." The gunman was herding his captives out onto the beach where there was virtually no cover behind which a desperate man could dodge. The sand became a further barrier to quick movement, dragging at Conn's shoes and causing Honor to stumble occasionally.

"Mr. Granger don't like the way you conduct business, slick. He said to tell you that you won't be getting in his way again after tonight. It's me that's got a deal with Granger," the punk added with pride.

Conn seized on the hint of arrogance. ''Granger trusts you to take care of us?''

Beside him Honor gasped as her foot collided with a stray piece of driftwood. Other than that she hadn't said a word, Conn realized grimly. She was scared to death, but she wasn't panicking. He felt a possessive admiration for her self-control. The last thing he needed right now was a hysterical woman. The next few minutes were going to be extremely precarious.

''Granger's sent word that he's giving me my chance to prove I can handle jobs for him,'' the gunman explained. ''And you can bet I ain't gonna let him down. Getting in with Granger's a quick way to the big time and I ain't gonna do nothing to blow my chances.''

Honor spoke for the first time, glancing over her shoulder to search the man's face in the watery moonlight. It was cold and there was a stiff breeze snapping the air from off the waves. She shivered again under Conn's hand. ''You're the man in the black pickup truck who followed me home the other night, aren't you?''

''You got it, lady.''

''And you also followed her out of Pasadena?'' Conn put in coolly.

''Had to see where you were heading. We knew that wherever the broad went, you'd be sure to follow.''

Conn thought about that for a few seconds. ''Is that right?''

''You should of stayed in your own league, Landry. Shouldn't have tried to mess around with Granger. He's big-time.''

''I didn't realize he was extending his scope of activities to include this kind of thing,'' Conn admitted dryly. ''But I guess it's safe enough for him. After all, you're the one taking all the chances.''

The gunman's eyes narrowed in the moonlight. Conn saw the hot, tense anger in the man's face and the uneasy way he lifted the weapon. ''I ain't taking no chances, Landry. I told you, Granger's big. He's got this all planned out. All I got to do is carry out instructions and everything's going to be just fine. No sweat."

"The only reason Granger got to be big-time is because he pays people like you to take the risks for him," Conn pointed out calmly.

"Shut up, unless you want it here and now," the punk rasped.

"I take it here and now isn't the way Granger wants it done?" Conn retorted. He felt the fury in himself and wondered at it. It wasn't just that he knew he'd been stupid for having allowed this situation to occur. It went beyond that, centering around his self-disgust at having failed to properly protect Honor. She was his woman, he thought tautly. It was his responsibility to protect her. Yet he'd allowed the reckless passion and the conflicting feelings of betrayal and inexplicable trust to swamp his normally cold-blooded, clear thinking to the point where he'd put Honor in jeopardy. It was traumatic to realize just how deeply involved he was with Honor Mayfield.

"Granger was real particular about how he'd like this done, but if you get tricky, I'm supposed to go ahead and finish things any way I can."

"Where are we going?" Honor asked softly.

"What's that?" the punk demanded suspiciously.

"I asked where we're going," she repeated obediently.

"Down to the far end of the beach. The water's supposed to be dangerous down by the point. Couple of bodies might not resurface for days, if ever."

"I see," Honor muttered.

Conn felt her drawing in deep, even breaths, trying to control her fear. The knowledge that she was so frightened enraged him further. Savagely he clamped a lid on his emotional reaction. It wouldn't help matters if he allowed his own control to disintegrate. He was unaware of how roughly he had begun to grip Honor's arm until she looked up at him questioningly. He relaxed his hold but he didn't release her. It was cold out here, he thought vaguely. The water would be unbearable.

''You seem to know a lot about the ocean currents around here,'' Conn managed to observe as they reached the water's edge and turned toward the rocky point at the far end of the beach. There wasn't much more time. The point was only about fifty yards away, looming dark and forbidding in the shadows. Around its base white water foamed evilly.

''I got all the instructions,'' the gunman informed him sullenly. ''I told you everything was planned.''

''Were you the one who moved the screen in my bedroom?'' Honor asked tightly.

''I don't know what the hell you're talking about, lady. I ain't never been in your bedroom.''

Conn slanted a quick, curious glance down at Honor but she was concentrating on her footing. It seemed to him that she was having more than the normal amount of trouble walking in the sand. After all, yesterday morning she'd been running on the beach without this degree of awkwardness. Her present lack of coordination suited him perfectly, however. So perfectly that he wondered whether she was stumbling on purpose. There was no doubt that the gunman wasn't paying much attention to her troubles as long as she stayed on her feet and kept moving. But he must be accustomed to her awkward progress by now. If she were to suddenly stumble to her knees, he probably wouldn't panic and pull the trigger.

Tentatively, uncertain how to get the message across to Honor, Conn tugged at her arm. Was it his imagination or did she actually incline her head slightly? His right hand tightened around the object he had palmed back at the cottage when he'd tugged Honor off balance the first time. He was only going to get one chance, so it would have to count and count heavily. Beside him he felt Honor's new level of tension as she seemed to pull herself physically together.

She was going to do it, Conn realized. She knew what he wanted. He felt another overwhelming rush of pride in her perception. Honor Mayfield was quite a woman to have beside you in a crisis, he decided.

"Let's move it, you two. Hurry up, lady. What's the matter with you? Can't you walk straight?"

"I'm a little scared," Honor retorted flatly.

"Tough. That's your problem, ain't it?" The gunman sounded pleased with the power he was wielding. "If it makes you feel any better, Granger wants this to look real romantic."

"Romantic!" Honor repeated, sounding horrified.

"Yeah. You know. A lovers' quarrel. What the cops like to call a *domestic*."

"My heavens," Honor breathed. And then she stumbled to her knees.

Conn released her at once, making no attempt to break her fall. Instead he swung around in a smooth rush, hurling the metal star-shaped object that had been nestled in his palm.

"Damn you—" the gunman began to yell at Honor, outraged at her clumsiness. But he never finished the sentence.

The razor-sharp blades that formed the points on the star sliced into his shoulder, cutting through the denim shirt he wore as though the material were delicate silk.

The punk screamed in fear and rage. His arm jerked spasmodically and the gun went flying. It landed on the wet sand at the water's edge and an instant later was lost below a breaking wave.

Conn didn't waste any time looking for the weapon. He was on top of the other man in an instant, his body uncoiling with controlled violence.

"Conn!" Honor shot to her feet, her eyes going from the sight of the two men locked together on the beach to the gun that appeared briefly, half covered with wet sand. She started to reach for it but stopped when Conn's gritted words halted her. Even as he spoke another wave covered the weapon.

"Forget the gun. It's useless now. And our pal here isn't going anywhere."

Honor swung back to see Conn releasing his captive. The

man on the sand was whimpering softly, clutching at his bleeding shoulder. Conn was wiping the star-shaped weapon against his jeans. Honor realized it was blood that was leaving the damp streaks on the denim fabric. Then he dropped the lethal object into his shirt pocket. There was a respectful casualness about the way he handled the object that spoke volumes.

''On your feet.'' Conn nudged his victim with the toe of his shoe. ''I'm afraid that your fast-track route up Granger's corporate ladder just met with a delay. Probably a permanent one. Young, ambitious executive types like you don't usually get second chances from people like Granger.''

The man glowered in mute rage but stumbled to his feet. He didn't let go of the bleeding wound in his shoulder. ''I got to have a doctor,'' he muttered.

''I don't think they make house calls anymore,'' Conn said easily. ''And since both our cars are out of commission...''

''My truck,'' the man gasped, shambling ahead as Conn pushed him forward. ''I got my truck parked down the road a ways.''

''Good. We can use it to drive you into town and turn you over to the cops.''

''Granger will take care of me,'' the punk declared. His own uncertainty about that fact was quite clear in his voice. ''The guy who hired me said Granger always takes care of his people.''

''Which brings us to an interesting question,'' Conn murmured, glancing back at Honor who was moving beside him without her former clumsiness. ''Just who did hire you? Not Granger himself, apparently.''

''I ain't talking,'' the man informed him haughtily.

Conn didn't bother to persuade him to make the effort. He turned his attention to Honor.

''Are you all right, honey?'' he asked as they neared the cottage.

''I'm okay.'' But she couldn't disguise the stark, too-flat

tone of her voice. Nor could she understand why she was still trembling. Reaction, she decided. It must be reaction.

"You handled yourself well back there," Conn went on, his voice husky with approval and pride.

"Gee, thanks. Maybe I've missed my calling somewhere along the line." The flippancy didn't feel any more natural than the tremor in her limbs, but Conn seemed to understand.

"It's all right, Honor," he soothed as he waited for her to open the door of the cottage. "You'll be fine in a little while."

He stayed back for a moment, watching the wounded man carefully as he followed Honor through the door.

It was Honor, therefore, who first realized there was another visitor to the cottage that night. She stopped short at the sight of a familiar face studying a photo of Stylish Legacy.

"Ethan!" she whispered.

Ethan Bailey glanced up and then swung around to cover the trio in the doorway with the gun in his hand.

"So things didn't go quite perfectly, I see," he noted in pained resignation.

"They rarely do," Conn said, sighing.

Ten

"It wasn't my fault, Mr. Bailey! I swear it wasn't. You got to explain that to Mr. Granger. I did exactly like I was told. I put the cars out of commission. I took the two assignments out to the point where the water's rough. I did my part exactly right. But you never told me about that knife thing he carries. He cut me bad. Real bad. I got to have a doctor."

"Knife thing?" Ethan favored Conn with a mildly questioning eyebrow. "Oh, yes, that fancy letter opener you said was a souvenir. Let's have it, Landry." He didn't point the gun at Conn but at Honor instead.

Honor stood very still, alert to the fact that without the element of surprise Conn would not be able to use his weapon before Ethan could shoot her. Wordlessly Conn removed the star blade from his pocket and dropped it down on the floor.

"Much better," Ethan approved. Then he turned his attention to the wounded man. "You'd better go find yourself a doctor. Although it's going to be tricky explaining that wound to an emergency room medic, isn't it?" He shook his head. "I should have realized you wouldn't be able to handle this by yourself."

"But you said Mr. Granger had everything planned out, right to the last detail. You said nothing could go wrong," the man whined.

"Well, son, I was wrong. It happens occasionally. The older you get, the more you realize that." Ethan waved the gun encouragingly. "On your way."

"I don't know if I can drive like this. I'm bleeding pretty bad."

''Try,'' Bailey suggested coolly. ''Try real hard. Mr. Granger doesn't like screwups. If I were you, I think I'd get out of his vicinity. Find some new territory, Tony. I think it would be healthier for you if you did.''

The man called Tony stared at Ethan's mildly implacable face and then he turned and walked out of the cottage without another word. The door closed behind him.

Honor stood staring at Ethan Bailey as a strange silence descended on the small room. She felt the renewed tension humming through her, mingling with the reaction from the first incident out on the beach. All of her nerves felt as though someone had seared them with a flame. Over and above her own shaky, unnatural sensation of fear and anger, Honor could have sworn she felt Conn's fierce reaction. But he seemed under control, as always. The knowledge steadied her on the one hand and raised grim questions about his past on the other. Conn's self-control was unnerving. What had he done to learn it?

''I take it,'' Conn said finally, ''that poor Tony is under a slight misconception?''

''About the identify of his real employer?'' Ethan nodded blandly. ''I'm afraid so. Seemed simpler to have the boy think he was working for Granger. Kid was so anxious to make it big in a hurry. I couldn't resist taking advantage of all that drive and ambition. There he was, hanging around the fringes of Granger's crowd whenever Granger appeared at the track. I heard through the rumor mill that the boy was looking for work, Granger's kind of work. I decided that since I needed some temporary help, I might as well use him. He seemed happy enough with the job until a few minutes ago.''

''I don't understand,'' Honor said in a whisper. ''Isn't Granger involved at all?''

It was Conn who answered. ''No. He was just a very convenient red herring, wasn't he, Ethan?''

''Yup. Would have been even more convenient if old Tony hadn't made a mess of things. But I learned a long time ago that a man has to be flexible, has to take advantage of his opportunities and be prepared with a backup plan when things go wrong. Didn't get where I am today without practicing what I preach.''

''You want us dead,'' Honor said in a remote tone that didn't sound at all like herself, not even to her own ears.

''It would have been mighty convenient if you two had played your parts out correctly,'' Ethan explained. He stood easily, the gun in his hand held at a relaxed but alert level.

''You mean if I'd really believed she was the one who tried to poison Legacy?'' Conn put in casually. He moved slightly, taking a few steps away from Honor.

''Stay where you are, boy. That's far enough.'' Ethan's gun hand tightened fractionally. Conn stopped.

Honor hastily interrupted, trying to divert Ethan's attention to herself. ''You wanted Conn and me to distrust each other, didn't you? You wanted us to quarrel.''

''It set the scene nicely. Everyone at the track saw Conn leave this morning and knew he was in a rage. Couple of owners had even seen him drinking purty heavy the night before. They knew the two of you had ties that went back a long, long way.''

Conn's eyes slitted. ''They know it because you made certain they found out, right?''

Ethan shrugged. ''You know what racetrack gossip's like, son. Especially when it concerns a stallion like Stylish Legacy and the men who owned him. Bound to be some talk when one owner's son shows up with a colt sired by the famous horse. When you started dating Honor, here, why folks were just downright fascinated. Leastways, they became fascinated after I reminded them of the old story.''

''Do you mind explaining just why you're going to all this trouble, Ethan?'' Conn asked coolly.

''I'm afraid it's a long tale. And I'm not sure we have time to go into it tonight. I looked up the tides before I set this whole plan in motion. The high tide will be peaking right soon. I want you and the little lady here following it out to sea.''

''Assisted by a couple of bullet holes?'' Conn tossed back.

''Something like that. Might as well head back down to the point. Looks like I'll have to take care of the little job I hired Tony to do. Hard to find good help these days.''

Honor felt Conn tense. He would make a suicidal effort, she knew. He would do anything he could to protect her. That knowledge was as sure and solid in her mind and heart as the knowledge of his passion. She had to act first or risk having him throw himself straight into Ethan's gun.

''You can take care of us, but it's going to be tough to stop the gossip that will be hitting the track when this is all over,'' Honor told Ethan with sudden conviction.

Ethan frowned. ''You don't have to worry about the gossip. You won't be around.''

''I'm not talking about what people will say of Conn and me. It's what they'll be speculating about you that should interest you. My sister, Adena, knows everything I know. I called her this afternoon and left the information on her telephone-answering machine.''

Conn shot her a startled glance, fully aware that she hadn't used the telephone. His attention went back to Ethan almost immediately.

''Now just what the devil are you talking about, little lady?'' Ethan demanded impatiently.

''I'm talking about the fact that Adena won't keep her mouth shut. When I don't return from this little jaunt she's liable to go straight to the police.''

''With what?'' Ethan snapped, more of his patience disintegrating. On the opposite side of the room, Conn stood balanced and poised. Ethan was focusing entirely on Honor.

Honor drew a deep breath and played her one and only card. ''With the information that there was another owner of Stylish Legacy fifteen years ago. A silent partner named Ethan Bailey.''

The effect on Bailey was electric. The easy, good-old-boy image disappeared in a flash, leaving the face of a raw, embittered and infuriated man.

''You're lying, bitch,'' he breathed tightly. ''You don't know what the hell you're talking about!''

''Don't I? It's all there,'' Honor said, gesturing calmly toward the wood-and-iron locker that sat in the corner, draped with the folded horse blanket. ''All the proof anyone could ever need.''

''What proof?'' Bailey hissed, his gaze momentarily riveted on the locker. But he seemed to sense that Conn was waiting for an opening. Ethan kept the nose of the gun firmly pointed at Honor. It would still be a simple matter for him to pull the trigger before Conn was halfway across the room. *''What proof?''*

Honor sucked in her breath and tried to think logically. She had to make this sound good. She badly wished the fear-inspired adrenaline racing through her system would calm down. As it was she could see the tips of her fingers trembling as she bent down toward the locker. Awkwardly she patted the black-and-white blanket lying on top.

''Dad was a businessman. First, last and always. As excited as he used to get about Stylish Legacy's wins, he always claimed the horse was really nothing more than an elaborate tax shelter. Nothing more than a business matter. And because it was a business matter, he kept very good records.''

''I don't believe you,'' Bailey snarled. ''If you knew anything you would have put it all together a long time ago.''

Honor shook her head. ''I didn't put it together all these years because I never wanted to go through all the records and souvenirs my father had left to me. It was too painful. Every time I looked at this trunk I was forced to remember what had happened to Dad. On the other hand, I couldn't bear to throw it all away, either. So I told myself I was putting the various mementos to good design use by decorating the cottage with them.'' She gestured at the photos and racing paraphernalia on the walls. ''Creates just the right ambience, don't you think? Casual but chic, rustic but elegant. It's made the cottage very popular, you know. I rarely have any trouble keeping it rented.'' Her voice broke a little on the last word and Honor quickly stopped talking while she regained her control.

''If you haven't investigated the contents of that trunk in all these years, why would you have done it on this visit to the cabin?'' Ethan challenged.

''If I hadn't met you at the track, I would never have recognized the third man who always seemed to show up in Stylish Legacy's winning photos,'' Honor told him simply. ''I've rarely studied the pictures, anyway, but after Conn arrived yesterday and became so interested in Legacy's sire, I started looking at the photos a little more closely. And when I look at things closely, Ethan, I tend to see things. I've been trained to see details,'' she added with a wry touch of apology. ''It's something designers get very good at, I'm afraid. The smallest details make all the difference in a well-designed room.''

''You little bitch,'' Ethan breathed.

Honor plowed on determinedly. Ethan was still holding the gun with far too much concentration. She turned back to the trunk. ''Once I realized you were in so many of those winner's circle shots and once I saw the expression on your face—''

''The expression on my face!''

Honor inclined her head ruefully. ''It's always the same, the expression on the face of the owners and trainers. That look of satisfaction and victory and excitement. It's really unique. Look around, Ethan. That expression is on my father's face in all the photos. It's on Richard Stoner's face, too. I saw it on Conn's face the other afternoon when Legacy won. And it's on your face in all the photographs of Stylish Legacy in the winner's circles. No matter how hard people try to keep it on a business level, racing seems to get into the blood. It's always more than a business."

"That proves nothing! Absolutely nothing!"

"True, but it was enough to make me curious. I opened the trunk, Ethan. I started looking through some of Dad's records and papers. As I said, he was a businessman. In his own fashion, he paid as much attention to detail as I do. It's all here, Ethan," she concluded, hoping she wouldn't have to fake it any further. It was very difficult being creative on your feet when someone was holding a gun on you. Out of the corner of her eye she saw Conn advance on catlike feet, making no sound as he approached Ethan. The older man's attention was still zeroed in on Honor.

"You're lying," Ethan muttered, his eyes moving uneasily now from Honor to the trunk. "There's nothing in that trunk."

"Want to see the records?" Honor taunted, her hand hovering just above the horse blanket.

"You're damn right, I want to see them! Show me your fancy proof, little lady," Bailey growled furiously.

Honor bent down and lifted the heavy wool horse blanket.

"Bailey!" Conn snapped loudly.

Instinctively Ethan swiveled around at the clipped command. He panicked as he realized that Conn was much too close to him. But Honor already had the blanket in motion, whipping it toward Bailey.

"Damn you!" Bailey shouted, pulling the trigger reflexively. But the blanket was floating over him, settling around his head and shoulders, and the shot went wild.

In the same instant Conn was on him, propelling the older man to the floor and wrenching the gun free. It was all over in a moment. Conn was far younger and stronger than Bailey and the struggle was fated to end in only one way. Ethan lay still, sagging with the knowledge that he had lost. Slowly Conn rose to one knee and picked up the weapon. He stared down at the fallen man and then he flicked a quick, assessing glance at Honor.

''Are you all right, honey?''

''Peachy keen,'' Honor mumbled, sinking down onto the top of the trunk. ''Just peachy keen. Except for my knees. They don't seem to be functioning properly.'' She took several deep breaths, willing herself to calm down. ''I don't think I can take too much more of this tonight, though, Conn. A little seems to go a long way.''

He was on his feet now, squeezing her shoulder tightly. ''I know what you mean. Why do you think I gave up those cushy security jobs overseas in favor of a little consulting work and real estate investment? This sort of thing gets to you after a while. I've never been so scared in my life as I was this evening. Twice someone held a gun on you and I was terrified I wasn't going to be able to protect you.''

She glanced up at his ravaged features and her love for him shone softly in her eyes. ''That's funny. I never had any doubts at all. I just don't tolerate the tension well.''

Conn looked at her, his gaze unreadable. ''No doubts?''

''I knew you'd do whatever you thought had to be done,'' she said quietly. It was the truth. Conn would have given his life for her tonight and she was fully aware of that. She had been equally determined that he wouldn't make the sacrifice.

''Thank you, Honor,'' he said softly.

''For what?''

He shrugged. ''For having faith in me.''

Honor touched his hand but she couldn't find any words. Her eyes met his in a silent communication that was shattered by Ethan Bailey's groan. She turned to look at the man as he sat up slowly. There was something different about Ethan now. He looked like a broken man. Or one who has come to the end of a long road. It was Conn who spoke first.

''I think,'' he said, ''that it's time we had some answers.'' He sat down on the trunk beside Honor, the gun held almost casually in his right hand. There was a grimness to him that was frightening. ''Were you really a silent partner in Stylish Legacy?'' he asked, staring at Ethan.

''Ask her, she seems to know all about it,'' Bailey muttered, massaging the back of his head.

''It was an educated guess,'' Honor confessed. ''I've never looked inside the trunk. I made a stab in the dark, based on your appearance in all those photographs. No one can resist getting into the photo when the horse wins, least of all the owners.''

''You might as well tell us everything,'' Conn suggested, watching Bailey with a brooding expression. ''Now that the connection has been made, it shouldn't be too difficult to dig into the past and find out the whole truth. It just hinged on knowing there was an association between you and our parents. I have a hunch that association involved more than a racehorse. There was something more, wasn't there, Ethan? Something you had to cover up, even if it meant killing the son and daughter of Stylish Legacy's original owners.''

Bailey glowered at him and then went limp. ''If you really start digging you'll probably find it,'' he admitted. ''For fifteen years I've been afraid of what would happen if someone went looking for answers. I thought I was safe because no one seemed inclined to probe too deeply. The most dangerous time was right after the *incident.*''

''Incident?'' Honor demanded. ''You mean after Stoner and my father died?''

Bailey nodded. ''I thought that if I got through that part okay, I'd be home free. I had to let you sell Stylish Legacy, of course. I didn't dare come forth with a claim on the horse. That would have been too risky, because I'd taken such pains to make sure no one knew I was involved financially.''

Conn thought about that for a moment. ''You didn't want anyone to know you had a financial interest in the horse,'' he finally repeated carefully. ''Because if someone knew that he might suspect that you were involved with our parents in other ways?''

Honor shot him a swift, questioning glance. What was Conn after?

Bailey nodded with a dismal air. ''Couldn't take any chances. It hurt to lose Stylish Legacy. Best colt on the West Coast in those days. Could have made a fortune off of him. I didn't even dare to buy one of his offspring. I didn't want to risk it. But I kept track of how the runners he sired were doing. Couldn't help myself. When I learned one of his colts was picked up by Richard Stoner's son, I had a feeling...'' His voice trailed off sadly.

''A premonition that something was going to go wrong?'' Honor suggested.

Bailey nodded. ''It seemed dangerous. As if fate had stepped in and forced me to get involved with everything I'd closed the door on fifteen years ago. I thought I'd just make contact with you, Landry. Easiest way to do that was transfer a couple of my horses over to Humphrey's stable. It was simple to introduce myself to you as a fellow owner using the same trainer. I could keep tabs on you that way. Make sure you never got too curious. Or at least have some warning if you did.''

''And then I got in touch with Nick Mayfield's daughter,'' Conn murmured. ''You must have really gotten nervous then.''

''It all seemed to be getting too dangerous, too close. Fate.''

Honor frowned. ''You tried to plant a few seeds of doubt at first, hoping I'd back away from any relationship with Conn, didn't you?''

''If you'd backed away from him everything might have gone back to being safe.'' Ethan sighed. ''But you didn't. I could see the two of you getting more and more involved with each other. I knew that once you knew who he was, you'd probably get angry,'' Bailey explained. ''And I thought that if Landry realized you had betrayed him by trying to poison Legacy, he'd be furious.''

''So you set up the situation and then you hired good old Tony to pull the trigger, right?'' Conn growled. ''Okay, I can figure that much out for myself. But why don't you save us all some time and explain why you didn't want your association with my stepfather and Mayfield to come to light? Seems to me, there could only be one reason for that.''

Honor held her breath as her mind leaped to the same intuitive explanation. ''You killed them?'' she whispered tightly, staring at Ethan. ''You killed my father and Stoner?''

A forbidding silence settled on the room and then Bailey nodded once. ''Had to, don't you see? They found out I'd been running guns, using their connections and facilities in the Middle East. The night they got wise, I had to act. There wasn't time to think,'' he went on, his eyes becoming remote as he looked back fifteen years. ''It all happened so quickly. I didn't know they'd been suspicious. I thought they believed I was just curious about the operations. After all, they'd let me put a lot of money into their business.''

''Once again as a silent partner?'' Conn asked with ice in his voice.

''Had to insist on that. I didn't want anyone connecting me with the guns if they were ever discovered. I'd been small-time until then. Don't get me wrong, I'd made money selling weapons to anyone who'd buy them and I'd made a fair amount of money, but I wanted to expand. I needed a safe cover for really big shipments. There was so much more money to be made in that line. Somewhere in the world there's always someone wanting to go to war, you know. Big wars, little wars, guerrilla wars, revolutionary wars. Bandits with political motivations and just plain outlaws. A never-ending market. A businessman's dream. But you got to take precautions.''

''You needed a legitimate cover and you needed reliable transportation facilities.'' Conn nodded with a degree of understanding that rather shocked Honor. ''You needed an established business that had contacts in places like the Middle East.''

''I met your father and Mayfield when they first got interested in buying a racehorse together. I used to own a couple of horses back then, although none of them were in Stylish Legacy's league. But I've always been involved with the track. And I kept up with track rumors. I knew your fathers were international businessmen and I made friends with them. I'm the one who put them on to Stylish Legacy. I'd planned to buy him myself, but when I suggested we all go in as partners, they were happy enough to agree.''

''One kind of partnership led to another, I suppose?'' Conn said.

''That was right about the time when Mayfield and Stoner were thinking of leaving the big corporation they'd been working for. They planned to set up their own business. I offered to pour some money into it. Any new business needs capital, and they agreed to let me invest. Things worked real well for a while after they'd established their new business operation. I greased a few palms, used a few contacts, and the first thing I knew, I had shipments of rifles riding right alongside the steel piping and oil field equipment your fathers were shipping overseas. No one looked too closely at the other end because Mayfield and Stoner were trusted. They knew folks. The right folks.''

''And if anyone had looked too closely, you'd have been in the clear because you were just a silent partner,'' Conn finished. ''No one knew you were involved.''

''I made sure my name was left off all the paperwork. Just a private gentlemen's agreement.''

''Then one night Stoner and Mayfield became suspicious.'' Conn's thumb moved with a hint of restlessness on the grip of the gun.

''They set up a trap,'' Ethan snarled with a trace of returning belligerence. ''One of the men I'd bribed talked, and they found out when I had another shipment due to arrive overseas.

They knew I had to be there in order to conclude the deal. They got there ahead of me. What they didn't realize was that the man who'd sold them information also sold me information. He was playing both sides of the fence, and I got lucky."

"You were able to set up your own trap," Honor hazarded bleakly. "You made it look as though my father and Richard Stoner had been smuggling the guns and had quarreled over a shipment. You killed them both."

"After that I got nervous," Bailey admitted. "I figured my luck was running out. Decided to get out of the gunrunning business altogether. After all, I'd made a pile. Time to invest it in more legitimate things. Investments people wouldn't be inclined to question."

Conn and Honor looked at him for a long time. Bailey seemed unaware of any of their emotions. He was lost in his own world, examining where it had all gone wrong.

"You bastard," Conn finally said but there was no heat in the words. Only a weary acceptance that the past could not be changed.

"I knew," Honor said softly. "I knew there was something wrong with the notion that Stoner and Mayfield had betrayed each other. It never felt right."

Conn nodded. "I know. Too many loose ends. Too many unanswered questions. That's one of the reasons I came looking for you, Honor. I can't deny it. And I don't regret it, because otherwise we would never have met."

"The questions needed to be answered," she agreed quietly.

He looked at her. "That was pretty slick, the way you pulled the basic connection out of thin air. If you hadn't realized that Bailey's association with Stylish Legacy was a solid one, the rest of it wouldn't have fallen into place so neatly. You're fast on your feet, lady. You've got guts."

Honor smiled shakily. "Coming from you, I'll assume that's a compliment."

Conn blinked in surprise. "Of course it is."

"You moved fairly rapidly yourself when the occasion warranted," she returned dryly.

He lifted one shoulder in a gesture of dismissal. "I spent a lot of years learning to do it. It was just part of the job."

"Some job!" Honor broke off thoughtfully, glancing back at Ethan. "What do we do now?"

"We've got all the evidence we need to get Bailey here out of our lives," Conn began slowly. "But I'm not sure we'll ever be able to pin the past on him. Unless there really are some incriminating records in this old trunk."

"I doubt it," Honor said. "I did glance briefly through the stuff when I moved it here to the cottage. I don't recall anything that might be useful in connecting Bailey with what happened fifteen years ago. But who knows? I didn't realize the significance of Ethan being in all those photographs until yesterday. Maybe there is something buried in this trunk." She paused. "It was all a long time ago, wasn't it? It's over now."

Conn glanced at her. "We know the answers. There aren't any more loose ends." He sounded strangely satisfied.

Honor understood the feeling. There was a deep sadness underlying the sensation, but also a sense of peace. No more loose ends.

Well, maybe one. Honor remembered the question that still hovered at the back of her mind. She turned to Ethan. "Was it you who moved the screen in my bedroom?"

He came out of his gloomy reverie long enough to appear vaguely startled. "How did you know I searched your room? I hardly touched a thing!"

Honor's mouth twisted wryly. "One thing slightly off is all it takes, I'm afraid. I'm beginning to think my eye for detail is going to be the bane of my existence."

Bailey slipped back into his memories. "I just wanted to see if you had any stuff on Stylish Legacy lying around. I needed to know how much you knew about the horse and who had owned it. Didn't realize you had all the answers here at the beach house.''

It was midmorning by the time Ethan Bailey had been taken into custody and the necessary paperwork completed. The authorities notified the hospital emergency rooms in the area to be on the alert for a man of Tony's description seeking care for an odd knife wound.

Honor and Conn returned to Pasadena late that afternoon.

They talked quietly over dinner at Honor's apartment, both of them coming to grips with the results of the traumatic events. Gradually they both began to relax and accept what had happened. There was a feeling of companionship, of being bonded together, Honor thought at one point. She and Conn now shared a past and the secrets that had been buried there. It deepened the sense of commitment she felt about the future, but something was missing. Something wasn't right about the way they were preparing to face that future.

It wasn't until later that evening that Honor realized that soon she would have to deal with the problem that had precipitated the entire matter: her relationship with Constantine Landry. If she didn't confront it directly it would haunt her, leaving an element of uncertainty deep in her mind. And it was a cinch that Conn himself would never of his own accord resolve the gray area because he simply didn't admit it existed. But by the time the thought flitted through her mind, Honor was slipping rapidly into sleep. Her body curled deep into the comforting warmth of Conn's as they lay together in her bed.

Tomorrow, Honor promised herself just before she closed her eyes. Tomorrow she would find a way to make Conn understand that what he felt for her was love. He needed to acknowledge that fact for both their sakes. He had to know that what they shared was something that went beyond an amalgam of want and need and desire.

Unless he took that final step, Honor realized, Conn would

never be able to give himself as completely to her as she was willing to give herself to him. There would always be a part of him that was remote and untouchable.

Was it selfish, she wondered, this need she had to make him understand that he was vulnerable to her? Possibly. No, *probably*. Perhaps it wasn't right to expect him to lower his guard as far as she had lowered hers. He had been alone a long time in a harsh world, and the barriers he had built around himself made sense on many levels. She had seen the fierceness in him at the beach house, had come to know the relentless, utterly determined side of his nature. The predatory part of him had helped save their lives; she could hardly quarrel with its existence.

But the hunter in him made it difficult for Conn to admit to love. He could commit himself; she didn't doubt that. He could also give passion and protection. In turn he demanded a great deal. Loyalty, respect, commitment, passion—all of those and more he wanted from Honor. She had given him more. She had given him her love. But so far he hadn't shown any willingness to take the dangerous step himself. He wasn't able yet to admit that he was vulnerable and that what he felt for her was love.

Until Conn could do that there would always be loose ends in their relationship.

Eleven

Honor awoke with the conviction that there were still matters remaining to be settled between herself and Conn, but she hadn't even begun to formulate a plan for resolving the uncertainties when he unwittingly pushed her into a corner.

Honor opened her eyes to find Conn sitting up against the headboard, the sheet carelessly bunched at his waist. He wasn't wearing anything that she could see but he'd obviously arisen earlier because he had a mug of coffee in his hand.

"You're certainly bright-eyed and chipper this morning," she complained, stretching languidly. "Isn't it a little early to be looking so alert? After all we've been through during the past couple of days, I think we deserve some extra sleep."

"I've been thinking," he told her very seriously. He didn't respond to her light greeting.

A small warning bell went off somewhere, but Honor couldn't imagine why. "Oh?" She eyed the coffee with increasing interest.

"We can fly to Vegas this afternoon, spend the night in one of the big hotels and be back here in time to see Legacy run tomorrow afternoon."

Honor tried to assimilate all that. "I suppose we could. Any reason why we should? And did you make me a cup of coffee while you were at it?"

Conn frowned and reached around to lift another mug off the end table. "Here. And the reason we should go to Vegas is because it would be the quickest and easiest way to get married."

"Married!" Honor nearly spilled the hot coffee on the

sheets as she accepted the mug and struggled to a sitting position. As it was, a few drops struck the bodice of the black-and-white-striped nightgown. She dabbed at them furiously while she tried to think. ''Married?''

Conn reached out to hold the mug while she finished attending to the small drops. ''I suppose we could go ahead and apply for a license here in California, but there's a waiting period, and I'd just as soon take care of things as quickly and neatly as possible.''

Honor finally ceased her efforts at cleaning the nightgown and went still. She seemed to be having a problem focusing on the main issue. Her mind was skittering around in circles, looking for an escape. In that moment Honor didn't bother to question why she wanted to escape.

''Are you quite certain you want marriage, Conn?'' she asked slowly.

His expression grew even more implacable. ''It's the only logical conclusion. We could simply live together but somehow that doesn't seem *formal* enough for what we have. You belong to me now. We belong together. There's a commitment between us. Obligations, duties, responsibilities. All those things go with marriage, not a casual affair. And I think you know it.'' He took a sip of his coffee and added blandly, ''After all, aren't you the one who keeps saying you love me?''

Honor paled beneath the well-aimed thrust. The man was, indeed, a hunter. He knew exactly where to strike. Frantically she rallied her forces.

''Yes, I'm the one,'' Honor agreed bleakly. ''I'll take my coffee back now.''

He handed it to her, faint wariness flickering in his eyes. ''Honor? What's the matter?''

She took a long swallow of hot coffee. ''Nothing, Conn. But I need time. We both need time.'' Her mind seized on the only escape it could find. ''There's so much to work out, so many plans to make. Where are we going to live, for example? I have a business established here in Pasadena. I can't just pick it up and move it elsewhere. And I imagine you have your business headquarters well established up in the San Francisco area."

"My business is movable," he interrupted flatly. "I can shift my operations to Pasadena without too much difficulty."

Honor blinked uneasily, sensing he had deliberately acted to forestall her protest before she could even get it properly outlined. She rushed to find another excuse. "There's Adena to consider."

"Believe me, from what I've seen of Adena, she wouldn't care at all if you got married. I think she approves of me."

"Well, it wasn't exactly her approval I was worrying about. I just thought it might be nice if she were invited to the wedding!" Honor flared.

"You can invite her if you wish. I don't mind picking up an extra airline ticket for her," Conn said.

"The police may have more questions for us to answer during the next few days," Honor fretted.

"They know where to find us."

"I have clients to see," Honor went on doggedly. "I really shouldn't take any more time off just now."

"We can plan a honeymoon for some other time. You won't be away from Pasadena except overnight. Not unless you want to take some time off again to go away for a few days."

"My mother—"

"We'll notify her," Conn said promptly. "Later, when we take the honeymoon we can visit her, if you like."

Honor groped for other excuses and found she had exhausted the lot. Except for the truth. "It's just too soon, Conn. I need time."

He drained his coffee and set down the mug with an air of finality. "You're stalling."

"Well, maybe I am!" she blurted, feeling cornered.

"Why should you want to stall?" he challenged softly.

"You love me, remember? I can make you come alive with passion. I've saved your neck. We share a bond that goes back fifteen years. We're committed to each other. Are you going to deny it?"

"No, I'm not denying it but I'll be darned if I'll let you push me into marriage when you don't know how you feel toward me!"

He stared at her in astonishment. "What the devil do you think you're saying? I know how I feel toward you. You're mine. I'll take care of you, protect you, make love to you. What more to do you want from me?"

"Love! I want you to understand that what you feel for me is love!" She could no longer control her tongue. Her emotions overwhelmed her, causing her to say things she was very much afraid she would regret later. Already she could see the anger beginning to burn in Conn's eyes. It frightened her, but she couldn't stop.

He reached out and caught her wrist, removing the coffee mug from her fingers and dragging her across his chest. Beneath dark lashes he gazed grimly down at her. "I asked you once if you wanted me to lie to you. You said no. Have you changed your mind?"

"No, of course not," she gasped.

"Then are you trying to blackmail me into saying the words you want to hear? Are you setting a trap of your own, Honor? Trying to push me into a corner by saying I can't have you unless I do things your way?"

"Typical of you to decide that I'm trying to trap you. You're the one who's so skilled at weaving webs, remember? I fell into all the nets you strung, all down the line, but it stops here. You want everything from me but you're not willing to give everything of yourself. I want a man who is as vulnerable to me as I am to him. I don't want a one-sided relationship, Conn."

"Vulnerable?" he grated. "I doubt you even know the meaning of the word. Vulnerable people don't survive long in this world unless they've got someone else to take care of them.''

''I'll take care of you,'' she promised rashly. ''I won't betray you or hurt you. I love you.''

''If you meant that you wouldn't be playing word games with me.''

''You don't understand,'' she cried.

''You're trying to force me into conforming to your mental image of a husband and a lover. You want to know you have power over me. That's what you really mean by *vulnerable,* isn't it? You want to know I'm weak when it comes to you.''

''You seem to enjoy your power over me,'' she flung back furiously.

''So you're trying to even the score?''

''Maybe I don't happen to like unbalanced accounts, either! You're not the only one with a monopoly on keeping the score even.'' By now she was no longer making any attempt to keep her words rational and calm. Honor's emotions had taken over completely as she sensed herself being pushed into yet another of Constantine Landry's intricate webs.

''You don't have any choice in this case,'' he told her savagely. ''You belong to me.''

''It works both ways.''

''All right, so I belong to you. That's grounds for marriage, lady.''

''It's grounds for an affair,'' she retorted. ''Not marriage.''

''You're going to split hairs over a four-letter word?'' he demanded.

''Love is more than a four-letter word. If that's all it was, you wouldn't have so much trouble dealing with it!''

''I'm beginning to realize exactly what it does mean,'' he said grittily. ''In your mind, at least. It means vulnerability and weakness and a knowledge of your own power over me. Admit it, Honor. That's what you're looking for.''

She stared up at him helplessly. ''If that's what you think

it means, then there's not much point in continuing this discussion, is there?''

His jaw tightened as he sensed her weary withdrawal from the argument. ''Oh, no, you don't, Honor. You're not backing out of this that easily. You're going to marry me. I'll make you a good husband. There will always be honesty between us. Honesty and commitment. And passion. Nothing else matters.''

She fought for composure. ''You mean it wouldn't bother you at all if I stopped loving you? As long as I continued to supply my share of the honesty and commitment? Oh, and the passion, naturally.''

He looked slightly startled. The expression was immediately replaced with a taut frown. ''What you call your love for me is really your sense of being vulnerable to me. And you can't change that, honey. By marrying me you'll be admitting that you trust me with that kind of power. I won't abuse that trust.''

''You're the one who's playing word games.'' Freeing her wrist, Honor slipped away from him. He let her go, watching through narrowed eyes as she tugged a robe out of the closet and tied the sash. When she dared meet his gaze again she realized that all the soft, gentle comfort she had known from him during the night had vanished. The predatory challenge was radiating from Conn in a way that effectively destroyed her last hopes.

''You're throwing a tantrum because you can't find a way to reassure yourself that you have as much control over me as I do over you. That's all this is about, isn't it?'' he asked icily.

''From the beginning you seem to have been manipulating me,'' she said, sighing. ''You've woven so many webs around me that I haven't always been able to think straight. I suppose that's why you now assume I'm trying to reverse the process. I'm not, Conn, but I've got to draw the line somewhere.''

''So you can keep the books balanced?''

''You taught me the importance of that.'' She turned and walked into the bathroom, not trusting herself to stay in the same room with him any longer. Mingled despair and anger were causing her to be almost as unsteady as fear had the previous night. Honor decided she was sick and tired of being at the mercy of such strong emotions. They took too much out of a person, sending her to euphoric highs one moment and despairing lows the next.

As she switched on the shower, she lectured herself on control. The kind of self-control Conn seemed able to exert much of the time was suddenly an enviable attribute. She'd work on it, Honor vowed as she stepped under the spray. She'd work very hard to develop it. No more would she allow herself to be swept up in her responses to Conn. Never again would she allow him to manipulate her or weave nets around her. She was a strong-minded woman, or at least she always had been. You didn't make a success out of yourself in Southern California without a fair degree of fortitude and determination. She could handle Conn Landry on her terms. She would force him to acknowledge his true feelings, force him to become really emotionally committed to her. She didn't want a man whose sense of commitment seemed to stem almost entirely from the harsher sides of his masculine nature. Possessiveness, sexual satisfaction, a feeling of protectiveness were strong factors, important factors. But they fell short of love.

Honor was still telling herself that fifteen minutes later when she stepped out of the bathroom and discovered Conn had left the apartment.

Twenty minutes after he'd stormed out of Honor's apartment, Conn walked into the barn where Humphrey stabled the Thoroughbreds in his care. Two grooms with whom he was on friendly terms took one look at the expression on his face and discreetly disappeared. A goat that had free run of the stables because it had a calming effect on the high-strung horses showed the intelligence goats are noted for and ambled off out of range.

Conn found Legacy's stall and came to a halt. The colt turned inquiringly and didn't seem particularly put off by the dark tension in the man. He shuffled to the door and thrust his nose into Conn's hand.

''Sorry, fella. Absolutely nothing special for you today. You have to run tomorrow. Can't take any risks,'' Conn murmured, stroking the sleek neck. The horse's ears pricked at the approach of another man.

''Hello, Landry,'' the trainer said easily as he came to stand in front of Legacy's stall. ''Come to check up on your horse?'' Humphrey peered perceptively at his client. ''He's looking very good. Very good indeed. No reason he shouldn't do as well for you tomorrow as he did in his last race. I've scheduled Eddie Campbell to ride him. Told him to hold him back a bit at the start and then just let him have his head.''

Conn nodded, only half listening to the familiar trainer patter. If Legacy lost tomorrow there would be an equally reassuring patter listing all the reasons why: The track was muddy, the horse was too nervous, the jockey didn't handle him right on the course and so on. It was all part of the horse-racing scene. Just like the rumor mill. Conn wondered if any rumors about Ethan Bailey had filtered into the network yet. Apparently not, because Humphrey didn't mention them. The trainer came to the end of his analysis of the horse and then arched an eyebrow inquiringly at his client.

''Did you have a question?''

''No.'' Conn shook his head, unable to come up with any form of idle conversation. What he really wanted right now was to be alone. He probably shouldn't have come to the track. But the thought of going back to his hotel room was depressing. ''Just wanted to take another look at Legacy. Do you think he has the potential of his sire?''

''Stylish Legacy? I believe he does.'' Humphrey nodded toward the colt. ''Legacy got the best of Stylish Legacy's genes, if you ask me. Good shoulders, strong hindquarters. Smart. Fast. Likes to run. Can't ask for more from a horse.''

How much could you ask of a woman, Conn wondered silently. How much could a woman ask of a man? Legacy was a friendly animal, willing to give his all on the racetrack. He'd respond with everything that was in him when called upon. But that didn't mean he was emotionally involved with human beings.

Damn it, Conn thought violently, *I'm going crazy. How dumb can you get, Landry? You can't draw parallels between animals and humans. Not when it comes to relationships.*

''Well, I'll be around if you need me,'' Humphrey announced with a nod of farewell. ''Want to use the box today?''

''No thanks. I'm not going to watch the races.''

Humphrey nodded again and departed, leaving Conn alone with his horse. Absently he continued to stroke Legacy's nose.

Honor wouldn't be able to maintain the distance she had put between them this morning, Conn told himself. He had been saying the words in various formats since he'd left the apartment. In her own words, she was vulnerable to him. She wanted him, needed him. Hell, she loved him! And she knew he was committed to her. She *knew* it! She had to know it in the depths of her soul. He'd never felt like this about any other woman. The impact she had made on him had thrown his whole life off balance.

He knew his impact on her had been equally strong. He was sure of it in his bones. She couldn't hide the completeness with which she surrendered in his arms. Yet she had balked at taking the final step of marriage. Conn racked his brain trying to understand why. He had accused her of wanting power over him, but now he wasn't so certain. Another infinitely more devastating possibility flashed through his thoughts.

What if she was nervous about formalizing their relationship for the simple reason that she still didn't trust him?

Conn's hand stopped moving on Legacy's nose as the knowledge exploded within him. Of course she trusted him. She had to trust him. She'd said she'd trusted him, damn it!

But something was holding her back from making the final commitment. She claimed she wanted love, and Conn had told her that she was using the word to mean power. But perhaps he had been wrong. Perhaps what the word really meant was trust.

Legacy nuzzled Conn's shoulder in a puzzled fashion, seeking more attention. When Conn didn't oblige, but simply stood staring unseeingly into the stall, the colt moved philosophically back to his feed.

It was intolerable to think that she might not trust him after all they had been through, Conn thought, dazed. Absolutely intolerable. The realization that she might lack faith in him was shattering in its intensity. Didn't she understand that he would do virtually anything for her? Protect her with his life?

Conn turned away from the stall and walked as if in a dream to the far end of the long barn. There he found a bench. No one was around. Slowly he sank down onto the hard wood surface and tried to understand what was happening to him.

He trusted her, he thought. Completely. At least he assumed he did. But perhaps he hadn't actually trusted her to know her own mind. She'd said she was in love with him. And he hadn't really trusted her to know what she meant.

She must think him incredibly arrogant. And he was, Conn realized. Unbelievably arrogant. How could she trust him totally if she knew deep in her heart that he didn't even trust her to know her own mind? When you gave something, you wanted something equally valuable in return. He hadn't given her what she needed.

Instinct guided Honor as she drove out of the underground garage and headed toward the freeway. Conn would head for the track. She knew it intuitively. It was where she would go if she were he. He wasn't the type to sit and sulk in his hotel room.

What a fool she had been this morning. She'd risked so much for so little. Conn was right. She'd been playing word games, searching for reassurance when all along she'd known intellectually that he was giving her everything he had to give a woman. She would find him and tell him that it was enough, more than enough. She loved him and what he felt for her had to be very close to that emotion. What did it matter if he couldn't or wouldn't verbalize it?

If only she'd kept her head this morning and not allowed emotions to rule her tongue. Bitterly Honor castigated herself for the way she'd handled Conn's proposal of marriage.

Except that it hadn't actually been a proposal, she reminded herself with a rueful sigh. Perhaps if he'd actually asked her properly instead of arrogantly assuming she would want to marry him as quickly as possible she wouldn't have lost her temper and her head.

Life with Conn was not going to be entirely uncomplicated. The man was made of iron, and he surrounded himself with almost invincible emotional barriers.

But they weren't totally invincible and that was what she had to keep in mind. It would take work getting him to trust her to the point where he could lower them, perhaps years of work. Honor told herself she was more than willing to make the effort to gain his complete, unqualified trust. She had no choice because she loved him.

She parked the car in the lot and made her way to the barns, flashing the visitor's badge Conn had provided for her. Then Honor turned toward Legacy's stable. Blinking a little as she walked from brilliant sunlight into cool shade, she glanced around and saw the horse looking out of his stall. There was no sign of Conn. Slowly she walked toward Legacy, wondering if she'd been wrong in her guess as to where Conn had gone.

''Hello, Legacy,'' she murmured soothingly. ''Have you seen him?''

The horse went into his attention-getting routine, nuzzling her shoulder. Honor obliged for a few moments, her gaze searching the shaded interior of the long barn. It took a while before she realized Conn was watching her from a bench at the far end of the building.

He didn't move as she turned to look at him, but his eyes absorbed the sight of her standing there in the jeans and bright-coral sweater in which she had hastily dressed. Honor had been so certain of what she wanted to say when she left the apartment, but now she couldn't seem to get the words straight in her head. Slowly she lowered her hand from Legacy's muzzle. Then she started toward Conn.

He stood up as she approached, the lean, tough quality of his body outlined beneath snug jeans and a white long-sleeved shirt. He let her come to him, not moving as she walked forward. There was a moment when Honor feared she had made the wrong decision, taken too big a risk. It seemed to her in those few seconds that the predatory side of him was the ruling side and that she stood no chance of suppressing it. Then she was close enough to read his eyes and at that point nothing could have kept her from going into his arms. She ran the last few steps, coming into his waiting embrace with a small rush. His arms tightened around her with reassuring urgency.

''I'm sorry, Conn,'' she whispered breathlessly. ''I never meant to push you this morning. Of course I'll marry you, if you'll still have me. We belong to each other. I don't know why I doubted it. I know you'll give me everything you can of yourself. I realize you wouldn't talk of commitment unless you meant it. What more could I ask for?''

His hands moved roughly on her back. ''How about a little trust?'' His voice was hoarse with barely controlled emotion.

She lifted her head from his shoulder, her eyes widening in shock. ''You trust me, don't you?''

"I thought I did, Honor," he groaned, pulling her head back down against his shirt. His fingers tangled in her hair. "I sure as hell trusted you more than I've trusted anyone else for longer than I care to remember. But in the final analysis, I guess I didn't trust you completely."

Panic surged through her. "But why? What have I done to make you think I'd betray you? I thought everything was resolved between us. I love you, Conn."

"That's the part I wasn't willing to believe. I didn't give you credit for knowing your own mind because you were talking about an emotion I've never really believed existed. I stormed out of the apartment this morning thinking that you were simply trying to push me into saying the words you wanted to hear, that you wanted to hear them because they would give you some assurance of your own power over me."

"No—" she began desperately but he silenced her gently with his hand.

"Even though I was furious, I had to admit that you had the right to know that I wasn't going to dominate the relationship completely. It must seem to you that I've been running things between us from the beginning. I tracked you down, engineered our first meeting, kept tightening the strands of the web until there was nowhere for you to turn except into my arms. I thought that by demanding some wild declaration of love from me, you were really just trying to reassert yourself in the relationship."

"I was, but not because I wanted to control you," she explained in despair.

"I realize that," he admitted thickly, lacing his fingers at the nape of her neck and bending his forehead down until it touched hers. "Now I realize it. I didn't trust you enough to give your feelings and emotions full credit. I kept trying to assume that what I felt had to be what you felt. You were either mislabeling or dramatizing or looking for a wedge. I didn't trust you to simply have fallen in love with me."

Honor heard the aching unhappiness in him and her arms

went around his waist. ''And now?'' she whispered tremulously, her eyes bright with unshed tears.

''I trust you, sweetheart. Really trust you.'' He caught her chin under his thumbs and lifted her mouth for a quick, hard kiss that conveyed the full scope of his feelings. When he freed her mouth he went on huskily. ''I want everything you can give me, including this thing you call love. I'm not altogether sure just what you mean by it but I want it.''

''It's yours, Conn. It will always be yours.''

He shook his head once. ''I'll give you everything I can in return, honey.''

''I know.''

''I'm not sure yet just what that includes. Will that hurt you? I can't bear to hurt you.''

''No,'' she denied. ''You won't hurt me if you give yourself as completely as possible. And I know you will. With you, there is no other way.''

He exhaled slowly, as if a great weight had been lifted from him. Then Conn folded her close, holding her in silence for a long moment before he spoke again.

''Vegas?''

She nodded her head against his chest. ''Yes.''

''I'll get the tickets this afternoon. Do you want Adena to go with us?''

''It's not necessary. She'll understand. I was just using her as an excuse this morning.''

''You were looking for a way out,'' he growled.

''I guess I wasn't able to trust you completely at that point, either.''

''And now?''

''Now I do,'' she told him simply.

''I thought we'd settled all that at the beach cottage.'' He sighed, easing her against his side so that he could start them back down the length of the barn.

''We talked about trust and we promised it to each other, but we didn't think about all that it meant. We assumed it was only a matter of telling the truth about facts. We didn't realize it also meant trusting each other's emotions and feelings,'' Honor said with a small smile. ''But I expect we can make a few excuses for ourselves. After all, everything has been happening so quickly. It's no wonder we were still feeling our way with each other this morning.''

Conn nodded wryly. ''I was sitting there on that bench a little while ago, trying to think of how to approach you. I've finally realized just how arrogant I must seem to you.''

''Terribly arrogant at times,'' she agreed cheerfully.

He winced. ''I'm going to try very hard to control that part of me.''

''Uh-huh.''

He slid her a sidelong glance. ''You sound skeptical.''

''Oh, I believe you'll try,'' she told him with a tiny grin.

''But not that I'll succeed?''

''I think it's a very basic part of you. And I think it's been well tempered over the years.''

''You don't seem worried about it any longer,'' he noted with interest. His gunmetal eyes softened, and Honor could have sworn there was both relief and amusement in his gaze.

''I imagine I'll be obliged to point out the error of your ways occasionally to you in the future. Part of my wifely duties.''

''You can yell at me until doomsday as long as you marry me,'' he assured her emphatically. Then he brought them to a short stop in front of Legacy's stall. The colt thrust his head out again and eyed the two humans curiously.

''You're going to win tomorrow, aren't you?'' Honor asked the animal.

''He'll run his heart out,'' Conn said quietly. ''He'll give it all he's got out there on the course.''

Honor glanced at Conn as she patted the horse. His face had reset into harsh, all too familiar lines. ''Legacy's a fine horse,'' she observed tentatively.

''But he'll run because he was born and trained to do exactly that. And there's an instinct in him that makes him want to lead the pack. That makes him a winner. But he doesn't run and win to please me or Humphrey or the guy on his back. He doesn't do it for any of us. He does it because that's just the way he is.''

Honor hesitated, trying to read between the lines. ''Are you trying to tell me something, Conn?''

Conn swung his gaze from the colt to Honor's face. ''Legacy's not emotionally involved with humans except on a very superficial level. He enjoys our company but he could get along fine without any of us as long as he had access to food and other horses.''

Honor felt as though she were missing something important, but she couldn't put her finger on it. ''Well, he is an animal, after all.''

''Just an animal,'' Conn repeated in a low voice.

''And he operates on his own kind of logic. I understand.'' She smiled. ''Still, if he does win tomorrow I'd like to think he's doing it as a wedding present for us.''

Conn relaxed and took her arm again. ''Speaking of a wedding, I have to go get one arranged. Why don't you go on back to the apartment? I'll meet you there as soon as I've made the reservations.''

''All right.''

But Honor still had the feeling she had missed a crucial piece of communication from Conn. He walked her out to the parking lot in silence. She nodded in the direction of her car and he turned to guide her toward it. She was struggling to find a way to ask him if there wasn't something more he wanted to say on the subject of Legacy when two men dressed in a style that was strongly reminiscent of Granger walked out from between a row of parked cars.

''Damn.'' Conn stopped abruptly, yanking Honor to a halt beside him. ''Why is it that just when I think everything's finally settled with all the loose ends tied up, something like this happens?''

It was clearly a rhetorical question and neither of the two men seemed inclined to respond to it directly. Large diamond rings flashed in the sunlight as one of the men made an apologetic gesture.

"We're here on behalf of Mr. Granger," the first man began.

"I was afraid of that," Conn groaned.

Honor felt the tension in him, but it wasn't the coiled, lethal kind of tension she had sensed when they had faced first Tony and then Ethan Bailey. This time Conn seemed wary but not unduly alarmed. Honor wished she could be that much at ease around two men who had openly stated they worked for a loan shark, but it was impossible. Living in Southern California might give one a certain amount of panache, but there were limits.

"Mr. Granger would like you to know that he's really sorry about the inconvenience you've recently experienced at the hands of a certain person named Tony," the second man said very civilly. "Mr. Granger don't do hits. And he don't like people saying they're on his payroll when they ain't. He told us to keep an eye out for the aforementioned person here at the track. Just in case. We been watching most carefully. Me, I said old Tony would be heading for the border, but Joe here figured he might just try to sneak back. Looks as if I lose another one to Joe."

The man called Joe grunted but said nothing.

"Mr. Landry?" the first man said with an air of grave politeness. "Mr. Granger says to tell you he's really sorry about all this. He'll take responsibility for cleaning up the mess. Says you and him had a deal and he don't want you to think he reneged."

Conn kept his fingers wrapped around Honor's arm. "Tell Mr. Granger I appreciate his integrity. Tough to find businessmen with integrity these days."

"Mr. Granger looks after his reputation," Joe remarked

with a certain air of pride. He obviously appreciated the fact that he worked for a man with a good business reputation.

''I'm aware that Mr. Granger's word can be relied upon,'' Conn said coolly.

''Good.'' The other man nodded. ''He'll be pleased to hear that. Well, no sense holding you folks up any longer. Just wanted you to know Mr. Granger has taken care of things.''

''Do I assume, then, that you've picked up Tony?'' Conn asked quietly.

''Got him trying to sneak into the barns,'' Joe said with obvious satisfaction. ''Mr. Granger was real pleased. Picked him up an hour ago.''

''You picked him up?'' Honor broke in, startled. ''You've got Tony?''

''Yes, ma'am. No need for further worry.''

''But what are you going to do with him?'' she gasped, ignoring Conn's suddenly tightening grip.

''Why, ma'am, we intend to make certain Tony don't go around misrepresenting himself in the future,'' she was told very gently.

''If...if I might suggest,'' Honor began carefully.

''Honor, shut up,'' Conn hissed under his breath.

She licked her lips as the first man and Joe turned polite, inquiring gazes on her. ''Just...just a thought,'' she managed weakly.

''What's that, ma'am?''

Behind her Conn groaned and his fingers dug into her arm. She knew he was ready to yank her back against him and shut her mouth completely if she said anything dangerous.

''The police are already looking for Tony. They want him in connection with a certain, uh, incident over on the coast. You say your Mr. Granger doesn't do, er, hits?''

''We can handle Tony,'' Joe explained as though she weren't very bright.

''Honor, these gentlemen know what they're doing,'' Conn began firmly.

"I was only going to suggest that they turn him over to the cops. Then Mr. Granger wouldn't have to worry about him and neither would we. It would certainly keep things cleaner for your boss," she added helpfully to the one called Joe. "He wouldn't have to get his hands dirty protecting his reputation. He could let the police do it for him. Don't you think he'd appreciate that?"

To everyone's apparent astonishment, Joe seemed to find the suggestion mildly interesting. "I'll pass your notion along to the boss," he finally said with a nod. "He might like it. Might at that. Appeal to his sense of humor. Come on, Carl. Let's go see Mr. Granger."

The two men disappeared down the row of parked cars.

Honor was left shivering in Conn's grasp. She turned stricken eyes up to meet his wry expression. "Do you think they'll kill him?" she asked uneasily.

"Honor, you're a babe in the woods." He sighed. "Too naive for your own good."

"I am not naive! I'm from Southern California. No one is naive out here!" she exploded.

"It's all right, honey," he soothed. "I'll take care of you."

"Well, if your lack of naïveté is due to the fact that you've been dealing with people like Granger and Joe and Carl and Bailey and Tony all your life, then you're the one who needs protection. I'm the one who's going to have to take care of you. I'll keep you from getting mixed up with bad company."

He glanced down at her in surprise as he opened the door of her car for her. "I never thought of it like that. You may have a point."

He bent down to kiss her possessively and then slammed the door shut.

Twelve

Legacy won by a full three lengths the following afternoon. No sooner had the results flashed on the board than Conn was dragging his new bride at a dead run toward the winner's circle. Adena, who had attended the races with Conn and Honor, grinned delightedly as she hastened along beside her sister.

Laughing with excitement, Honor allowed herself to be swept up in Conn's wake, her new gold band sparkling in the sunlight. Breathlessly she stood beside Legacy's proud owner as the photograph was taken. The usual assortment of gawkers, pranksters and miscellaneous folk crowded into the shot but no one minded. Least of all the colt who tossed his head with spirited arrogance.

"Are you quite sure he isn't emotionally involved in all this?" Honor murmured to Conn as she watched the groom and trainer lead the horse back toward the barns.

Conn's mouth curved briefly. "I'll admit that at the moment it's tough to tell just what that horse is thinking."

"He gave you both a great wedding gift," Adena observed. "When are you leaving for the beach house?"

"Just as soon as I can get Honor back to the parking lot and into the car," Conn vowed determinedly.

"Don't you just love a forceful man?" Adena cooed mockingly to her sister.

"Just this particular forceful man," Honor replied so softly that no one heard her.

"How long are you going to be gone?" Adena went on interestedly.

"Just a couple of days." Conn was striding briskly through the crowd, towing the two women behind him. "Honor has to get back to work. She's finishing some projects and can't afford to be away too long."

"That was great news about the police locating that awful Tony person, wasn't it?" Adena commented. "Imagine finding him locked inside a tack room. Makes you wonder how he got inside in the first place, doesn't it?"

"It certainly does," Conn said with great feeling. "Racing gear is expensive, though. They have to keep it locked up. I suppose Tony went into one of those rooms and someone came along behind him and shut and locked the door, not realizing he was inside."

"Sure." Honor grinned. "And then a casually patrolling guard just happened to check the tack room and find him. Recognized him instantly and turned him over to the cops. Very neat."

Conn slanted her a look. "Very." He paused. "You're looking a trifle smug, darling."

"Am I?" Honor feigned surprise.

"Listen," Adena broke in, waving energetically at a young man dressed in leather and silk, "I see someone I know. He'll give me a ride home. Have a good time at the beach and I'll see you when you get back. We'll throw a real bash. 'Bye!"

Conn swung an assessing glance at the young man in the exotic clothes. "You know him?"

"Oh, yes. That's Jason. He's very sweet, really. Works in the men's department of a local high-style boutique. Adena's dated him on and off for ages. Quite safe, Conn. You don't have to play big brother."

He shrugged and turned back to the task of getting her out to the waiting Porsche. "I only do it for your sake," he explained almost apologetically.

"What? Play big brother?" Honor smiled. "I know. You're trying to assume the responsibility so that I won't have to watch out for her. But I've been keeping tabs on Adena for years. And she's really getting to be quite grown-up. Soon she won't need anyone watching over her."

"As long as you worry about her, I'll worry about her, I suppose." Conn reached the Porsche and opened the passenger door.

"I know." But she wound up saying the words to herself because he'd already closed the door. He would worry about Adena because he was in love with Honor and what affected Honor, affected Conn. It was an intricate, tightly woven web, one neither of them could escape. And one day, Honor promised herself, Conn would know that the kind of emotional involvement he was feeling was called love.

Conn slid into the driver's seat and thrust the key into the ignition. There was a strange mixture of satisfaction and hunger in his expression. The combination had been there since last evening when he'd slipped the ring on Honor's finger and repeated his vows. She still shivered when she remembered the passionate, possessive way he had made love to her later in the elegant hotel room.

The drive back up the coast to the beach cottage was a pleasant one. The sun was shining but the clouds were gathering far out at sea. There would be a storm later, Honor knew. The thought of a pleasant fire in the fireplace and a glass of warm brandy made her smile. By the time she and Conn unlocked the front door of the cottage she was feeling surprisingly content with life.

The first thing she noticed as she walked back into the cottage was that she no longer experienced that vague air of depression she had always sensed in the past. The beach house felt right, now. No lingering questions or disquieting memories. It felt good.

Conn took her for a long walk on the beach before they sat down to a home-cooked meal of paella and wine. Honor teased her new mate about his ability in the kitchen and he assured her she had gotten a real bargain of a husband.

It wasn't until they were sitting together on the sofa in front of the fire, sipping brandy, that Honor's gaze fell on the old iron-and-wood trunk. She stared at it thoughtfully for a long moment.

''What are you thinking, honey?'' Conn asked softly.

''I was just wondering what, exactly, might be hidden in that old trunk. I never really did go through Dad's stuff properly. It was just too painful a process. Maybe it's time I took a look.''

Conn watched her for a moment or two and then without a word he got to his feet and went across the room to unlatch the iron lock. The top groaned as he pushed it open. Honor stood up and went across the room to join him, looking down into the trunk.

''Just more photos and form books and copies of the racing trade journals,'' she observed. Kneeling, she began to lift out some of the yellowed papers. Conn dropped down onto one knee beside her.

They spent nearly two hours going through the contents of the trunk. Much of the time was taken up by Conn who paused to read everything he found on Stylish Legacy.

''Humphrey says Legacy might do just as well as his sire in another year or so,'' he told Honor proudly. ''Then we'll retire him to stud.''

''Legacy will probably enjoy that.'' Honor grinned, reaching for yet another folded copy of the *Daily Racing Form.* ''Being a male, he probably does a lot of thinking and fantasizing about that sort of thing.''

''There you go again,'' Conn complained. He stopped as a small, leather-bound book fell from the folded newspaper. ''What's that?''

''Looks like a diary or a notebook,'' Honor said, turning the volume over and over in her hands. She opened it cautiously and stared at the bold scrawl on the pages inside. ''My father's. I'm sure of it. It looks like some sort of financial record.''

''Here, let me see.'' Conn reached over to take the book

from her hand. ‘‘You’re right. It’s a running account of a debt. Want to take a guess who was being systematically paid every three months?’’

‘‘Ethan Bailey?’’ Honor leaned over his shoulder to peer down at the page in front of him.

Conn nodded. ‘‘There had to be some record. You just don’t borrow a huge sum of money from a man like Ethan Bailey and not keep track of the payback. It’s all here. A good accountant could probably trace the whole history of the transaction, given this book.’’

‘‘And prove that Bailey was involved with Dad and Stoner,’’ Honor concluded. ‘‘I don’t know how far that would get us, though. It’s been so long.’’

Conn kept turning the pages, working his way toward the back of the volume. The precise account of the debt continued to be recorded, but now there were remarks at the bottom of the page. Conn paused so that he and Honor could read them.

‘‘ ‘Dick says he’s getting uneasy feelings about Bailey. Says there’s something about the man he just doesn’t trust,’ ’’ Conn read.

‘‘Dick was your stepfather?’’ Honor asked curiously. ‘‘Short for Richard?’’

‘‘Right. Listen to this.’’ Conn picked another passage and read it aloud.

> I have to agree with Dick. This business with Bailey needs to be checked out. I’m going to start leaving more complete notations in this account book. It will serve as a record in the event that what Dick and I fear is taking place is actually happening. If we’re wrong, Ethan will never need to know we distrusted him. If we’re right, the new firm of Stoner & Mayfield is in big trouble. A scandal of this size will be difficult to smash.

From there on, the details of suspected weapons smuggling were given along with the name of the man who was selling information. There was a brief description of the trap that had been set and then there were no further entires in the leather volume.

Honor sighed a long time later as Conn closed the book and set it back inside the trunk. "It's all there."

"Do you want to make it public? I still don't think we could make it stick. It's an old tale and it happened in a foreign country a long time ago."

"I wonder what story Bailey is giving the police?"

Conn shook his head. "I doubt he'll open up that weapons-smuggling scandal. He's too smart to raise more questions about his past than necessary."

"But what if he does, Conn? He could drag our fathers' names through the mud again."

"This time around we'll have the book." He indicated the leather volume.

"That might not stop him," Honor fretted. "Bailey might decide he's got nothing to lose. We never really thought about that aspect of it. If he talks, really talks, it will open the whole mess up again."

"I think we could both survive another round of scandal, don't you?" Conn asked softly.

She smiled gently. "I think we could survive just about anything together."

He reached out to close the trunk. "This is such old news now that very few people would be interested, anyway. Except, naturally, for the folks who hang around racetracks. It would probably just focus a lot of attention on Legacy. Make a mystery horse out of him or something. Might be just the touch of magic he needs to make his name in racing circles. Great horses always have stories and myths told about them."

Honor couldn't help it; she broke out laughing. "You're one very determined owner, Conn Landry. You've got the fever."

He straightened and reached down to pull her into his arms, his gunmetal eyes suddenly intent. "Not nearly as bad as the fever I've got for you, Honor Mayfield Landry. And I think I've finally got a word to describe it. It's been burning in my mind ever since I made you my wife."

She went still in his arms. "Has it, Conn?"

"I love you, Honor." The words came from him in a thick, husky voice that shook her to the core. "I don't know why it took me so long to realize it. But I know. I'm sure now. So very sure."

"I'm glad, Conn," she whispered, touching the side of his face with gentle fingertips. "I love you so much."

"I'm sorry it took me all this time to get the words straight. I was worrying about other things, like trust and honesty. I didn't stop to realize until tonight that I wouldn't have been so concerned about those other things if I wasn't already in love with you. It's all so simple once you look at it from the right direction. Heaven only knows why I was so blind."

"As you said, you had other things on your mind." She smiled invitingly. "But I was sure that you weren't a race-horse."

"What?" He looked blank.

"That's what you meant earlier, wasn't it? When you talked about the reasons Legacy runs and wins? You told me he wasn't emotionally involved with humans. He gives them his best when they ask it of him, but he does it because that's just the way he is. But you're involved with me, Conn. You don't protect me and care for me and occasionally yell at me just because I ask it of you. I never did actually ask it of you, as I recall," she added thoughtfully. "I knew you did all that because you were involved on some deeper level than even you realized. At least, that's what I kept telling myself."

"Completely involved. I've never been so involved with another human being before in my life! I know it sounds ridiculous but I knew I didn't want it any other way with you. I didn't want to be separated from you in some manner. I didn't want to be like Legacy. I'm a human being, not some Thoroughbred who doesn't really need people." He seized her abruptly, lifting her high into his arms with a fierce joy. "I knew I needed you, honey, but I thought most of that need was tied in with the way I wanted you physically. But it's so much more. I never understood. I just never understood."

His surging wonder was contagious. Honor's own happiness was shining in her eyes as Conn carried her into the bedroom.

The storm that had been building out at sea broke just as Conn came down onto the bed alongside Honor. He gathered her into his arms, all the words that had once been so alien to his tongue tumbling forth in a glorious litany of love.

"Hold me," he breathed as he flowed over her body and let himself sink into her welcoming warmth. "Hold me, Honor. I love you so much."

Honor held him, giving herself up to the passion that was binding them together as Conn proved beyond a doubt that he was, indeed, emotionally involved with her.

Conn Landry knew how to love.